IVAN

KIT ROCHA

IVAN

Edited by Sasha Knight
Cover Artwork by Gene Mollica

ISBN-13: 978-1986818278
ISBN-10: 1986818276

to everyone brave enough
to be scared

1

The sun dipped toward the western horizon, painting the sky in dozens of vibrant streaks of red and violet that Ivan couldn't bring himself to appreciate. As beautiful as a sunset in Sector One could be, for the past two weeks, it had meant only one thing to him.

Ivan was going to have to be the bad guy. Again.

Maricela was still bent over a makeshift drafting table, her head close to Nita's as they traced their fingers over the various floor plans and debated the practicalities of each one. Behind them, a grizzled contractor named Murphy shifted his nervous gaze between Maricela and Ivan. Maricela's royal pleasure could make his career, but her bodyguard's cold stare had kept him on edge.

That was fine. Ivan was used to keeping people on edge. He was used to a lot of things—instant respect and wariness wherever he went. Immediate deference. Swift obedience. He was a Rider, a personal representative of Gideon Rios himself. A warrior with a fierce reputation and the son of a revered saint. People prayed to his father. They hung portraits of him in their homes and tattooed his image on their skin.

Maricela was a princess, daughter of two saints, granddaughter of the Prophet. Her sister ran their grandfather's religion. Her brother controlled all of Sector One. She didn't like having a bodyguard—or a curfew. But it was Ivan's duty to get her back to the estate before the sun set, and if that meant being the bad guy...

Well, Ivan had always performed his duty.

"I don't know," Maricela said. "Even if we build a loft space for the beds, we *still* don't have room for a kitchen."

"But they need one," Nita insisted, smoothing her hand over the paper with a frown. "It's so much cheaper to feed a family when you can cook your own meals."

They continued studying the designs, both sporting equally fierce expressions of concentration. Behind them, the first of the retrofitted storage containers they'd reclaimed from Sector Two stood as a model of what could be.

Windows had been cut into the side to let in light. The heavy metal doors had been replaced with simple wooden ones. Inside, the contractor had done his best to transform cold steel into something welcoming— pine floors and adobe plaster walls, with a few pieces of furniture, bright, colorful curtains, and even vases of flowers staged to appeal to two idealistic young women.

The homes wouldn't be fancy or spacious. But they'd be sturdy, easily constructed, and they'd keep out the bite of winter a whole lot better than the flimsy tents currently housing the hundreds of refugees still struggling to piece together a life after the war.

Ivan had lived in worse places.

But Maricela and Nita hadn't. The two of them had grown up in palaces luxurious beyond what most people in the sectors could imagine. When they wanted food, it appeared. Discarded dirty clothing made its way back into their closets, clean and pressed, with little effort on their part.

Their intentions were beyond reproach. Their logistics, on the other hand...

Solving their dilemma would be the quickest way to get his charges moving, so Ivan stepped forward and pointed to the simplest floor plan, one that provided sleeping space, a sitting area, and a bathroom. "This is all you need," he said, tapping the page. "For every five or so of these units, build a communal kitchen. For every ten, give them a communal space for laundry. A lot of the tenements are designed that way. People are used to sharing those spaces."

"They shouldn't *have* to share them. Surely we can come up with something better than a tenement." Maricela's brow furrowed for a moment, then relaxed as she sighed. "But probably not before winter." She turned to Murphy. "Draw up some new plans incorporating Ivan's suggestions. But I want each home built with future expansion in mind—come spring, we can add on to complete them."

No, Maricela would never settle for anything less than perfect.

Relieved, Murphy bobbed his head in something that fell just short of a bow. "As you say, Miss Rios. I'll have the final plans ready for you before the summer festival."

"Good." Nita started rolling the preliminary

sketches. "My family's hosting the solstice ball this year. We can convince all our rich relatives to open their pockets and contribute."

"So at least one good thing will come of it," Maricela murmured.

"That's what I keep telling myself." Nita offered the sketches to the contractor, who gave her another of those nervous almost-bows. The eldest Reyes daughter might not command the same deference as Maricela, but her family's vast estates ensured crafters and merchants tripped over themselves to keep her happy.

She wasn't going to like the curfew much either, but Ivan couldn't afford to care. "If Murphy has everything he needs, it's time for us to head back."

Maricela didn't even look at him. "Hardly. I have plenty more to do before I can go home."

"We should look over the furniture..." Nita started, but her gaze drifted to Ivan. Even though her big brown eyes were deliberately innocent, he'd known her brother long enough to recognize that look—Reyes got that same tilt to his head and slight pursing of his lips when he was pondering whether a fight he was about to pick was hopeless.

Her brother usually threw himself into the fight either way. Nita was a lot smarter. "We can make most of those decisions at home. It is getting a little late."

Maricela propped her hands on her hips. She drew in a deep breath, bracing for an argument, but all she said was, "Fine."

It sure as hell wasn't fine. Ivan would probably hear all about how not fine it was later. But Maricela was a Rios, and the Rios family maintained appearances in public.

Most days, Ivan counted on it.

A pointed look at the contractor convinced the man

to keep his farewells quick. He bowed to each girl—actual bows this time—with promises and assurances spilling from him as he backed away.

That left Ivan to herd his charges toward the Jeep. Nita linked her arm through Maricela's as Ivan trailed behind them. Once they were out of the shelter of the shipping containers, the warm summer wind stirred their hair and tugged at the edges of Maricela's white dress. The hemline had grown dirty during an afternoon spent exploring the boundaries of the land set aside for refugee housing, and Ivan's gaze caught on it between repeated scans of their surroundings.

Maricela could be at home, lounging by her pool or strolling through her gardens. She could be curled up next to the hearth in her suite with her favorite book. If she wanted to be productive, she could have joined the acolytes studying under Del at the temple and picked a craft—sewing, weaving, needlepoint, even art.

Those activities would have been safer, and most of them would have kept her white gowns pristine. But Maricela was a Rios, and a Rios wasn't happy unless they were tromping around the sector, trying to save everyone.

He should know. Twenty-three years ago, her big brother had saved him.

He'd parked their vehicle in the middle of a clearing just off the main road. No opportunities for an enemy to conceal themselves nearby, and no way they could be lying in wait. But fifteen feet from the Jeep, Ivan spoke for the first time. "You two wait here for a second."

Maricela made a noise that sounded suspiciously like a long-suffering sigh.

Ivan ignored her.

The Jeep looked undisturbed. There were no new

footprints in the dirt surrounding it, no indication it had been tampered with. But Ivan still dropped to the ground and slid under it, taking his time to examine every spot where an enterprising assassin could have hidden a bomb.

Nothing.

Partially mollified, he rolled back to his knees and scanned the area again. Maricela looked impatient, Nita exasperated. The breeze brought scraps of their low-voiced conversation to him as he rose and opened the hood, enough to know they were still discussing whether the refugees could survive until spring without their own kitchens and laundry rooms.

Ivan knew the answer. For two bitter years, he'd lived with his mother in conditions that would horrify his perfectionist princess. The memories were blessedly hazy, but checking the engine for sabotage didn't take enough concentration to distract from them. He could still remember the cold on the nights the temple shelters had been too full, or his mother had been too ashamed to seek one out. The nights they'd spent huddled together in a park or against the wall of a shop, as if they could soak up the heat through its surface.

Sector One was generous to a fault sometimes, but when people thought you had conspired to kill one of their princesses, doors tended to close in your face. His mother had seen a lot of closed doors before Gideon rescued them.

So Maricela could frown and sigh and roll her eyes all she wanted. Ivan was *not* taking chances with her safety.

He finished his inspection of the engine by checking the brake lines a second time, just to be sure. When he was convinced nothing had been tampered with, he slammed down the hood and raised his voice. "All right. Let's go."

"Maybe we should walk everywhere." Maricela paused by the Jeep to brush some dirt from his shoulder, genuine affection curving her lips into a smile. "It would be faster, and you wouldn't have to crawl around on the ground."

Her absentminded touch tightened his skin, and her smile was a Sector One miracle all on its own. Maricela was always striking, with her light brown skin, bronzed by long hours under the summer sun, dark brown eyes, sharp, high cheekbones, and the elegant arch of her brows. She had a face meant to be carved into statues—and she would be. In generations to come, children would leave offerings at the feet of the beloved Santa Maricela and pray to her to heal all their hearts' ills.

Children today didn't have to pray. They just had to wait for her smile.

He couldn't let her distract him, so he was gruffer than necessary when he opened the Jeep door for her. "I don't mind."

Shrugging, she climbed into the vehicle. "Suit yourself."

Nita offered him a bright, beaming smile that reminded Ivan too much of the way her brother smiled when he wanted to charm some overawed young man or woman into blushing. "Thank you, Ivan," she murmured in that husky voice that made all the newer guardsmen stupid.

Which was exactly why Ivan couldn't trust the guardsmen around these two. They'd leap to obey Maricela's slightest whim and fall over themselves trying to impress Nita, and probably not notice danger until it was pissing on their boots.

If then.

When both women were settled into the back seat, Ivan shut the door and circled to the driver's door. He didn't love the openness of the Jeep, or the fact that his passengers were out of his direct line of sight while he was driving. But a slight adjustment of the rearview mirror kept them visible, and the route he'd planned home was short and kept mostly to roads few people even knew existed.

Maricela was as safe as he could make her, but he'd still breathe easier once they were back within the well-patrolled walls of the Rios family estate. He could control the variables there. He could stay close to her. If worse came to worst, he could put himself bodily between her and danger.

His uncles might have been responsible for the death of a Rios princess, but before that, his father had taken a bullet to save one.

Ivan had been raised to emulate him.

2

Maricela had a plan.

It wasn't a great plan, seeing as how it hinged on somehow securing Ivan's cooperation, and he wasn't going to like any of it, not one bit. But she was desperate, tired of being locked up like a child after dark.

And she was *horny*. God above, she was horny.

Maybe if she broached the subject casually enough, Ivan wouldn't realize she was fomenting revolution until he was neck-deep in it. With that in mind, she sat quietly at the small dining table in her sitting room and waited for him to finish his security sweep of her suite.

It took a while. The suite was large, and Ivan was thorough. She had to mark his passage by the soft click of doors opening, because even on the tile floors of her bathroom, his boots were silent. But eventually he returned, having traded his light body armor for a black T-shirt and shoulder holster. Silver glinted from the knife tucked into his boot, and she knew he had more weapons hidden away.

He sat across from her—silent, as always—and Maricela regarded him thoughtfully. "You need a day off."

His brow furrowed. "No, I don't."

"Of course you do. Everyone does, from time to time."

Ivan shrugged one shoulder. "I've taken time off. Two afternoons. I'm fine."

"How did you spend your afternoons off? If you don't mind my asking," she added hurriedly. She had to, or he might tell her even if he resented the question.

He fixed his gaze on the table and remained silent for so long that she started to think he minded very much. "Personal obligations," he said finally.

Her stomach knotted. Maybe he was already taking care of this stuff, and she was the only one left suffering alone in her gilded cage with her early bedtime.

She propped her elbows on the table, leaned forward, and rested her chin on her hands. "Naked obligations?"

He flinched. From Ivan, it may as well have been a violent recoil. "Absolutely not."

She had no idea why he was upset. Sexual desire could be a physical need just like thirst or sleep, and there was no shame in having physical needs. And she knew he liked sex—it had been the talk of the temple a year ago when he'd finally ended his long-term under-standing with a widowed blacksmith who lived near the market. The acolytes had spent weeks tittering and giggling, making predictions about the next woman to catch his eye.

No one had, at least not that Maricela had heard. Which was unthinkable—he was young, vital, and he wouldn't lack for willing partners. He *couldn't*. Plenty of people found his icy blue eyes and strong features attractive, and surely some of them would find his brooding seriousness equally appealing.

Maricela would know. She was one of them.

But this wasn't about that. Not entirely, anyway.

She took a deep breath and tried again. "I know you don't date, but there are other ways to...pass the time."

He blinked at her and tilted his head a fraction to the left. "I understand how sex works."

She wouldn't grit her teeth. She would *not*. "Then why don't you take the night off and go have some so I can, too?"

That wiped away his confused expression, and her stern bodyguard was back. "Maricela..."

The note was still crumpled up in her pocket. She smoothed it out on the table, and Colin Visscher's bold scrawl stared up at her.

My place, ten o'clock tonight.

I'll use my tongue.

Ivan craned his neck, and she slid it across the table toward him. "Let's forget about your needs for a minute," she mumbled. "Maybe you don't have any. Maybe you take care of them yourself. Who knows? All I know is I'm tired of taking care of mine by myself."

His face might have been carved from the stone they'd built the temple from. His eyes were chips of ice. He put a finger on the very corner of the note, as if he didn't want to touch it at all, and slid it back to her. "If you want to see Colin Visscher," he said in a bland voice, "you can invite him here."

Because that went so well last time. "Even if you're in the next room, Ivan, you're *there*. Listening." She shrugged helplessly. "I can't do this with you listening."

"You didn't have a problem with that last time."

"That was different." That was back before her tiny little crush on Ivan had had a chance to explode. But the past few weeks had turned that vague interest into a fierce, almost brutal craving for his touch—and she had to head it off *now*.

The best way to do that was surely to distract herself, right? Colin was convenient, appealing, and the only thing he wanted from her was exactly what she wanted from him.

What she *wanted* to want from him.

"I'm sorry, Maricela. I can't let you go out alone." The muscles in his cheek worked, as if he was having to force his next words out. "If having me in the next room is that upsetting, I can ask Ana to come and take my place for a few hours."

It would help, but he looked so hurt that she couldn't tell him so. She opened her mouth to deny it, but the chime on her door cut her off.

"Dinner," she said instead, trying to sound cheerful. "Could you, Ivan?"

Looking as if he'd been granted a stay of execution, Ivan all but leapt from his chair and crossed the room. With his hand hovering close to his gun, he opened the door a few inches, angling his body to block the hallway. Only then did he pull it wide and allow two familiar servers from the kitchen to enter, both laden down with massive trays.

She hated to put them through the hassle of serving meals in her private quarters. In the absence of a family dinner, she'd always eaten in the kitchens. It caused the least amount of trouble for the staff, and it was a welcome chance to get away from the some-times-unavoidable formality of her life.

She couldn't do it anymore. Not since Donny, one of the kitchen staff, a man she'd laughed and joked with, traded family stories with, had tried to murder her brother.

It wasn't fear that kept her out of the kitchens, not exactly, but they sure as hell didn't feel like a safe haven anymore. Not with the memory of that day fresh in her mind...and Donny's blood still on her hands.

"Maricela?"

When she blinked and looked up, Ivan was seated across the table from her again. The door was safely closed, the kitchen workers gone. Dinner was spread out between them, the silver lids already removed and set aside.

And Ivan was watching her with concerned eyes.

Having him look at her like that, with something dangerously close to pity, was unbearable. So she smiled and picked up a serving spoon. "Chicken pot pie, that's your favorite. Looks like you have some admirers in the household."

He let the change of subject go, and even unbent enough to hold out his plate so she could give him a healthy serving. "The cook knows all the Riders' favorites. She makes a point of learning."

Of course she did. The Riders were heroes, beloved by everyone. They carried out Gideon's orders, acted as the living embodiment of his will. Their word was law, their deeds unquestionable.

Maricela usually accepted that without question. But this time, she had to try. "My curfew doesn't make any sense."

"I'm not the one who gave the order," he replied as he added steamed green beans to his plate and snagged a couple of dinner rolls.

"But Gideon would listen to you if you argued against it."

"I don't *argue* with my leader." But as he broke a roll in half and spread butter on it, he finally lifted his gaze to hers. "Why don't you think it makes sense?"

"Everyone knows, right? That I'm confined to quarters after dark."

"You're not confined to quarters," he protested. "You can go anywhere you want in the palace, and even over to the temple if you want."

With him as her ever-present shadow. "I'm confined, Ivan," she told him flatly. "So anyone who wants to hurt me already knows that it probably has to happen during the daytime, when I'm out." She paused, gripping her fork. "I suppose."

"You suppose?"

"Yes. Well, I mean..." She met his gaze. "We're operating on the assumption that I'm safer at home. But the last two assassination attempts on a Rios have happened here, within these walls. So maybe our assumption is faulty."

His eyes softened. Not with pity, but something else—a protective warmth she'd only seen one other time. The first night he'd stayed with her. The night he'd talked her to sleep.

"No one is making assumptions," he said gently. "New precautions have been put in place. Ashwin has interviewed all the guards and done extensive risk assessments on everyone who works on the estate. And Kora has helped with her intuition. Nothing is going to happen to you inside this house. Even if someone tried, I'm here, Maricela."

For a single, ridiculous moment, she considered telling him the truth, that his proximity was doing unbearable things to her libido—and, worse, that the more she talked to him, the more she *liked* him. But he'd already let her down easy once, and she couldn't go through that again.

She could go straight to Gideon and ask him to assign another one of the Riders as her guard. Ana, perhaps, or Lucio. But no matter her reason for asking, Ivan would consider it a slight, a condemnation of her faith in his ability to protect her, and nothing could be further from the truth. She trusted him more than anyone else.

That was part of the problem.

"Never mind," she whispered. "It's fine. Everything is fine."

He watched her for a few moments before nodding and turning his attention to his plate. He devoured a serving of pot pie and two more rolls before casually saying, "My mother. That's who I visit when Ana comes to stay with you. I visit my mother."

"Your mother? I didn't know—" What, that he still had one? That he had one at all? She bit her lip.

Oddly, the words made the corner of his mouth tilt up. "Most people don't. My mother values her privacy. She hasn't had the easiest time."

Aside from his sainted father, Ivan's family carried mostly shame. His uncles had been instrumental in the Rios family kidnapping that had instigated a bloody civil war. Maricela's aunt Adriana and cousin Mad had been held for days, and only Mad had walked away from his captivity alive. He'd lost his mother and father that day, and he still carried the scars.

Maricela tended to think of it that way, in terms of its impact on her family. She rarely spared a thought for the people on the *other* side of the conflict. "Your uncles were her brothers."

"Her older brothers," he confirmed, staring at his plate as he chased a green bean across it with his fork. "When my father died, my mother moved back in with them. She needed help. I was still so young."

"What happened to the two of you after your uncles were—" She couldn't bring herself to say the word *executed*. "Once they were gone?"

Ivan picked up his glass of ice water and drained half of it in two huge gulps. "Things were rough for a while. People didn't trust my mother. Most people didn't want to give her work, and sometimes when she got it, they wouldn't pay her."

Without thinking, Maricela reached for him. She slid her hand over his, squeezing when he finally looked at her. "I'm sorry."

"It's fine." He cleared his throat but didn't pull his hand away. "Gideon found out what was happening and came for us. He got us a place to live until I was old enough to help support her. And when I became a Rider, he found my mother a quiet job in the north temple. She goes by her middle name, and most people probably don't even know who she is. Who she was."

Mortification swept through Maricela. She'd been complaining about her situation, never once stopping to consider how much worse it could be. Yes, everyone from her brother to the palace cook was smothering her a bit, but it was out of concern for her safety, not malice.

And Ivan? All he wanted to do was protect her, and she was making things harder than they needed to be, all because she couldn't control her stupid *urges* where he was concerned.

No more. "Thank you for telling me." She squeezed his hand again. "It means a lot."

He returned the squeeze for a few seconds, his

fingers strong and warm around hers. Then he eased his hand away. "Gideon and Kora are the only ones who know. It's not as bad as it used to be, but some people can still be unkind."

She didn't know what to do with her hands anymore, so she folded them in her lap. "I understand. I won't say anything."

"Thank you." He refilled both their water glasses, then nodded to her plate. "You should eat more. You and Nita had a light lunch."

Out of duty more than hunger, she picked at her dinner. Her mind was still reeling over Ivan's revelations, all the intimate details of his life that he'd shared with her. Naturally, it could have been nothing more than her status that prompted the admission. Her being part of the royal family—and the younger sister of their religious leader—sometimes made people feel like telling her things was tantamount to confession. A way for them to absolve themselves of their sins.

But with Ivan, it had felt like a *revelation.*

She shook the thought out of her head and focused on finishing her dinner. It was easy to see the things you wanted to see, whether they were grounded in reality or not. And she had—had, *had*—to remember that.

3

Of all the places Maricela's duties took her, Ivan found the temples the most stressful.

They shouldn't have been. Each temple had its own trained guard, devoted men and a growing number of women, all superbly trained. Even more so now that the most promising members of each squad were attending weekly lessons with Ashwin, where the Makhai soldier pressed them to their limits and taught them to be flexible and creative with their thinking.

But in the end, training was just that. Practice. An exercise. Even when you were staring down Ashwin's most intimidating glare across the practice ring, it wasn't the same as a fight with real blood and real killing.

A temple guardsman could go days or weeks without being forced to use their skills in earnest. Some went months. Even then, the kind of trouble they saw was rarely lethal, usually petty thefts or fights breaking out between angry or grieving penitents.

Some guardsmen never had to take a life.

Ivan had stopped counting the ravens on his arm that marked the blood he'd spilled. As long as Del etched his sins onto his skin for a thorough accounting, Ivan didn't want to think about it. He'd accepted his damnation a long time ago.

His only concern was staying alert to the potential dangers surrounding them, and that meant not letting the familiar scents of wax and spice and incense lull him into complacency. It meant not trusting the temple guardsmen to protect his charge.

"Don't you think so, Ivan?"

And it meant not letting Maricela drag him into her conversation when he should be focused on the three doors that led into the vestibule, or the knot of acolytes that had gathered in front of the wall of candles to ruin his line of sight. "Uh-huh."

She sighed. "He's not listening, but it's true. It's a surprise to see you here, but such a *good* one."

One of the acolytes shifted enough to give Ivan a clear look at the door. After ascertaining no one had snuck in behind them, he glanced back to the women in time to see Avery Parrino smile.

Ivan wasn't surprised to see her. The Riders made a point of knowing Avery's typical schedule. Gideon hadn't insisted that she remain within the safe boundaries of the estate once the war ended, but Ivan suspected that he'd wanted to. Though Gideon would shroud it in political practicality all day long, the truth was that he worried about her.

And the Riders protected Gideon. Even when he hadn't asked them to.

"It's good to see you, too," Avery murmured. "This isn't your usual temple visitation time, is it?"

"No, it's not, but Reyes told me I had to shake up my routine a little."

Ivan caught movement out of the corner of his eye and turned his head enough to watch a priestess step out of the back room, a basket full of offering cards swinging from her arm. The potential threat dismissed, he caught himself frowning.

Reyes hadn't said anything to *him*.

Avery made a soft noise of amusement. "Reyes? Really?"

"Oh yes. He gave me this big lecture about how I couldn't rely on others to protect me completely, not even the Riders. So I had to take some responsibility for my own safety."

"How wise," Avery observed. "Uncharacteristically so, some might say."

Maricela snorted. "Some who aren't paying attention. If Reyes is crazy, he's crazy like a fox."

Ivan resisted the urge to snort. That, at least, was true. But Reyes shouldn't have been heaping *more* responsibility on Maricela's delicate shoulders. Ivan hadn't realized how much was already there until he started following her around.

Fighting rogue mercenaries again might seem like a vacation.

"How are things at the Houses?" Maricela asked, then immediately continued talking. "I have an ulterior motive for asking, bear that in mind. But I'm also honestly curious."

Avery arched one eyebrow. "They're fine. Good, actually. Many of the girls from Two don't feel like refugees anymore. They've been pitching in to help out some of the newer arrivals from Eden and the other sectors."

"Excellent." Maricela smiled. "Think they could spare you for a few weeks? As long as we're increasing security for the family, I think we should include you."

The woman who had arrived in Sector One battered and broken would never have contradicted a Rios. But the months had begun to heal Avery, so that's exactly what she did. "As far as I'm concerned, it's unnecessary. I'm no one."

"You lived with us," Maricela argued. "You were practically part of the family."

"I'm telling you, it's not an issue."

"And *I'm* telling *you*, maybe it is."

Both women looked at Ivan for support. He cleared his throat. "I think the only reason Gideon hasn't already requested that you come back is that he doesn't want to make you uncomfortable. I know I'd feel better if you were staying somewhere secure."

Avery hesitated. "No one would target me. I have no value as leverage against Gideon."

Ivan might argue that point, but he didn't have to. He'd been there at the City Center during the final battle in the war, when Lex Parrino had threatened to shoot an innocent person in the face if that was what it took to protect her lover.

No one wanted to find out what Lex might do to protect her sister.

"Your sister leads Sector Four with Dallas O'Kane," he told her gently. "If someone wanted to convince them to hurt Gideon or the Riders, you would be extremely valuable leverage. Even failing to protect you could cause friction between the Riders and the O'Kanes."

"That's true." Avery rubbed her collarbone absently, then shrugged. "All right, I'll come back for a while."

"Thank you." She was speaking to Avery, but Maricela shot him a grateful look as some of the tension melted out of her shoulders. "It'll be fun. We'll—"

A scream ripped through the temple.

Ivan moved.

In seconds, he'd shoved Avery at the nearest startled guardsman and locked one arm around Maricela's waist. The alcove he'd mapped out in his earlier assessment was four feet behind them and two to the left, and her feet didn't touch the ground the whole way.

Her gasp of shock was still ringing in his ears when he spun them into the alcove and pressed her into the most protected corner, plastering his body in front of hers so any projectiles would hit him instead.

Her fingers closed on his arms with enough force to bruise. She opened her mouth to speak, but all that emerged were those gasping, shocked breaths. He needed to turn around so he'd be facing any potential threat. But she was clutching him so tight, her entire body trembling against his, so he leaned into her just to keep her from shaking apart.

Mistake. Her halting gasps caught on a whimper of gratitude, her lips so close to his throat that her breath skated warm over his skin with every exhalation. She was soft, so soft. Even after he pushed away he knew he'd still feel her, the sensation burned into his skin— her breasts crushed to his chest, her hips against his, her long legs surprisingly strong.

A bodyguard shouldn't know how it felt to press his charge against a hard surface and have her welcome him.

Her heart was racing, and when she nervously licked her lips, her tongue grazed his skin.

Fuck.

Shuddering, Ivan tried to push back from the wall. Her fingers only tightened more, her nails pricking his skin.

"It's okay," he whispered, tilting her head up with one hand so that her wide eyes met his. "I've got you."

Her gaze locked on his mouth. "I know."

"Open your hands, Maricela. I need to check what's going on."

She blinked and shook her head, but she let go of him. "Sorry."

The ghost of her touch lingered as he turned around, keeping his body in front of hers. One of his throwing knives balanced lightly on the tips of his fingers, but no enemy rushed around the corner to confront him.

Instead, one of the guards called out. "Ivan?"

He recognized the man as Alrik, the guard he'd pushed Avery toward. A solid man with a long history of service, and smart enough not to step into the path of Ivan's blade. "Yeah?"

"It's all clear out here. One of the girls saw a spider."

Ivan took one step forward, then turned and held out a finger to Maricela. "Wait here, okay?"

"It was a *spider*, Ivan."

"Maricela." He rarely let a commanding edge enter his voice—you didn't order around a Rios—but thwarted adrenaline made his words sharper than he intended. "*Wait*."

Her eyes sparked with something hotter than simple irritation, but she relented.

He stepped to the edge of the alcove and gave the room a single sweep. Alert guards hovered in front of each entry point, still waiting for the command to stand down. Alrik stood next to Avery, his hand on the wooden baton at his hip.

A few feet away from the candles, one acolyte stood with her arms around her waist, her cheeks bright red with embarrassment. The laughter of the other girls broke into a string of yelps as one of the younger guards herded the spider toward the door. They broke ranks and scampered in the opposite direction as the tarantula skittered across the marble. It was almost as big as Ivan's palm, hairy and poisonous—and even though a grown person was unlikely to die from its bite before they could find help, it would *not* be a pleasant experience.

Killing it inside the temple would be considered terrible luck, but Ivan wouldn't take chances when Maricela left. "When you get it outside, kill it," he told the harried-looking guard, who nodded and leapt to block the spider's abrupt change in direction.

Confident that the boy had it under control, Ivan raised his voice. "Okay. You can come out."

When she did, her expression was pleading. "*Ivan.*"

He could order her around when her life was on the line, but when she begged him for something... Ivan bit back a sigh and called after the guard. "Wait. Don't kill the spider. Just get it out of here."

Maricela took a step closer, gratitude in her low whisper. "Isn't there enough death?"

She brushed past him before he could answer, the gauzy fabric of her gown dragging over his skin in a shivery caress he felt long after she'd reached Avery. Their low conversation melted into the sound of the acolytes laughing over the adventure and the guards settling back into their routine, and Ivan spent a few precious moments locking down his physical responses.

Reaction to the proximity of a beautiful woman was to be expected. But he could still feel the eight little pricks of heat where her nails had dug into his arms and shoulders. He could still conjure up the sensation of her body pressed tight to his.

Distraction was unacceptable. Because Maricela thought there'd been enough death, enough killing. And Ivan might be able to indulge her with spiders and bugs, but the more serious threats...

There was a reason Gideon needed the Riders. Everyone in Sector One extended their hands in peace and welcome. Everyone got a chance. Sometimes a second chance, or even a third. But some threats couldn't be tolerated. Some people were so dangerous, you couldn't give them an opportunity to hurt you.

Where Maricela's safety was concerned, Ivan would never hesitate to strike first.

4

When Maricela needed to have difficult conversations, she planned them out in her head.

It wasn't a perfect strategy. She couldn't account for how another person would react or what they would say, but it helped her feel more confident, more in control. She could center herself by imagining where she would first broach the subject, whether she would sit or stand. How she would start.

So it was just as well that Avery rode with them back to the palace, because Maricela needed to have a difficult conversation with Ivan, and she wasn't ready for it, not at all. Instead, she made small talk with her friend, watched the back of Ivan's head as he drove, and tried to make her plans.

It didn't work. By the time they reached their destination, she was no closer to knowing what to say to him than when she'd begun. Not that it mattered, after all, because cars lined the drive circling the fountain in front of the house.

She'd completely forgotten about their family dinner.

"Maricela!" Mad was there, beaming at her, by the time Ivan opened her door. Her cousin pulled her out of the car and into an enthusiastic hug that lifted her feet from the ground. "I thought you'd abandoned us."

"Never," she vowed. Jyoti had come out behind him, and Maricela hugged her next. "You brought Dylan and Scarlet, I hope?"

"Of course." Jyoti kissed her cheek and then laughed. "Your sister's children are fighting over who gets to talk to him first. Uncle Dylan is very popular."

"Isabela's already here, then?"

"The whole caravan pulled in just after we did," Mad told her as Jyoti turned to greet Avery. "Ashwin and Kora are here, too. We might actually fill the table tonight."

Ivan hovered behind them. She'd spent weeks growing more aware of him by the day, and that moment in the temple had only heightened the feeling. If she closed her eyes now and concentrated, Maricela thought she might be able to determine the distance between them precisely, down to fractions of an inch.

She shoved away the fanciful thought and turned to him. "Will you be joining us?"

Ivan shook his head. "I'm going to eat at the barracks and catch up on some things. I'll be back before you go to sleep."

He said it like he expected her to argue. He probably did. "Say hi to Ana for me."

"I will." After another hesitation he extended his hand to Mad. "Good to see you, Mad."

"You too, Ivan." After clasping hands, Mad pulled the other man into a back-pounding hug. "Thanks for taking care of her."

"Of course."

Ivan flashed her one last, strangely blank look, then turned toward the path down to the barracks. Maricela only realized she was staring after him when Avery took her arm and gently steered her toward the front door.

The not-so-low hum of noise hit her as soon as she walked in, and it only grew louder and more boisterous as she neared the dining room. Isabela's family had already taken over one end of the table, with Isabela at the end and her spouses interspersed around the older children. Dylan sat next to them, the baby on his lap, her chubby little fingers tangled in his beard.

Scarlet sat across from him, laughing, and Maricela slipped into the seat beside her. "Sorry I'm late."

Kora looked up from her futile attempt to lure the tiniest Rios away from Dylan with a breadstick. "You brought Avery, so all is forgiven."

At the opposite end of the table from Isabela, Gideon smiled at Maricela before inclining his head toward Avery. "Welcome, Avery. Sit wherever you can find a chair."

"Sit by me," Jyoti urged her as she slid into the seat at Gideon's left hand. "We can catch up as soon as Gideon and I are done talking business."

Maricela opened her napkin with a snap. "Business? At family dinner?"

Jyoti smiled as she lifted a water goblet. "Running this part of the sectors *is* the family business. But I just wanted to hammer out the arrangements for the shipping containers we're giving you. I'm so excited about your project, Maricela."

"So am I." It had started as a way to do *something*, if only to assuage her conscience over the huge divide between her privileged existence and the struggles of the refugees. But it was turning into something that might really make a difference. A sustainable community. "Ivan has been helping a great deal."

"Ivan's a good resource," Mad said from his seat across from Jyoti. "He's handy, you know. He and Deacon have built half the new houses the guards live in. He even built some of the furniture in the barracks."

"Right." She'd been thinking more of his insights. His personal history made him uniquely aware of the challenges faced by the displaced and homeless—but he'd told her that in strict confidence, and she'd eat her silverware before she betrayed that. "I like him. He's not stuffy and glowering *all* the time. Ninety percent, tops."

"Ivan's a good soldier," Ashwin said abruptly. "He's not glowering. He's prepared."

Maricela hid a smile behind her water goblet. "Oh, I think he's both."

"Maybe a little." Mad winked at her. "So what else have you been up to, when you haven't been single-handedly solving the refugee crisis?"

A blush heated her cheeks. "Don't tease, Adrian. I *wish* I could say I'd done that, but I haven't."

"Don't sell yourself short," he chided her. "You saw an opportunity where most people saw empty, rusting metal. Be proud of that."

She'd seen *desperation*, a need that made her heartsick to consider. And that feeling had grown worse now that she knew about Ivan's history. "I just want to have all the plans in place before the Reyes house party so work can begin." She tilted her head and batted her eyes at her cousin. "You are coming to the party, aren't you?"

Scarlet choked on her wine.

"Not for anything," Mad told her cheerfully. "And don't bat those big eyes at me. If Jyoti couldn't sweet-talk me into taking her so she can work on trade deals, no one is getting me there."

"Now, Mad." Gideon sighed and shook his head. "This will be Kora's first house party, and you're making it sound terrible."

"It's only terrible if you don't like stuffy rich people smiling stiffly at one another while they negotiate how many of their relatives they can marry off."

"Adrian." Isabela's stern voice carried down the table, over the babble of young voices. "You're speaking of my children's aunts and uncles."

He raised both hands and relented. "I know, I know. I'm just surly. Kora, you're going to have a great time. Have you ever ridden a horse before? The Reyes family has the best horses in the sectors, and they love to go riding during the parties."

Kora's clear laugh rang out like a bell as she turned to Ashwin. "How adorable. He thinks you're going to let me anywhere near a horse right now."

A muscle in Ashwin's cheek jumped, and Maricela could almost *hear* the internal struggle between his desire to find a way to let Kora ride a horse if she wanted and his increasingly intense need to protect her as her pregnancy progressed. "Horses involve... too many variables," he said finally. "There's no way to manage the risks."

No wonder Ashwin and Ivan got along splendidly. They sounded just alike. "I won't be riding any horses, either," Maricela told them. "If Adrian isn't going, then I'm only going for the ball."

"Oh no, you're not." Gideon leaned back in his

chair, his water goblet dangling from one hand. "If I'm stuck there the whole week, so are you."

The thought of it was enough to make her stomach clench. An entire week of being someone else's guest meant being on her unrelentingly best behavior. And while the festivities usually more than made up for the emotional toll, this time would be different. This time, she'd have suitors dogging her every step. And after that breathless moment of connection with Ivan at the temple, that was the last thing she wanted him to see.

She tried again. "Half the week?"

Sympathy filled his eyes, and she could tell he was hovering on the edge of compromise.

Apparently, so could Isabela. "Maricela. In this family, we enjoy privilege and luxury beyond the telling of it, with so few duties asked of us in return. Don't be stubborn about this one. No one's forcing you into a betrothal. But acting like it's beneath you to meet with suitors who only want to impress you is unkind."

Mad's eyebrows drew together. "Isabela—"

"It's fine," Maricela cut in. She gripped her hands into fists in her lap to still their trembling and addressed her oldest sister. "It isn't that the attention is beneath me. It's just that it's unwanted."

Her sister's expression softened somewhat. "Surely they're not *all* so bad. And if any bother you too much, you can have Ivan scare them off."

Perfect. Maricela fell silent, picking at her food until another snatch of conversation caught her attention.

"You and Kora should definitely come visit, now that the chaos from the big reopening is past," Mad was saying as he heaped a second serving of rice onto his plate. "I know Cruz would love to see you. And the twins are growing like weeds. Isaac has the cute baby babble going nonstop. Probably Ace's influence."

"How old are they now?" she asked wistfully. Maricela missed the days when the palace had been overrun with Isabela's babies. Only a few were still toddling around now, and there always seemed to be someone else commanding their attention.

"Just about three months." Mad leaned back in his seat, and Maricela caught him sneaking a look down the table at Dylan, who had charmed Isabela's youngest into falling asleep on his shoulder. "It's a cute age."

He was making googly eyes at Dylan—but then again, so were Jyoti and Scarlet. The minute Dylan started being parental with one of the little ones, his three lovers lost their *minds*. If Mad didn't deserve this kind of happiness so much, it would have been vaguely disgusting.

Gideon's voice interrupted her thoughts. "Maricela, pass me the stuffed peppers."

The dish was closer to Avery, who wordlessly picked it up and handed it to Jyoti, who passed it to Gideon. He murmured his thanks and transferred two to his plate before glancing at Avery. "I'm glad you joined us tonight. We've missed having you around."

"I'll be staying," she told him quietly.

Gideon froze for one moment, his fork halfway to his mouth, surprise obvious in his brown eyes. But he recovered quickly, setting his fork down and gesturing to one of the guards standing against the far wall. "Ronan, will you ask the housekeeper to prepare Avery's room? Thank you."

It was a strangely charged moment, and Scarlet stepped into it boldly. "Maybe we should go to this party, Mad. It sounds like fun."

He shot her a dark look. "Traitor."

The chatter continued as Maricela focused on her

meal. After a few carefully measured deep breaths, the knot in her stomach uncoiled enough for her to be able to eat.

It didn't matter if the party was fun or not. She'd go because she had to, and because it was the closest thing she had to a job. She only hoped that it wouldn't be *too* awkward, dealing with an endless stream of suitors with Ivan at her side.

As honored as Ivan was to have been entrusted with Maricela's safety, a small, traitorous part of him missed being in the Riders' barracks.

There was an indescribable sense of *belonging* that washed over him every time he stepped into the common room. It didn't matter that, more evenings than not, he sat quietly in the corner with his guns or his knives or a book on tactics. The other Riders accepted his rare contributions to the conversation, and they accepted his silences.

They never asked him to be anyone he wasn't. They just gave every indication of liking who he was.

Dinner was fancy tonight—maybe even fancier than what he would have gotten staying at the palace. Gideon preferred simpler fare in his home, but the girls training under Del were being prepared to host great banquets and elegant dinner parties.

Hunter's cousin must have been in charge of the kitchen this time. Ivan didn't even know what to call half of the things she cooked, they were so fucking fancy, but they always tasted delicious.

The bowl in his hand was no exception. Tangy radishes covered creamy rice, and both were topped with some sort of spicy fried shrimp. Every bite was an explosion of flavor, but it was the *shrimp* Ivan couldn't get over.

The seafood in his bowl could have paid for a tenement apartment for a month. Maybe two, if it wasn't one of the nice ones. The Petrov family had made a name for themselves in recent years by specializing in aquaponic farming. Their massive greenhouses turned out blueberries in the middle of winter, and fish that tasted better than anything you could get from the river or reservoir.

But their real money came from the novelty items. Lobster. Tropical fruit.

Shrimp.

No doubt they'd tithed a certain portion to the Rios family, who had blithely allowed one of the temple acolytes to practice her skills with them, because why wouldn't they? There was always more.

But even when the people around Ivan seemed oblivious to this kind of bounty, it never shook his sense of belonging. Because Ana was across the room, savoring each bite of shrimp like a tiny miracle. And Zeke had poked dubiously at one with a fork before eating around it, clearly unconvinced.

Some of the Riders had come from luxury, some from squalor. But it never seemed to matter when they sat back in the common room together.

They were different. They were still family.

"You've got to be fucking kidding me." Reyes was stretched out on the couch, glaring at the ceiling, his empty bowl resting on his stomach. "If I wanted to go to my family's fucking parties, I would have married Maricela and *gone to their fucking parties.*"

Sometimes, they were closer than actual family.

Deacon growled low in the back of his throat. "Gideon feels—and I agree—that this is our best opportunity to gather intel on who might have hired the

Suicide Kings to get rid of us. Everyone who stood to gain anything with that stunt will be there. For that reason alone, so will we." He looked around. "Anyone else need it explained to them in small, easily understood words?"

"I only have one question." Ana popped another shrimp into her mouth with a pleased hum and grinned at Deacon. "Do I get to wear a fancy dress?"

"I don't give a damn if we're all in fancy dresses, so long as we're there—and ready to work."

"I'd look amazing in a fancy dress," Zeke announced as he transferred his shrimp to Ana's bowl. "Who's going to take me shopping for one?"

"You think you're joking," Gabe said. "But this will probably go more smoothly if you're dressed less..."

He trailed off, his gaze taking in Zeke's ripped jeans and pre-Flare T-shirt emblazoned with the fading logo of some obscure video game. A Rider would always stand out in a crowd because of their tattoos and their calling, but there was standing out, and then there was showing up at a fancy event dressed like a street kid straight out of Eden.

"Cool," Zeke supplied. "You were going to say I look cool, I'm sure."

Laurel didn't look up from the magazine she was browsing. "My money's on, 'less like you just pawed your way through a city sewer grate.'"

"Takes one to know one, baby."

Laurel arched one eyebrow. "So is this a bad time to tell you I'm wearing your girlfriend to the party?"

"Which one?" Zeke rested his chin in his palm and studied her. "Lusira would look cute on you."

"Only in your wildest dreams, son."

"Stop bantering." Reyes sat up with a grumble. "This is no time for banter. This is a serious goddamn situation."

Apparently. Ivan wasn't sure he'd ever seen a situation so dire that Reyes wouldn't crack a joke. "Most of us have never been invited to one of these fancy noble parties," he pointed out as he set his bowl back on the table. "Maybe you should explain it to us."

"What, the dog-and-pony show? It's wall-to-wall insufferable rich people." Reyes finally grinned, an expression devoid of mirth. "You're gonna hate it."

"Fernando—" Hunter began.

Reyes cut in with a snarl. "Call me that again and I'll stab you with my fork."

Fernando was a common name in Sector One. Dozens of boys were born every month and given some variation of the Prophet's name, just as Gabe had been named after the Prophet's son, and Ana was named for his daughter. Ivan had never wanted to ask if Reyes's rejection of the name was tied to his clear discomfort with his family, or if the aversion went deeper.

Asking people about an aversion to the Prophet danced perilously close to blasphemy.

Gabe stepped into the awkward silence, his expression serious. "There's one party per season. The Reyes family always hosts the summer solstice party. My family hosts the winter one. You know about the Rios' spring festival, and then Hunter's family holds the harvest celebration. And it's not just the central families—*everyone* goes. All the cousins, all the cadet branches..."

"Yeah, basically every person who makes important decisions for the sector spends a week crammed into one central, easily bombable location." Zeke made a rude noise. "Has anyone explained this to Ashwin yet? Because he's gonna spank our asses, and not in the fun way."

Ivan would be shocked if Ashwin hadn't arrived having memorized a list of every important social event and cultural quirk unique to Sector One, but pointing that out would only activate Zeke's paranoia again.

Reyes rose and dropped his bowl to the table with a clatter. "Ostensibly, it's a chance for the noble families to show their appreciation for the bounties of the seasons. Just like the street festivals."

The street festivals had been one of the lone bright spots in Ivan's memories of growing up. Entertainers crowded every corner, showing their skills by juggling improbable things and exhibiting feats of dexterity and strength that had awed him. And most of the vendors had sympathetic hearts and baskets full of broken cookies or imperfect meat pies that could find their way into a hungry young boy's pockets, even if he didn't have the coin to pay.

Somehow, he doubted the noble parties would share that innocent, sweet purity.

Hunter rubbed his chin. "So we're attending as Riders. Will we be providing extra security or investigating?"

"Both. Except for you two." Deacon pointed at Ivan and Bishop. "Your orders haven't changed."

Ivan flexed his fingers. "I stick with Maricela?"

Deacon nodded. "Same as here."

Except it wouldn't be the same at all. He'd be in an unfamiliar location where he couldn't control any of the variables. And he'd have to maneuver a political minefield with nuances he wasn't remotely equipped to understand.

It would be smarter to assign her protection to Gabe or Hunter. Even Reyes, for all his grumpy reluctance. They knew the terrain. They knew the potential threats. They'd be able to navigate the turbulent political waters.

But people would notice them. *Nobles* would notice them. And if Ivan had always been good at one thing, it was fading into the background. That could give him the edge he needed.

It was a pretty excuse, anyway. Ivan didn't know how he'd sleep at night knowing that someone else was responsible for Maricela's safety. He trusted all the Riders with his life.

The only person he trusted with Maricela's was himself. "All right."

"I know this isn't what we usually do." Deacon shot Reyes a pointed look that silenced his grumbling. "But it's important. Not just for Gideon and his family, but for us, too."

Bishop aside pushed his empty bowl and leaned against the table. "Instead of whining about it, Reyes, make yourself useful. Ivan and I need to know how to plan for security in your family's house."

Reyes pulled a battered notebook from his back pocket and slapped it down in front of Bishop. "I made some notes already. Didn't realize I'd be going with you bozos."

Hunter grinned and ruffled Reyes's hair. "We love you, too."

Ivan reached for the notebook as they traded more banter back and forth, letting the teasing jokes and the affectionate insults form a soothing, familiar babble as he flipped open the notebook and studied the pages.

The Reyes estate was huge. *Massive.* Page after page detailed multiple wings, floors, inner courtyards, and hidden nooks. Outbuildings and guest suites. Servants' quarters and secret hallways. Reyes had broken it all down in neat, organized sketches and lists highlighting potential danger and routes of escape. There were plenty of the latter—but far, far too many of the former.

The man liked to bitch and moan and spend way too much time talking about what he did with his dick, but when it came time to get a job done, Reyes was meticulous, thorough, and deadly.

Hopefully, it would all be unnecessary. If Gideon truly thought there was any danger to Maricela at this gathering, she wouldn't be attending. But it was Ivan's job to consider every scenario.

And if a threat did arise, he'd take care of it. By any means necessary.

5

True to his word, Ivan arrived back at the palace just before midnight.

As the doorknob to her suite rattled softly, Maricela sat at the table, a bottle of tequila and two empty glasses in front of her. She'd resisted the urge to open the bottle and down a little liquid courage, but as the door swung open, she bitterly regretted her decision.

Ivan stepped in and stopped, his gaze sweeping the room before settling on her at the table. His brow furrowed. "You didn't have to sit up. There was a guard keeping an eye on your room."

"I know. I was waiting for you." She pulled the chair next to hers away from the table. "Have a seat."

He obeyed, dropping a battered notebook on the table in front of him. "Did you have a good family dinner?"

"It was nice." She opened the bottle. "How are things down in the barracks?"

"The same as usual. Laurel's visiting again. She was talking like she might come to the house party with us."

"Oh?" She filled one glass with way too much tequila and slid it toward him.

He accepted the glass but didn't drink. "Have you met her yet?"

Ana liked her so very much, and so did Gideon. If they could manage it, they'd probably talk her into joining the Riders and staying permanently. "Not yet."

"I'd like to introduce you before we leave. If there are going to be any activities where a male guard is impractical, Ana and Laurel can step in."

"All right." He was making small talk, something she knew didn't come easily to him, and the effort was almost enough to change her mind. She could hold her tongue, pretend that she'd waited up only because she wanted to see him. It wasn't far from the truth.

But it wouldn't be fair—to either of them.

So she filled her glass and picked it up. "We need to talk about what happened at the temple today."

His fingers tightened on the glass. "Okay."

When she'd tried to imagine this conversation, this was as far as she'd gotten—*we need to talk*. But now she didn't know what to say. "We had a...moment."

He didn't deny it, just lifted his tequila and sipped it. "I'm sorry."

She wasn't sure blame was the issue. If it was, it might be easier—for both of them—to let him take it. But nothing about the situation felt *easy*. "You were far from alone. I mean, *I'm* the one who licked *you*."

The muscles in his arm tightened again. His lips parted, drawing her gaze, but it took another few seconds for any words to emerge. "It was a tense situation. It's not unusual for adrenaline and fear to provoke unexpected physical reactions. It wasn't your fault."

Only biting down mercilessly on the inside of her cheek kept her from bursting into nervous laughter. "That's what you think? That I lick people when my fight-or-flight responses kick in?"

His too-serious gaze roved over her face, so intense she could *feel* it. "No, I suppose not."

"I wasn't frightened." The confession should have embarrassed her, but the flush that heated her cheeks was something far more visceral. "I was turned on."

Still no obvious response. Ivan's ability to keep a stony expression was legendary, but the lack of reaction was nerve-wracking.

The silence grew as Ivan finished his drink and set the glass down with such rigid control, it barely clinked on the table. "What do you need, Maricela?"

What a tricky, tricky question. "I don't know. Your help, I guess."

He swallowed, the strong muscles in his throat working. "You can say anything you need to say. Ask for anything you want. I won't be upset. I'm here to take care of you."

Oh yes, he would give her anything she asked him for—and that was the problem. "Exactly. We can't have a relationship, even something casual based on sex. Normally, it might not be a problem, but this isn't a normal situation. You're acting as my personal guard."

"Yes, I am. And that means not crossing the line." He reached out and covered her hand with his. His calloused fingers scraped over her skin in a rasping tease. "You can feel whatever you need to feel. Trust me to hold that line. To protect you."

"I do trust you." There was no one she trusted

more—and that just made things worse. She *liked* Ivan. She liked him too much.

"Then we only have one relationship. Bodyguard—" he pointed to himself, then, with his lips quirking into a hint of a smile, pointed at her, "—and a very sleepy princess. We have a couple of big days of packing and preparation before we head out. You'll want plenty of rest."

He was taking this all with perfect, utter calm, and she wasn't sure whether his composure inspired confidence or indignation. But that was her bruised ego talking, the part of her that needed to know it was just as difficult for him to keep his distance as it was for her.

The *selfish* part of her. A good person would be glad that at least one of them had a little self-control. That one of them wasn't suffering the aches of thwarted lust.

Maybe she wasn't such a good person, after all.

She downed her tequila in two burning gulps. "I'm going to bed."

"All right." He swept up his notebook. "If you need anything, I'll be up for a while longer."

"I need..." For a single preposterous moment, she considered telling him the truth. "You're right. I need sleep."

She'd curl up in her bed, alone. By the time the morning sun streamed into her windows, she'd know that she'd made the right decision.

It was amazing how a tiny bit of context could change everything.

Maricela was tucked safely into bed, behind a pair of closed doors. Ivan sat in the antechamber he'd converted into a bedroom, his various sets of knives spread out on the table. He was glad he could clean them by rote because his mind was stuck back in the temple.

Wide eyes. Rapid breaths. Trembling. Clutching fingers.

He could close his eyes and imagine that moment in the alcove with crisp, perfect clarity. He could remember every noise and move she'd made, every reaction he'd interpreted as fear.

Wide eyes. Rapid breaths. Trembling. Clutching fingers.

All signs of arousal.

He should know. He'd been exhibiting most of them since he'd gotten the bedroom door shut behind her.

Ivan shifted in his chair, as if that could relieve the discomfort of an erection that seemed unwilling to subside. Somewhere around the fourth mental replay of the scene in the temple, his imagination had started to add details. Her parted lips grazing his jaw. Her fingers trailing up the back of his neck. Her mouth opening, eager for a kiss.

By the sixth replay, she moaned as his tongue stroked hers, coaxing sounds from her that echoed off the stone walls around them. By the ninth, he'd edged her dress from her shoulder, revealing smooth, light brown skin he had to taste.

If he let himself get to twelve, he'd be on his knees in front of her, making her sob with pleasure as she came on his tongue.

After twenty years of trying so, so hard to overcome the legacy of his uncles, Ivan had discovered that blasphemy did, indeed, run through his blood. Because fantasizing about putting his hands and mouth all over the sheltered Rios princess had to be a least a little bit treasonous.

Maybe he should focus on that. The treason. Add Gideon to his mental image. More specifically, Gideon finding out that Ivan wanted to do dirty, dirty things to Gideon's baby sister. After all, Sector One might embrace love, but big brothers were frequent hypocrites.

He tried to adjust his mental image to add a furiously disapproving Gideon. But the fantasy twisted. His leader faded. Maricela's tongue touched his ear, her voice dropping to that husky whisper he'd never forgotten, the command she'd given the last playmate to crawl into her bed. *"Use your tongue."*

Shit.

Ivan dropped his knife with a clatter and curled both hands around the table's edge until the wood bit into his palms. Maricela might want him, but she didn't *want* him. She'd all but begged him to help her keep the lines nice and crisp and clear.

Princess and bodyguard. Rios and Rider.

They could never be anything more. Because her destiny was to marry some rich man or woman—or both, or a few of each—and become the matriarch of a sprawling clan that bound the important families of Sector One together in shared blood and shared purpose.

And his job was to keep that family safe. Not to imagine himself worthy of joining it.

gideon

Estela Reyes was a formidable woman.

Unlike plenty of the men in other sectors, Gideon had never been threatened or discomfited by formidable women. His aunt had been legendary for her passion and her temper. His mother's strength might have been quieter, but Juana's sharp mind and fearless heart had shaped Gideon's perception of what courage was.

Estela Reyes was every bit as sharp as Juana, but her cunning was extremely focused and relentlessly mercenary. She'd planned the seating for her welcome dinner with the careful strategy of any general, dividing the Rios family between various tables. The people she'd placed next to them revealed her priorities for the week.

Poor Maricela had Ivan as a buffer on one side, but

the rest of her table was heavily slanted toward eligible Reyes cousins who would spend the evening competing for her attention. At any other meal, Ivan's stern-faced glower might have chilled the flirting, but noble sons of the Reyes family weren't likely to be easily intimidated.

Estela's husband, Diego Reyes, was seated beside Isabela at a different table. No doubt they were exchanging fond stories of the early days growing up in the Prophet's palace, when Diego's father had stood at their grandfather's right hand as his most trusted advisor. Estela knew how much Isabela valued tradition.

But Estela had saved Gideon for herself. She sat at his left, her long black hair held back from her face in an intricate mass of braids that offered the illusion of a crown. Her complexion was slightly darker than his, and her smooth skin showed only the tiniest wrinkles around her eyes. Her spine was perfectly straight, her smile pitch perfect for an honored hostess, and it wasn't hard to believe she'd been the most celebrated beauty of her generation.

Which had caused plenty of men to underestimate her. Gideon might not find her threatening, but he wouldn't make *that* mistake, either.

Gideon had already considered the possibility that she might have used her considerable wealth to hire mercenaries to kill his Riders and weaken his position. A man in a weakened position might grasp for allies, or even agree to a marriage proposal. But for all of Estela's elegant ruthlessness, Gideon couldn't imagine her doing *anything* that would endanger her precious, beloved son.

Then again, the easiest way to wipe out the Riders would have been a bomb dropped on the barracks. The fact that the Kings hadn't taken such a simple opportunity might indicate their orders had included a command to keep one particular Rider alive. Or it might simply indicate that their leader's obsession with Deacon had been his downfall, after all.

The sparse evidence they had didn't point to Estela, but Gideon couldn't rule her out, either. Of one thing, there was *no* doubt—the Reyes matriarch had marriage alliances on her mind.

"Aren't the dishes lovely?" Estela asked, indicating the dip-glazed setting in front of him with a flourish. "Anita made them, you know. She's very skilled."

Nita looked like she wanted to sink through her chair and be swallowed up by the earth. "Mother—"

"They're beautiful," Gideon cut in, rubbing a thumb along the edge of his plate. It wasn't even a lie—Nita *was* very skilled. The plate in front of him somehow captured the glory of a Sector One sunset, pinks and purples in the middle that spiraled out into blue and then midnight, with tiny specks of white mimicking a thousand stars.

Exquisite, and no doubt capable of commanding an incredible price. Most of the nobles present would leap at a chance to add Nita's skills—and her inheritance—to their families.

Estela had other ideas. She always did.

"Beautiful, yes, but also functional." Estela tilted her head and smiled. "Beauty fades. True strength will always endure."

Gideon's usual gracious smile didn't come naturally. He had to summon it, responding to Estela with the expected compliments about the wisdom of her pithy words. He could only hope Nita was oblivious to the subtext—but a glance to his right showed a fixed smile and Nita gesturing for a servant to refill her wine glass.

That kindled a spark of anger. Nita was a beautiful

young woman. Maybe not the type of petite, fragile beauty her mother was, but undeniably gorgeous all the same. Del often expressed amused exasperation over the string of lovesick guards and gardeners who wrote Nita terrible poetry and brought her gifts and woke up half the acolytes by throwing pebbles at her window.

And three days after she'd been born, Gideon had attended her christening with his mother. Cute, adorable baby Nita had cooed and then thrown up on him.

He would always be fond of Nita. And nothing on earth would compel him to marry her, not even Estela Reyes.

As the conversation continued, his gaze drifted to the opposite side of the garden, where Avery had been seated so far away she was practically in the trees. Zeke was at the table with her, and Lucio, along with several West and Montero cousins so distant they barely qualified as noble.

They looked like they were having a lot more fun than he was.

Estela's subtle knife may have sliced Nita to the bone, but it cut Gideon deeper than he wanted to admit. Estela was too smart a woman to pass up the opportunity to forge a relationship with Avery. Avery's sister wasn't just the co-ruler of Sector Four, but one of the most influential women in their world. Anyone who valued power as much as the Reyes matriarch should have been working hard to ingratiate herself to Lex Parrino's only sister.

Unless, of course, she saw Avery as a threat to her plans for Nita.

His patience for political games had waned since the war, but this week he'd have to play them fiercely. He'd have to be charming and personable, wise and just. He'd have to ferret out who might wish him ill and who might have paid to hurt his Riders.

And he'd have to flirt with the eligible men and women thrown into his path enthusiastically enough to dispel any rumors. Because if Estela Reyes had noticed his...weakness for Avery, it was only a matter of time before other people did, as well, turning her into a target.

6

By the time dinner wound to a close, Ivan wanted to break a few noble jaws.

Alexei Petrov was the only one at the table who *wasn't* slobbering all over Maricela with his eyes. The three Reyes cousins and two Reyes uncles—old enough to be Maricela's father and grandfather respectively—took turns flirting, bragging, and using barely concealed innuendo to present their qualifications as consort.

At least they kept their hands above the table and to themselves. Not that Ivan hadn't entertained a few fantasies of what he'd do with those potentially wandering fingers anyway—pondering the damage he could do with a lobster cracker had gotten him through an endless dessert.

Now, his job was going to be exponentially harder. Dinner had ended, and people were rising from their assigned tables to have drinks and mingle in the gardens. The Reyes uncles and cousins were drifting away, but before Maricela could leave the table, someone else claimed the seat beside her—and took her hand.

"My favorite sister-in-law's sister." Javier Montero looked like a softer, prettier version of Gabe. They both had inherited their father's height and broad shoulders, but instead of Gabe's stern features and lean strength, Javier had his mother's silky black hair, big brown eyes, and far-too-charming smile.

And he wasn't just slobbering all over Maricela with his eyes. He was doing it with his mouth, kissing the back of her hand in a lingering fashion that tightened instant dislike in Ivan's gut.

"Javier." Maricela smiled but extricated her hand by reaching for her water goblet. "How is your mother?"

"Good, good." He tossed an arm across the back of her chair and leaned in so close that Ivan considered dragging him back by his pretty hair. "I was just telling her we should have you over. Uncle David says the new lambs will be born any day now. Nothing so cute as the first time they stand up on their wobbly little legs."

"I'm sure they're adorable. Perhaps Isabela should take the children to see them."

Ivan had to press his lips together to avoid smiling at how deftly she sidestepped him. But the momentary urge to smile faded almost instantly—she hadn't gotten this good at skillful evasion without years of practice navigating a minefield of overly friendly men.

Dinner must have been exhausting for her.

Pushing his chair back, Ivan stood just as Javier's fingers left the back of the chair, no doubt headed for Maricela's shoulder. Ivan clamped a hand around the man's wrist, squeezing hard enough to provoke a grunt of surprise, then released him. "Sorry," he lied, gripping the back of Maricela's chair so he couldn't put his arm back. "Are you ready to go meet your brother?"

"Very," she murmured, rising to slide her arm through Ivan's. "Thank you for the invitation, Javier. I'll be sure and pass it on to Gideon."

Javier's pleasant smile slipped the moment Maricela's back was turned. Ivan met his irritated glare with a blank expression of his own before turning to lead her away from the table.

Her fingers dug into his forearm. "Will you even believe me if I tell you the parties aren't usually this bad?"

"Are they not?"

She shook her head as they passed under the shadow of a tree at the edge of the garden maze. "When I was younger, they were almost fun."

The yearning in her voice spoke of a desperate need for respite. Thanks to Reyes's thorough little notebook, he knew how to provide it. He steered them through the maze's entrance and let the stillness and shadows of the high hedges wrap around them. "Before you had to deal with suitors?"

"Honestly? It's hard to remember a time before I had suitors. But they're going to be more plentiful and more insistent this year." She shrugged. "Isabela has decided it's time for me to get married."

"Does Isabela get to decide that?"

Maricela didn't answer. Instead, she reached out and plucked a leaf from one of the hedges.

The maze had a trick to it. Reyes had written it out, and Ivan had dutifully memorized it. After two right turns made in silence, he steered Maricela to the left at the next fork and spoke again. "Do you *want* to get married?"

"What I want doesn't matter. I mean, it *does*, but

it also doesn't." Her thumb brushed the inside of his elbow as she released his arm. "It's what I'm supposed to do."

The Rios streak of responsibility ran deep. He'd spent enough years watching Gideon to understand that, but some things seemed too personal to accept out of duty. "Your brother hasn't gotten married yet."

"No, not yet." She turned to face Ivan, her long gown tangling around her legs as she walked backwards before stopping. "I lied to you."

"You lied? About what?"

"Last training day. I let you believe that I wanted an escort to the festival, but I—" Even in the moonlight, the flush on her cheeks was visible. "That's not what I wanted."

All the emotions he'd locked down so carefully gave one, violent kick.

Odd, how much the shading of memories could change with new context. Not that he was any stranger to the idea. He'd had good memories of his uncles. Being lifted onto a knee so he could sit at the table with the grownups. Being scooped up off the ground when he fell. Pats on the shoulder and ruffled hair, the short, blurry-around-the-edges recollections of a young child.

But after he'd grown old enough to understand, shadows had seeped in around the edges. Those memories were darkened by the cold chill of nights sleeping on the street, curled against his mother, because he was being punished for the crimes of men he'd never realized were bad.

Now that Maricela had confessed her physical attraction to him, the memory of their interaction at the training day shifted subtly. He knew that he'd looked at her with fondness and reverence. With devotion. He never would have imagined crossing that big, bright line. Not even in his head.

He couldn't help it now. She wanted him. Had been wanting him. Now that he knew *wanting him* wasn't a whim or adrenaline, it was hard not to be pleased by that. But he couldn't.

He would not.

He'd never had any trouble controlling his mouth before. He didn't even *like* to talk. But the words slipped out without his permission. "What did you want?"

"A lover." She turned and stepped farther into the shadows. "I should have been honest with you then. Now it's too late to find out."

Yes, too late. Far too late. Because she'd asked him to hold them to what was right, and she was sweet. Sheltered. Too innocent to realize that murmuring the word *lover* while it was just the two of them, standing in shadows deep enough to disappear into, was actual, literal torment.

Ashwin would be envious of how efficiently she was torturing him.

They came to another intersection, and he had to swallow hard to get even one word out. "Go right. That should bring us to the center of the maze."

"Have you been here before?"

"Reyes drew me some diagrams. And I did some recon while you and Ana were with the seamstress."

She made a soft noise of amusement. "It took me a week to find the center of this maze. I was probably seven or eight years old, and I spent every afternoon of our visit meticulously mapping this damn thing." She cast a quick glance over her shoulder at him, her expression unreadable. "I'm starting to think it would have been a bad idea, anyway."

His emotions kicked again. "Us becoming lovers?"

"Yes." She emerged into the center of the maze,

where benches made of quarried rock and stone surrounded a large, ornate fountain. Water shot into the air and cascaded down, the droplets catching the moonlight like tiny diamonds.

The music from the party was a distant hum. The voices had faded away completely. It was peaceful here, with the gentle music of water over stone and the wind through the leaves on the hedges and nothing but the clean smell of earth and plants and nature.

Maricela belonged in a place like this. Outside, under the stars. Not trapped in her house or stuck between swaggering suitors who leaned too close and whispered constant invitations she had to pretend not to understand.

The breeze tugged at the ends of her long hair, tossing it across her face, and his fingers itched to smooth it back into place. Before he could give in to temptation, she reached up and tucked the rogue strand behind her ear.

The silence between them wasn't comfortable. It was charged, her last words hanging there like a tense challenge. "We can't be lovers," he said softly, a reminder as much for himself as for her. "But we can be friends."

"Yes." She smiled, and the tension dissolved. "What did you think of the dinner?"

A lifetime of habit almost had him locking down his reaction, as was proper in the presence of a Rios. But the word *friend* still hovered in the air, so he reacted like he would have to a Rider.

He rolled his eyes.

Her laughter rang through the small courtyard. "I'll have you know, that was some of the finest seafood money can't buy. Didn't you notice the Petrov heir at our table? The one who wasn't being a creep?" She sank to one of the benches. "I'm sure that's how Estela got her hands on enough lobster to feed fifty people."

He straddled the opposite side of the bench so he could look at her but keep the maze entrance in his peripheral vision. "So that's how the seating arrangement works? People bribe Estela Reyes to get close to you?"

"That's how this whole week works." She ticked the list off on her fingers matter-of-factly. "Basic line of sight, that's cheap. But you have to pony up if you want your son or daughter seated next to me at a meal or concert. And don't even *ask* how much it costs to get them a room assignment near mine."

Disgust at the sheer *awfulness* of it all rose, and Ivan didn't try to hide it. "They better not think they're getting into your room without an invitation."

"Oh, no. Never. It's not about force." She leaned closer and lowered her voice. "It's about access. The opportunity to influence. The same thing happens to Gideon and Isabela, for different reasons. Hell, Deacon and Ana weren't shoved at a table in the corner with the rest of the Riders who don't come from noble families, were they?"

He thought back, summoning the placement of the various Riders from memory. He'd expected Gabe, Hunter, and Reyes to be seated prominently, of course, but Deacon had been at a table next to the West matriarch, and Ana had been tucked between Gabe's parents. "Because Ana's father's going to be sainted?"

"Maybe," Maricela allowed. "William belonged to the Riders, but I'm not sure it matters. We talk about how your families give you up when you take your vows, but those ties never really seem to die. Not on a gut level."

No, they didn't. Not the ties to the saints *or* to

the traitors. In his life, Ivan had faced both—younger people who begged him to ask his father for a special blessing, and older people who eyed him with wariness, no doubt remembering the havoc and pain his uncles had wrought on their beloved royal family.

"It's complicated," he murmured. Normally that would have been all he said, all he cared to say, but talking to Maricela was...easy, somehow. "There's only just the two of us, you know. Me and Ana. And Gideon hadn't even officially formed the Riders before my father died. We don't fit into the rules and customs. So people see us the way they want to see us."

"How do they see you?"

The marble bench had a tiny crack along one side. Ivan traced it with his thumb. "All I ever wanted to be was a Rider. But when I first showed up to a trial, people were furious. They didn't want the traitors' nephew in Gideon's inner circle. It had been more than ten years, but that's all they saw when they looked at me. Bad blood."

She sucked in a breath. "That's horrible."

It hadn't felt horrible. It had felt deserved, a guilt he'd internalized after a lifetime of lessons from his mother, who had never forgiven herself for not seeing what was happening all around her. It had taken him years to understand that the intensity of her guilt was the product of a chemical imbalance in her brain.

Maybe his was, too. Ivan wasn't sure he wanted to find out, wasn't sure there was even a point. Guilt had never gotten in the way of his job—if anything, it made him a more dedicated Rider.

Proving the whispers wrong had always been *very* good motivation.

He couldn't say any of that to Maricela, not with outrage all but vibrating off of her. "Your cousin Mad stepped up. Even though my uncles had kidnapped him and killed his parents, he stood up for me. No one was willing to fight him over it." Ivan shrugged and glanced up at her. "Becoming a Rider means your family is supposed to give you up. It doesn't mean the sector will let you give up your family. Just ask Reyes or Gabe or Hunter."

"That's true." Her stormy expression cleared as she patted his hand. "I'm glad you were able to find your way."

Her fingertips burned over his skin, and she didn't even realize it. If being friends meant Maricela planned to shower him with sweet, oblivious touches, he'd drastically miscalculated.

This was torture.

He tensed, consciously exerting control. He had to find a way to go back to before she'd tilted their world on its side. He couldn't help imagining Maricela's husky command to use his tongue and thinking of just how easy it would be here. He could stretch her back on the bench and coax her dress up her long legs. Use his tongue anywhere and everywhere until her hoarse cries drowned out the sound of the fountain and the stars were dancing above them.

He could take care of her.

He could go to hell.

"Maricela!" Nita's voice drifted toward them on the wind, coming from somewhere east in the maze.

"Over here!" she answered, her gaze still fixed on Ivan's face.

"I'm glad you know your way through this thing." Grace's voice, tinged with laughter. "I would be hopelessly lost."

"I think my coach is turning into a pumpkin." Maricela rose with a soft sigh. "Except now it's time for me to get *back* to the ball."

He had no idea what the words meant, but he didn't get a chance to ask. Nita appeared at the break in the hedges, the intricate jeweled beading on her bodice catching the light. She beamed at Ivan before winking at Maricela. "C'mon. Let's go get the annoying dances out of the way first so we can flirt with cute guards and dance with pretty girls."

"Of course." But Maricela's smile didn't quite reach her eyes as she slid her hand into Nita's.

The three girls headed back to the party, with Ivan trailing a few feet behind, all his thwarted desire replaced with frustration of a different kind.

He could protect Maricela from physical harm, but he couldn't protect her from the demands of who she was. No matter how much he wanted to.

Over the years, Maricela had learned to treat dances as reconnaissance.

There was a lot you could glean about a person in a few minutes of chatter on the dance floor. So far this evening, she'd learned that Gabe was her favorite Montero for a very good reason, because most of his uncles and cousins were pushy as hell. She'd also found out that tongues were wagging about the fact that Gideon had chosen to bring his entire family—plus all the Riders—to the Rios gathering. Rumors of an impending engagement had already begun to circulate.

Which was probably why the Monteros were being so damn aggressive.

Still, in between the stilted conversations and stomped toes, she discovered some lovely things. Alexei Petrov was a polite, witty man who seemed to be genuinely interested in talking to her, and dancing with him proved a welcome reprieve from the thinly veiled declarations of intent. And her friends were having a good time, something she couldn't help but appreciate with snatches of their laughter blending into the music.

Mostly, she realized that she was aware of Ivan. Not in that way where she always knew where he was, or how his proximity made her skin prickle. She could feel him watching her, the soft weight of his stare like the barest brush of a hand. And every time she glanced over to test the sensation, she was right.

That was new.

So was the look in his eyes. His expression was set in the same blank mask she'd become accustomed to, but his dark blue eyes followed her with a barely contained heat she told herself she had to be imagining.

"Your bodyguard's cute."

The words jerked her attention back to Alexei a moment before their meaning sank in, and she blushed furiously. "I suppose so."

"All stern and broody." Alexei grinned and twirled them so Ivan wouldn't see her blush. "I used to have a weakness for the type. It's irresistible, you know. Finding out what's lurking beneath all that brood."

She fought a smile. "Teasing people is just mean."

"Hey, now. I thought we were becoming friends. And friends get to tease." He leaned closer. "Anything that gets us through the week, right?"

"You're right." She lowered her voice to match his. "But it's a sore spot."

"Ah. Nothing more tragic than star-crossed lovers."

He spoke with enough melancholy to convince her he knew this from personal experience, which was the only reason she didn't step down firmly on the arch of his foot.

"So," he continued, his tone lightening again.

"Maybe you can help me out with something."

"After you've teased me so mercilessly? How brash."

"Consider it a business opportunity." He looked around quickly. "You know one of the Montero chauffeurs is taking bets on which of us get married off. The odds are all over the place on you, and I'm a lost cause, but your friend Nita..." He waggled his eyebrows and tilted his head toward where Nita was dancing with one of Hunter's brothers. "Any hint of romance in the air you want to tip me off about?"

The odds of someone successfully wooing Nita were perfectly calculable and exact: zero. Nita would never, ever marry anyone, not even under the fiercest pressure Estela Reyes could muster—not while Hunter was alive. She'd never said it, not in so many words, but Maricela had watched her friend's infatuation with him kindle and grow into something that nothing, not even him joining the Riders, seemed to shake.

Alexei was still watching her, so she shook her head. "My advice? Save your money."

"Now that's what I needed. The good intel." They spun in another lazy circle as the music swelled toward its climax. "Tell me the truth. Does this whole thing get any less awkward?"

"Hmm." He'd only been attending the parties for a year or so. He'd never experienced them without the burden of searching for a spouse he didn't want. "Ask me again in the fall, Alexei."

"What will be different in the fall?"

"Nothing, probably. But maybe I'll be able to give you a better answer by then. Because right now, the truth is *not so far*."

"Pity." His dark hair fell across his bright blue eyes as he offered her a smile. "Well, I would tell you that you make it slightly less awkward, but then you'd think I have designs on you. So I'll just say you're a terrible dancer and this isn't any fun at all, and I hope we can continue to not enjoy each other's presence tomorrow at the picnic or the horseback riding or whatever we're supposed to be doing."

"Likewise, Mr. Petrov. Likewise."

The music wound to a close, and a tall stranger with tanned skin, black hair, and a neatly trimmed beard appeared at their shoulders. "Can I claim the next dance?"

She didn't know him, she was certain of that, but he seemed so familiar that she smiled reflexively. "Of course."

Alexei relinquished her with a bow and a wink, and the newcomer slid into place, clasping her hand in his as the musicians began to play a slow waltz. He was tall enough that she had to reach up to settle her hand on his shoulder, but when he guided them into the dance, he moved gracefully. "I'll try not to step on your toes. I've only done this a few times."

Taken off guard, she answered honestly. "I don't believe you."

He laughed, his brown eyes twinkling. "All right, I've only done it with someone who isn't my mother a few times. She taught me because she loved to dance, but I haven't had much opportunity to practice."

Maybe that was it—he was the distant cousin of someone at court, but she knew his parents. "I'm Maricela."

"I know." He spun her around, giving her a brief glimpse of Ivan watching warily. "I'm Lucas."

The name didn't prompt recognition, but he did, so profoundly that she *knew* she knew him. "Have we met before?"

"Oh, I doubt it." He tilted his head. "I grew up away from the sectors. In a survivalist commune in the mountains, actually. Hence why I haven't had many chances to attend formal dances."

"But your family is here. They must be." More than money, Estela Reyes valued status. There was only one way to win an invitation to her yearly house party: to have a name or position she prized highly enough to merit it.

"Antonio Montero has taken me under his wing. He was kind enough to bring me with him this week."

That would do it. Gabe's uncle wasn't the patriarch of their family, but he was well-respected and genial. More than that, he'd developed a reputation as having a keen head for business. If anyone could socially elevate a new arrival from the communes, it was Antonio. "Then I hope you enjoy your visit to Sector One."

"Well, it will be hard to top the pleasure of dancing with Maricela Rios."

His smile was just right, wide and appreciative without treading too close to artifice. But there was something else going on behind his eyes, something calculated and nervous that left her instinctively looking around for Ivan.

Her gaze snagged on Isabela instead. Her sister gasped, and her champagne flute slipped between lax fingers to shatter on the stones beneath her feet.

The music tapered off with a discordant screech of strings. Murmured voices buzzed around the room, but Maricela couldn't look away as her sister raised a shaking hand to her throat, her lips forming a single word.

"Abuelo."

She swayed, and Maricela dove toward her. "Isabela—"

Gideon was quicker. He caught Isabela around

72

the waist, steadying her as his gaze raked over Lucas. Emotion flashed across his face almost too fast for Maricela to track—rage, pain, regret—before he locked it down.

When he spoke, his voice was perfectly even. "I suppose you're Teresa's son."

"Indeed." The glint was back in Lucas's eyes. He smiled at Maricela again before sweeping a bow to Gideon. "Fernando Lucas Rios. It's so nice to finally meet you, cousin."

7

After a late night of wine, dancing, and frantic gossip, most of Estela Reyes's guests were crashing in their borrowed beds.

The Riders didn't have time for that.

As the hallways quieted and servants finished attending to last-minute needs, Gideon assembled his people in the generous suite he'd been provided. Kora and Maricela were next door in Isabela's suite, waiting under Bishop's watchful eye, but Ivan was anxious to return to her side.

He was just anxious in general.

Laurel tagged along to the meeting with Ana, and Gideon's nod of welcome all but confirmed his plans to woo the sniper from Sector Three into the ranks of the Riders. Ivan still wasn't sure that was wise. He liked Laurel, but she reminded him of a skittish, wild creature. She seemed easygoing and confident on the surface—especially when she was verbally sparring with Zeke or poking at Gabe—but she got a look in her eyes sometimes. A well-hidden but undeniable panic, as if the walls were closing in and she was searching for the closest exit so she could disappear and never return.

Ivan didn't trust Laurel to stick around if shit got too weird for her. But he trusted her to have their backs while she was here, so he settled into a seat with a strong cup of coffee and braced himself to have the darkest parts of his childhood torn open.

"So." Reyes brushed his hair out of his eyes. "The lost heir of the Prophet's bastard son. This should be fun."

Zeke made a rude noise. "Only the *really* out-there conspiracy theory nuts in Eden bought into this one. I can't believe it's fucking true."

"It looks like it could be," Gideon said reluctantly. "His resemblance to my grandfather in his youth is uncanny. Kora says it's possible cosmetic surgery could have replicated the features, but a simple DNA test will reveal the truth either way, and that would be nearly impossible to fool."

"Nearly," Ashwin interjected. "The Base has experimented with retroactively altering DNA, but their only successes have been at a microscopic level. Nothing sophisticated enough to counterfeit a familial connection."

"It would be risky for an impostor to make such a public claim." Lucio didn't move from his spot by the window, and he gazed out over the lawn below as he spoke. "Then again, potentially being exiled from One might be worth the gamble."

Deacon gestured toward Gabe. "Your uncle

brought him. What did he have to say about it?"

Gabe's eyebrows drew together in a stormy frown. "Uncle Antonio wasn't very forthcoming. He's never been shy about asking me for favors, but now suddenly this is *family* business, and I'm not technically family anymore."

Hunter scoffed. "Come on. You didn't let him get away with that, did you?"

"Of course not. I made it clear he could explain the situation to me or directly to Gideon. But he still just spewed a lot of shit about forgiveness and grace and how if Gideon wanted to hold the sins of the family against the next generation, then he never should have—" Gabe cut off abruptly, but his gaze slid to Ivan.

There it was.

"Then he never should have let me become a Rider," Ivan said as evenly as he could manage.

"That's a load of shit," Reyes growled.

"Oh, fuck," Zeke exclaimed suddenly, sitting upright. His wide eyes locked on to Ivan, and the expression there was familiar and demoralizing. "I mean, I learned about the bastard heir and the civil war and everything, and I guess I knew your uncles were involved, I just never..."

"*Zeke*," Deacon snapped.

Laurel, who had been surveying them all with silent interest, cleared her throat and raised her hand. "A little background here? For the new kid?"

Half the Riders looked at him. The rest looked at Gideon. Ana was the one who cleared her throat. "About twenty-five years ago, some people decided they didn't agree with the way the Prophet was running things, so they found a convenient figurehead. The grown son of one of the Prophet's mistresses."

"He had plenty of choose from, I assume." Laurel

glanced at Gideon. "No offense."

Gideon lifted one shoulder. "The idea of group marriages had become popular by that point, but my grandmother drew a firm line. The Prophet had many consorts, but only one wife. I expect Abuela Ana is the reason our inheritance traditions are so rigidly defined. She had no intention of seeing her children usurped by the many, many offspring her husband fathered in his later years."

"Which is logically inconsistent," Ashwin said, his brow furrowing. "If any specific divinity could be inherited, all of his children should have equal claim to it."

Reyes barked out a laugh and batted his eyelashes at him. "You're so cute when you're being stupid."

Ashwin glowered at him.

"Don't start, you two." Zeke leaned forward, grabbed an entire tray of pastries—probably meant for the next morning's breakfast—and dragged it towards him. "It's too late to be punching each other."

"You're straying off topic," Ana chided them, then turned back to Laurel. "Anyway, there was a civil war. Fighting, on and off, for years. But it started when the main agitators kidnapped Gideon's cousin and his aunt."

Laurel absently reached for one of the pastries and drew back her hand when Zeke smacked it. "You mean Mad and his mother."

"Yeah." Ana glanced at Ivan, her gaze almost apologetic. He inclined his head to give her permission to say the worst of it.

At least then he wouldn't have to do it.

"It got bad," Ana said softly. "They made a ransom demand, and the Prophet refused to negotiate. He said he'd had a vision, that he was being tested. So they sent him his daughter's finger."

A horrifying detail, but still so sanitized. Ana probably didn't know how it had really gone down. Ivan did. When he'd been old enough to understand, he'd made Mad tell him all of it. How they'd held Mad and his mother in a dark room, shut away from light and food and water. How they'd come into that stinking cellar with a gun, but couldn't bring themselves to point it at Santa Adriana, the beloved princess of Sector One. They certainly couldn't bring themselves to cut her. So they'd ground the barrel of the gun into Mad's temple and ordered him to cut off his mother's finger.

And, in a dull voice numb with trauma, Mad had told Ivan how his mother had begged him to do it, so desperate to save her son's life that, in the end, she gave up her own.

Ivan's family had done that to him. His Uncle Scott had bounced Ivan on his knee and let him steal the bacon from his plate, and then he'd gone to a shitty, dank basement, wrapped his fingers around a pistol, and shoved it against the temple of a thirteen-year-old boy, forcing him to take a knife to his own mother.

No wonder Ivan's mother had gone a little crazy. Finding out that the people you loved were capable of evil left wounds that never healed.

Ana was still talking, her voice too warm and bright for the story she was telling. "...eventually they got Mad out, but both of his parents died. That's when the war broke out in earnest. The bastard heir had a pregnant wife, but she disappeared in all the chaos, and then he died pretty dramatically."

"But the war never really did," Gideon added. "I formed the Riders officially five years after the kidnapping, and it took us another eight to bring the sector back to order. A lot of people died on both sides. I guess I always figured that if Teresa had gotten out, there was no way she'd risk coming back."

"To be fair, it seems she hasn't." Lucio finally turned toward them all, his arms crossed over his chest. "The question is, why did her son? Is he looking to reconnect with his roots, meet his cousins? Or are his intentions more...revolutionary?"

Ivan almost held his tongue. Shame still burned in his gut, and he wanted nothing more than to escape this conversation. But he had a job—a duty—one that mattered more than personal comfort. "I think his intentions are obvious. He went straight for Maricela."

"Assuming he's being honest about his identity, she *is* his cousin," Hunter said mildly. "And less intimidating than Gideon or Isabela."

And more useful as a kidnapping victim. If someone snatched Maricela, Gideon and Isabela wouldn't make up some shit about being tested. They'd sacrifice whatever was necessary to get her back.

He didn't say it out loud. Gideon was already giving him that *look*, the one that peeled away all the walls you tried to hide behind and saw into the darkest corners of your heart.

Lucas was the son of tragedy, just like Ivan. He hadn't even been *born* when the events that had defined both of their lives had transpired. The people who loved Ivan would be horrified to know how quickly he condemned Lucas for the sins of his father, because then they'd know the truth.

Ivan had condemned himself a long, long time ago.

"Lucas isn't responsible for what his father did," Gideon said slowly, his gaze never leaving Ivan's face. "I won't damn him for someone else's crimes. But Teresa was in the thick of the rebellion, and we don't know what he grew up hearing about *us*. So caution seems wise. Zeke?"

"On it," Zeke said around a mouthful of donut. He reached into a bag at his feet and pulled out a sleek tablet that unfolded on the table into a wide square. "Check this out. I got the new prototype out of Eden. The best thing about the war being over is that innovation is booming."

He swiped a hand over the edge of the tablet, and a holographic display appeared above it. "Sweet, right? I'll get my group on it, tracking down any whispers. I might even be able to sweet-talk Penny into running some facial recognition scans inside Eden. See if he's been around for a while and what he's been doing."

"Good. Ashwin? Do you know anyone in the mountain communes?"

"I don't. But I know a Makhai soldier who's cultivated an extensive network of contacts there. I can ask for a favor." He hesitated. "The Makhai don't take favors lightly. Indebting myself to him will mean he can call on us for assistance later."

"That's fine," Gideon said. "We need all the information we can get."

"What do we do about the kid in the meantime?" Deacon asked.

"We watch him. Feel him out. I'll let Isabela take the first run at him. Most people aren't prepared for how devious she can be." Gideon sipped his coffee and glanced around the room. "Reyes? You and Hunter should find a chance to talk to him, too. Flatter him as a fellow noble. Make him feel accepted."

Reyes groaned, and Hunter elbowed him in the ribs.

"Reyes." Gideon said it mildly, but it was still a reprimand. "You don't have to enjoy your status, but it's a valuable tool. Use it."

After a moment, he relented with a shrug. "All right, all right. I'll talk to my mother. She's probably already running intel and surveillance ops that would make us weep with jealousy."

"I don't doubt it for a moment," Gideon replied with a hint of a smile. Then he turned to Ivan. "Maricela's safety is your only concern."

It wasn't just an order, it was a quiet declaration. Ivan didn't have to give voice to the doubts in his heart for Gideon to see them. But his leader still trusted him with the most precious thing in his life.

Ivan swallowed hard. "Yes, sir."

Laurel looked up from Zeke's dancing holographic display. "Anything you want me to do? I mean, I'm nobody...but sometimes that helps."

Gideon tapped his fingers against the table. "Watch him, especially when he doesn't think he's being watched. It's hard for a Rider to go unnoticed, but if you can get an idea of who he's talking to, what he's doing..."

"You bet."

"Good." Gideon took a deep breath. "I want to believe this is just an innocent coincidence. But having the lost heir resurface a few weeks after someone attempted to eliminate the Riders? It would be reckless to disregard the potential danger. So if anyone *does* find something, no matter how small, you come to me immediately. At the first hint of trouble, I want my family out of here. I'll deal with the political fallout later."

And that was the Rios sensibility to the bone. Gideon would risk his own life for the sector, but that carelessness didn't extend to the people he loved.

Unfortunately, in Ivan's experience, Maricela felt the exact same way.

The suite the Reyes family had offered Maricela was large and luxurious, with a parlor, a sitting area, and an attached bathroom. As she stared up at the murals on the ceilings and gilded cornices, she tried to calculate how many acolytes must have been shoved into much smaller rooms together just to afford her this extra space.

Ivan came out of the bathroom, running a towel over his freshly shaved face. Damp strands of hair stuck up in spikes, and he'd changed into loose jeans and a thin white T-shirt. He paused next to the bed, a sympathetic half-smile curving his usually stern lips. "Are you doing okay?"

The suite was big, but not big enough for the two of them.

Maricela swallowed a groan and sat up—no small feat, with the thick, fluffy duvet trying to swallow her whole. "I'm fine."

He gave her a doubtful look before perching on the corner of the bed—something that might have been more intimate if the bed wasn't so massive. "It's okay if you're not."

"I'm just tired," she confessed. "It's been a long, weird day."

"It has." He rubbed the towel over his hair, which only served to dishevel it more. "Gideon's going to find out as much as he can about this Lucas guy, see if we can figure out why he's here and what he wants."

"I don't want to talk about him right now." She needed to think about something else. Anything else. "What do you like to do? You know, when you're not working twenty-four hours a day."

The corner of his mouth ticked up again. "I'm a Rider. I'm always working twenty-four hours a day."

She stretched out and nudged him with her foot. "You know what I mean. It can't all be keeping the peace and polishing your knife collection—which you do *a lot*, by the way."

"No, I don't," he corrected, straight-faced. "Sometimes I'm sharpening them."

"They're already sharp."

"Maybe." He shrugged and leaned against the bedpost. "The knives *are* my hobby. When I was a kid, there was a blacksmith who used to do knife throwing at all the street festivals. Mostly flashy tricks to attract attention so he could sell them his kitchen knives."

"You mean Ed." Just imagining the burly man's infectious smile was enough to make Maricela feel a little better. "I love Ed."

"He's a good man." Ivan tilted his head back against the post and closed his eyes. "I never had any money to spend at the fairs, so Ed brought me into his booth and taught me how to polish and sharpen the knives. He overpaid me, too, but it meant I had money to buy candy and presents to try to make my mama smile."

Sharp, sudden pain twisted in her chest. "It wasn't fair, what people did to the two of you."

Ivan didn't open his eyes, but his jaw tightened for a moment. "It wasn't as bad for me," he said quietly. "I was a kid, and people knew I was a kid. Maybe they didn't help me as much as they should have, but they usually weren't *mean* to me. But people were sure my mother had to have known something. That she couldn't have lived in the house where the kidnapping was plotted and just...been oblivious."

Nothing felt more helpless than understanding how your life could spin out of control with no warning. People needed to *know* that Ivan's mother must have been an accomplice, because accepting that she honestly may not have known about the plot would mean admitting that the same thing could happen to them, and they would be powerless to see it, much less stop it.

"It wasn't fair," Maricela said again. "And it wasn't her fault."

"No." He flexed his fingers and finally opened his eyes. "I don't talk about it a lot because it makes me mad. My mother always had...moods. But they told her she was bad and told her and told her, and eventually she started to believe them."

Maricela almost reached for him. With any of her other friends, she would have offered a hug or some other soothing physical contact to help ease the pain that old memories could carry. But that seemed dangerous here, with Ivan. She already wanted to touch him in ways that had nothing to do with comfort or friendly support. Crossing the line might prove a temptation too great for her to resist.

She settled back against the padded headboard instead. "I have another brother, you know."

He tilted his head, one eyebrow raised. "Another brother?"

"I wasn't an only child when my birth parents died." How could her own family history seem so unreal, like she was talking about characters in a story instead of her own life? "They had a little boy before me. Relatives took him in, but they couldn't handle a baby, so."

"I didn't know." Ivan studied her, obviously hesitant to ask what was bound to be a personal question. "Have you met him?"

"No. I know that he lives in Sector Eight. He's married. They might have kids by now." She shrugged. "The idea of contacting him doesn't feel right. What if he doesn't even know I exist?"

"But you know he exists."

"I do."

"Do you *want* to meet him?"

"Yes and no." How could she decide when she didn't know if a meeting would cause the man joy or pain? "I'm not sure it's worth the chance. What if he doesn't even know about our birth parents? I could ruin his life, Ivan."

"Maybe," he allowed after a moment. Then he shrugged. "I'm not exactly good with family. I don't know what I'd do. But anyone who wasn't happy to get you as a sister would be a fool."

Tears stung her eyes, and she blinked them away with a grin. "You're sweet. Why does everyone else in this sector think you're such a hard-ass?"

"Because I am." He rocked to his feet and slung the towel over his shoulder. "I'm not sweet, Maricela, not even a little. I'm just telling the truth as I see it."

"Then you're biased." She watched as he walked over to the sofa where the servants had left his bedding. It was only a dozen feet away, with nothing separating them. "Is this going to be weird? The sleeping arrangements?"

He paused with the blanket in his hands, his gaze sweeping the room as if looking for an alternative. "Will it bother you?"

She rolled to her side and propped her head on her

hand. "Do you realize that when a question is tricky or delicate, you answer it with another question?"

His mouth opened. Closed again. His brows drew together in a frown.

"Uh-huh. It makes me wonder how different your answers would be if you couldn't buy yourself enough time to consider them."

"You want the truth?"

"Always. There's no other reason to ask questions."

Ivan's sudden smile transformed his entire face. "I spent a bunch of years sharing a room with Reyes. I don't care how weird it gets, it's not gonna get Reyes weird."

The words—and the smile—were irresistible. "Explain, please. Did he drag you headfirst into his debauchery?"

He snapped the blanket out and let it float down to cover the couch. "Maybe once or twice."

Envy roared up inside her. He'd *lived*. For better or worse, regrets and all, he'd experienced things that she couldn't even imagine.

All Maricela had ever done was exactly what had been expected of her.

She sank to the bed and went back to staring at the slightly garish ceiling. "How depressing."

The springs of the couch creaking softly were followed by his soft sigh. "I know this is hard on you..."

"No, it isn't." People went through far more difficult things every day. *She'd* been through far more difficult things. "It's stupid."

"Stop it." His voice was still low, but the lack of deference was new. He sounded almost firm. "You don't have to do that all the time, you know. Shove down every bad thing you feel."

She wasn't sure about that. Some people struggled

so hard, every day, and she had everything. She always had. She was a literal goddamn princess. "It's indulgent. My life is nearly perfect. What more can I want?"

"It's not a contest, Maricela. We've all got our own shit. Yours is different, and most people won't understand it. And if you went around whining to refugees that it sucks having to have a bodyguard all the time, you'd be a pretty big asshole. But that doesn't mean you can't admit it in the privacy of your own damn bedroom. Just say it. It's shitty not to have any freedom."

She struggled back up on her elbows. "I have freedom—"

"You can't even have sex with your boyfriend without a guard sitting outside the door," he interrupted. "That's *shitty*, Maricela. Say it. Say it's shitty."

There were a hundred things she wanted to say instead. That Colin Visscher wasn't her boyfriend. That it wasn't having a guard sitting outside that was the problem, it was having that guard be Ivan. That he didn't have any idea about what she wanted, because what she wanted was a bunch of things he wouldn't even let himself think about.

"You want to know what's shitty?" The covers were so heavy she could barely lift them, but she needed *something* between them. Some sort of shield. "You kicked him out. There was no good reason for Colin to leave my bed that night, but you made him do it anyway."

He was silent for a long time. The answer, when it came, was honest and blunt. "Yeah, that was shitty. Like I said, Maricela. I'm not sweet."

"Right." Maybe he was something else, something better and worse than sweet. Something Maricela could relate to, one hundred percent.

Maybe he was infatuated.

8

It was a perfect day to be outdoors.

Maricela stretched out on a padded blanket in the shade of a gnarled old oak tree, her eyes closed against the afternoon sunlight. Beams pushed through the branches and leaves anyway, turning the darkness behind her closed lids into a patchwork of dappled shades.

Laughter surrounded her. All the younger Reyes children—plus the little ones who had accompanied their families to the party—were tearing around the courtyard, their voices melding together into an unintelligible cacophony of noise.

It shouldn't have been peaceful, not in the slightest, but it *was*. Maricela smiled and opened her eyes, shading them with one hand. "How can they have so much energy? I ate too much lunch, and now all I want to do is sleep."

"Easy." Grace sat a few feet away, barefoot in denim overalls, her legs crossed and a sketchpad on her lap. "They didn't stop long enough to eat."

"And some of them only ate dessert." Nita's skirt held a rainbow of wildflowers deposited by various children, and she was absently weaving the blooms into a crown. "We used to be worse. We're just getting *old*."

"Speak for yourself," Maricela protested.

"What, about the old part? Or the misbehaving?" Nita flashed her a grin. "I remember the time you helped me replace all the sugar meant for the lemonade with salt."

"I remember the *lectures* I got." It didn't matter that her momentary amusement over the prank had almost instantly turned into remorse at causing people discomfort. Isabela had taken her to task, admonishing her about the importance of trust and reminding her that the delicate balance of power in their sector could easily be upset. "Even Gideon didn't think it was funny."

"Neither did my mother, believe me." Nita wrinkled her nose as she twisted two stems together. "My aunt wanted to wallop me. My mother made me write out the entire Reyes family tree twenty times to give me an understanding of the legacy I was squandering."

Maricela's mother probably would have smiled before quietly, gently chiding her. Of course, if Juana had still been alive to smile at her, Maricela never would have been acting out. And Isabela wouldn't have been so determined to prove that she could manage her baby sister. And Gideon...

Well, Gideon might have laughed, after all.

She shook off the memories and sat up. "This is nice, isn't it? Peaceful."

"You mean the distraction?" Nita tied off her crown with a flourish and leaned over to drop it onto Grace's hair. "I wonder how long the gossip can keep the other nobles busy. Maybe we'll get a whole day or two."

The crown slipped down over Grace's eye, and she laughed as she righted it. "I swear, the way you two talked about this party, I thought it'd be hell. But so far it's been fun."

Because she wasn't being stalked through the halls like a gazelle by a bunch of noble wildebeests. Maricela snorted. "Enjoy your relative anonymity while you have it, McKinnon. People will see you sitting here with us. And when they see our ball gowns and find out that *you* made them, then—"

"Then absolutely nothing will change," Grace cut in with a shrug. "Jaden may have secured a temple commission for me because he wanted me to stay in One, but I highly doubt my brother ever intended for me to marry into nobility. He knew me too well."

"It's cute that she thinks that makes a difference." Nita started in on her next masterpiece, her gaze focused on the bright petals spilling across her lap. "You won't have it as bad as we do, because no one's telling you that you *have* to marry one of them. But trust me, Grace. Gabe's parents will send every cousin in the bunch past you at least once, just to see if they can woo you by promising to make you queen of a textile empire."

"Never gonna happen."

Isabela had staked out a spot over by one of the larger fountains. Lucas was sitting with her, no doubt answering her questions in between visits from the steady stream of people drifting past. Everyone was curious about him, sure, but they were *more* curious about how the royal family would receive a long-lost member.

If they would receive him.

Nita caught the direction of Maricela's gaze and leaned closer, lowering her voice. "So what do we think about him?"

"I don't know yet." It took actual physical effort for Maricela not to glance at Ivan, who was standing silently by the tree—just like he had been for the last hour. "But I'm not willing to discount him without a chance because his father did a terrible thing. What kind of person would that make me?"

"That's gracious." Nita paused and tilted her head, examining Lucas. "He's handsome. And someone took the time to turn him out in style. How much do you think that outfit cost, Grace?"

"Hard to say." She tipped her drawing pad up and rested her chin on the top edge. "It's impeccably tailored, maybe even custom-made. That's not cheap."

"I was only five when the Prophet died. I don't know if I really even remember him, or just the paintings." Nita gestured over to where Gideon sat with his back against a tree, deep in conversation with Hunter's father. "He looks like your brother, though, only younger and prettier. My mother's probably already trying to decide if she can marry me off to him, or if that would seem like too much of a power play."

Maricela wasn't sure if she felt sympathy at his sudden infamy, or simply relief that the spotlight was off her, even if only for a little while. She decided to go with relief. She glanced over, found Ivan watching her, and winked.

His demeanor was usually so serious when they were out in public. But for a second, she thought she saw the corner of his mouth twitch up. And his eyes were warm, meeting hers with silent understanding, as if he knew exactly what she was thinking.

Her cheeks heated, and she looked away. *Careful, Rios.* She was walking a dangerous line, but it was so much safer to indulge in a tiny bit of flirtation when they were out like this. It had to be light, and it couldn't go anywhere. It wasn't anything like flirting with him while they were alone, when the tension between them twisted tighter and tighter, until it felt like the tiniest thing might make it explode.

A little girl with jet black pigtails and Nita's big brown eyes stopped at the edge of their blanket, her shy gaze falling on Maricela as she silently held out a full white rose with red-tipped petals.

"Thank you, Alene." Maricela took the bloom by its stem and twirled it between her fingers. "Do you know what my mother used to do with roses?"

Nita's youngest sister shook her head.

Carefully, Maricela plucked a single petal from the outer edge of the rose and ran her finger over its velvety surface. "She told me rose petals were the softest things in the world. And then she would show me, like this." She rubbed the petal against her cheek. "You try one."

Very seriously, Alene tugged one of the petals free and touched it to her cheek. Her sudden smile of delight showed two missing teeth. "It *is* soft."

"Of course it is. Maricela would never lie." Nita dumped the petals out of her skirt and caught her sister around the waist, hauling the giggling girl down to her lap. "Grace, this adorable little brat is my baby sister, Alene. Last time I saw her, she was covered in mud, but someone must have dumped her in a horse trough."

Grace held out one hand. "It's very nice to meet you."

Alene accepted Grace's hand with a practiced

shake, but her gaze was fixed on the pad of paper balanced on Grace's knee.

As soon as her hand was free, she leaned in and whispered something to Nita. Sadness flashed across Nita's face, gone almost as soon as it appeared, and she repositioned Alene to face Grace. "Go ahead and ask, sweetheart. It's okay."

Alene's voice barely rose above a whisper. "Are you drawing? Can I see?"

"Sure." Grace flipped the sketchbook around, revealing the vague outline of a knee-length dress. "I make clothes, but before I can sew them, I have to draw out my ideas. Would you like to help me?"

Alene hesitated until Nita beamed encouragement at her. "Go ahead. Show her how good you are already."

They stretched out on their stomachs on the blanket, their heads together, the pad and pencils between them. With Alene's attention firmly locked on her task, Maricela moved closer to Nita and lowered her voice. "What's wrong?"

Nita picked up one of her discarded flowers, but instead of braiding it, she slowly shredded the leaves and petals. "She loves to draw. She's loved it since she got big enough to wrap her fist around a pencil. But my mothers think drawing is frivolous."

The arts were prized in Sector One, but sometimes the focus tended more toward crafts—especially amongst the noble families. If an artistic endeavor couldn't reliably produce practical goods for sale, it wasn't encouraged. In fact, sometimes it was discouraged.

Which made sense, in its own claustrophobic way, for the older children. But Alene was so *young*. "She's just a baby."

"Estela isn't taking chances with the younger

ones. Not after Reyes ran away to join the Riders, and Mateo—" She bit off the name of her brother who'd been disowned, a frown darkening her face. "And I utterly failed to trap you into a marriage neither of us wants, so I'm a big disappointment, too. And Alene is the one who pays for it."

Their culture was rooted in honoring traditions, but at what cost? "I can ask Gideon to speak with her—"

"*No.*" Nita exhaled, visibly struggling to regain her usual composure. "The last thing any of us need is Gideon showing an interest in anything related to me. That'll only encourage her."

"You're right, I know you're right." But watching Alene's face light up at the simple pleasure of dragging a pencil across paper broke Maricela's heart.

Obviously, it did the same thing to Nita. She looked away—and Maricela wasn't surprised when her gaze drifted to where Hunter was kicking a ball around with some of his cousins. "I'm going to have to do it, you know. Pick someone rich and biddable, so I have access to my inheritance and can support my brothers and sisters if they want a different life."

"You wouldn't. You *couldn't.*" But even as Maricela breathed the words, she knew they were lies. Nita could, and she would—if it meant securing her younger siblings a future where they could live as they pleased instead of wilting under the pressure of immutable expectations. If they never had to quietly yearn for the impossible while woodenly satisfying their duties.

Nita picked up her discarded crown, but half the flowers had been crushed when Alene had rushed to Grace's side. Her fingers lingered over the bruised petals. "We do what we must."

But they couldn't help what they wanted, either. Especially when those desires were only intensified by the lure of the forbidden.

Maricela didn't have to look to know where Ivan was standing—about four feet behind her, a little to her left. She *felt* the distance, as clearly as if she'd measured it.

Physical attraction aside, he saw her as an icon, a figure, a piece of their culture and religion. She wasn't a woman to him, she was a living milagro, a thing to be touched only in respectful worship. Maricela clung to that thought, embraced it. Because if that ever changed...

She wasn't sure she could stop herself from sinking into rebellion, no matter who she hurt in the process.

Five minutes on the back of a purebred stallion was all it took for Ivan to miss his motorcycle.

Granted, his bike wouldn't have been a lot of use galloping across untamed fields and along wooded paths and over crystal-clear brooks. And the horses were incomparable. The Reyes family's primary business might have been their ranch, but their secondary passion was breeding horses for speed and fearlessness.

Kind of like Reyes and Nita. Three of Maricela's would-be suitors had already fallen out of their damn saddles trying to compete with Reyes, who barely seemed to need the reins to control the fire-spitting monster he'd claimed. They'd long since left the rest of the guests behind, and the concentration it took Ivan to keep up with the three of them was tempered by Maricela's smile as the stress of performing for everyone else slipped away.

Hopefully, Maricela wouldn't get competitive with Nita. Ivan wasn't even responsible for the girl's safety, and his stomach still clawed its way into his throat as she jumped her horse across a river that seemed about five hundred yards wide for the endless moments she was airborne.

Maricela, thank God, slowed as they approached the river. But Ivan's relief sputtered out as she laughed and let her horse prance into the shallow water. It splashed everywhere, kicked up by the horse's hooves, soaking her loose white pants until they clung to her skin.

In the bright afternoon sunlight, all that thin white fabric was basically see-through. And now they couldn't go back until she dried off, or he'd have to punch half of the guests for gawking at her.

She laughed and patted her mount's neck as he turned circles in the stream, sending fresh waves of sparkling water up over her. "I know, I know. It's hot today."

Nita circled back, an equally bright smile on her face. "Having fun splashing around?"

Reluctantly, Maricela guided her horse up onto the bank. "If he gets much wetter, he'll shake me right off into the dirt."

"He has better manners than that." Nita patted the satchel thrown across her shoulder. "Since we're out here, I'm going up river to find some clay for my glazes. You guys mind hanging around?"

Maricela looked longingly at the gentle hill that rose before them. "We might ride ahead a little."

Ivan crossed the river more sedately, reaching the far bank with wet boots just as Reyes galloped back to them. "Nita wants to go look for clay," Ivan told him. "Maricela and I are going to go on ahead. We'll wait for you at that pond over the border into the Rios land."

Reyes waved him off.

This close to Maricela, Ivan could see that the

water had splashed up so high that tiny droplets clung to her bare arms. Her sleeveless white tunic was probably clinging to her body in enticing spots, too, but he refused to look as he guided his horse toward the hill ahead of them.

"Thank you," she murmured.

The soft gratitude in her voice hurt. Because after three days at this party, it had become rapidly clear that guarding Maricela physically wouldn't be a problem—but that nothing Ivan could do would protect the rest of her.

Other people's needs pressed in on her constantly. She couldn't set a toe outside her room without being mobbed by them. The suitors who were eager to court her. The ones who weren't, but were being pressured into it by their families. The lower nobles who had no chance but still stared at her with adoring, worshipful gazes that were uncomfortable to witness from the outside, because Ivan had watched her with the same awe...

And now, seeing her shoulders slowly bend under the pressure, he knew how much that had hurt her.

Everyone at this damn party wanted something from Maricela. Even her sister. Even *him*.

But not Nita. Nita had given her exactly what she needed—a swift departure from the crowd and some time alone. And as Maricela urged her horse to pick up speed until the wind tugged at her hair, Ivan almost regretted that he couldn't give her the true solitude she must desperately crave.

The best he could give her was silence and the illusion of freedom.

"I think you're loosening up," she continued. "Just a week ago, you would have insisted that we go back for an entire complement of royal guards before an outing like this."

She probably thought it was true. He wouldn't tell her that having Reyes within shouting distance *was* like having an entire complement of guards on standby. "I'm familiar with this area. Your family's land is on the other side of the hill."

"Adrian's estate." She brought her horse in line beside Ivan's, so close her leg brushed his, sparking electricity. "It's being run by a solicitor right now. Waiting for him to claim his inheritance."

The inheritance her cousin only had because Ivan's uncles had killed his parents. Even the sizzling contact of her thigh against his couldn't stop the familiar surge of guilt. Adrian Maddox was never going to claim his inheritance. The seemingly endless grain fields would no doubt go to whoever married Maricela.

No wonder Estela Reyes wouldn't leave her alone.

They reached the top of the hill, and Ivan reined in next to Maricela and stared down at the gently rolling wheat fields laid out in a well-irrigated pattern along the upper branch of the river. "It's beautiful land."

"All of Sector One is beautiful." Shrugging, she flashed him a look that was both sheepish and brutally self-aware. "If I say I want it, I sound greedy, don't I? But if I say I don't, then I sound spoiled. Like even this bounty isn't good enough for me."

"So don't worry about how you sound." His horse shifted, and his thigh pressed more firmly against hers. He could feel the heat of her skin through the wet fabric of her pants and the denim of his jeans. It made his voice hoarser than he intended. "I'm the only one here to listen."

"That's worse. You grew up with so little, and here I am, a woman with everything." Her words dropped to a whisper. "Hating her life."

She wasn't hearing him. Maybe she *couldn't.* Christ knew he'd listened to Gideon talk often enough about the responsibilities that came along with his privileges. Maybe the whole family had ground it into her so deeply that she couldn't acknowledge any other reality.

Touching her was a terrible idea. He couldn't reach over and cover her hand with his. He couldn't brush that wild lock of hair away from her forehead. He had to fix this with words, and words had always been his bluntest, clumsiest tool.

So he was blunt and clumsy. "Fuck, Maricela. After the past three days, I hate your life, too. I don't know how you stay so damn calm."

A laugh tore free of her. "Do I? I don't feel calm sometimes." She twisted the supple leather of the reins around her fingers. "I don't hate it, not really. My life. I have responsibilities and duties, yes, but even those have up sides."

Walking the knife's edge, he gently tugged the leather away from her fingers. She'd twisted it hard enough to leave an indention on her index finger, and he rubbed it with his thumb.

An innocent touch, until he imagined stroking his thumb across her cheek. Her chin. Her collarbone. "Have you ever been outside the sector? Gone *anywhere* where people don't know who you are?"

Her brow furrowed. "I can't believe *I'm* the one saying this to *you*, but...that doesn't seem safe."

That wasn't entirely true. There were places he could take her now, after the war—places secured by the legend and reputation of the O'Kanes. But safety wasn't the point. "Then you don't know what you're missing, do you? You don't *know* if you really have everything."

"Wait, are you—?" Another laugh. "Are you trying to make me feel better or worse?"

He barely held back his scowl of frustration. "Fine. I'm not good with words. I just want you to quit beating yourself up. You're too hard on yourself."

"I'll concede the point as yours." She moved, guiding her horse in a circle around his. "Take it while you can. I don't admit defeat often."

The spark was back in her eyes, that teasing light that had slowly diminished over the past few days. Relief flooded him.

Clumsy and blunt had gotten it done.

Of course, now he had a mischievous Maricela circling him, all bright and smiling and happy, and he could still see the line of her underwear through her transparent pants and trace the sweet curve of her breast where her shirt clung to it.

It was blasphemous to enjoy the view.

His body didn't care.

It was wrong to want to ease up on the reins enough to let his stallion dance toward hers. It was downright *reckless* to imagine how easy it would be to get near enough to grab her from her horse. To pull her into his lap. To ride away from all of this with her body tucked so close to his that every movement was the sweetest agony.

She tensed. That was his only warning before she urged her mount into motion. The horse took off, his mane and tail streaming, galloping down the hill with reckless speed.

The urge to chase her was uncontrollable.

It was also his job.

Thank fucking hell.

He'd learned to ride on the mules the Riders sometimes used to navigate the canyons and mountain paths on the edge of the sector. He'd practiced on the horses in Gideon's stables. He was proficient—Reyes had made sure of that—but the placid, agreeable mounts he was used to couldn't compare to the stallion he'd been given.

Given his head, the horse *ran*. The world turned into a blur, and for a few precarious seconds, Ivan's focus narrowed to staying in the saddle instead of being left behind on his ass. Maricela's brown hair flowed behind her, and her laughter floated to him on the wind, high and joyous.

Happy.

When they slowed down—and he was sure he could walk without his knees buckling—he was going to drag her over his lap and spank some sense into her. Because this speed was *insane.* If her horse put a foot wrong, if she lost her balance, if the slightest thing went amiss—

But it didn't. She moved with the animal like she'd been born to this, and the tiny part of his brain not drowning in adrenaline wondered if that was why her thighs felt so strong whenever she pressed them against him. Maybe she rode like this all the time.

Maybe she'd ride a man like this. Fast and confident and full of joy.

After what seemed like an eternity—or maybe just a few of his frantic heartbeats—she slowed and turned. Her chest heaved, and her face was pink and flushed.

She was so damn happy with herself, he didn't know how to yell at her.

He eased his horse to a walk—no simple feat, now that the stallion had a taste of exhilaration and wanted to keep running—and stopped in front of her. "Where did you learn to ride like that?"

She turned the question around on him. "Where

did you?"

The idea that he could ride as well as she could was laughable, but he accepted the compliment. "Reyes taught me."

"Me too. I spent a lot of time at their estate, growing up." Her flush deepened. "Everyone encouraged it. I *was* supposed to marry him."

The tangle of emotions that evoked was too messy and ugly to examine closely. Stupid, to be jealous over a woman he couldn't have and a man who hadn't taken her. He still wanted to drop an elbow into Reyes's ribs.

Probably because of the color in her cheeks. "Did you want to marry him?"

"You know, I never really thought about it. Not until he jilted me." She shrugged. "But no. I don't want to marry anyone who doesn't love me."

It shouldn't have sounded sweet and sad. Their sector was built on sincere reverence for the very idea of love. For the common folk, it still held true. They married who they wanted, when they wanted. In pairs or in trios, as many people as it took to build a family and a life.

The nobles had probably started out that way too, but it hadn't taken long for power and practicality to take over. Ivan had seen plenty of emotions in the eyes of Maricela's most aggressive suitors.

He wouldn't have called any of them *love*.

"What about you?"

He tore himself out of his thoughts and turned to find her close again. Close enough to touch. "Me?"

"You." She leaned forward and absently stroked her horse's shoulder. "Most Riders don't get married or have families. Will you miss it?"

He opened his mouth and barely managed to snap it shut before the truth came out. She was good at making it easy to talk, at lulling a man into dropping his guard. No surprise—she'd been taking people's spiritual confessions from the time she was old enough to speak in complete sentences.

But some confessions were too personal.

Besides, Ivan didn't know a damn thing about families. All he knew was betrayal and grief and the bleak times when he came home from work to find his mother sitting in darkness, wrapped in a blanket, cradling a tiny saint's painting of his father against her chest.

"Be like your father," she'd whisper as he moved about the room, changing the solar-powered batteries in their lamps or lighting candles if she'd forgotten to put the batteries out to charge. "Promise me. Be loyal. Be a protector. Be *good*."

Irena Wolff had been a strong woman. *Was* a strong woman. She worked herself into exhaustion, year after year, to provide Ivan with the barest scraps of normalcy in a sector that wanted to forget she existed. Her bouts with melancholy only underscored how much Ivan owed her. She'd fought her own inner darkness to make a home for him.

He was going to be what he'd promised. Loyal. A protector.

Good, like his father.

Even when he felt as broken as his mother at her lowest.

The wind caught Maricela's hair again, teasing it across her face. He curled his fingers toward his palm, but it wasn't enough. She was staring at him with those big brown eyes, all open and earnest, and he had never wanted so much to be someone else. Someone who could envision a future with her. A family with her. Someone without treason and shadows and who knew what else running through his veins.

Hell, he'd settle for being worthy to reach out and brush that hair from her forehead.

He wasn't, but he did it anyway. Her skin was so soft under his fingertips, and he hated how big and rough his hand looked next to her face. He was a weapon, a tool shaped for one purpose, and it sure as hell wasn't touching precious princesses.

She sucked in a breath and lifted her hand. It hovered over his for half a heartbeat—then it touched his, pressing his palm against her cheek. "Ivan."

Her cheeks were flushed again. Her thin white shirt was drying rapidly in the hot sun and the warm summer breeze, but it couldn't hide her immediate physical reaction. Her next breath in was shallow, ragged, as if he'd already slid his hand down her throat to cup her breast and roll his thumb over the tight tip of her nipple.

"We can't," he whispered.

"I know," she agreed instantly. But she was leaning toward him anyway, and if he didn't stop her she'd sway close enough for his mouth to find hers. It was inevitable. Impossible, reckless, blasphemous. A violation of the oath he'd sworn to Gideon.

And *inevitable.*

She jerked away at the sound of hoofbeats as Reyes rode into view. Ivan let his hand drop to his reins and told himself Reyes hadn't had time to see anything incriminating.

Then he turned his horse and caught sight of his fellow Rider's baffled expression.

Shit.

"Have a good ride?" Reyes called, his brow still furrowed.

"Very nice," Maricela answered brightly. "Ivan?"

He was seriously fucked. "Is Nita ready to go?" he called back.

"She said something about dress fittings."

"Oh *no*." Maricela urged her horse into a run, leaving Ivan behind to drift into line beside Reyes.

The other Rider squinted at him. "Is she trying to get in your pants?"

"Don't be an asshole, Reyes." He picked up the pace so he could easily keep Maricela in sight.

"What? It looked like a thing." But Reyes let it drop. "How are you handling the festival tomorrow? Want to team up?"

Ivan wrenched his mind back to his job—a harder challenge than he would have liked. "I could use some backup. Though if Kora's going with the girls, Ashwin will be there. But he's been...focused lately."

"Never fucking mind, then." Reyes snorted. "I'm not getting within fifteen feet of Kora until she has that damn baby. Ashwin's getting *mean* lately."

"You could stop picking fights with him, you know."

"Leave it to you to pick the least fun solution to the problem."

Everyone always talked in hushed whispers about Ivan's death wish, but Reyes was the one who seemed determined to find a swift exit out of the world. "Yeah, I'm a real downer. How's the search for intel going? Have you gotten anything out of any of your family?"

That made him laugh. "They don't know anything, and it's pissing my mother off like you wouldn't believe. She's spitting nails."

"What does that mean for her?" Maricela topped the hill, and Ivan held his breath until they reached the crest and he could see her again as she rode down the other side to meet Nita. "Politically, I mean. I'm never sure how the nobles are gonna react to shit like this."

"Eh, who the hell knows? Or cares?"

Most people cared. Maricela did, because Lucas could be family. Gideon cared because the man could be a threat. Nita probably cared because if Estela Reyes could see profit in it, she'd be trying to marry her daughter off to the lost Rios heir.

Ivan cared because political unrest might endanger the person whose life he'd sworn to protect. Which made keeping his mind on the job imperative.

And keeping Maricela out of his pants vital.

9

The summer festival was an explosion of light and color, of sound and joy. Everywhere Maricela turned was chaos, a cacophony of laughter and shouts, and the air was heavy with spices and delicious smells. It wasn't quite dusk yet, but the children were already running around with lit sparklers, darting in and out through the growing crowd.

A few of them passed by her so closely that Ivan reacted, wrapping an arm around her as he placed his body between her and the fiery but harmless sparkles popping off their handheld fireworks.

"Relax," she murmured.

His grip on her eased, but only slightly. "I am relaxed."

"Right." On this one night, at least, his job was supposed to be easy. By tradition, no one approached the royal family on festival nights to ask for blessings or air concerns or offer felicitations. Maricela was simply another reveler tonight.

The street leading to the main marketplace was lined with brightly decorated booths, selling everything from simple charms and milagros to palm-sized holograms that projected tiny images of the saints. Grace and Nita gravitated toward a booth laden with bolts of cloth, while Maricela lingered beside one showcasing necklaces and bangles.

Ivan stopped beside her, running a finger over a pendant made of carved wood that had been polished to a shine. As Maricela stared, he skimmed his thumb over the smooth, gleaming surfaces.

She shivered.

"Maricela." Lucas stepped up on her other side, his expression almost tentative, as if he wasn't sure of his welcome. "I'm surprised to see you here."

"I wouldn't miss it." She picked up one of the bangles and turned it over between her fingers. "Couldn't miss this one, in fact. A friend's father is being sainted tonight."

"The Rider they're all celebrating?" His eyebrows pulled together in confusion. "I didn't think Riders *had* children."

Ashwin would be the first. "It's not typical, but this is a special case. Ana was born before my brother formed the Riders. William was one of the original members."

And a friend of Ivan's father's. Though Mischa Wolff had already died by the time Gideon gathered his men and christened them his Riders, people still sometimes acted as though Mischa had been one of them. Like his portrait was on the temple wall alongside the others—and they'd afforded Mischa the same reverence, even before his sainthood.

Did Ivan forget sometimes, as well? Or was he acutely aware that he was treading new ground in continuing his father's legacy?

Glancing at him gave her no insight. His thumb was still resting on the carved wood, but his entire body was tense. One sudden move, and he'd have Lucas facedown in the dirt.

Maybe that was why Lucas seemed so much more subdued today. "I have a lot to learn about the sector," he admitted. "And I should apologize for the way I approached you."

"Oh, don't," she said wryly. "I imagine you accomplished your goals quite handily with that. It was very theatrical."

He winced. "That wasn't how I wanted it to go. I thought I could introduce myself to you. I certainly didn't think my resemblance to the Prophet was so... pronounced." He picked up a little necklace bearing a framed miniature of their grandfather. In it, Fernando Rios was depicted as a smiling man with silver hair. "All the pictures I've ever seen looked like this."

Most of the public portraits did. It was easier that way, for the people to have one enduring image of him—older, authoritative. Distinguished but still strong.

The treasure trove of family pictures at the palace told a different story. Instead of the smiling, benevolent leader on the pendant, they showed a much more complicated man. Snapshots obviously taken only moments apart veered wildly between joy and sullen brooding. Portrait sittings including the whole family were rigid, formal affairs, while candid shots of him alone were much more relaxed. And he never looked happier than when he was posing with cherished possessions or gifts his followers had bestowed.

After looking through all those photos, Maricela *couldn't* like the man. It was impossible.

But perhaps Lucas would feel differently. "We have a family collection at home. A few even predate the Flares. Maybe you'd like to see them sometime?"

"That would be an honor." He put the miniature back on its display and turned to face her. "To be honest, I wasn't sure I'd be welcome. It would be understandable if the bad blood between our parents was impossible to overcome."

"I don't think that way. What matters to me is your behavior. Your intentions."

"Can we start over, then?" He offered her a smile and extended his hand.

She took it. "Cousin."

"Cousin." He clasped her hand. "So tell me, as an insider. What part of the fair should I be sure not to miss?"

Nita was calling her name from across the street, so Maricela pulled her hand free. "The food. Now, if you'll excuse me—"

A shock ran up her spine as Ivan cupped her elbow, but before she could turn to him, he spun her in the opposite direction to face Nita and Grace, who carried a bolt of luxurious, honey-colored silk beneath one arm.

At her baffled look, Grace sighed. "I know, but I had to. I'm running out of time."

"It's for her dress." Nita linked her arm through Maricela's. "Apparently, she's just going to whip up a fabulous gown before the ball. Because she's *that* amazing."

She wouldn't have time to do anything else—literally. "You'll be glued to your sewing machine until the party," Maricela protested.

"That's okay." Grace handed off the bolt of fabric to a guard, who hurried away with it. "To be honest, I'm getting a little tired of fancy people. Present company excluded, of course."

"Of course." Then Maricela leaned in and told her the truth. "I'm getting a little tired of us, too."

"We're exhausting," Nita agreed as she steered them down a path between two rows of booths. "I need to get some fried dough with sugar and chocolate before we go back. My mother abhors messy food you eat with your fingers. *So* uncivilized."

"Mrs. Petrillo makes the best," Grace observed.

Not in Maricela's experience. "Better than Mr. Cason's?"

"By a *mile*."

Only one person could decide this. "Ivan?"

He glanced between them, but only hesitated for a moment. "Mrs. Petrillo."

He could barely bring himself to disagree with her, even over something as inconsequential as dessert. But maybe he was getting there. "I stand corrected," she murmured.

They reached the end of the alley and turned again, spilling out into one of the broad main roads. Larger booths from more established merchants lined the prime real estate, and just ahead of them on the right, a rhythmic *thud* announced Ed's presence.

The burly old bearded man was tossing knives casually through the air. Each one sank into the painted red heart of a target, so close to its brothers and sisters that the handles scraped together.

Ivan's steps slowed, and he glanced at Maricela. "Do you mind?"

"Not at all."

He waved to Nita and Grace. "We'll catch up with

you at Mrs. Petrillo's stand. Don't leave it until we get there."

Nita rolled her eyes but dropped a kiss to Maricela's cheek. "We'll be good girls."

They disappeared into the crowd, and Maricela turned to Ivan. "I could have gone with them."

"You know better than that."

"They have guards." And Ivan deserved a moment to himself, so he could catch up with an old friend.

He reached up, his hand hovering over her elbow but not *quite* touching. "I'd like for you to come."

Her muscles tensed, and she locked them in place to keep from unconsciously leaning closer to him. "All right."

His hand hovered a moment longer. Then it dropped, sliding slowly to rest at the small of her back. The lightweight summer fabric of her dress wasn't thick enough to block the warmth of his hand, and Maricela could focus on nothing else, no matter how hard she tried. She fixed her attention on a group of temple acolytes breezing past, intent on matching their faces with names, but then one of Ivan's fingers shifted, and her entire world collapsed to that one tiny spot.

She shivered.

The final knife thudded home as they stopped in front of Ed's stall. He turned to greet them, his face breaking into a wide smile even his bushy beard couldn't hide. "Ivan, my boy! It's good to see you."

"Ed." Ivan tilted his head and pulled his hand away from Maricela's back, leaving a cold spot. "You know Maricela?"

She dropped a quick curtsy, and Ed returned it with an even deeper bow, folding his big body nearly in half. "Always a pleasure to see you, Miss Rios."

With the formalities behind them, Maricela peered

down at his table. "Did you make me something?"

"I do have something special..." He pulled over a display case with an impressive dagger almost the length of her forearm. The wavy pattern in the blade indicated that it was forged from his prized folded steel, finished with an intricately carved pommel and a large chunk of polished amber embedded in the handle. "It had a twin, but your sister already bought it. As a gift, I believe, for Bishop."

"It's beautiful." She held out her hand. "May I?"

He flipped open the case, eased it from the stand, and offered it to her, handle first. "Maybe we can talk Ivan into giving a demonstration while you look. He's always been good at luring in the customers."

Maricela had watched him, spellbound, often enough to believe it. "A charming thought, but I don't need to look." She turned the dagger over in her hand, testing its weight and balance. Both were perfect. "I'll take it."

"Excellent." He reached for a matching sheath studded with smaller chunks of amber. "Ivan, how are those knives treating you? The ones I modeled off your new friend's?"

"They're good." Ivan slipped a knife from his belt and held it up so its gleaming surface reflected the light. "You were right about the cut-outs. They're perfectly balanced." He bounced the knife on his fingertips, then tossed it up and caught it by the blade. With a flick of his wrist, it flew through the air to sink into the target right next to Ed's knives. "I can throw it from either end."

"I told you," Ed said with a deep-chested laugh. "Someday, boy, you'll listen the first time. Always did have a head harder'n any steel."

"Some things never change," Maricela muttered

under her breath.

Ivan half-turned as if he'd heard her, then strode to the target to retrieve his knife. Ed, on the other hand, huffed out another laugh. "He's not giving you grief, is he, Miss Rios?"

"Of course he is. But I probably deserve it."

"Nonsense." Ed tucked the sheath into a box and tied it shut with a long piece of twine. "Ivan, you'd better do your mother proud. I know she taught you manners."

It could have been a harsh admonition, but the affection in Ed's voice turned it into something warm and comfortable. And Ivan's disgruntled look seemed more like a habit or an inside joke than genuine displeasure.

She'd never seen him this relaxed or unguarded. He didn't even open up like this with the Riders, and they were his brothers. It left her feeling...not quite sad, but a little envious and lonely, as if she were standing on the other side of a thick pane of glass, able only to watch them interact.

The melancholy illusion lingered even when Ivan gestured to one of the guards to sign the payment ledger and retrieve Maricela's purchase. "We have to catch up with her friends. I'll stop by as soon as I can to talk about the next set of knives."

"I know you're busy. Whenever you find the time." Ed leaned over the table to squeeze Ivan's shoulder, then inclined his head once again to Maricela. "Keep him on his toes, Miss Rios."

"I can only promise to try."

Ivan's hand returned to the small of her back as he hastily steered her away from the table. As stern as his expression was, humor kept snapping in his deep blue eyes. "People who knew you when you were a grubby little kid never really believe that you've grown up."

She barely managed to keep a straight face. "Really? I wouldn't know anything about that."

His lips twitched. "Can you imagine how much Reyes would torture me if he heard Ed?"

"I don't think he'd tease you at all. I think he'd find it unbearably adorable."

Ivan answered with a rough noise midway between a laugh and a grunt. But his touch on her lower back turned firm. His fingers splayed wider. For the first time, she realized how *large* his hand was— large enough that he could almost span the distance between her waist and her shoulder blades.

And if she thought about that too closely, she'd embarrass herself.

She breathed in deeply, but instead of clearing her head, she only filled it with his scent. "Do you like the dagger I chose?"

"It's beautiful."

"I'm glad you think so, because it's yours."

His fingers flexed on her back, five points of heat blazing against her skin. "That's too much. Too precious a gift for someone like me."

Maybe so—but Ed, God bless his soul, had given her the perfect excuse. "It's a properly suitable gift, one Isabela obviously felt Bishop deserved. And you've worked just as hard as he has."

"Are you saying you're as much trouble to look after as a woman with four lovers and nine children?"

The words stung—not her vanity, but her conscience. "Probably. I know I'm not the easiest person in the world to deal with. I'm too stubborn."

A Montero cousin appeared a dozen paces ahead of them, his eyes lighting up when he caught sight of Maricela. He took two steps toward them before Ivan froze him with a glare that sent him veering sharply between two booths.

"No," Ivan said as he guided her past the end of the row of stalls and into a square filled with brightly colored tents. "You're not stubborn enough by half. I know how often my security precautions frustrate you, but you never try to make my job harder."

"No. I have other ways of doing that." She trailed her fingers through the fringe hanging from the corner of a tent as they passed. "A better person would have handled all this differently. I'm sorry—"

"There you are." Grace was standing beside one of the tents, a cup of wine in one hand. "We didn't make it to Mrs. Petrillo's stand. Nita got distracted." She tilted her head toward the sign above the tent's entrance.

FORTUNES AND SEEINGS.

"She's visiting a fortune teller?" Maricela asked dubiously.

"Oh, yes. She was very excited about getting her cards read, or something like that."

It didn't sound like Nita at all, but she sometimes got a little unpredictable when she'd been dealing with her mother for extended periods of time. It was like the woman's claustrophobic expectations were a stifling blanket, and Nita had to shake it off.

That didn't explain why Grace was waiting outside. "You didn't join her?"

"Not a chance in hell."

"Because you don't believe in this sort of thing?"

Grace snorted. "Because I do."

The flaps of the tent opened, and Nita appeared, her eyes sparkling with repressed laughter. "She's *good*," she said, stealing Grace's wine to take a sip. "Definitely the best fortune teller I've ever seen. I mean, I know nobles are easier marks because everyone already knows everything about us, but she actually had me going for a bit."

Grace reclaimed her cup. "What did she say?"

"Oh, you know. I'm a heartbreaker. Men will keep throwing themselves at me, and I'll throw them back until I'm ready to risk everything on love." She grinned at Maricela. "You guys should go in."

"Absolutely not." Grace drained the rest of her wine and shook her head. "Nope."

"Guess it's just me, then." Maricela turned to Ivan. "Is there any point in asking if you'll wait out here?"

He raised one eyebrow at her.

"Right." She ducked into the tent.

The air inside was warm, scented with candles that lit some of the space brightly while leaving the rest in deep shadow. Everything was red, from the cloth draped over the table and chairs to the embroidered pillows.

A woman sat at the table. In the oddly colored light, it was impossible to tell much about her—she was younger than Maricela had expected, with long, curly hair the same shade as the fabric draped over everything, and she wore heavy layers of makeup.

Her head was bent over a set of cards, which she was turning over slowly in her hands. Maricela had seen psychics reading tarot cards at a few of the festivals. It seemed harmless, but it was also strangely uncomfortable. Many of the cards incorporated Sector One's saints into their iconography—people Maricela had *known*, even members of her family.

She never could help a cold little shiver at the thought that, one day, they'd be painting *her* face on those cards.

The woman glanced up, revealing brown eyes ringed with thick black liner and glittery bronze eyeshadow that caught the candlelight. One dark brow rose as her gaze slid from Maricela to Ivan, who had followed her into the tent and positioned himself in front of the flaps like a silent wall.

"A Rider," the fortune teller murmured. Her gaze returned to Maricela. "And a Rios. I'm honored by your patronage."

"Hello." Maricela offered her hand, and the woman reached out her own gloved hand to shake it.

Her grip was firm but brief. She waved to the fabric-covered chair across from her before spreading the cards out on the table to shuffle them. "What weighs on your heart today?"

"No cards, please." Maricela settled into the chair. "I don't—it's odd for me."

Her movements stilled. "Of course it is." When the cards were in a neat stack, she slowly peeled off her gloves and held out both hands, palms up. "May I?"

Maricela had obviously been spending too much time with Ivan, because her first instinct was to hesitate. But that was silly—how could an apparently unarmed woman harm her with a Rider standing three feet away?

Maricela laid her hands on the woman's open palms.

The fortune teller stiffened, her fingers closing around Maricela's as her eyes drifted shut. "Oh—"

Maricela glanced back at Ivan, who rolled his eyes. She bit her lip to hold back a giggle, but any urge to laugh vanished as the sound of a single gunshot cracked through the air.

Or did it? Ivan just stood there—on guard, but nothing out of the ordinary. Uncertain, Maricela stared at him.

He stared back, arching one eyebrow when she

continued to watch him. "Are you okay?"

The words echoed strangely, like he was at the other end of a long tunnel. Maricela blinked, and the tent was gone. She was still sitting on the cushioned chair at the table, and she could still feel the warmth of the woman's hands around hers.

But she was also at home, stumbling in slow motion through the twisting, paneled hallway between the solarium and Gideon's study. Fear clenched tight around her heart, because she already knew what she'd find when she reached the room—her brother, bleeding on the floor. Dying, with his attacker standing over him.

A faulty memory. That wasn't how it had happened at all. She'd strolled down the hall that day, curious but unalarmed, because who could ever have imagined that one of his followers—a longtime member of their household staff—would try to assassinate Gideon? Certainly not Maricela, whose entire world up until that point had been so sheltered that she literally could not conceive of that sort of danger, not even with the sound of gunfire ringing through the house.

But dreams had a way of distorting memory, and that's what this was—her nightmare. The way her conscience recalled that day with the strictures of waking thought stripped away.

She fell into the study. Gideon was sprawled on the floor, his skin sallow and gray. Long dead. His eyes were open, fixed. Staring out into nothing with a terrifying expression torn between horror and...

Relief?

She recoiled from the sight, and a worse one greeted her—the man who'd shot Gideon, kneeling in front of the fireplace, both arms outstretched in surrender. Donny had worked in the kitchens for years.

His face was as familiar to Maricela as some of her own family, and a shudder wracked her as he stared up at her.

This was wrong. They had struggled, she knew that much—first over the gun, and then over the knife he'd pulled from his belt. He had hit her, and she had hit him back, both of them careening off the walls and desk. Bloody fragments of memory flashed before her as she moved across the carpet.

As Donny offered her his knife and tilted his head back, baring his throat.

As she took it, turned it. Pressed the sharp edge of the blade against his skin.

No.

"Maricela!" Ivan was there at once, his voice pulling her dizzily from her memory. The fortune teller gasped and released her as welcome reality crashed in around her once again.

Her chair fell to the floor, where Maricela almost tripped over it as she stepped back. Ivan still held the other woman in an iron grip, and Maricela spoke through numb lips. "Let her go."

Ivan was pale and tight-jawed. Trembling. "Are you all right?"

Not by a long shot. Not even close. "Will you pay her, please? I want to go."

After another moment, he opened his fingers. The fortune teller slowly pulled her hands away and laid them on the table. "Payment isn't necessary."

With a grunt, Ivan dug a gold temple coin out of his pocket and tossed it onto the table. It clattered heavily, the noise still echoing through the tent when he reached Maricela's side and slid a protective arm around her shoulders. "Come on."

Her hands wouldn't stop shaking. "I need to leave."

He steered her out of the tent. Grace and Nita had drifted toward a stall selling hand-dyed scarves. Before they could turn and see her, Ivan guided Maricela between the two tents and stood between her and the world like a solid, protective wall. "Take a breath."

She tried. She tried, but it seemed like no matter how much or how fast she breathed, the air wasn't reaching her lungs. "I can't."

"Shh." He cupped her cheeks, his hands warm and careful. "Look at me."

His eyes were so blue, like a clear summer sky—until she looked closer. Darker blue ringed his irises, and there were little flecks of gold near his pupils.

"That's it." The words were a soft whisper that wrapped around her. He took one of her hands and pressed it to his chest. "Breathe with me. Nice and slow."

His heart thumped under her hand, fast and hard but *steady*, like everything else about him. She matched her breathing to his, following the rhythm of the gentle rise and fall of his chest, until she was able to draw in one massive gulp of air.

"Good." He held her hand to his chest as he inhaled again, more slowly this time, and held it before exhaling. "You're safe, Maricela. I've got you."

The words comforted her, but the intimacy of the moment sparked an almost painful longing deep in her belly, and she pulled her hand free. "It's okay. I'm okay."

"Yes, you are." When his hand dropped away from her cheek, she felt the loss. "I can make your excuses to the priestess—"

"No." She couldn't miss William's ceremony. She had to be there for the people, for *Ana*—and besides, what excuse could Ivan offer? *Maricela let herself get sucked into a fortune teller's theatrics?* It was worse than embarrassing. It was humiliating.

She forced a smile. "I'm fine. Really, I'm fine."

If she said it enough times, maybe that would make it true.

sara

The Rios princess left, herded away by her bodyguard, and Sara held her breath and counted to sixty. Then she rose on shaking legs and held it together long enough to put out her hand-painted CLOSED sign and tie the flimsy tent flaps in a feeble attempt to shut out the world.

That task complete, she collapsed into her chair, dragged the trash bin between her legs, and hunched over, pretty damn sure the meat pies that had seemed so delicious a couple hours ago were about to come back up.

Her skin crawled. Her lizard brain howled. Her muscles were locked in endless spasm as instinct demanded that she kick over the table, grab her bag, and run. She still had a clean bolthole in Sector Eight. She could disappear into it and not have to come out for a month, at least. The freeze-dried rations she'd stored there wouldn't be great eating, but malnourished was better than dead.

And dead was better than discovered.

Her stomach lurched. She sucked in an unsteady breath, but the candles that lit the tent's dim interior provided more than ambience. They filled the air with sharp spice and a cloying sweetness that only twisted her gut tighter.

It was stuffy and too warm in the tent. Breathing shallowly through her mouth, she reached up to drag off her headscarf. The wig came with it, a heavy fall of auburn curls that she tossed onto the table on top of her tarot cards.

She'd gotten reckless. So reckless.

Why hadn't she just kept to the game? People wore their desires and fears and hopes painted across their faces. A few strategic words to draw them out, and observation combined with logical deduction did the rest. People saw in her fortunes what they wanted to see. It was the easiest money Sara had ever made, her latest iteration of telling people what they so clearly needed to hear.

But then the Rios princess had wandered into her tent, and a ravenous need for actionable intelligence had opened up inside Sara, driving her to do the one thing that always, *always* ended badly.

Her discarded gloves peeked out from under the wig. The tent was claustrophobically warm, but she still yanked them free and tugged them back on.

Who could have guessed that sheltered, soft-looking Maricela Rios had such dark memories seething just below the surface? Did Sector One know that their beautiful, white-clad princess had killed a man with her bare hands?

If she closed her eyes, Sara could reconstruct the memories she'd taken. They were jagged, fuzzy around the edges in a way that meant Maricela had recalled them many times, and they were wrapped up in a sprawling tangle of nightmarish variations that seemed almost as real.

Memory encoding and recall were imperfect. The simple act of remembering could change a person's perception of what had happened, especially when the human brain couldn't always separate dream from reality.

Well, a *normal* human brain couldn't.

Sara's brain had already teased through the variations, cataloging and cross-referencing based on context clues. She knew the official story of the assassination attempt—that God himself had struck down Gideon Rios's attacker for his audacity—but she'd always subscribed to the cynic's theory: that Gideon himself had done the dirty work. After all, Gideon's hands were hardly clean of blood.

Apparently, neither were his baby sister's.

Sara could still feel Maricela's rage like an echo in her blood. She could feel the handle of the knife, the resistance of the assassin's body as she thrust it into him. Unlike Sara, Maricela hadn't been trained in the most efficient places to stab a man. She'd been messy, driving the knife home again and again until some combination of shock and blood loss had finally rendered him unconscious.

The nightmares were even more telling. Sara had enough of those to know how *her* brain shaped her fears—helplessness. Hopelessness.

Maricela's deepest fear was her own power.

It was a valuable insight into the royal family, and if it had ended there, the risk of touching her might have been worth it. But Maricela had startled, and her bodyguard had leapt into action, grabbing Sara's bare wrist with his fingers—

Another wave of nausea hit her, riding a fresh surge of horror.

Darkness didn't *begin* to describe what writhed beneath the guard's placid exterior.

His memories overlapped hers for a dizzying moment. She was a small boy, shivering in the dusk, watching other children delight in the fat snowflakes trickling from the sky, knowing they'd mean a cold, miserable night if he couldn't find a place to sleep—

—a man, surrounded by gunfire, lunging to shove someone out of the path of a bullet with a fierce joy that bled into disappointment when he hit the ground, unscathed, still alive—

—a youth, his chest tight as his mother turned to the wall, the sobs she fought to muffle still evident in her heaving shoulders—

—a man, slashing a blade across an enemy's throat and feeling nothing as the blood splashed him, nothing except cold resentment—

—a boy again, shivering until his body ached, pressing tight against the brick wall behind him as the night grew colder and colder—

Sara shook her head violently, as if she could shake her way free of the borrowed memories. She'd never spent a night on the streets. Her father had prepared her for the likely eventuality of orphanhood with precision and foresight. By age seven, she knew how to hack the city's network to give herself a new identity. By nine, her father had helped her establish an untraceable safe house in every sector. He'd drilled her on evasion tactics. On strategy, on network security, on disguising herself. She had credits stashed under half a dozen different aliases, and she knew how to vanish into the chaotic mass of humanity that lived in and around Eden.

The one thing he couldn't teach her was how to deal with being a freak.

As soon as she thought the word, her mother's voice rose from the depths of her too-perfect memory, warm and chiding. *"You are not a freak. You're my miracle."*

The recollection brought warmth with it, enough to combat the lingering chill of that snowy night and the shivering little boy. Sara closed her eyes and focused on it, sinking into the crisp, bright edges of it like watching a vid.

Her mother gathered her close, even though at eight she was too big to sit on her lap like a baby anymore. "Our brains run on electricity," her mother explained, tilting her tablet so Sara could see the illustrated brain scan with bright bits of light flashing like fireflies.

"Neurons?" she asked, and her mother stroked her hair with a laugh.

"Yes, neurons transmit and process the electricity. That's how we store memory. Most people will never be aware of it. They can't see or sense the electricity without special equipment. But you're different. It's like in the wintertime, when you wear your socks on the carpet and then touch a doorknob. You get a shock, because the built-up electricity finally has somewhere to go. You're like me, except I only get a little prickle. A hint of what's going on in their heads. When people feel strongly, you get a spark, and you can see what they've seen. You're like the doorknob—you're a conductor."

"A freak," Sara muttered again. But the second the word was out, she regretted it. The last thing she wanted to do was hurt her mother, whose big brown *eyes sometimes overflowed with tears—*

The memory twisted. Her mother's brown skin and dark hair blurred. Blue eyes and limp blond hair and a deathly pale face superimposed themselves over her mother, and Sara hovered, torn between her past and the bodyguard's.

His mother had also curled into herself and turned to the wall sometimes. Somehow, Sara doubted it was because the guard's mother was also a genetically enhanced neurosurgeon on the run from a secret military program.

Chemical imbalances of the brain plagued plenty of people who had nothing to do with experimental gene modification, and in the sectors, such disorders still frequently went untreated. It was conceivable the bodyguard's mother had suffered from one, possibly exacerbated by whatever had resulted in those dark, helpless memories of sleeping in the streets. The memory was coated with too much resigned recognition for his mother's grief to have been a sporadic or rare occurrence.

Sara could empathize. Her mother may not have been a conductor, but she'd taken in the pain of the world, collecting it like static that had no way to discharge. Sara had known early in life that Mama had bad days, and Papa would do anything it took to make them right, except that sometimes, he couldn't.

Her father hadn't accepted defeat well. Makhai soldiers rarely did.

Sara's stomach nearly heaved again as she imagined what her father would have said about today's fiasco. She was only eleven when the Base came for her tiny family, but her parents had spent every second before that day preparing her to live an invisible life. To hide in plain sight, to use her rapid processing skills and uncanny instincts to earn the right amount of money in the right ways—enough to be comfortable, but not so much as to be noticeable.

To never be someone the people in power took seriously or remembered.

Well, she'd fucked that up.

10

As a child, Ivan had learned to sleep lightly.

During his mother's worst dark periods, he would awaken at the slightest whisper or creak of floorboards. Sometimes, if he left his room and caught her wandering, he could head off a spiral. He'd lead her back to bed, or to the overstuffed chair in the corner of their tiny sitting room. She'd gather him close and bury her face in his hair and tell him to be like his father, to be *good*, over and over, until sleep dragged her back down.

Maricela's nightmare started with a whimper.

Ivan's eyes shot open at the first sound, and he stared at the darkness above him until he heard it again—soft and terrified, a low noise ripped from an unwilling throat.

He tossed his blanket aside and was over the back of the couch before it came again. In the dim moonlight filtering through the window, he saw movement on the bed—Maricela twisting fitfully, tangled up in her ridiculous duvet.

Her face looked stricken, and his heart clenched.

"Maricela." No response as he crossed to the bed and slid one knee onto it so he could reach her in the middle of its vast expanse. His fingers encountered a bare shoulder, and her skin felt feverish. He shook her gently. "Maricela, wake up."

"No." Her fingernails raked over his upper arm as she clawed at him. "*No.*"

"*Maricela.*" He dragged the heavy covers away from her and pulled her upright. "It's Ivan. Look at me."

"How—" Her voice, thick with emotion, broke. "How could you?"

She still wasn't *seeing* him. He cupped her flushed face, his heart thudding painfully as he choked back panic. He smoothed his thumbs over her tear-streaked cheeks and lowered his voice to a soothing murmur. "Come on, Maricela. Come back to me."

After what seemed like an eternity, her gaze focused on his face, and she mouthed his name.

"Yes, it's Ivan." He stilled his thumbs, but he couldn't pull his hands away. Not when she looked so lost. "Do you know where you are?"

She nodded. "I'm okay. Just a bad dream."

Reluctantly, he released her and sat back on the edge of the bed. "It sounded really bad."

After a moment, she sighed. "Yes. But I don't know how to talk about it." She drew her knees up under her chin and wrapped her arms around her legs. "What do you know about the day Gideon was almost assassinated?"

Not a comfortable topic for a Rider. Ivan had been

in Sector Three that day, tasked with helping to get the new joint hospital operational. "I know that Eden used the family of one of the kitchen workers to pressure the man into trying to kill Gideon. Donny shot Gideon, but Gideon managed to take him down before he collapsed."

"And I found them and called for help." Maricela nodded. "It's a nice story. Plausible, with no holes. It fits the timeline. It could have happened."

His heart had been racing. Now it felt frozen in his chest. "It didn't?"

Her throat worked as she swallowed. "I was working in the solarium when I heard the gun go off. Gideon's study is just down the hall, so I went to ask him if everything was okay. He was—he was bleeding, but conscious. And Donny had the gun."

She didn't say anything else, and Ivan had the sick feeling he knew where this was going. But it was hard to look at her like this—so small in the middle of the huge bed, curled in on herself, fragile in spite of all of her strength, because she never, *ever* gave herself a break. "What happened?"

"I had to stop him from hurting Gideon again." She licked her lips, and her eyes lost focus, like she was looking at something very far away. "I tried to disarm him, and he hit me. We struggled. He must have dropped the gun somewhere, because he pulled a knife. I took it, and I stabbed him with it. I stabbed him until he stopped moving."

The mental image of Maricela lunging at a man with a gun was its own special brand of nightmare fodder. He could see it so vividly, too. She was fearless in defense of the people she loved, reckless with her own safety.

He wanted to shake her. He wanted to wrap his arms around her and hold her until the fear at what might have happened that day stopped eating him up inside.

He wanted to make that lost look in her eyes go away. "You shouldn't have had to do that."

"I didn't," she mumbled. "At least, that's what everyone thinks. That God struck Donny down, or Gideon killed him, or the guards or one of the Riders. No one suspects the truth because it's so *unfathomable*."

Of course it was. Who could look at her like this, or when she worked in the gardens or handed out sweets to children or walked among her people, granting blessings, and think that she was capable of taking a knife and plunging it into a man until he bled out?

She hunched further in on herself, and he realized that his shocked silence was only proving her point. That if anyone learned her dark, violent secret, they'd never be able to look at her the same way again, because murder was incompatible with Sector One's princess.

Ivan shifted more fully onto the bed and opened his arms. "Come here."

"No." She started unbuttoning the top of her nightgown, then paused. "Can you keep a secret?"

After all the burning tension that had passed between them, watching her bare the tops of her breasts should have been seductive. But her pain seethed in the air, and the moment felt like it was balanced on the edge of something dangerous, as if one wrong move would send her into a fall he couldn't protect her from. "Of course."

Wordlessly, she shrugged her arms free of her gown, then clutched the white fabric to her chest and turned away from him.

The smooth skin over her ribs was interrupted by a splash of black ink so unexpected that he simply stared at it, his mind unable to process the meaning.

Clarity hit him like a knife to the heart.

Maricela had a raven.

She took a deep breath. "Del didn't want to do it. She tried to set a penance for me instead, but I couldn't take it. You understand why, don't you?"

"No." Surely if anyone deserved leniency, it was Maricela. A year of service to wipe the stain from her soul would have been nothing. Her entire *life* was service. "I don't understand."

"Only through contrition of heart and deed may you find absolution," she recited woodenly. "You can't repent unless you regret your actions. You have to be sorry for what you've done." Slowly, she turned to him, her dark eyes burning with intensity. "I'm not sorry. I'd do it again if I had to. Every day."

Now he was the one balanced precariously on the cliff's edge. There was nothing fragile about Maricela now. With the weight of the secret gone from her shoulders, she was fierce—less like her gentle mother and more like her aunt, Santa Adriana, the woman who had fought alongside her bodyguard more often than she'd hidden behind him.

Maricela was glorious. She was a little intimidating.

She was waiting for him to say something. "I'm going to make sure you don't have to do it again."

The banked fury in her gaze eased, and she smiled as she reached out. "You know what? I believe you."

Her fingers brushed his cheek, and Ivan remembered something else about Adriana.

She'd fallen in love with her bodyguard.

Warmth spread out from the tips of Maricela's fingers. He was so damn attuned to her now that his body stirred from that contact alone. She was only using one hand to hold up her nightgown now, and the fabric dipped low, revealing the outer curve of one breast.

It would be so, so easy to fall into this. In the darkness, in silence. If neither of them spoke, neither could say *we can't*. Just hands and mouths and finally, *finally* getting more than stolen, forbidden touches.

His hand flexed in anticipation of stroking her. But her fingers trembled on his cheek, and he knew he couldn't. Not with the weight of her revelations between them, or with her vulnerability still so close to the surface.

Ivan could survive a lot of sexual frustration. He couldn't survive being something Maricela regretted.

Moving slowly, he reached out and caught the edges of her nightgown. He coaxed it back up, guiding her arms back into it before carefully refastening each button.

The bed was so big that three more people could have joined them with room to spare. He shoved two pillows up toward the headboard and scooted up. Then he held out his arms. "Come here," he repeated.

She curled up against him and rested her head on his shoulder. Sweet. Trusting.

His chest hurt again.

Her hair spilled across his arm. He drew his fingers through the silken strands, coaxing them away from her cheek, and she relaxed with a soft noise of pleasure.

It loosened the band in his chest. It tightened other places. But Ivan smiled and let his fingers sink deeper into her hair, until he could drag his fingernails lightly over her scalp. "Want me to talk?"

"No, just..." Her hand clenched in his shirt. "Don't leave me."

That was the one promise he could make to her, for as long as he was alive. "I won't."

11

Nita's suite was huge, a sprawling collection of rooms that eclipsed Maricela's in their grandeur. The royal palace, after all, hadn't been expanded since the days of the Prophet. Gideon thought the mansion was too big as it was, and Maricela couldn't argue. She had a wing to herself, more than sufficient space, and that was enough.

Estela Reyes, on the other hand, had things to prove. It wasn't a practical need for space that drove her to build a house grander than the royal palace, but it was practicality all the same. Her majestic home was a statement of prosperity.

And her heir's massive suite? Well, that was a promise—a promise that anyone lucky enough to marry Nita would share in these riches.

Laurel ducked out of a closet, shaking her head,

and narrowly avoided a collision with two servants pushing a rack of gowns. "My entire fucking apartment could fit in your closet."

"Which one?" Grace asked around the pins clenched between her teeth.

Bewildered, Laurel tilted her head. "Which apartment?"

"No, which closet."

"She has more than *one*?" Laurel stalked away, presumably to take full inventory of Nita's storage space.

Nita rolled her eyes skyward before zipping up the back of Ana's slinky, glittering dress. The fabric looked like the midnight sky with a dreamy scattering of stars across it—but the slit in the front was high enough to flash the knives strapped to Ana's thigh. "Wait until she finds the bathroom."

"You should just give her the grand tour, Nita." Kora paused in applying Maricela's mascara to wink at her. "Shouldn't take more than an hour or two. You'll barely be late for the ball."

"Yeah, yeah. My rooms are ridiculous." She finished with Ana's dress and jabbed a finger at the Rider. "Don't go anywhere. Jewelry next."

Ana turned and held up both hands. "No, no way. I don't want to spend ten years paying you back if I lose an earring in a fight."

"Wait until you see it," Nita countered before raising her voice. "Inga, can you get the set from my debut, please?"

One of the maids who'd been arranging snacks on a wide table nodded and hurried off in the direction Laurel had gone.

Kora slipped the wand back into the mascara pot and rearranged the protective smock covering

Maricela's dress. "You've been quiet."

"Have I?"

"Mm-hmm."

Maricela sorted through the various blush palettes, taking her time to choose one. She couldn't tell her sister that she was still reeling from the events of the previous day—or that she'd woken up in Ivan's arms.

She especially couldn't say that last part with Ivan and Ashwin standing only a few feet away.

She deflected with a half-truth instead. "I was just thinking about how beautiful you look tonight. Pregnancy agrees with you, and so does that dress."

Kora smoothed her skirt over her stomach. The ice-blue fabric showed no change in her shape, but her skin glowed with health and happiness. "Thank you. But you're avoiding something."

"Miss Nita!" The maid was back, staggering under the weight of a massive jewelry box. Ivan jumped to take it from her, hoisting it onto the table next to the pre-party snacks.

"Thank you, both." Nita flipped up the lid and unfolded the trays that swiveled out from each side. "Maricela, did you pack your own jewelry? I can have Inga bring out the rest of it."

"Thank you, but I'm fine. Isabela—" She paused as Grace reached past her for a sewing kit with a murmured apology. "Isabela came fully prepared. She brought our mother's wedding jewels for me to wear."

"Oh, that's subtle." Nita lifted a velvet tray out of the box and turned it to reveal a necklace and matching earrings made of wrought silver flowers accented with pearls and diamonds. "This will look perfect with that dress, Ana."

Ana stroked the delicate petal of one silver flower.

"Are you sure? If something happens..."

Nita waved a hand. "If a fight breaks out in the middle of my mother's carefully planned ball, she won't be fretting over jewelry. Trust me." As if that settled the matter, Nita set the tray on the table and pointed to a chair. "Now let Maura fix your hair and makeup. And where the hell did Laurel go? She needs to get dressed. *Laurel!*"

Nita stalked toward the far side of the room, and Ana obediently dropped into the chair next to Maricela with a laugh. "This is more intense than gearing up for a fight. And she might be bossier than Deacon."

"You have no idea." Grace glanced up from the dress draped across her lap, though her fingers never stopped flying as she tacked up the seam with a row of stitches. "She spent the last few days subtly offering me gowns from her closet. She was *sure* I wouldn't be able to finish mine."

Maricela had no idea how she had. Grace's dress was simple, certainly—a wrapped bodice with twisted spaghetti straps that fit her tightly through the waist before draping loosely for the rest of its length. But the wrap created a dramatic, extremely flattering plunge halfway to her navel, and the fitted parts clung to her like a second skin.

"It looks good." Laurel emerged from another door, a length of black fabric draped over her arm. "Maybe we should trade, or something." Before Grace could answer, she dropped her dress over the back of a chair and started unbuttoning her vest as she kicked off her shoes.

In moments, she had stripped to the waist, and Ivan cleared his throat and turned his back on them. Ashwin's brow furrowed, but Ivan made a quick gesture, and Ashwin obediently turned.

Laurel laughed like it was the cutest thing ever, then dropped her jeans, swept up the dress, and pulled it over her head. It fell to mid-thigh, the stretchy fabric skimming her curves.

Maricela covered a smile. "I don't think you need anything tailored, Laurel. Our hearts might not take it."

"Flatterer." Laurel pushed her hair back out of her eyes and squinted at Ashwin and Ivan's backs— or maybe their asses. "Nothing like a well-made tux, though."

Ivan's shoulders stiffened, as if he felt her gaze.

Ana laughed. "I thought about wearing one, but I couldn't resist a slinky dress. Plus, no way was I going to the fittings. Zeke was being *so* dramatic about having to dress up."

Ivan couldn't have been thrilled about it, either, but he hadn't complained. Maricela folded the smock covering her dress, careful not to smudge the white satin, and set it aside. She rose and circled the table to stand in front of him.

His bow tie was slightly crooked, and she reached out to straighten it. "Laurel's dressed now."

"Thank God," he murmured. He lifted his hand to the tie. "Did I do it wrong?"

"Not at all. You look..." The only words that came to mind were far too revealing. She couldn't say them to Ivan, much less in the company of so many others, so she bit her tongue. "You look fine."

He tugged lightly on the bow tie, knocking it askew again. "I feel ridiculous."

"You'll be dressed exactly like dozens of other people tonight. Trust me, you'll blend in." A lie, but only a tiny one. Gideon had mandated formalwear for the Riders in lieu of their official dress uniforms in hopes that they would do exactly that—blend in with Estela's guests.

But Ivan could never be mistaken for one of them. It wasn't just that he was uneasy in the tuxedo. He exhibited a leashed strength that the fine fabric couldn't hide, and a prowling energy it couldn't contain. He might look like one of them, but he wasn't. He was a warrior, and a fancy party didn't change that one bit.

Right now, all that energy was focused on her. The clink of dishes and the chatter of the other women felt distant. Even the sound of Nita trying to drape Laurel in more of her diamond-studded jewelry faded away.

It took a hundred years for Ivan's hand to close the distance between them, and his fingertips lingered on her bare shoulder as he brushed back a lock of her hair. For a moment—an eternity—they were alone in the world.

The illusion ended with a low cough at her elbow. It was one of Nita's chamber servants, holding a calling card that bore Alexei's name. "Ma'am."

Maricela stared at the cream-colored paper, unable to make sense of it. "He wants to see me? Now?"

"He asked if you had a few moments."

Nita appeared and glanced over Maricela's shoulder. "Well, he's one of the only nice ones here. Take the library, if you want."

He could only want one thing—to press his suit before the ball began and others started proposing to her, as well. She could deny him now, but she couldn't outrun this all night. "Yes, of course. Please show him to the library and tell him I'll be along in a minute." That task complete, she turned to Ivan. "I need to speak with him alone."

Ivan studied her face, as if trying to judge how serious she was. "I'll stay outside the library," he said finally. "But the door stays open."

She could hardly bear the thought of hearing all these proposals herself. The idea of *Ivan* listening to them as well was intolerable. But she couldn't argue with him about it, not here. "Very well."

Alexei was waiting by the fireplace—which was laid with a fire that was not only unnecessary in summer but downright stifling. His tuxedo was elegant and perfectly tailored, accentuating his lean frame and strong arms. He smiled self-consciously, his gaze skipping over her shoulder to the open door—and to Ivan, hovering a few feet beyond it. "Don't worry. I won't make this miserable."

She didn't see how he could make it anything else. "You don't want to marry me, Alexei."

"No," he admitted readily. "No more than you want to marry me. You deserve to be happy, and so do I. But we are who we are. We can fight it with everything in us, but in the end, we'll both give in." He shrugged. "And I'm the best person you could ever choose to grudgingly marry."

Her chest tightened until just drawing a breath ached. "It's not funny."

"Oh, I'm not laughing." His cheerful expression faded, and she got her first glimpse of the bleakness in his eyes. His voice lowered until there was no chance it would reach Ivan's ears. "I didn't get to bring my star-crossed love. Hugo is a genius. People say he was blessed by your mother. He could make a garden grow in dead, salted earth. He just has one flaw."

"You can't marry the gardener." There was no advancement in that for his family, no way it would help them climb the social ladder or generate new business contacts.

"Maybe if I already had an appropriate spouse or

two." His lips twisted into a bitter smile. "There are four great families. The best chance we have of becoming the fifth is if I marry you."

"And what about Hugo?"

"My only hope is to marry a man or woman who understands. Who might even come to appreciate a surly genius who seems brooding and rough at first, but underneath is just a teddy bear." Alexei's gaze held hers. Serious. Intent. "And if you appreciate men like that, I would be understanding, too."

The future he offered stretched out before her, all the more dismal and depressing because he was right. It *was* their best-case scenario—a practical marriage full of affection but devoid of passion, where they each were free to seek solace in the arms of others. He could have Hugo at least part of the time, and she could have—

Would Ivan agree to such an arrangement? Or would he consider it beneath the office of a Rider, to carry on with a married woman, even if everyone involved knew what was going on and why?

And could it ever be worth it?

She didn't realize she'd asked the question aloud until Alexei looked away to stare into the fire. "I don't know. I want to believe it could."

Or they'd end up hating each other over it. "No. I like you too much for that. I know you had to ask, but now that you have, I'm going to forget it happened. Sound fair?"

He managed to look disappointed and relieved at the same time. "Absolutely. I'll even make you a deal— you save me from overeager suitors, and I'll do the same for you."

People had probably already started to gather downstairs. "I'm afraid it's much too late for that. I'd rather have a promise that you'll step in and save my toes if they're getting trampled on."

"Consider it done."

She accepted his arm and began walking him the back way toward the suite's exit. "I know this ball is about courtship, so everyone is focused on marriage, but I also make a pretty good friend. If there's anything I can do to help you—"

They turned the corner, and a brash voice rose in a tipsy slur. "There she is! Enough of this babbling about announcements."

The maid guarding the door turned to give Maricela a pleading look. Javier Montero filled the doorway behind her in a rumpled tux, looking drunk and extremely affronted—and, for once, absolutely nothing like his brother. In all the years Maricela had known him, Gabe had never once worn that expression of angry entitlement.

"It's all right, Lindsey." Maricela put herself between him and the maid. "I'm afraid I have to finish getting ready now, Javier, but I'd be happy to save you a dance later."

Javier's gaze raked over Alexei in accusation. "You had time for *him*."

Only years of practice kept the vague smile on her face. "A waltz, perhaps?"

Alexei stepped forward. "Javier—"

"Shut up." Gabe's brother swept his arm wide as he stepped into the suite, knocking Alexei back. He loomed over Maricela. "You know his family just wants to use you to claw their way to relevance. You should be spending your time with a better class of people."

Her spine stiffened. "How ugly. If you insist on offering opinions like that, I'm afraid I'll have to skip that dance."

Javier's breath stank of liquor, and something desperate stirred behind his eyes. Maricela didn't know what family ultimatum had driven him here, but the bitterness in his expression made it perfectly clear how much he resented needing her. "I don't want a dance," he snapped as he clasped her upper arm with bruising strength. "I want to *talk* to you—"

"Hey!" Alexei reached for Javier in protest.

He didn't get a chance to do anything, because Ivan burst into the foyer in an explosion of movement so fast Maricela barely had time to free herself from Javier's grip. The man yelped in pain as Ivan grabbed him and bore him back, through the open doorway and across the hall. Ivan slammed him against the wood paneling with his forearm across his neck and lifted him until Javier's toes only just scraped the floor. He clawed at Ivan's arm, but no words could make it past the pressure on his throat.

Ivan stood there, an immobile statue carved of hard muscle and anger that seethed beneath every word he managed to bite out. "Don't touch her."

Javier's red face was taking on a decidedly purple tinge. If Maricela didn't intervene, Ivan might hold him there until he passed out—or worse. She stepped forward and touched the back of Ivan's shoulder. "Put him down, please. You have to put him down now."

He tensed but obeyed—a little. Javier's shoes touched the floor as Ivan eased the pressure enough for him to gasp in a breath.

"Ivan, put him *down*."

After another trembling moment, Ivan abruptly stepped away. Javier slid partway down the wall before locking his knees, embarrassment and rage battling on his face.

Rage won. He glared at Ivan as he straightened,

tugging his tuxedo into place. "It figures you'd be feral. Just like your uncles."

Ivan's stony expression didn't waver. "And I'll kill anyone who lays a violent hand on a Rios. Just like my father."

"Go ahead and bare your teeth like the rabid dog you are." Javier stepped into Ivan's space. "Someday you won't heel when she tells you, and I'll enjoy watching them put you down." When Ivan stared at him without reacting, Javier turned to Maricela. "I hope you know I just wanted to talk about our future."

"We don't have a future." Her hands were shaking, and she clenched them in her skirt. She didn't care if she crushed the delicate satin. "I knew you could be petty, Javier, but I didn't know you were cruel. Good night."

"Maricela, be reasonable—"

"Enough." Ivan grabbed Javier's arm and turned him around roughly. "Maricela, go back to the others and finish getting ready."

Maricela watched them retreat down the hallway and disappear around the corner. Tears threatened, and she kept her eyes open, wide and unblinking, until the burning subsided.

She didn't have time to ruin her mascara.

A soft touch on her shoulder tore her attention away from the end of the hall, and she turned to find Avery eyeing her with concern. "Are you all right?"

The compassion in her friend's voice was enough to shake her careful self-control. As it was, it ripped past every polite, automatic assurance, and the truth slipped out. "No. I want to go home."

hunter

The seasonal celebrations thrown by each of the four most powerful families in Sector One were as different as their hosts. Estela Reyes had always preferred a more formal occasion, which was why Hunter was sipping champagne, making small talk, and resisting the urge to tug on the bow tie constricting his airway.

He was the only one of the Riders who seemed to be suffering. Reyes looked as comfortable as ever, as if he didn't even feel like his range of movement was severely limited in a tuxedo. Gabe looked his usual level of broody. And Zeke, the traitor, even though he'd fought the idea of being custom-fitted for something so stuffy and expensive, was actually enjoying himself.

All the minor heiresses giggling at him from behind their fans probably didn't hurt.

Hunter sincerely missed the days when he was too

young to officially attend the ball. He and Reyes and Gabe would sneak down from their rooms while the servants were busy setting up and hide beneath the buffet tables. They'd spend the entire evening under there, sneaking treats and peeking out to watch for hints of scandal at the edges of the ballroom.

Reyes grinned and lifted the edge of one pristine white tablecloth with his heel. "I think you can still fit, if you want to give it a go. I'll cover for you."

"Shut up," Hunter grumbled.

Reyes saluted him with a fresh glass of champagne, only to have it plucked from his hand by Deacon. He didn't look uncomfortable in his formal clothes, either. In fact, he didn't look any different than usual. He was just like Ashwin and Lucio—he wore the tuxedo like a uniform or tactical fatigues.

Like he was still a soldier, even in this stuffy, restrictive getup.

Deacon eyed the crowd with a frown. "Anything?"

"Not a peep." So far, all of Hunter's best intelligence-gathering efforts had come to nothing. If anyone at the house party was responsible for hiring the Suicide Kings, they were keeping the information close enough to avoid even hints of gossip. "No chatter about anyone's liquid assets or spending habits changing. Just the usual—who's sleeping together, who's *not* sleeping together. Who drinks too much."

"If we get lucky," Reyes observed, "that last one will help us out tonight. Champagne does tend to loosen tongues."

And inhibitions. Hunter lowered his voice. "There was one situation. A personal one."

Zeke glanced at Gabe and raised both brows in a prompt so unsubtle, Gabe sighed. "My brother got drunk and pushy with Maricela, and he and Ivan scrapped."

Deacon's frown deepened. "He did what?"

"Said some dumb shit. Tried to talk her into marrying him, I guess. The maid who was with them told me he grabbed Maricela's arm to keep her from leaving, and Ivan threw him out of the room and into a wall. Then they...exchanged words." Gabe's grip on his champagne flute tightened until Hunter half-expected the delicate stem to snap. "I don't know what's going on. None of that is like him."

Reyes rubbed his shoulder. "It's just the pressure. It gets to everyone sometimes. He'll be all right."

Hunter hoped it was true. Javier had often joined their close-knit group as a youngster. He was witty and fun, and as one of the youngest children of the family, he'd grown up carefree and wild. His only responsibility was to marry well one day, making some fine connections for his family in the process.

But then, one by one, his older brothers had scattered. John married Isabela, effectively becoming part of the Rios family. Martin had died in a riding accident, and Gabe had joined the Riders, and pretty soon only Javier was left to carry on the family business *and* secure their legacy.

It was enough to make anyone a little nuts.

The band started playing, and the crowd turned in unison to the wide staircase that dominated the foyer. Their hosts came down first, and Hunter stifled a smile when Reyes threw his mother a lazy salute.

Gideon was next—alone and unsmiling, nodding instead of waving to the gathered guests. Isabela and her family followed, and Hunter spared a wink for his sister as she accompanied her wives and husbands past him, into the crowd.

A handful of gasps and murmurs drew his attention back to the top of the stairs. Ivan stood there stiffly, with Maricela on his arm. Her strapless dress was sewn with crystals on the bodice, completely covering the fabric around the top but slowly thinning in number as the white satin flowed into a full skirt. The crystals caught the light as she moved, and half the crowd broke into applause.

Laurel appeared out of nowhere, nudging past Hunter to steal Zeke's glass of champagne. "No offense, but the rich people in this sector are *weird*."

"Rich people are weird, full stop," Zeke retorted, snagging another glass from a passing server. "That's what happens when you don't have to spend your time worrying about how you're gonna eat every day. You get weird."

The temple acolytes began to make their entrances, and Hunter turned to Laurel. "Any luck with the lost heir last night?"

"Nope. The guy was stone cold." She shrugged. "Maybe I'm not his type."

"I'm taking a run at him next," Ana murmured, stepping up next to Deacon. "If he won't flirt with me, I say we send Zeke."

"Better to send one of these louts," Zeke said, jabbing his thumb toward Reyes, Gabe, and Hunter. "You know, someone whose family can buy half a sector."

Reyes slapped his hand away. "I already took a shot. He kept steering the conversation around to Maricela. I'd say he's a man on a mission."

"Is there anyone here who *doesn't* want to marry her?" Laurel asked.

"Marry a Rios," Hunter corrected.

"Huh?"

"They all want to marry a Rios." He shrugged. "I don't think they much care which one it is."

"Charming."

"Oh. *Oh.*" Reyes stared past them at the staircase. "Oh, there is a God."

Grace was coming down. Instead of her usual ponytail, she'd curled her hair to tumble down over her mostly bare shoulders, and her dress was made of thin, clingy silk, the kind of thing that danced back and forth across the border between *sweet* and *scandalous.*

Zeke's mouth fell open.

"Yeah." Ana couldn't hide her laughter. "She looks like that, *and* she made the damn dress in, like, two hours this morning. After making Maricela's and Nita's. She'll have to beat Gabe's cousins off with a bat."

Reyes groaned. "Please don't talk about beating off right now."

Zeke flushed and jammed an elbow into Reyes's side. "Shut your foul fucking mouth. That's Jaden's baby sister."

"Hmm. Sister, yes. Baby? No." Laurel shook her head. "That is a grown-up goddamn woman."

"*Laurel.*"

Reyes leaned over Zeke's shoulder. "So, hey. Are you gonna...? I mean, I figure you've got dibs and all, but if you're not gonna, then I'm *definitely* gonna."

Zeke had turned an alarming shade of red, and Ana took pity on him. "Don't worry, Grace is too smart to fall for Reyes. Plus, if he annoys her, she'll tell Nita, Nita will tell me, I'll tell Ashwin, and Ashwin will break so many parts of him, he won't be able to make jerk-off jokes for a month."

Reyes snorted. "Frankly, I think you're underestimating me—on many counts—but whatever."

The music changed as Nita appeared on the second-floor landing. If Grace really had made her dress, then Ana was right—the families who dealt in textiles and clothing would be eager to fold Grace's skills into their businesses. The dress was deep purple, with a jeweled bodice that hugged Nita's breasts and a voluminous skirt that seemed to be made of miles and miles of floating fabric.

She looked beautiful. She always did. But the smile on her lips as she gazed down at the partygoers sent a chill sliding up Hunter's spine.

At one time, they'd been close. Not exactly friends, maybe, but close enough for him to look at her and know whether she was happy or sad, amused or horrified, no matter how well she'd schooled her expression into a polite mask. But her masks had gotten better over the years, and now not even he could see through them.

She descended the stairs like she was floating, her back straight, her smile fixed. As her gaze drifted across the crowd, it clashed momentarily with his. He raised his glass in a silent toast, and something softened in her eyes. She inclined her head to him in the tiniest of gestures.

"Damn, Reyes," Ana murmured. "If you want to talk about hot sisters..."

"Hey, you'd be lucky."

"Nita is a sweetheart," Zeke said loftily. "And I, for one, am not going to make lewd comments about her amazing rack just because her brother's a fuckhead."

Reyes grabbed his head and planted a smacking kiss on his cheek.

"You guys are impossible." Ana brushed her fingers lightly over Deacon's, a gesture so subtle most of the others missed it. "I'm going to go work the room. C'mon, Laurel."

"Later, boys." Laurel paused long enough to step on Reyes's foot and wink at him as she walked past.

He winced. "Wicked, wicked woman."

Gabe turned silently, his gaze following Laurel

as she sauntered away. He wasn't being subtle—not to anyone who knew him the way Hunter did—but he was being way too subtle to catch Laurel's attention.

He sidled up to Gabe. "You could go with her, you know."

Gabe started and whipped his head back around. "No, I need to focus on the job. Figure out what's going on with my brother."

From where Hunter stood, Javier's problem was the same as everyone else's—he couldn't pin Maricela down long enough to plead his case for matrimony. He only hoped she was outmaneuvering them on purpose, playing the game better than they ever had. For her own sake.

But Gabe's genuine worry tugged at him, and he wrapped an arm around his friend's shoulders. "Come on, then," he urged. "Let's get to work."

12

The night was passing in a blurry whirl of dances, faces, and champagne. Maricela felt numb to it, like the whole ball was very, very far away—and happening to someone else. Someone who could still smile and make small talk, even though she wanted to run away.

All her attention—her *real* attention—was fixed on Ivan. He somehow managed to always be within her line of sight without *looking* like he was lurking. He ghosted through the crowd, his former discomfort gone and his focus absolute.

It was his job to watch her, but not like this. The weight of his unceasing gaze was anything but practical. It was tangible, *hot*, and it had nothing to do with objectively ensuring her safety.

It had everything to do with sex.

Her dance partner, the second son of one of the

lesser noble families, was saying something. She smiled and nodded, then immediately regretted it when his face lit up.

"Oh, I can't wait to show you my workshop." He beamed down at her. "I know it's not how things have always been done, and my father thinks mass production is crass and cheap. But when I heard what you were doing with those shipping containers—making homes for the refugees? Well, just because they can't afford handblown glass doesn't mean they don't deserve nice cups."

"That's so true," she murmured. "I look forward to it."

It was enough to launch him into an enthusiastic description of the process. It sounded like a sales pitch, though not an overly personal one. He only wanted her patronage, and she almost promised it to him on the spot. Money was simple. Easy, especially for her.

But she couldn't choke out the words, because everyone wanted something from her. The demands were so unrelenting that she felt sincere relief when someone only asked for a bit of her time or an influx of cash for their business venture.

How fucked up was that?

The song ended and bled into another one, and her partner didn't even notice. He was deep in a loving description of synthesizing glass when Zeke appeared and gave the man's shoulder a firm tap. "Can I cut in?"

He blinked, but immediately stepped back and gave Maricela a little bow. "I'll send the details to your estate."

"I look forward to it." Then she fought a wince, because she'd said that already, but her companion didn't seem to notice. He was still smiling when he melted into the crowd, and she turned to Zeke. "You didn't bring me any booze, did you?"

"No, just my sparkling personality. And how hot my ass looks in these pants." He grasped her hand and her waist. "Plus you looked like you needed a break."

"You have no idea. But I am glad to hear that you've learned to appreciate what some skilled tailoring can do for your butt."

"I'd check out what it's doing for yours, but I don't want Ivan to knock out my teeth." He grinned, flashing them at her, then whirled her around so fast that the room swam dizzily. "Hold steady, kiddo. We'll be out of here in another few days."

She clutched at him for support until the room righted itself. "So everyone keeps desperately reminding me."

"Yeah, well, it's the truth." They swooped again, nearly colliding with a West cousin who was dancing with his husband. Zeke's dancing was more energetic than skilled, but he was clearly having the time of his life—until he caught sight of Reyes spinning Grace around with significantly more finesse.

His eyebrows drew together as his lips flattened into a stern line. "That is not okay."

"What, Reyes dancing? Or with Grace?"

"That's not dancing. That's plotting a debauched seduction."

Maricela let her head fall back with an inarticulate groan. "Ugh, so what? Humor me for a moment—just a moment—and answer this: what if that's what she *wants*?"

"With *Reyes*?"

Probably not. Grace hadn't said anything, not in so many words, but in her less guarded moments, she looked at Zeke with a bewildering, complicated mix of emotions that could only mean one thing. "You could dance with her instead."

His eyes narrowed suspiciously, and his next dizzy spin was a bit petulant. "Not like Reyes, I can't. It's a miracle I haven't broken any of your toes."

"Okay, so you completely missed that I was talking about sex, not dancing. I see."

This time, Zeke stopped entirely. Another couple almost crashed into them, but he barely seemed to notice. "*What?*"

"Never mind." Maricela urged him into motion again with a grin. "If you want to learn, I can teach you. About dancing, not sex."

"I should hope not sex. Your brother would murder me. Slowly and creatively." Zeke found the beat of the music again, settling into the steps of an awkward waltz. "And I know how to dance *normal*, you know. But that doesn't help with these fancy rich people gigs. Gabe tried to teach me, but he's not very patient."

Gabe was currently holding court on the center of the dance floor with one of Hunter's sisters. People had actually stopped to watch them as they glided across the ballroom in a spectacle of elegance and skill.

Maricela snorted. "Gabe's a fabulous dancer. Terrible teacher, though."

"So why don't you do what he couldn't? Make me a fabulous dancer."

"Oh my *God*, come on." She dragged him through the crowd by the hand, ignoring the whispers and the curious stares.

If she wanted to leave the floor in the middle of a number, she damn well could. No matter what they thought, they didn't own her.

The back balcony overlooking the garden was deserted, probably because the couples looking for real privacy had already disappeared into the hedge maze.

Maricela propped her hands on her hips and surveyed the space. "This will work."

"Will it?" He glanced over her shoulder and grinned. "Better hurry. Ivan's getting nervous."

"Keep it up," she muttered as she manually corrected his frame and posture. "I may normally be very sweet, but right now I'm tipsy. Who the hell knows what's liable to come out of my mouth? Tease me at your own peril."

"Yes, ma'am."

Quickly, she ran through instructions for a basic box step, then nodded to him when they could start moving in time with the music drifting through the open doorway. "Eyes up. And remember—my legs are shorter than yours."

The reminder helped. Zeke was smart, coordinated, and trained for combat. Once he moderated his stride so he wasn't dragging her around, the dance was far more graceful.

After a few moments of silence, he spoke. "You know Ivan means well, right?"

"Of course he does."

Zeke's face was uncharacteristically serious. "We all poke fun at him for being so serious, and having him follow you around has to be a little claustrophobic. But he's the most loyal person I've ever met. You're safer with him than anyone else in the world. Even me."

"You're preaching to the converted, Zeke." His intensity didn't abate, so she sighed and tried again. "In a perfect world, I wouldn't need a Rider as a guard. But the world isn't perfect right now. And if I had to choose one of you, it would be Ivan." For so many reasons. So many things.

"Good." His fierceness eased. "I just get protective. A lot of people don't understand Ivan."

"Don't apologize. I'm glad he has friends looking out for him." She lifted one eyebrow. "My turn?"

"To do what?"

"To play the overprotective friend." Maricela stopped dancing but kept hold of his hand. "Grace has been through a lot, and she deserves to have some fun. If you want to be the one having it with her, go for it. But if all you want is to stop her from having it with someone else, please don't. Just...let her be."

For once, Zeke didn't have a witty retort. He studied her face as they resumed their waltz, then finally nodded. "You're a good friend."

"I do my best." The curtain billowing in the doorway moved a little, and she caught sight of Ivan standing in the shadows. Watching, his expression momentarily unguarded.

Envious, like *he* wanted to be the one dancing with her.

Her breath caught. But before she could make her excuses to Zeke, a loud group of revelers drifted through the open door at the other end of the balcony. Even if Ivan cut in now, it wouldn't be a private moment, with just the two of them.

So she grinned up at Zeke and tilted her head toward the ballroom. "I could use a break. Are you ready to try your skills with a new partner?"

"Damn right, I am." He offered his elbow and escorted her through the door.

As they passed by Ivan, Maricela slowed and leaned toward him. She didn't *mean* to do it, but he was like a magnet—every time she got too close, the pull overwhelmed her. She squeezed her eyes shut and started to move away, but his fingers drifted over her arm.

She shivered, caught between the chill of the

evening breeze and the heat of his hand. Then her eyes flew open and the heat took over, because he was stroking down, tracing a path of goose bumps down to the sensitive skin inside her wrist.

The contact lasted only a moment, but Maricela's entire world shifted on its axis.

Zeke didn't even notice. He steered her back into the party and relinquished her to a request by Gabe's father. She danced with Miguel, smiled at him, almost certainly made small talk with him, but her attention was once again centered on Ivan.

He drifted through the crowd, and even when she wasn't looking at him, she felt his gaze. She felt it on the inside of her wrist, on the back of her neck—on every spot he'd already touched her, and the places he hadn't yet.

Yet.

nita

Every year, when Nita stepped out onto the landing to descend into her personal hell, she spared a moment of silence to perform her most tragic ritual.

Ten years. Tonight, it's been ten years.

One should always mark the anniversary of the night one had fallen hopelessly in love.

At least this year, Nita had a distraction available. Managing Grace and Laurel and Ana as they prepared for their first ball had given her an outlet for all the simmering tension she'd stored during the long days trapped in her mother's clutches. She had orchestrated their entry into the world of Sector One nobility like a leader preparing her rawest recruits for their first battle. Dresses and makeup were armor, and the jewels adorning perfectly displayed cleavage were weapons.

Their own personal charms were doing the rest.

Nita watched from beside a convenient potted tree as Laurel and Ana cut a swath through the hapless nobility. Ana had one of Gabe's great-aunt's hanging off her every word, while Laurel had entranced two of Nita's twenty-year-old cousins. Both boys looked torn between lust, awe, and fear.

Nita empathized. Laurel provoked all three feelings in her, too.

Grace wasn't faring so well. The Monteros had reacted with predictable speed to the unveiling of the gowns she'd made. Gabe's younger father was twirling Grace around the dance floor, his handsome face all smiles and charm. They weren't wasting time by sending in the cousins and uncles—if Grace wanted, she could leave the Reyes estate as Gabe's newest mother.

Somehow, Nita doubted Grace wanted that at all.

Maricela was stuck dancing with the Montero patriarch, which might have been even worse. No doubt Miguel Montero was trying to smooth over any ruffled feathers caused by his son's drunken idiocy. He probably thought he was succeeding, too. Maricela's smile was gracious and warm and utterly convincing...if you hadn't grown up with her.

Or if you weren't a broody, obsessed bodyguard.

Nita sipped her champagne as she watched Ivan drift through the crowd like a moon orbiting Maricela. Pretending that she hadn't noticed the way they were circling one another had grown difficult, but she and Maricela had a silent understanding, born of who they were and the lives they were expected to lead.

You never, ever talked about someone else's hopeless love.

A ripple of murmurs spread through the crowd, and habit had Nita skimming the crowd for the source of the disturbance. It wasn't hard to find. Gideon had taken to the floor for one of his rare dances, and on his arm...

By all the saints, Avery was *stunning*.

Her brown hair was piled on top of her head, baring a graceful neck and black pearl earrings. Her body wasn't all that different from Nita's—they were both big in the chest and bigger in the ass, with wide hips and solid frames. But Nita was short, with muscles under her generous curves, thanks to a childhood spent in a saddle and subsequent years of wrestling with clay and throwing huge pots.

Avery was...softer. More graceful. *Elegant.* She walked like she was dancing, and when she started to dance, it was like her feet didn't even touch the floor. Her black gown hugged her body. The skirt flared as she spun, and every movement was liquid poetry.

Even her makeup was a work of art. Simple, smoky eyes, dramatic eyeliner, a hint of blush, and heart-stopping red lips. Classic and sophisticated. Perfect. As a master of the game of personal presentation, Nita couldn't help but respect Avery's skill.

And try to find an exit before—

"For heaven's sake, don't lean against the wall. You'll crush your gown."

Oh, *shit.*

Satisfied that her admonition would be heeded, Nita's mother followed her gaze and pursed her lips. "She dances well. I suppose she had lessons."

Avery had come from Sector Two, from one of the infamous training houses that had turned out the most skilled courtesans in all eight sectors. No doubt dancing had featured prominently among the many things she'd been forced to learn.

Desperately, Nita tried to shift the vector of the conversation. "I suppose so. But you must be pleased to see Gideon dancing. He didn't dance once at the Monteros' winter ball."

"And why should his sudden appreciation for the activity please me?"

"Because you threw the best party. Everyone will be talking about it, Mama."

Estela smiled and touched Nita's cheek. "You always see the silver linings, don't you?"

Her mother's voice was so warm that familiar guilt curled around Nita's gut and squeezed. When they were apart, it was easy to build Estela into a monster who wanted to wreak havoc on her children's lives, but then Nita came home and her mother smiled and hugged her and praised her latest pottery work. She was protective and fierce, loving and brilliant. Nita loved her mother. She even *liked* her mother.

But she could feel the sword, too. Dangling over her neck, waiting to drop.

Still, it always felt good to be at the center of Estela's regard. She couldn't stop herself from smiling in return. "I try."

"Now..." Estela tapped her chin thoughtfully. "The question is, what do we do about *her*?"

Nita followed her mother's gaze back to Avery, and there was the sword. Blissfully swift, she supposed. "Her sister is Lex Parrino, Mama. The queen of Sector Four, a war hero. I imagine we shouldn't do anything."

Her mother scoffed. "Relax, Nita. I'm not talking about having her killed. But there must be some way we can turn his head."

She wanted to say so many things. The words tangled in her chest until it hurt, and she clenched her jaw to prevent any of them from bubbling up.

For all you know, that could be an innocent dance. But who cares if it's not?

I hope it's not.

I don't want him, Mama, and he doesn't want me, and this is never, ever going to happen. Stop, please stop.

She'd tried everything. Her mother brushed away objections like annoying flies, because she loved her daughter and knew what was best, and what was best was thrusting Nita to the pinnacle of their world, even if the dizzying height would be too much for her to bear.

Estela made a soft noise of contemplation. "Perhaps Gideon suspects that your...practical education is lacking."

"My practical education?"

"Sex, darling," Estela answered absently. "Miss Parrino *most certainly* had lessons."

A flush of embarrassment washed over Nita, followed by hot humiliation. Her face was on fire. How many times would she do this? How many *times* would she let down her guard, allow herself to be wooed by scraps of affection?

An actual sword would have been merciful. This was torture.

"Oh, don't look at me like that." Her mother made a face. "Do you honestly think you'd be the first noblewoman to receive professional instruction? Or noble*man*, for that matter? For the saints' sakes, Nita."

There was no graceful escape. If she argued, her mother would push back, dismantling every protest until Nita wasn't sure which of them was right. The easiest thing to do was to nod, even though her neck was so stiff it hurt. "I'll think about it," she managed through numb lips, then pushed away from the wall. "I should get back to the dancing."

"Of course." Estela smiled as she straightened the heavy necklace Nita wore. "You are a vision, darling.

Just perfect."

Nita endured the kiss on the cheek, returned it, and used every scrap of training to keep her expression serene as she drifted—*drifted,* not *fled*—through the crowd and out the back door.

The revelry had spilled down the steps and into the garden. On a normal night, the maze might have been her refuge, but no doubt its various secluded corners were already full of lovers stealing moments together.

She turned sharply to the left instead, following the path around the side of the main wing. The music grew softer as she lifted her ruffled skirts and hurried deeper into the shadows. The path skated the edge of the kitchen garden, and Nita cut through it to her destination—an arch that led to a tiny courtyard that was nothing more than two stone benches and a tumbled-rock fountain that burbled cheerfully in the darkness.

Alone, *finally,* she collapsed on the bench, bent over, and struggled against the tight lacing on her bodice to take a full, cleansing breath.

Soft footsteps echoed on the stone behind her. "Are you all right?"

Any air she'd managed to suck in whooshed out again.

Of *course* it was him. Why wouldn't her humiliation be absolute?

Nita straightened and smoothed her skirt over her legs, glad that the fabric was voluminous enough to hide her trembling hands. "I'm okay."

Hunter rounded the bench, a skeptical frown creasing his brow. "Did something happen?"

She met his gaze, and Nita's heart flipped in her chest. The golden light spilling through the windows around the courtyard gilded Hunter's dark brown skin, and the shadows sharpened his chiseled features. He was huge, not just tall but *muscular*, and his tuxedo was so lovingly tailored to him that he wore it effortlessly. He made powerful elegance look natural.

He made it hard to breathe.

Ten years ago, tonight.

It had been the first summer festival after her fifteenth birthday. Her debut into grown-up society—and the marriage market. She'd spent hours preparing for that first descent down the staircase, for the *moment* when her adult life was supposed to start. She'd had the perfect gown, like a midnight sky fading to dawn with glittering bits of glass spilling down like a thousand stars. Her hair had been flawless, her jewels breathtaking.

And, two steps from the bottom, lightheaded from the nerves and the tight bodice and the fact that she hadn't eaten all day, she'd caught her heel in her dress and gone sprawling across the polished marble floor to a symphony of hastily muffled laughter.

Her mother had been horrified. Her brother had rushed to help her to her feet, his glare fierce enough to silence the few remaining snickers. No one had dared to enrage the Reyes heir, of course.

But the heir had duties beyond protecting his baby sister all night. So Nita had retreated to a protected alcove, her cheeks still flushed with humiliation, her gut churning with the certainty that she could never, ever face any of them again.

Hunter had followed her that night, too. He'd drifted into her corner with his big, gentle smile and easygoing nature, and she'd been *certain* someone had sent him to coax her back out to dance, because that was what her mother would want. To force her back onto the horse that had thrown her.

Instead, he just...talked to her. About his family's newest trade contracts, how they'd found an exclusive source of *real* coffee, and how much better it tasted than the stuff they made in Sector Eight or the commune's attempts to grow it in their greenhouses. Easy topics. Low pressure. And when her stomach had growled audibly, he'd left her for a few minutes, only to return with two glasses of champagne and a pilfered tray of stolen snacks.

She'd eaten for the first time that day, hidden in the shadows with him as the champagne bubbled to her head and their conversation drifted. She'd told him about her pottery, and the minerals and clay she harvested to make her own glazes. They'd talked about books and music and the adorable baby foals sired by her brother's favorite horse.

She'd told herself over and over that he was just being nice to his friend's baby sister, but he'd been so earnest, so kind, so *handsome* that she'd ended the night dizzy in love and determined to talk her mother into opening negotiations. She was fifteen years old, naive, and convinced her happy ending was within her grasp.

By her sixteenth birthday, Hunter had joined the Riders, and Nita gave up on happy endings.

Knowing it could never happen should have killed this longing. Instead, somehow, it only seemed to grow deeper every year. Probably because Hunter still did things like follow her out into the night to gaze at her with earnest concern and ask if anything was wrong.

Everything was wrong. But that wasn't an answer she could give him. "You know how it is. My mother's anxious to find me a suitable spouse."

"You mean Gideon." At her look, he shrugged one shoulder. "Estela Reyes doesn't think small."

"No, she doesn't." Nita stared back down at her hands, tangled in the deep purple ruffles of her dress. "She would have settled for Maricela, but she's going to see me married to a Rios or... Well, I don't think there's an *or* for her."

Hunter remained silent as he sat down beside her, careful not to rumple her skirt. "She's determined, I'll give her that." He paused. "But why is it so important to her?"

His tuxedo sleeve grazed her bare arm, and she fought a shiver. "We're the only ones not tied to the Rios family by marriage."

"Yes, but what would it accomplish? It can't elevate the Reyes family. You're already the second most powerful in this sector."

No, if it had just been about that, Nita suspected she would have found herself married off to Isabela years ago. Estela's dreams were much grander. If she could slip Nita into Gideon's bed—and into the coveted spot of first wife—the Reyes family wouldn't be second anything.

They'd be well on their way to tied for first.

"I don't know how long I can do this," she admitted in a whisper. "I'm the oldest acolyte at the temple. I can't hide there and pretend I'm courting Maricela anymore. My mother's lost patience. Now she's suggesting—" She bit off the words, hoping it was too dark for him to see the flush in her cheeks.

"Do I want to know?"

Maybe if she said it, they could both laugh, and it wouldn't have this sick, horrifying power over her. "Oh, you know. She wants to hire someone to teach me about sex so Gideon won't have to worry that I'm bad at it."

He did chuckle, but it was a reflexive noise that

didn't sound genuinely amused at all. "Well, then."

"Yeah." Her cheeks were still burning. The humiliation wasn't fading. If anything, the helplessness in her chest was twisting tighter. She covered her face with her hands, unsure if the sound they muffled was the start of a laugh or a sob.

"Hey." He touched her shoulder, his hand big enough to engulf it and still so gentle. "It won't ruin your family if you tell her to shove all this up her ass. It won't hurt them. Only your mother's pride."

"That might be the worst thing of all." She stiffened her spine, refusing to let herself lean into him. His strength was a comfort she couldn't afford to rely on. "I can say no and risk being cut out of the family, but if I do that, I won't be able to help my younger sisters. I need to find someone to marry. Then I'll have my inheritance, along with enough money to make a safe place for them."

"That doesn't seem fair to you."

It wasn't. Somewhere, in some alternate universe that had been fair to her, they were still sitting on this bench together, but they were married. In love. They'd snuck away the way they did every ball, just like the first, and their children were tucked upstairs in bed under the watchful eye of their nanny. They'd steal a kiss, and Nita would lean into the warmth of Hunter's body, secure in the knowledge that she was safe and loved. That happiness wasn't just possible, but guaranteed.

In a fair world.

She rose, and his hand slipped away from her shoulder. She locked down the part of her that immediately missed the contact, imagining that ice flowed beneath her skin instead of blood, and nothing could touch her. "Thank you for listening, but we should get back. I promised Grace I wouldn't abandon her."

He stood as well, wordlessly offering his arm. She accepted it, and they started back to the party in companionable silence. Two casual friends, sharing an evening walk. Nothing more. Never, ever anything more.

It would be nice to live in a world that was fair. Unfortunately, Nita was stuck in this one.

13

Ivan had been involved in drawn-out gun battles that left him less on edge than the Reyes ballroom.

A gun battle might have been welcome, honestly. He knew what to *do* in a gun battle. Cover Maricela's body with his own, get her to safety, fight back. He longed for a tangible enemy with an actionable solution. Smacking Gabe's brother into a wall had been the least frustrating part of his night so far.

But Ivan couldn't fight the demons plaguing Maricela. He couldn't march over to where she endured Gabe's father's chatter with an increasingly fixed smile and drag *him* off her and into a wall. It didn't matter that he was watching something bright inside her die a little more with every dance—she was a Rios. She would willingly martyr her happiness, then be angry with herself for feeling a moment's resentment over the loss.

He was starting to wonder if Maricela could even see the bars on her cage. How could she? She'd grown up trapped inside them, so carefully sheltered she rarely glimpsed the outside world.

Each dance she endured only strengthened his desire to rip open those bars and drag her out into the real world, even if it was only for a night. Just to *see* freedom, so she could understand the depth of her sacrifice. Maybe then she'd stop punishing herself.

Or maybe it would be a singular cruelty, to show her a world she would never be allowed to touch.

By the time the dance ended, a queue of hopeful men and women had already formed. But Maricela excused herself from the knot of potential partners and turned toward Ivan.

At first, he thought she was finally taking a break. But her gaze clashed with his as she moved toward him with purpose, and he knew. All the other Riders had taken their turn spinning her around the dance floor, but he'd stayed carefully on the sidelines where he wouldn't be the focus of everyone's attention.

Ivan didn't know if he could dance with Maricela without giving his feelings away.

She held out her hand boldly, though her words acknowledged his hesitation. "You can't say no. Just this once, I'm pulling rank." Her voice dropped to a whisper. "Dance with me, Ivan."

He clasped her hand, the contact shocking in its directness. After so many glancing brushes of skin, it felt almost obscene to hold her hand so openly. The feeling intensified when they reached the floor and he dropped his hand to the spot where her waist flared into her hip. The beading on her dress abraded his palm, and the floral scent she was wearing filled his senses.

This close, she had to tilt her head back slightly to meet his eyes. Hers were big and brown, soft with desire and *want*. She was as dizzy with it as he was, and Ivan wasn't sure how they'd manage a dance like this. He could barely remember the steps Gabe had taught him.

"Thank you," she murmured.

"Don't thank me yet," he replied just as quietly. "I might step on your feet. Zeke's a mess, and he's still better than I am."

"You exaggerate." Her hand tightened on his shoulder. "I don't think it's possible for you to be less than graceful."

The music started, and he stepped to the right, torn between the need to concentrate on his footing and the fact that he could feel each individual fingertip pressing into his shoulder. "It's a different kind of grace."

"No." She moved with him, as naturally as breathing. "Don't you feel it?"

"Feel what?"

"What to do."

He did. He was so attuned to her touch that she barely had to lead. The slightest pressure on his shoulder guided him to one side, the faintest squeeze of his hand to the other. Moving with her was effortless, because he'd been watching her for weeks. He'd memorized her gestures, her movements, her breathing. He'd grown an entire set of nerves that answered only to her.

His guilty, furtive imagination hadn't done the fantasy of sex with her justice. If they moved like this through the steps of a dance he didn't know, how would they move together at one he'd mastered?

Not something he could afford to ponder with the eyes of all the most powerful people in the sector glued to them. This tuxedo fit him a little *too* well, and he doubted it would hide a punishing erection.

Maricela's gaze roamed over his face. "You're frowning."

If he was, it was only with the effort to keep from doing the opposite. "That's just my face."

She laughed. "You shouldn't tease me. I consider it an unavoidable challenge."

"Maybe that's why I do it," he countered.

"Because you want to be teased back?" Her head tilted to one side as she considered that. "How curious."

It wasn't something he would have put into words, but it made sense. The only people who'd ever teased him were fellow Riders. "You tease people you care about."

Her eyes widened, and her fingers clenched around his. "Ivan…"

Too far. He'd taken it too far, and he didn't know how to pull back. The whole night felt surreal. With the champagne and the music and the glittering lights and this ridiculous tuxedo, he might as well be a different person. One who was allowed to twirl Maricela through the steps of a dance and smile at her. "Shh. We're dancing."

She returned his smile, and neither of them talked as they moved with the music. The silence was heavy, but instead of being awkward, it just felt *full*—of pleasure, of longing.

Of all the things they weren't saying.

Ivan was starting to like dancing.

But a commotion was sweeping through the crowd, mutters and gasps so obtrusive that he couldn't ignore them. A few of the couples stopped dancing altogether and drifted to the edges of the ballroom.

Maricela squeezed his hand again. "What in the world—?"

A scream from the other side of the room cut off her baffled question, and Ivan reacted on instinct. Within moments, he had her off the dance floor, his body between hers and the source of the disruption. Zeke and Reyes pushed through the crowd toward them, and Ivan steered Maricela in their direction. "What's going on?"

Reyes caught his shoulder. "Get her out of here. Gideon's orders."

He reached for Maricela immediately as his brain switched gears to tactics. "What happened?"

Reyes only shook his head. "It's not important right now. Just go."

Maricela didn't move. "*Fernando.*"

Sighing, he met Ivan's gaze. "It's Javier."

Oh, *God.* Ivan's stomach sank into his boots, and he regretted asking. He wanted to drag Maricela away before Reyes could speak the truth Ivan could already read in his eyes.

But the other Rider's bleak, damning words didn't stop. "He's dead."

14

The Reyes house was in chaos.

Numb, Maricela went where Ivan steered her. People spoke to her, but she couldn't hear them. She was only vaguely aware of being urged into a car, and of Avery, pale and somber, pulling her close until she stopped shaking.

Javier Montero was dead. It didn't seem real. None of it seemed real.

In hushed tones, Avery told Ivan what she'd managed to glean from the gossip spreading through the party like wildfire—they'd found him in one of the studies. There was no sign of struggle or obvious injury...

But he did have a nasty bump on the back of his head.

That made Maricela start shivering all over again. This was all some terrible thing happening very far away to people she didn't know. Silently, she repeated the lie to herself as the car sped toward home. As Ivan practically carried her inside and up to her room. As Avery helped her take off her dress and replace it with a nightgown.

Ivan hovered in the doorway to her suite, carrying on a low-voiced conversation with someone in the hallway. The words blurred into meaningless sound as Avery carefully laid her ball gown over the back of a chair. The conversation ended, and Ivan appeared at the door to her bedroom. "One of the royal guard is waiting for you in the hallway," he told Avery. "He'll stay with you for the time being."

"Thank you." Avery framed Maricela's face with her hands, gave her an encouraging smile, and slipped out of the room.

Somehow, that smile grounded Maricela. She rubbed her hands over her arms as she stared out into the dark antechamber. "This is really happening, isn't it?"

"Yes." Ivan went to secure the doors, his footsteps nearly silent on the carpet. When he returned, he closed the door that separated his antechamber from the sitting room and turned to hover in the doorway to her bedroom. "Are you okay?"

Her stomach lurched. She was being worse than self-absorbed. She was being a complete dick. She wasn't the one who'd fought with Javier, who might have—

She shook away the thought. "I should be asking you."

His expression remained impassive. Closed off. "I'm fine."

He didn't look fine. He was wound so tight she thought he might shatter. "Ivan, listen to me." She reached for him. "Whatever might have happened—"

"No." He sidestepped her so fast, he was halfway across her room before he stopped. His fingers flexed at his side, and he stared at the floor. "You can't touch me. Not right now. Do you know what it *does* to me when you touch me?"

Her heart wedged in her throat. It was the sort of declaration meant to flatter and seduce...except that Ivan didn't sound infatuated.

He sounded tormented.

She tried to draw a breath, but it turned into a sob. "What are we doing to ourselves?"

"Fighting it." He reached up to rip open his bow tie. "You don't understand, Maricela. I didn't want to kill him, but I'll take the raven. I'd do it again. He shouldn't have touched you."

"You don't mean that."

He shed his jacket next, letting it fall to the floor in a heap. Then his shirt, one intent button at a time. He dragged it off and turned, displaying his arm to her. "Look. Look at who I am."

Ravens covered his skin, dozens of tiny tattoos that each represented the unfathomable value of a life taken. He had so many, more every year, but she couldn't be horrified by the deaths he carried.

After all, were his dozens any worse than her one?

She approached him slowly, carefully, the way she would a skittish animal. He watched her, his eyes burning, as she reached out again, but he didn't move. He barely breathed.

Her fingers trembled on his arm. "I know who you are." Before he could deny it, she bent her head and pressed her lips to one of the ravens that marked his shoulder.

"Maricela." Her name came out on a hoarse groan.

"You have to stop touching me, or I'll start touching you."

Her stomach clenched again, this time in anticipation. "You should. Because I think we're already lovers—in every way but one." She tilted her head back, entranced by the sheer ravenous hunger on his face. "Am I wrong?"

He stared at her for so long, she feared he was gathering his self-control. That he'd turn his back on her and put the door between them, and she'd never, ever know what it felt like to be honestly, nakedly *desired*.

Instead, he sank his fingers deep into her hair and cradled the back of her head. "This might be blasphemy," he murmured, but she didn't get a chance to argue.

Because he was kissing her.

She'd been kissed before, polite pecks on the cheek and hesitant caresses and eager, lusty explorations. But nothing like this. Ivan's mouth moved confidently over hers, as if he didn't have to discover what she liked because he already knew.

Somehow, he was right. She clung to him as his tongue slid over hers, momentarily distracted by the sensation of touching his bare skin, smooth and hot over hard muscle. His hands dropped to her hips, and her nightgown wasn't thick enough to block the heat of his grip. He pulled her closer, right up against the hard ridge of his erection.

Her head was spinning. She broke the kiss to draw in a desperate breath, and Ivan just kept kissing her. Her jaw first, then her throat, lingering when she gasped to scrape the spot with his teeth before sucking lightly. The backs of her legs hit the edge of her bed, and Ivan smoothly lowered her to the mattress, following her without taking his lips from the hollow of her throat.

All her previous sexual encounters had been a little awkward, a lot of bumped noses and nervous laughter and *is this all right?* But Ivan didn't stumble. He didn't hesitate.

And he was *everywhere*.

He settled half over her, his chest blazing hot as he pressed her down into the bed. His mouth found her ear, murmuring something she couldn't even understand because his hand had settled low on her leg, just under the hem of her nightgown. His calloused fingertips traced her skin, rough and gentle at the same time.

"I know what to do," she whispered.

Ivan lifted his head, his hand stilling on the outside of her knee. "What do you know, Maricela?"

Her cheeks heated. "How to make you feel good." She nuzzled the spot where his neck met his shoulder, then bit him gently.

He stiffened against her, a groan escaping him. "Do it again." So she bit him harder, her teeth lingering on his skin until he gripped her thigh and threw his head back. *"Fuck."*

He drove his fingers into her hair again, this time tightening to tilt her head. This kiss was rougher, almost bruising. *Perfect*, because it felt like something she'd always needed but never knew enough to miss.

One lover worshipping another instead of a supplicant kneeling before a saint.

He rolled them, his fingers still tangled in her hair, and urged her to straddle his hips. When he broke the kiss this time, he reached for her tangled nightgown. "Take it off," he rasped, somehow making it sound like an order and plea at the same time.

She peeled the gauzy nightdress over her head,

acutely aware of the flexing, leashed strength of his body beneath hers. "Ivan..."

But she didn't have time to be shy about stripping naked in front of him. He was looking at her like he'd been starving for this. Just to *see* her. His gaze roamed over her body and, with every passing heartbeat, his breathing sped.

Then, frowning, he traced the single raven tattooed onto her side. "You shouldn't have to carry this."

"No one forced me." She caught his hand and laced her fingers with his. "It was my choice."

His muscles flexed as he sat up, pressing his chest to hers. His erection ground insistently up against her, and Ivan caught her gasp with his mouth, kissing her deeply as his free hand slid up her spine.

He pulled her lower lip between his teeth, eliciting a whimper that turned into a moan when he tugged at her hair. Maricela let her head fall back, torn between a dozen different sensations—her scalp tingling, his hand on her hip, the heavy pressure of his cock rubbing against her through the fabric of his pants.

Warm air on her naked skin.

His mouth on her collarbone.

He pulled her hair harder, arching her back. "Tell me," he murmured against her breastbone. "Tell me what you want."

It would take her all night to answer. Every inch of her was aching to be touched, and she barely knew where to start. Then his cheek brushed the curve of her breast, his stubble scraping lightly over her skin, and the words spilled out with a shudder. "I want your tongue. On my nipple."

He gave it to her. No teasing, no waiting—just heat, a pleasure that jolted through her as he dragged his tongue over the tip before drawing it between his lips.

No, he wasn't a fumbling boy. Not in the slightest.

"What about—" She cut off with a cry as he sucked, and now the whole world was fuzzy. Swimming. "What do *you* want?"

"This." He switched to her other breast, licking and sucking until he drove another helpless sound from her. His hand tightened on her hip, urging her to move against him. "You. All of you."

It was a different sort of dance, and this time he was the one leading. She arched against him, gritting her teeth when pleasure shuddered up her spine. He hauled her upright, pressing his forehead to hers with a groan at her next squirming rock. "Just like that."

She clutched his shoulders with trembling hands, desperate to steady herself, but she couldn't stop shaking. It was like all the tension that had built up between them had never dissipated—it was all knotted up inside her, twisting tighter with every passing heartbeat.

Ready to explode.

He turned his head just enough for his lips to brush her ear. "I've been imagining this," he whispered roughly. "How you'll sound when you come. Show me."

His breath on the sensitive spot behind her ear tipped her over the edge, and she came with a cry that she had to muffle against his jaw. It was fast but not easy, a blazing flash fire so hot and wild that it should have receded in an instant.

Instead, it burned her alive.

His arms locked around her as he rose and twisted. The brief sensation of falling ended with her back on the mattress, Ivan's hard body pressing her down into the plush quilt. He braced his weight on either side of her head and ground his hips against hers, provoking another startling burst of pleasure.

Maricela opened her eyes. Ivan stared down at her, his face in shadow, his blue eyes wracked with a hunger that instantly renewed the empty ache between her thighs.

He hovered there for a moment, his gaze tracing her face as if he needed to fix it in his memory. Then he slipped silently down her body. He trailed kisses in his wake—to her jaw, her collarbone, the spot between her breasts. When he reached her ribs, he lingered over her tattoo again, but only for a moment.

Warm breath ghosted over her belly button next, and he curled his fingers under the lace edging her panties. She lifted her hips out of instinct, and he tugged the fabric down her legs, then settled onto his knees as he dropped her panties over the edge of the bed.

Then he just...*looked* at her.

She tried not to fidget under his scrutiny, but none of her previous experiences had ever been this intense. Those men and women had been happy with simple, easy pleasure, and eager to soothe her when it all threatened to overwhelm her.

They never *demanded* anything from her. Not the way Ivan would.

He stroked the sensitive skin just above the inside of her knee. "You're perfect," he murmured, pressing gently to urge her legs apart. Anticipation eclipsed her nervousness as his lips brushed her knee, her thigh. Higher.

She choked on a moan as his tongue touched her. Soft, at first, just a tease, followed by his fingers grazing her clit. He stroked lower, parting her flesh to his inescapable, devouring mouth.

No, no one had ever demanded this much from her.

And no one would ever, *ever* give as much in return.

She slid her fingers into his hair, gripping the short strands, utterly focused on the sinuous movement of his tongue. He groaned, a sound she felt more than heard as the low noise vibrated through her, and she arched toward his mouth, chasing that sharp little jolt of pleasure.

And he gave her more. Ivan had always been serious and intense, but now his focus had shifted. He pursued her pleasure with single-minded deliberation, finding the spots that had her yanking on his hair and lingering there with endless patience and unwavering attention. His tongue lashed over her. His fingers stroked lower. One dipped inside, pushing into her with slow, languid strokes that matched the rhythm of his mouth.

She choked on a moan. "Ivan..."

He groaned again, the vibrations melting into another bright shock as his tongue circled her clit. But she needed something harder, *deeper*. Something to assuage the empty ache inside her.

She didn't realize she was pulling him up until he loomed over her, his eyes burning with hunger and one finger still deep inside her. "Tell me what you need."

Always so ready to give her what she asked, everything else in the world be damned. Her heart thudded painfully as she stroked his cheek. "Your fingers," she whispered.

"You want more?" He watched her face intently as he slipped his finger free. For a moment she was left alone, bereft, and then his touch returned with two broad fingers pressing slowly into her. His jaw clenched as he rocked them back and forth. "They're big. Is it too much?"

No. She tried to say it, but all that came out was

a tight whimper, and she gripped his shoulders in case he tried to pull away.

"Shh," he soothed, pressing his temple to hers. His lips hovered over her ear as he eased his fingers deeper, filling her a fraction of an inch at a time. "Move your hips. Take me as deep as you can."

The hoarse command left her trembling, and she obeyed without thinking, arching up. He moaned his encouragement, curling his hand so the base of his palm pressed down on her clit. "Yes. Ride it."

Her lungs were on fire, her pulse pounding in her ears. Every movement was torture, and she couldn't get enough. Her body had taken over, greedily seeking what her mind could barely comprehend. She clenched around his fingers, tighter and tighter, until she imagined she could feel them trembling inside her.

She bit his jaw. Scratched his shoulders. Bucked beneath him—anything to release the nearly painful tension that wracked her. When it finally splintered, she threw back her head to scream. Ivan caught her mouth instead, muffling her cries as she shuddered beneath him.

The world barely existed, and Maricela was in a million pieces. The only truly real thing was *Ivan*, and she clung to him even as she broke the kiss, gasping. Even as pleasure crashed over her in drowning waves.

Once the waves started to recede, she floated there, giddy with relief. A laugh bubbled up inside her, but then she opened her eyes, and the urge vanished. Along with the rest of the breath in her lungs.

Ivan was braced above her, both arms locked, his muscles trembling with the effort of maintaining control. His chest heaved once, twice. He shuddered. "My pants."

Mesmerized, she reached for them without looking,

though he shuddered again when her fingers trailed over his stomach before reaching the double buttons. She managed to free the first one, but her impatience got the better of her, and the second button popped off as she tugged at the fabric.

His breath hissed out as he rocked against her hand. "Hurry."

The zipper stuck halfway down, and Maricela shoved his pants and underwear off his hips, pushing them down his legs with her feet. He lowered his weight without warning, settling on top of her with his shaft slicking against her clit.

She had to bite her lip to hold back a cry. "Please."

"Put your legs around my hips."

A momentary flash of nervousness seized her, and she squeezed her eyes shut as she locked her legs around him.

"Maricela." His chest touched hers as he lowered himself to his elbows, and she felt the softest brush of his lips over hers. "Look at me."

How could she? Everything about this moment threatened to overpower her with its intensity, and she still wanted it more than her next breath. She was standing on the edge of something vast and inescapable, and she was *eager* to fall into it.

How was she supposed to explain that she was terrified—not of him, but of how much he made her feel?

She met his gaze, and the tenderness there eased her apprehension. "I'm all right."

"You're safe." He shifted, and the head of his erection, broader than his fingers and *so hard*, pressed against her as he watched her face. "I'll take care of you."

"I know." He would hurt himself before he hurt

her.

Maybe that was part of what scared her.

Then he thrust into her, sliding deep with one slow, relentless movement, and thought became an impossibility. It didn't matter, anyway. Nothing mattered but *this*—naked intimacy and dazzling pleasure and the look on Ivan's face as his iron control fractured.

"Fuck." The word seemed torn from him as he began to move. Slowly at first, his arms trembling with the effort. Every time he sank into her, another layer of control chipped away, until his thrusts became demanding, insistent. A little rough.

Yes.

Everyone else who'd ever touched her had been careful beyond reason, because they were touching a princess—the prized youngest Rios child, adored member of the royal family. Future saint.

Ivan was only touching *her.*

She sobbed in a breath as another thrust drove her up the bed. Pleasure wasn't a word that fit anymore. This was something more desperate. Visceral. She tried to caress him—his shoulders, his back—but she couldn't stop herself from curling her fingernails into his skin, so she dropped her hands and clenched her fingers in the coverlet instead.

"Don't," he groaned, fucking her deeper. "Don't hold back."

The words jolted through her in a white-hot flash, and she remembered his reaction when she bit him. Maybe she wasn't the only one who needed to feel that sweet edge where control didn't exist. She dragged her nails down his back and moaned when his hips jerked.

He pushed up again, locking his arms, and the new angle of his thrusts shattered the tense pressure. The orgasm went on and on, curling through her like ink in water, spreading outward until her entire body was quaking beneath his. Too much, and Maricela embraced it, *exulted* in it.

So did Ivan. As if her release had stripped away the final shreds of his control, he gripped the bed on either side of her head and plunged into her, fast and deep. Finally, with a choked groan, he went rigid above her.

She could feel his cock pulsing inside her. It was a breathless moment of almost unbearable intimacy, and she never wanted it to end.

But it had to. Ivan dropped his forehead to hers for a few shuddering breaths, then rolled over in one graceful flex of muscles. He brought her on top of him, sprawled across his chest with her head tucked under his chin.

His heart pounded beneath her hand, echoing her own racing pulse. It only intensified the feeling that they were alone in the world, just the two of them. No one and nothing else.

Ivan settled one hand at the small of her back while the other stroked slowly up her spine. "You okay?"

She hid her smile against his collarbone. "Yes. Are you?"

"I should feel guilty." His fingers spread wide, spanning her back from one shoulder blade to the other, and the possessiveness of his touch made her heart race even faster. "I don't."

"Good." She lifted her head. "What do we do now?"

Ivan's gaze was serious. "If anyone finds out, Deacon will assign you a new bodyguard."

Odd, considering that no one had dared to suggest that Ashwin couldn't provide Kora with effective protection. Then again, perhaps no one wanted to risk that inevitable fight. "It might be easier—"

"No." His hand tightened on her back, but only for a moment. "Unless you don't want me anymore."

Her chest ached. "I always want you, Ivan. There's no one I trust more. But I don't want to lose this, either."

"You don't have to." One of his rare, precious smiles curved his lips. "I can't give you forever, Maricela. No Rider could. But I can give you this, for as long as you want it. We'll just have to be careful."

The ache twisted into a splinter of pain so sudden and sharp that she was surprised she didn't wince. Ivan was honest—maybe to a fault—and he was speaking a truth she already knew. He couldn't give her forever.

Too bad that was exactly what she wanted.

But she'd take what she could get. And if that meant her time with Ivan would be limited to a handful of stolen moments no one else could know about, she'd just have to make sure those moments counted.

She brushed a kiss over his chin. "It sounds like you're suggesting a torrid secret affair."

One of his eyebrows went up. "You want torrid?"

"Is there any other kind of secret affair?"

"Maybe not." He gathered her hair back from her face as he stared up at her. "I can show you torrid. I can show you a lot of things. You just have to tell me how far you want to go."

She didn't have limits, not where Ivan was concerned. Not where her *heart* was concerned. "I think... we should find out. Together."

"All right." He sounded so serious, like he was making a vow or a pledge. But his fingers tightened in her hair, drawing her mouth back to his.

The kiss was soft, slow. An opportunity to explore— and Maricela took it. She slid her hands over his body, every place she hadn't had the time or presence of mind to touch yet. The hard plane of his stomach. The sharp lines of his ribs. The strong cord of muscle that ran down the side of his neck.

And when she'd satisfied her curiosity, she started again—this time with her tongue.

His muscles flexed and tensed under her mouth, tighter as she drifted lower. He groaned when her teeth raked his skin, then shuddered and sank his fingers into her hair again when she licked his hipbone. "Maricela—"

"Shh." She teased her fingernails down his thighs. "Just say yes."

It came out as another groan. "Yes."

He made a delectable noise of pure pleasure low in the back of his throat when she wrapped her hand around his cock and touched her tongue to the crown, and Maricela silently added it to the list of things she was pretty sure she could no longer live without.

I can give you this, for as long as you want it.

It would have to be enough.

15

Ivan woke with the faint rattle of the door to Maricela's suite. Even with two more solid wooden doors between him and the sound, he was so attuned to it that his eyes snapped open.

The first warm glow of dawn filtered through Maricela's curtains, giving him just enough light to see. Maricela herself was a warm, yielding weight snuggled tight against his side, one hand resting on his chest and the other tucked under her chin. Her hair cascaded over his arm, soft as silk and more than a little disheveled.

His perfect princess looked debauched—and Ivan was *definitely* going to hell.

The familiar murmur of servants and the clink of serving trays eased his body back from high alert. The cooks' assistants would lay out breakfast for two and vanish again, and Ivan would have time to extricate himself and figure out how to present a cool, collected front to the world.

No one could know that he'd spent the night with his fingers and tongue inside Sector One's beloved princess. No one could know how quickly her shy desire had melted into eager hunger, a hunger he'd been all too willing to sate.

No one could know how many times she'd come around his cock.

Like many of his fellow Riders, Ivan had a contraceptive implant. He couldn't risk leaving any children behind on the day he inevitably fell in battle. Some women would have been willing and ready to carry his baby—especially knowing that Gideon would always provide for a child of a fallen Rider—but Ivan had grown up as the son of a self-sacrificing saint. He wouldn't put that pressure on a child of his own.

That's why he'd always picked practical lovers, women who only wanted convenient physical companionship with no emotional entanglements. Nothing more than a mild mutual affection.

He'd never had a woman stare up at him with huge eyes brimming with trust and naked adoration before. He'd never felt this *hitch* in his chest that followed Maricela nuzzling closer and pressing her nose to his shoulder with a sleepy murmur.

He'd never had his control shatter like it had the previous night. And he wasn't sure how to fit those pieces back together.

The back of his neck prickled and his muscles tensed, and it took him a moment to realize why. A new voice had joined those in the outer room, the words unintelligible but the tone and rhythm unmistakable.

Ana.

Ivan laid a hand on Maricela's shoulder and shook her gently. "Hey, wake up."

She barely stirred. "Unh-uh."

"Maricela." He put a little steel in his voice, as much as he could while keeping it barely above a whisper. "Ana's in your sitting room."

"She what?" Maricela rubbed her eyes, then sucked in a sharp breath. "Wait, she *what*?"

"Shh." Ivan gently extricated himself from the tangle of her arms and legs and slipped from the bed. "Gideon probably wants to see me, so he sent Ana to watch over you for the morning. I'll get in the shower, and you stall her."

She was already throwing back the covers and waving him away. "Go."

He spared a few moments to gather up his scattered clothing and hauled it with him into Maricela's massive bathroom.

The entire apartment he'd shared with his mother could have fit in this one room. Hell, his bedroom would have fit in her tub alone. It was the size of a small swimming pool, surrounded by tiled steps and lined with shelves full of oils, soaps, and who the fuck knew what else. Three massive spigots at one end could open to fill the thing with hot water pumped from the giant cisterns on the roof, which was probably a waste if you didn't have half a dozen friends who wanted to bathe with you.

The shower on the opposite side of the room was almost quaint by comparison. It was still borderline obscene—big enough for three with beautifully patterned tile and frosted glass doors, but at least the giant rainfall showerhead was efficient as well as luxurious.

Ivan stepped under the cascade of water and winced as the spray hit the deep scratches across his shoulders.

With a little encouragement, Maricela had expressed her passion directly and enthusiastically. She was so eager, so *hungry*—he'd barely cracked the bars on her polite little cage, and she'd flung herself straight into hedonism.

He knew it wasn't *him*. He reminded himself of that firmly as he tried to wash the scent of sex and Maricela's floral perfume from his skin. Last night had been the result of weeks of tension, driven beyond the breaking point by the stresses of the house party and the ball. The secrecy only made it more appealing.

He'd offered her an escape from the confines of being a Rios, a few precious moments of freedom where she could indulge herself in selfish pleasure. Those big, gorgeous eyes hadn't been staring up at *him* in adoration, merely at what he represented. Something wild, something forbidden. Something that was just for her.

Ivan could be that. For as long as she wanted.

By the time he was out of the shower, Maricela had gone through to the sitting room and closed the door to Ivan's antechamber behind her. He stashed his rumpled tux and hauled on clean clothes as well as his boots. The fabric of his T-shirt rasped over the fresh scratch marks, and he had to take a moment to exert enough rigid self-control to keep his body from reacting.

If he was headed to face Gideon, his body could *not* be reacting.

In the sitting room, Maricela was pouring tea. She'd slipped into a casual patchwork sundress done up in shades of pale yellow and deep blue, and she smiled up at him. "Good morning."

He nodded to her, then to Ana, who had sprawled in his usual spot at the table, her booted feet crossed at the ankle. "Ana."

"Hey." Ana waved at him with half a breakfast roll. "Deacon wants you over at the barracks ASAP, but I'll stay with Maricela until you're done. You probably have time for breakfast, if you want."

Breakfast with Maricela would be nice. Breakfast with Maricela under Ana's observant gaze, however? Not such a good idea. Ana had always had a knack for seeing more than Ivan meant to show, even before she joined the Riders. If anyone was going to catch them, it would be her.

Which meant Ivan had to get his ass moving. "No, I shouldn't keep the boss waiting. You two have a good morning."

Maricela acknowledged him only with an absent smile, which was smart and practical and the only way they'd be able to keep this damn secret longer than a day.

He still left wishing he could kiss her goodbye.

This was a bad, bad idea.

The farther Ivan got from Maricela, the more doubt intruded. By the time he was seated around the big table in the Riders' lounge, watching Deacon and Gideon finish their quiet discussion, the guilt was smothering.

He was a sacrilegious fucker who didn't deserve to look his leader in the eye—and Gabe's haunted expression reminded him that he was probably a murderer, too. Not that killing was anything new—

But he'd never killed a friend's brother before.

Deacon stepped up to the end of the table. "Javier Montero died last night," he said bluntly. "For everyone's peace of mind—ours *and* his family's—we need to figure out exactly what happened."

A few gazes swung toward him—including Gabe's. He was the one whose tortured eyes Ivan met. "I swear, Gabe, I knocked him around a little, but I don't think it was enough to kill him. We've all hit each other harder during training."

"It's not that simple," Kora murmured. "Like you said—you're a fighter. You train, so you know how to minimize injury." She paused. "And maximize it."

Deacon rubbed a hand over his face. "So you're saying that's what killed him?"

"No," she countered quickly. "I'm not saying that at all. Just that it's a possibility, one of many." She turned to Gideon. "I managed to get a look at the b—at Javier last night. He *did* have a bump on the head, but that doesn't mean he sustained it during the altercation with Ivan. If he was as drunk as everyone says, he could have taken a fall and hit his head then. Or it could have been something else entirely, and the head injury is a coincidence."

Lucio drummed his fingers on the table. "We need an autopsy."

"We do," Kora allowed. "But they're so far outside of religious practice that we won't get one, not unless Gideon demands it. And I don't think that's a good idea. We should respect the Montero family's wishes."

"We need a tox screen, at the very least," Ashwin argued. "Ivan and Javier's confrontation was widely known by the time the ball started. If I were targeting the Riders, I would have taken advantage of that and disposed of Javier in a way that left Ivan looking culpable."

"Poison," Reyes said flatly.

Gideon pinched the bridge of his nose. "Kora, is there a minimally invasive way to check for this? What would you need?"

"Minimally invasive? No. For a proper post-mortem toxicology workup, you need blood, hair, vitreous humor, stomach contents..." She trailed off, shaking her head. "I'd settle for the blood."

"Blood. All right. When we're finished here, Deacon can accompany you and Ashwin to the Montero estate. Invoking my name should be enough to get you that much. And, Gabe, if you feel up to it..."

"I'll go," Gabe said without hesitation. He had both hands resting on the table, and Ivan watched as his fingers curled toward his palms. "There are people there who will talk to me. Servants, some of the younger cousins. My little sisters. I know Javier has been stressed out, but the way he talked to Maricela last night... Something was *wrong*."

Reyes reached out to him. "Hey, everybody gets drunk and does shit they don't mean sometimes."

"Not Javier. Fuck, you know that, Reyes. How many times did he drink *all* of us under the table? And he's always been more of a stickler for proper manners than the three of us combined." Gabe clenched his fists. "Something's changed in my family. I need to figure out what's happening."

"Did he do that often?" Kora asked quietly.

"Do what?"

"Drink you all under the table."

Gabe's eyes narrowed, and his jaw tightened. "He didn't used to, no more than anyone else. But I... I haven't seen him much lately."

"It doesn't seem so crazy to me, your brother getting handsy with Maricela." Everyone turned to look at Laurel, who shrugged uncomfortably. "I mean, I don't know a lot about your customs here, or the way the Rios family is supposed to be treated, but...everyone at that party seemed to feel like they were entitled to a piece of the princess."

Nobody else would have said it to Gideon. The words hung in sudden silence, echoing with their bluntness, and the fact that no one immediately leapt to refute them was its own sort of damnation.

What argument could they offer? Ivan could hear Maricela's voice from the night of the first dance, casual and wry as she recounted all the ways Estela Reyes had sold access to her. Maybe it seemed unthinkable to imagine one of the nobles violating her physical boundaries, but nobody had protested the constant, unceasing violations to her mind and heart.

Not even Maricela.

"That's an astute observation," Gideon said finally. His expression remained bland, almost impassive, but his brown eyes held a struck flame of frustration. "It's never been this bad before. Isabela means well, but I'm afraid that her eagerness to make a match for Maricela has resulted in some unforeseen consequences."

Deacon frowned. "It wouldn't hurt for Maricela to lay low for a while, keep out of the public eye. She could probably use a break."

"I agree." Gideon glanced to Ivan. "How was she this morning?"

It took every scrap of Ivan's willpower, built over decades, to keep from squirming under Gideon's perceptive gaze. Part of him was certain that even if he kept his guilt from his face, Gideon would somehow pluck the truth from the air anyway—there was a reason people whispered that God spoke directly into his chosen leader's heart.

But Gideon was simply watching him, one brow raised, nothing more dangerous than worry shrouding his eyes. Nobody suspected Ivan because none of them could imagine a world where he would—

No. *No.* He wouldn't think about the things he'd done to Maricela. Not now. Not with Gideon watching him, waiting for a reply. "She's a little shaken up, but I think she's okay. But..."

When he hesitated too long, Gideon prompted him. "But?"

Telling Gideon the truth wasn't crossing any lines. This *was* part of his duty—protecting Maricela. "She *does* need a break. I don't think she'd ever admit it to you, but the party was wearing her down. Bad. I don't know if she would have made it the rest of the week."

Gideon sighed. "You're right. She probably wouldn't have told me. I'll talk to her, though. And in the meantime... I'm not saying you have to confine her to the estate, but let's keep a low profile."

Kora rose. "The sooner we go to the Montero estate, the better."

"Before you go—is there any update on the DNA test?"

She shook her head. "Not yet. Confirming a relationship between a single grandparent and grandchild isn't easy. I've compared Lucas's profile to the one on file for Fernando Rios, but it's not enough of the picture to judge conclusively. His mother has agreed to come in for testing, though. Once I narrow down which markers she contributed, I might have an answer for you."

"All right. Go on." He waved a hand to Gabe, who left the table and squeezed Ivan's shoulder on his way past. That was it—no words, no look, just a brief tightening of fingers. But a weight in Ivan's chest eased slightly.

When the four of them were gone, Gideon turned back to the table, his expression far more serious. "The DNA test is a formality, but a positive match might make Lucas even more dangerous. Isabela has invited him and his mother to stay with her as guests for the foreseeable future. Many people underestimate Isabela to their peril, but she'll be watching him."

"I dug deep into every system I could get my hands on," Zeke offered. "Nada. I even had my friend in Eden run a facial recognition scan. He pops up a couple times in the last few months, but nothing incriminating. Shopping in the market. Eating dinner with Antonio Montero. But we already knew Gabe's uncle sponsored him, so..."

"So, assuming he has bad intentions, he's either here to kill you or woo your baby sister." Reyes winced. "What's the more time-honored method of seizing power, murder or marriage?"

"Yes," Lucio answered.

"Both," Ivan agreed, not knowing if his conviction came from a warrior's instincts or a man's jealousy. Even the thought of Lucas oozing charm all over Maricela tightened every muscle that Gabe's silent acknowledgment had eased. "Even if his goal is to marry Maricela, there's no clear path to power while Gideon's alive."

Hunter sighed. "There *is* still a chance that he's just a guy looking to reconnect with his family."

"That's it, buddy," Zeke said, punching Hunter on the shoulder. "Keep hope alive."

"Zeke," Gideon chided mildly. "Hunter's right. *All* the children of the civil war suffered. I don't want him condemned. But I don't want us caught off-guard, either."

Reyes scoffed. "No matter what his intentions are, after a couple weeks with Isabela, he'll think twice about causing trouble."

"Let's hope." Gideon rapped his knuckles on the table. "Let's try to get back to business as usual around here. And, Ivan? I don't want you visiting Del for any new ravens until Kora's finished with her work. Understood?"

"Yes, sir," he said out of habit. But as the meeting broke up, a chill clawed its way up his spine.

Ivan hadn't been thinking about the raven. From the day he'd joined the Riders, each trip to Del's chair had been a solemn occasion, laced with a twisted kind of satisfaction. Each drop of ink in his skin solidified the truth he'd learned in childhood—that he was bad. That he was wrong. That he was damned.

He'd never rejoiced in taking a life, but he'd lived for those moments where the sharp pain of the needles clarified his own personal truth—there was no future for him but a good death, the best one he could wrench out of his undoubtedly short life. He'd been damaged goods since childhood, either cursed with his mother's bleakness or simply broken by it. Finding out which had never seemed important. He didn't have to be happy or even sane to go out in a blaze of heroic glory.

But now there was Maricela, with her soft touches and sweet smiles and gentle commands, who would grieve for him and miss him.

Maricela, who made him want to *live*.

Ivan just wasn't sure how.

16

It took Maricela a grand total of twenty minutes to realize that she was terrible at keeping secrets.

Every time Ana looked directly at her, she felt like her cheeks were flaming. Like it didn't matter if she said the words out loud or not, the truth was written all over her face—*by the way, I spent the whole night fucking Ivan.*

Plainly, there was only one way to deal with the situation—avoidance. So Maricela lingered in the shower after breakfast, then invited Ana for a very long, very pleasant walk through the sunny gardens.

They'd only just gotten back to her suite when Ivan returned from the barracks. He spoke briefly with Ana, apprising her of Deacon's current whereabouts, while Maricela kept her head down, pretending to be fully engrossed in the book on her lap.

"That sounds good," Ana said finally. "I'll see you later, Maricela."

She looked up. "Thanks for staying with me, Ana."

"Any time. Thanks for letting me eat Ivan's share of breakfast." With a wink, Ana slipped out the door.

Ivan closed it behind her and turned slowly. "Everything go okay?"

"Of course." She shut the book without marking her place and set it aside. It didn't matter anyway, because she couldn't remember anything she'd read. "You?"

"Well enough. Your brother wants you to step back from your public commitments. I don't think that's a bad idea."

He said it matter-of-factly, as if it had already been decided. "I see."

Ivan's brow furrowed. "You don't sound like you see."

"Sure, I do." She grabbed the book and headed for her small study to put it away. "There was a meeting that I wasn't invited to where the topic was discussed without my input and a conclusion reached. Business as usual."

When she turned, he was standing in the door-way, still watching her warily. "I don't think anyone wanted to worry you."

No one ever did. "Maybe what worries me is not being consulted about my own life." He filled the door-way. There was no room to brush past him, and he showed no inclination to move, so Maricela stopped in front of him and stared up at him. "Everything happens *to* me. I might as well be a table or a lamp. Just once, I'd like to *do* something."

He watched her in silence, then nodded once. "Do you want to get out of here?"

"Wouldn't Gideon rather have me stay home?"

"I asked if *you* want to get out of here."

Almost as much as she wanted to kiss him. "Desperately."

"Okay." As he stepped back, his gaze drifted slowly down her body. "You're going to need to change. Do you have any jeans?"

He took her for a ride on his bike.

At first, Maricela thought he planned to cruise around the sector for a little while, just far enough away from the palace for her to breathe a little easier. It would have been enough, to have the hot summer wind rush by. To cling to his waist and press as close to the hard, muscled lines of his back as she wanted. It would have been *heaven.*

But he kept driving, out toward the far edges of the sector, beyond the ranches and farms that made up most of the estates. Then they crossed a bridge over a wide river that sparkled in the sunshine, and she realized the truth.

He was taking her *away.* Not just from the palace, but from Sector One.

The world sped by in a blur, but the road was constant, a dark, sun-scorched ribbon of freedom winding through the dirt and scrub of the desert. Exultant, she threw her head back to laugh, but the wind snatched the sound and carried it away. The only thing it couldn't overcome was the rumble of the motorcycle, heavy with power as Ivan gunned the engine and drove faster.

He handled the bike as gracefully as he did everything else, guiding it through the curves like it was an extension of his body. Maricela leaned with him, relishing the simple, steady competence almost as much as the way his muscles tensed as she gripped his sides through his T-shirt.

Eventually, buildings started to appear ahead of them. Small, sad little shacks first, then sturdier ones. They topped a gentle hill and an entire settlement appeared on the other side, a mixture of wooden houses and reclaimed train cars and vehicles backed against each other at odd angles. Animals grazed in a communal pen, and children kicked a ball across an open, dusty bit of ground.

Ivan coasted down the other side of the hill and came to a stop near a cluster of cars. He kicked down the stand and waited for her to pull off her helmet before helping her off the bike. "I come out here sometimes when I need a break from people who recognize me," he said, placing the helmet on the seat. "Your cousin actually introduced me to it."

"Where are we?"

"Outside of Sector Four." He pointed toward another road that headed back in the direction of Eden, which was just visible to the northwest. "That road leads back into Four. Technically this isn't part of any sector, but the people here answer to the O'Kanes."

He said it like it was no big deal, this tiny cluster of life out in the wilds—and maybe it wasn't. Maybe he saw places like this all the time, all over, places she couldn't even imagine. "It's beautiful."

"In its own way," he agreed.

He dropped a hand to the small of her back and guided her toward a brightly painted van with a window cut out of one side. It opened as they approached, revealing an older man with sun-weathered features and a ready smile. "Ivan. It's been a long time."

"It's been a busy year," Ivan replied. "Shorty, meet Maricela."

No recognition showed in the man's face, and no instant worship. But his smile was plenty charming as he leaned out of the window and offered Maricela a big hand. "Well, Ivan's never brought a pretty lady to see me before."

"He hasn't?" She arched an eyebrow at Ivan, whose lips lifted in a tiny smile. "That's a shame, because the food smells fantastic."

"Of course it does! Fit for royalty. You know, the queen of Sector Four herself comes out here just for my tamales."

"Then I have to try them. Ivan?"

"Tamales are good. And two beers." He pulled some folded Eden currency from his pocket and traded it for two cold bottles. Then he tilted his head. "Come on."

He led her to a picnic table a short distance away from the truck, where he straddled one bench to sit. She did the same, facing him, as he opened her beer. "Adrian told you about this place, huh?"

"Yeah. Some of the O'Kanes really like it." He took a sip from his bottle and made a face. "The beer's not as good as ours, but the food is amazing. I don't know how he cooks shit that good in that tiny van."

"He must be a miracle worker." The beer washed over her tongue, bitter and sharp, but not unpleasantly so. "I like it."

"Yeah?" That little smile played around the corners of his lips again, as if he took pleasure from watching her enjoy something new. "I know you almost never get to leave One, so I thought it might be a nice break."

That smile was making her dizzy, lightheaded, like she was drinking champagne instead of beer. "You were right. Thank you for bringing me here."

"Maybe…"

He trailed off, and she waited for him to finish, but he just eyed her uncertainly. "Maybe what?"

"Well, your brother said he wanted you to drop your public duties, but he *did* tell me he didn't want to trap you on the estate. Maybe there's other stuff you've never gotten to do. Things you want to do."

There were a million—simple things and scary things, easy and complicated, and everything in between. "Like what?"

He tapped his beer bottle lightly on the table as he thought. "Go to a market where nobody knows who you are, maybe. You never really get to browse and haggle."

Where nobody knows who you are. All her life, everything she'd ever wanted had materialized as if by magic, gifted to her by her brother or sister or some dedicated believer who loved her because of her family name. The only thing she'd never had was the only thing she'd never been: *normal.*

"What are bars like?" she asked curiously.

Ivan almost choked on his beer. "Uh, usually dirty and loud. Rowdy. Full of fights."

It didn't sound safe, but it didn't sound boring, either. "I want to go to one."

Ivan's dubious look was interrupted by Shorty arriving with their food. He set a basket in front of each of them with a grin and took himself back to the van. Ivan pulled his food closer and studied Maricela. "Okay, how about a market first? And I'll figure out how to pull off a bar."

She toyed with the edge of the corn husk wrapped around one steaming tamale. "If you give me time, I can come up with a whole list of things I've never done."

"You should. What else would be on it?"

Only one thing that mattered with him looking at her like he wanted to lick her. "I've never kissed someone in public."

Ivan's gaze slid past her, wandering over the people going about their lives and the children shrieking with glee as their game escalated. There were people around, but no one who cared about *them*, and after a moment his eyes found hers again. "Do you want to?"

"Always with the questions." She leaned closer, close enough to lay her hand on his jaw as she pressed her lips to his. His mouth was warm and firm, but he made no move to deepen the kiss. Their lips brushed and parted as he slipped his fingers into her hair, the kiss slow and easy and endless.

It didn't matter that he was barely touching her. Her heart thudded, then skipped a beat entirely when he ended the kiss with a tiny nip of her lower lip. She stayed there, motionless, her eyes closed, unwilling to let go of the moment.

Someday, the memory of it would be all she had left.

"Maricela," he murmured against her lips.

She opened her eyes and smiled. "So many firsts. I'm not sure we have time for all of them."

He leaned back and dragged his lunch closer. "So we'll hit the ones you really want. Kissing in public. Haggling in a market. Visiting a bar."

Falling in love. "Don't forget Shorty's tamales."

"Why do you think they were number one on the list?"

"Because you, Ivan Wolff, are a genius."

17

They hadn't *technically* broken any of Gideon's rules by leaving the estate, but Maricela seemed so enchanted by the idea of sneaking back in that Ivan couldn't stop himself from indulging her.

Indulging Maricela was quickly becoming his favorite pastime.

"How." It wasn't even a question. She repeated the word, wide-eyed, as she dropped to the bench at the foot of her bed and tugged off one dusty boot. "I mean... the guards are everywhere, all the time. It's *impossible* to get past them."

She was so giddy he couldn't tell her that they hadn't. One royal guard had winked at Ivan from his secluded post—a new addition demanded by Ashwin, who had surveyed the residence's defenses and identified weak spots. If it hadn't been impossible to get into the Rios estate undetected before, it sure the fuck was now.

Makhai soldiers apparently got even scarier than usual when they were expecting babies.

But Maricela's flushed cheeks were adorable. Ivan settled in a chair and tugged at his own boots. "You should see me scale the outside wall sometime."

She paused, her cheeks growing even redder, then threw a sock at him. "Okay, now you're just teasing me."

He loved her blushes. And her laughter. "Are you doubting my stamina?"

Her other boot hit the floor. "Not after last night."

His body tightened. Desire slid through his veins, a heat as powerful as if he'd done a dozen shots of O'Kane's finest whiskey. He knew his doubts would return the second he stepped outside the intoxicating sphere of her magic, but it was *so easy* to rationalize here as he stripped off his boots and watched her eyes darken with anticipation.

She was sparkling. She was *happy*. How could anything that made her shine like this be wrong? The world owed Maricela Rios a little joy.

She swallowed hard as he stood and stripped off his shirt. Her eager gaze raked over him, but then she lifted a hand to her hair. "I'm grungy. I need a shower."

A beautiful image filled his head—Maricela, naked, water from the enormous showerhead cascading down the curves of her body. "That shower's big enough for two."

She opened her mouth, closed it again, then tugged at the top button on her shirt. "I've *definitely* never done that."

No, she probably hadn't. Her lovers were here to worship a saint, not have dirty, messy, hot sex with a woman. Ivan could all too easily imagine their horror at the idea of pushing the Rios princess up against the tiles of a shower wall and fucking her with their fingers until her knees gave way. Only a month ago, he would have been horrified, too.

Turned the hell on, sure. But horrified.

Weeks of close quarters had shattered all those saintly illusions. Not because Maricela wasn't as perfect as he'd imagined, but because she *was*, and all that damn worshipful distance was slowly killing her.

Maricela didn't need reverence. She needed the thrill that filled her eyes as he stalked toward her and pushed her hands away from her shirt. He found the second button, working it effortlessly as he backed her toward the bathroom. "Soap makes everything slippery, you know."

She moaned. "I can't tell if that's a promise or a warning."

"Both." He got her shirt open and took his time sliding it from her shoulders, savoring the soft skin on her arms and how she shivered at the slightest touch. "How much of a warning depends on you."

Her hands dropped to his belt. "On how far I want to go, you mean."

"Mmm." They stepped into the bathroom, where the tile was cool under his feet. "That's why I'm always with the questions. If you want to have really good sex, you have to ask the right ones."

She tipped her head back. "Such as?"

She was under his spell now, hanging on his next words. Ivan backed her up against the open shower door and leaned in, whispering into her ear as he cupped her breasts. "Does this feel good?"

"Yes," she breathed, then frowned. "Wait, were you asking me, or telling me the right question?"

"Both." Her bra was deceptively simple, lacking a lot of frills and ruffles but tailored to her and hand-stitched. He worked the hooks and drew it down her arms, baring her breasts.

Her nipples were stiff under his palms, and he caught them between his thumbs and forefingers and pinched hard enough to drag a gasp from her. "Do you like it a little rough?"

She shuddered. "I don't know."

Of course she didn't. How could she? No one would ever dare handle the precious princess with anything but the gentlest of touches. He tightened his fingers on her nipples until she was squirming between him and the shower stall, her breathing quick and unsteady. "Do you want to find out?"

"*Yes.*" The word tore free of her as she arched off the shower door. "Fuck, yes."

He released her long enough to pop the button on her jeans and haul the zipper down. "Take off my belt."

Maricela was tugging at the buckle before he finished the sentence, her fingers trembling on the leather. "Do you?"

"Do I what?"

Her eyes locked with his. "Like it rough."

He could still feel the scratch of her nails over his back. He wanted it again. "Sometimes, yeah."

Maricela hummed softly. She left his belt hanging open and stretched up on her toes, far enough to reach his mouth. Her teeth closed on his lower lip—gently at first, then hard enough to sting.

Pleasure rushed through him. Ivan shuddered and slid his hands into her loosened jeans, under her panties and down to cup her ass. He dragged her to him, grinding his painfully hard dick against her. "You learn fast, don't you?"

Her sigh blew over his ear. "Only from you."

He could get drunk on words like that. He nipped her earlobe and shoved her pants and underwear down over her hips to her thighs. "Get in the shower."

She reached in and turned on the water before shedding her clothes. By the time she was naked, steam billowed out of the open shower, and she arched one eyebrow in challenge as she backed under the hot spray.

Ivan kicked off his pants and followed her. He couldn't *not*. She was made of impossible contrasts, her eagerness to be taught clashing with a lifetime of giving commands. Her brazen curiosity about sex twined in and around a sheltered innocence. She was bold and blushing, pliable and demanding. Sometimes all in the same breath.

It was the hottest thing Ivan had ever seen in his life.

He dragged the shower closed behind him, and he'd been right—there was a *lot* of room in here. More than enough to maneuver as he backed her up against the swiftly warming tiles.

So many possibilities. Her skin was slick. Hot. He pressed his erection to her hip and let his hand glide over her curves, lingering to flick a thumb over her nipple and tease the indent of her belly button.

Every wriggle and squirm ground her harder against his dick, but that would only make it better when he finally sank into her. "Give me your hand."

"Just one?" She placed her right hand on the center of his chest, curling her fingers just enough for her nails to score his skin.

A prick of pain, but still gentle. He covered her hand with his and pressed her fingers harder into his skin. "Rougher. Scratch me up. I like feeling you the next day."

"Now that you mention it..." She wrapped her other arm around him and lightly traced one of the cuts she'd already left on his back with her fingertip. "I noticed."

That shiver of contact over the sensitive marks only wound him tighter. Ivan lifted her hand from his chest to his mouth and dragged his tongue across the pads of her first three fingers. Her eyes widened, and she murmured his name, but she didn't pull away.

She moved closer.

He nipped the tips of her fingers before guiding her hand down. The water beat against his shoulders, sliding down his arms as he coaxed her fingers to dip between her thighs.

Then he stepped back and leaned against the opposite wall. The view was stunning—the colorful tile was a vivid backdrop for Maricela's naked body. The water beaded on her light brown skin and sluiced down her curves in rivulets. Her long hair clung to her shoulders and breasts, but her nipples peeked through, tight little buds he wanted to taste.

Her cheeks were flushed with more than the heat of the water. Her chest moved with every unsteady breath, and her fingers trembled against her pussy.

His cock ached. He wrapped his fist around it, partly to remind himself to be patient and partly just to see her big brown eyes get even wider. "If you want it rough, first you have to get yourself ready for me."

She licked her lips. "How ready?"

The hunger in her expression must have stripped away the final controls on his tongue, because the words that came weren't suitable for a sheltered princess. "When you're riding three of your own fingers, I'll take you."

"That won't take long." Her fingers moved, a slow stroke that she met with a sinuous roll of her hips. "Or it could take all night."

"It could." He waited until her gaze dropped to his hand, then indulged himself with one slow, careful stroke. "But you won't have this inside you."

"True." Her voice caught. "I thought about this. At night, alone in my bed. What it would feel like to have you watching me."

That wasn't going to help him maintain his control. Now he was remembering the last time he'd distracted himself from a raging hard-on by polishing his knives—and imagining her on the other side of the door, stroking herself to a silent climax.

"Show me," he commanded, and it came out so rough it might as well have been a snarl.

She shuddered against the tile. Her hips moved faster, and she lifted her free hand to her breast. Her fingers squeezed tight on her nipple, twisting lightly.

Harder than he'd done it. He committed the preference to memory before his gaze dropped back to her other hand, and the rhythm he could already feel in his bones. She liked it steady, a long, careful build to an explosive, inescapable finish.

He could give her that. "Use another finger."

Her gaze flicked down his body, and she licked her lips again. "Getting impatient?" she panted.

"No," he lied. And because she seemed to like his inappropriate words, the cruder the better, Ivan channeled Reyes at his most obscene. "I just like watching you work those fingers into your pussy. I like imagining how much you can take."

Maricela froze. "You don't have to imagine it." Slowly, she angled her hips to his view and worked one slender finger into her body. "You could find out."

Another finger. "You might even help me discover that I can take more than I thought."

He'd do any damn thing she wanted. "I know you can."

She made a soft noise of anticipation that hit him like a caress. The rainfall sound of water hitting tile couldn't quite cover the slick sound of her plunging her fingers deep. Hers weren't as wide as his, and even three wouldn't be overwhelming. He locked his muscles to resist the urge to lunge across the shower and replace her hand with his own, to work his fingers into her and feel the tight clench of her body as she shuddered and came—

"Three," he rasped. "*Now.*"

Finally—*finally*—she obeyed, pushing three fingers into her pussy with a sharp cry.

It was too much. Not for her, but for *him.*

Ivan shoved away from the shower wall and all but fell on her. He caught her next cry with his mouth, muffling it as he kissed her. Wild, a little out of control, but the *noises* she was making—eager and frantic, trembling on the edge of release.

He tried to help her get there. Everything was slippery now. Her skin. His hands. He slid them up to her breasts and caught her nipples, tugging at them the way she had. Maricela went rigid against him, then started to shake, her back arching as she came long and hard.

Groaning, he dragged her hand away from her body and pinned it to the tile next to her head. "Last question," he ground out. "Are you ready?"

"Yes," she moaned. "Yes, yes, ye—"

He hauled her up the wall and drove into her.

And there was nothing but *her.* Her pussy clenching tight around his cock, still fluttering with the aftershocks of her release. Her strong legs winding around his hips. Her hand on his shoulder, her fingernails carving sharp little points of pain as she clung to him through his first rough thrusts.

She gripped his head, her nails raking his scalp through his wet hair. "Harder."

It was a royal command, and Ivan had never been happier to obey. He hoisted her even higher, bracing his legs wider for leverage, and drove into her. "That's it," he groaned. "Take everything. Everything you want. All of me."

"Don't." She yanked his head back. "Don't say that."

Because it was too much. He was a Rider, and a Rider's future was never their own. He couldn't make promises or give her more than this—a few weeks of raw, filthy fucking before his stint as her bodyguard ended.

But he'd give her as much of it as he could. The passion, the pleasure. A glimpse beyond her gilded cage.

He fought her grip on his hair until the pain slid through him, hot and intoxicating. He managed to seize her mouth, driving his tongue between her lips to part them as he fucked into her body. Maricela moaned into his mouth, lower and more intense with every thrust.

She bit his tongue when she came again, but even the sudden, bright shock of pain couldn't eclipse the sensation of her pussy squeezing him impossibly tight with every pulse of her orgasm.

He told himself to hold on. To fight the wave of pleasure, to fuck her harder. Longer. *Forever*. But Maricela had been studying him, too. Her nails scraped over his skin, her other hand jerked at his hair, and her teeth sank into his lower lip—three bright spots of pain that melded into the clenching, shuddering pleasure without getting lost in it.

His final thrust slammed her back against the tile, and fire flooded him. He groaned her name and buried his face in her throat as he came.

She stroked his back, whispered something against his skin, then lifted her mouth to his ear. "All of you."

It sounded like a promise. Ivan raised his head, serious words on the tip of his tongue. But staring down into Maricela's flushed face, he couldn't find it in him to remind her that *all of him* wasn't very much, not when most of what he could be was already sworn to the Riders.

He didn't have much, but everything he had was hers.

Moving slowly, he eased from her body and coaxed her legs down. When he was sure she was steady, he left her only long enough to find her shampoo and turn her so the water cascaded over her.

She was silent as he lathered her hair, speaking only as he rinsed away the shampoo. "Nita is coming tomorrow for a visit."

"Is she?" There was conditioner on one of the shelves, something sweet and floral. He worked it through the long strands of her hair. "Is she back at the temple, or still at her family's estate?"

"Still at home. That's why I invited her here."

Nita was a smart girl, but very few people in Sector One could go toe-to-toe with Estela Reyes and come out triumphant. "Is her mother giving her a hard time?"

"Always." Maricela leaned in to his touch. "It's too much pressure."

"I know." He wouldn't even resent Nita stealing a few of the precious hours he had with Maricela before this affair ran its course. "I could talk to Reyes. Maybe he can get their mother off Nita's back."

"No." She turned in his arms. "When he tries, they only fight, and that stresses Nita out even more."

Another unfixable problem. Heiresses seemed to come drowning in them. Ivan tilted Maricela's head back and drew his fingers through her hair to rinse it. "I'm better with problems I can punch. Or throw a knife at."

"Or kiss breathless."

His lips twitched, but he forced a serious expression. "I probably shouldn't kiss Estela Reyes."

Maricela squinted at him. "Don't joke. You might like it."

Ivan couldn't help himself. He laughed, and he couldn't remember the last time he'd done that. Sometimes Zeke and Reyes provoked groans or snorts or, at the most, reluctant chuckles, but a heavy weight had always existed somewhere inside him—a smothering blanket of darkness that numbed every emotion before it could fully form.

And he hadn't *known*. He hadn't known how much he was missing until Maricela crashed into his life, shining so bright the darkness didn't stand a chance.

He finished rinsing her hair and stood patiently as she found his soap and worked it into a lather. Her touch was light across his back and shoulders, a sensual tickle interrupted by the sting of hot water over the scratches she'd left.

No one had ever spent so much time *touching* him before. It wasn't even sexual. Her fingers slid over his skin, soft and gentle, petting and caressing until he felt like one exposed nerve. By the time he got them out of the shower and had her wrapped in a giant, fluffy towel, it was a struggle not to drag her to the tile floor and drive into her again just to drown all this sweet affection in something comfortably carnal.

It only got worse when she reached up and ran her fingers through his hair. "You've never let it get this long before."

The scrape of her nails over his scalp made it hard to keep his eyes open. "I used to do it myself, but Ana's aunt told me I was terrible at it. She usually cuts it when Ana and I stop in on our intel runs, but I haven't done one in a while."

"I can trim it for you, if you want."

He bit back the instinctive urge to agree. She made it too easy to forget why he was here. That he was a bodyguard with a mission, and this was only a temporary affair. For all her power, she was still so young, so *sheltered*. She could build this sweet, intimate little world where they acted like husband and wife, but at the end of the day...

He was still what he was. And so was she. The last bodyguard who'd dared to love a Rios princess hadn't just ended up dead, he'd been erased from the sector's history, an embarrassing, desperately ignored footnote.

One of them had to remember that.

So he distracted her with a kiss, deep enough that she let the towel slip down her body to pool on the floor. He followed it, dragging her to the cool tiles that quickly warmed under his back. He pulled her on top of him, showed her how to ride his cock to her pleasure and gritted his teeth against his own when her head fell back and she came hard around him, muffling her cries against her own hand.

It didn't help. Even with his thumb working her clit and her pussy squeezing him tight as he whispered the most obscene things he could imagine, the sweetness was still there. The intimacy. Fucking didn't drive it away, it made it *worse*.

When her fingernails pricked his chest and dragged downward in eight perfect lines of fire, Ivan gave up. He fell into the fantasy with her. And fell. And fell…

The landing was going to be a bitch. But Maricela was worth it.

18

The shed at the edge of the east garden had been used for a lot of things over the years. It had served as a chicken coop, a potting shed, tool storage—and, during some of Maricela's more imaginative childhood years, the headquarters from which she planned dashing adventures on the high seas, where she would rule her crew of salty privateers at the point of a sword.

Now, it had been converted to a workshop. Nita spent so much time at the palace these days, working alongside Maricela, that she needed a place to store her equipment, and the old shed was perfect. It was close to the courtyard where they preferred to spend their time, but roomy enough for her to work in it if she chose. A space that was *hers*, away from the temple and her family's home.

But, for once, she didn't look happy to be there.

Maricela watched her friend as she examined a line of freshly fired clay bowls, and finally spoke. "Are you all right?"

Nita cradled a bowl in her hands, her thumb working over the edge. "I'm wondering if it's time to pack this place up. I don't know if I'm coming back to stay at the temple."

"That's ridiculous." So far, Nita's mother had kept her close to home, claiming the need for support in a difficult time. But Estela Reyes was far too practical to pull her daughter out of prestigious service to the temple for too long. "She can't keep you at home forever."

"Can't she?" Nita set down the bowl and sighed. "She only let me stay here for so long because she thought I had a chance at marrying a Rios. You saw the way she was all week, throwing me at your brother."

Maricela wrinkled her nose. "We already knew she was delusional."

"I know. If Gideon wanted a nubile young bride, he'd have one." Nita turned to the next bowl and traced a crack along the side with her finger. "She doesn't see the world as it is. She never has. And she wants all of us to conform to her vision."

And why not? All her life, Estela had always gotten exactly what she wanted. "Some things never change, I suppose."

"No, they don't." Nita finally met Maricela's eyes and squared her shoulders, as if preparing for battle. "I talked to Alexei after you left. It's not precisely what my mother imagined, but Alexei's parents would pay a *lot* for a Reyes. I think Estela would come around. And Alexei is looking for the same thing I am. A pragmatic partner."

Shock left Maricela standing there, blinking and

confused. Nita had spoken before of giving in to her mother's demands, but always as a vague potentiality, not a *plan*.

"And he's rich," she continued stubbornly, and Maricela couldn't tell which one of them she was trying to convince. "Even if my mother refuses me my inheritance, he has so much money. He promised he'd set aside enough for me to provide for my sisters and brothers who want a different kind of life. I'll be able to take care of them."

Somewhere outside the shed, Ivan was waiting, watchful and observant but out of sight, giving them the illusion of privacy.

That wasn't enough, not right now.

Maricela quickly closed the door and turned to Nita. "You *can't*."

"I *have to*," Nita countered, her eyes shining too bright. "I'm twenty-five years old, too old to still believe in fairy tales. And—" Her voice dropped to a rough whisper. "And I can never have him, Maricela. Even if he wanted me, it's impossible."

The word should have stung. After all, wasn't Maricela tangled up in the same impossible situation? In futile, hopeless love with a Rider.

But it didn't *feel* hopeless. When she was lying in Ivan's arms as he slept, tracking his slow, steady breaths by the rise and fall of his chest beneath her cheek, it didn't seem impossible. It didn't even feel *possible*. It felt inevitable, as if it didn't matter what happened between them. Loving him was her destiny.

But this wasn't about her and Ivan. It wasn't even about Hunter. It was about Nita and what she could stand to do. What she could live with.

"You tease me about being an incurable romantic," Maricela whispered. "But you're even worse than

I am. And you might be able to accept making yourself miserable, but doing it to Alexei would break your heart all over again."

Nita looked away and began to stack the bowls. "They're only stories, you know. The tales of knights and ladies, all that pining love. It's not real. Or maybe it's just not real for people like us."

Apparently, calm arguments weren't going to get her anywhere. Maricela leaned against the door and took a deep breath. "I'm having an affair with Ivan."

Nita dropped the bowl she was holding.

It bounced off the edge of the table and crashed to the cement floor, splintering into three pieces. Nita didn't even seem to notice. She was staring at Maricela, her mouth slightly agape. "You're—"

"Uh-huh."

Nita snapped her mouth shut and stared for another few seconds before a muffled laugh escaped her. "Oh, saints above. I knew there was something going on, but I thought—I just assumed—"

"That he would never. I know." Maricela laughed, too. "No one was more surprised than me. Than *us*."

Nita clapped her hands together and pressed her fingers to her lips, like she was fighting to hold back a torrent of questions. When Maricela didn't say anything, her friend lifted both eyebrows and flung her hands aside. "Well? Are you going to *tell me?*"

She wasn't sure she could explain the weeks of tension. "We've been spending so much time together. I mean, I knew that I was attracted to him, but I didn't know…" She trailed off.

"That the sex would be hot? No, you knew it would be amazing. How could it not be?" Nita studied her, her brown eyes softening. "You didn't know it would be more, did you?"

Her heart ached. "It can't be, can it? I mean, that's what you were just saying." What *Ivan* had been saying. "It's just this, for as long as it lasts. Unless..."

But the light was already fading from Nita's eyes. She turned away abruptly and bent to gather the shards of pottery. "Why spoil what it is now by worrying about that?" she said with forced cheer. "It's about time you had a good lover. Don't let my gloom get all over you."

"Nita—" Maricela caught her arm. "I don't know what's going to happen, or how much it might hurt. But I had to find out, do you understand? The only thing that can possibly be worse is not knowing."

"I know, I know." Nita sighed and stood. "There's something I have to tell you. The rumors about Ivan were getting bad when I left."

A chill seized Maricela. "What kinds of rumors?"

"That he killed Javier for no reason, and Gideon's going to let him get away with it because he has a blind spot where Ivan's concerned. And..."

"And?" The chill was quickly being overtaken by anger. "You mean there's something worse?"

She flinched. "Some people are saying it wasn't on purpose. That Ivan killed Javier by mistake."

Maricela automatically opened her mouth to counter the lie, but the words wouldn't come. There was a reason every Rider prized self-control. The people of Sector One openly embraced the deadly mission of the Riders, and in return, they got that legendary control. Every life taken by a Rider was a life taken with calculated purpose. For the average citizen, killing someone by accident was lamentable, a death that would stain their soul, but it wasn't *murder*.

For a Rider to kill someone by accident was something worse than murder. It was sheer savagery, an unforgivable misuse of the tools and training meant to turn them into warriors. And the final fault would lie with Gideon, because the Riders were *his*. He hand-picked the candidates, oversaw the trials, and was responsible not only for every bit of their training, but for their actions, as well.

If people were saying Ivan had lost control, they were really saying that *Gideon* had lost control.

The implications were so terrible, and on so many levels, that Maricela wanted to deny it instantly—but she couldn't. Instead, Ivan's words echoed in her brain.

I didn't want to kill him.

"They don't know what they're talking about," she said finally. "If Gideon thought for a second that Ivan was out of control, he wouldn't let him anywhere near me, much less make him my personal guard."

"I know," Nita said quickly. "And no one will say flat out that Gideon's *wrong*. But the lost heir resurfacing has dredged up a lot of memories and talk about how the civil war started—specifically about Ivan's uncles. And about how Gideon overlooked all that when he made Ivan a Rider."

They thought Gideon had made a mistake. And if he'd made a mistake, then maybe he didn't have divine authority, after all. "People can be so fickle, can't they?"

"People can be greedy, selfish, ungrateful ass-holes." The pottery shards clattered against the side of her trash can as Nita tossed the remains of the bowl. "Maybe I shouldn't have told you. People always talk. Next week it will be something else."

It was such a lie that Nita couldn't even hide her skepticism. Maricela groaned and smacked her head against the door. "No, it's good that you said something. I need to know." So did Ivan.

So did *Gideon*.

Nita wiped the dust from her hands before

wrapping an arm around Maricela's waist and pulling her into a hug. "I'm glad you told me," she said softly. "Make a liar out of me, Maricela. Prove me wrong. If anyone can make a fairy tale come out right, it's a princess."

19

The rumors were spreading.

Maricela had resisted telling him the extent of them. Neither of them liked anything that dragged harsh reality into the moments they stole together. But Ivan couldn't afford to hide from *this* reality.

People were scared of him.

Like most Riders, Ivan frequently found himself at the sprawling temple complex situated on the edge of the Rios estate. Memorials were held there, as well as initiations for new Riders. The Rios family and other members of the estate gathered there to celebrate the saints on their holy days, or in quiet moments to pray in the smaller, more intimate alcoves.

And Riders visited Del there every time they took a life. They sat in her chair and contemplated the gravity of the blood they'd spilled while Del commemorated their extended damnation on their skin.

The wing of the temple that housed Del's students usually buzzed with activity. The younger girls ran through the halls, chasing each other from one lesson to the next. The older ones gathered in groups, whispering and laughing over their projects. And whenever a Rider showed up, all the ones old enough to flirt invariably did—even with Ivan, who never flirted back.

He didn't mind their flirting, but he never particularly wanted it, either. So he was surprised to discover he missed it as he waited for Maricela, who'd disappeared into Grace's room.

None of the acolytes rushed to him with wide, worshipful eyes. No one practiced awkwardly adorable pickup lines or stared at him for too long before dissolving into giggles with their friends. The students who did see him averted their eyes and hurried their steps, and the whispers they traded sounded somber. Even fearful.

Too many of the girls would have attended the ball. God only knew what stories they'd brought back—or how much the stories had grown in the telling. He was only getting the barest taste of censure and suspicion, and the muscles in his neck were already tight with strain.

He wasn't entirely sure how his mother had survived *years* of this.

"Ready!" Maricela emerged from Grace's room with a wide smile that faltered when she noticed two acolytes whispering at the end of the hall. She pinned them with a pointed look until they rushed off, chastened.

He had something his mother hadn't: a protective Rios hovering next to him. "It's okay," he told her softly as they started for the stairs.

"No, it isn't." A muscle in her clenched jaw jumped. "If they don't have anything better to do, they can pray." Her voice lowered. "Pray I don't find out what they were saying."

The fierceness of her response made his chest ache. Ivan had never doubted that his fellow Riders would drop everything to have his back in a fight, but no one fretted over inconsequential slights. Maricela looked fully capable of wheeling back around to deliver a blistering lecture defending his honor, and *that* wouldn't do a damn thing to kill the rumors.

It'd probably start a few new ones, though. Rumors Ivan couldn't afford. "Come on," he said, steering her toward the exit. "If we want to get there before it's too crowded, we have to leave soon."

She followed him without argument. "I can't believe we're actually going."

Neither could he. It had taken him three days to satisfy himself that his security precautions were sufficient, three days where he'd been careful to make his arrangements outside of Maricela's presence. It would spoil her glee in their secret, spontaneous trip to find out it was neither a secret nor spontaneous, and Ivan intended to protect her joy as ruthlessly as he did her safety.

Even with his plans, he was still walking a line. The only Rider who knew what he was about to do was Ashwin. And while Gideon hadn't expressly *forbidden* this...

Ivan was under no illusions. His leader would *not* be thrilled to find out that Maricela's trusted bodyguard was about to take her into the heart of the city.

The car he'd taken from the Riders' garage sat in the gravel parking area behind the temple. It was inconspicuous, black with four doors and subtly concealed solar panels to recharge its near silent engine. It would blend in with the other vehicles in Eden while looking too mundane to present a tempting target for thieves.

Thieves wouldn't know Ivan had stocked the trunk with enough gear to hold off a small army and survive a siege.

He opened the door for Maricela, and she climbed into the back with the linen bag Grace had given her tucked tight against her chest. The moment he slid behind the wheel, she leaned up over the back of the seat. "I forgot. I don't have any money."

"Don't worry." He started the car by pressing his thumb to the biometric key, then reached for the envelope he'd tucked between the seats. "Eden's citizens mostly use their bar codes to transfer money, but they have these credit sticks, too. A lot more people are using them now that trade's open with the sectors."

"You thought of everything."

"That's my job."

"Uh-huh. Hang on a second—" Her voice grew muffled, and he glanced in the rearview mirror just in time to see a flash of white as she pulled her dress over her head.

Ivan tightened his fingers around the steering wheel and forced his eyes to the winding road that led away from the estate. The tinted windows would keep anyone from seeing inside the car, but nothing protected Ivan from the soft brush of fabric over skin and the temptation to let his gaze drift back to the mirror as she stripped in the back seat.

"What's it like?"

Her words were still muffled. He snuck another look at the rearview mirror and caught a glimpse of her breasts hugged by her bra before her borrowed dress dropped down her body. "What, the market?"

"Eden." She climbed over the seat, her skirt riding up to bare one thigh only inches from his face. "The city."

Focus. He had to focus on the narrow road lined with sprawling apple trees, not the fact that he could smell the floral soap on her skin. "Like nothing you've ever experienced. You can see the skyscrapers from outside the walls, but it's not the same as standing at the base of one. They're massive."

She settled in the passenger seat and smoothed her dress. It was dark, dark blue, with a high neck and sleeves banded with black lace. She looked like a prim and proper Eden housewife—except for her hair. No demure, modest woman in Eden would have shiny brown hair tumbling wildly around her shoulders. "What about the people? I've only met refugees."

"They're reserved. Controlled." They reached the end of the long driveway, and Ivan turned onto the road that would take them to where the north gate had once stood. "Some of that's changing now, though. You should know that better than anyone."

"A lot of people are converting to the Prophet's religion," she agreed. "I suppose, after everything that's happened, they need to believe in *something*." Her hands curled into fists on the leather seats. "It makes me want to tell them the truth."

"The truth?"

"That the Prophet was a hypocrite. An opportunist. A con man, when you get right down to it. Everything that came out of his mouth was garbage." She turned toward him on the seat, drawing one leg beneath her. "I believe in what they teach at the temples—most of it, anyway. But only because Gideon and Isabela have tried to fix it."

It was casual blasphemy of the highest order, the

kinds of words that could still get a person shunned by their neighbors and all but exiled from the sector.

And Ivan had thought the same damn thing in his darkest moments. When he'd come home to find his mother curled in on herself again, too guilty and tired and numb to force herself into her daily routine.

He'd challenged her once, when he was thirteen and angry and starting to feel the bite of being a social pariah. He'd shouted at her that the Prophet was to blame for his daughter's death. Ivan's uncles may have kidnapped her, but the Prophet was the one who'd decided to sacrifice her, who'd thrown away his own blood because it wasn't *convenient* to save her.

It was the only time in his life his mother had struck him. She'd slapped him across the face, the shock of it doing more damage than the blow itself. And then she'd grabbed him by the collar and told him to never, *ever* speak ill of the Prophet again.

He never had.

Maricela worried her lower lip with her teeth. "I'm sorry. That was a stupid thing to say out loud, even for me."

"No," he said slowly. "No, it's just...I never expected to hear anyone say it."

"I guess not." She slid closer and laid her head on his shoulder. "But silence doesn't change reality. The Prophet wasn't a good man. Not like you."

That, he couldn't let stand. "I'm not a good man, Maricela."

"Yes, you are."

I kill people. I'm good at it. It's all I'm good at.

The words stuck in his throat. He'd worked so hard to give her this—the illusion of freedom, a few moments where she didn't have to be a Rios, where she wasn't responsible for any souls or lives but her own.

He couldn't ruin it for her with his guilty confession.

He wished he had Zeke's wit or Reyes's clever charisma. His attempt to change the subject was awkward and obvious. "Well, one thing I'm definitely good at is bartering. People are scared of me. Zeke says I have resting murder face."

Maricela laughed. "He's just jealous."

Ivan wasn't sure jealousy was a concept Zeke comprehended. He was perpetually impressed with himself in an easy way that felt alien to Ivan. He wouldn't have just accepted Maricela's compliment. He would have shot back that he was a *great* man, and he would have meant it.

Maybe *he* was jealous of Zeke.

The first signs of civilization appeared ahead of them, the newest constructions on the edge of the inner sector. The border was creeping out faster than Ivan could ever remember, devouring the scrubby hills and empty expanses. Soon, it would be encroaching on the borders of the smaller family estates, and Gideon would have some hard choices to make.

Ivan couldn't blame the people who wanted to flee the confines of the city. The closer they got to Eden, the narrower the roads became, and the taller the buildings climbed. It was claustrophobic here, this close to the city. And it only got worse as they drove onward.

For the first time in his life, he used words to distract himself. Not for the sound of his own voice, though—he craved the sound of hers. "Have you figured out what you're going to buy yet?"

"Maybe nothing." She shrugged one shoulder. "I don't really need more *stuff*."

His lips twitched. "Maybe wait until you see what kind of stuff they have to sell. Our markets don't have anything like it."

Her brows drew together and her nose wrinkled, as if the very suggestion that Sector One didn't have anything and everything a person might want or need was offensive.

The tickling urge to smile only grew. "Sometimes it's interesting. They have a lot of pre-Flare antiques. I'm hoping to find a new book for my mother."

"Really? What does she like to read?"

"Old cookbooks. That's what she does at the temple. She cooks."

"Then we have to find some. I'll help you look."

This time, the sensation in his chest was too sharp to be an ache, and he finally recognized it. Years of numbness stretched between now and the last time he'd felt this, as a young boy in a cold, dark street, his face and hands pressed to the baker's display window as his empty stomach rumbled.

Longing.

He ruthlessly forced it down as they rode through the open gates and past the empty checkpoint. He didn't have time to brood. Until they were back on the estate, his total focus had to be on keeping Maricela safe.

Navigating the slow-moving traffic in the crowded Eden streets took plenty of focus on its own. He'd mapped out the route in advance, but maps failed to capture the sheer cluttered chaos of Eden. Glass buildings shot dozens of stories straight up, blocking the sun one moment and reflecting a thousand painfully bright rays of it in the next.

And the *people*. They seethed on the sidewalks and bolted across the street, and Ivan nearly ran four of them over by the time he maneuvered his way to the market's parking deck.

Maricela stared silently out the windows, her eyes wide as she struggled to take it all in. Even once they were parked in the dark solitude of the deck, she twisted her hands in her borrowed skirt and said nothing.

Ivan slid his hand over hers. "If it's too much, we can go right back out the gate."

She shook her head. "I'm not scared, just a little nervous. But that's silly, isn't it?"

Eden had been the scary monster that sector parents used to frighten their children for generations. Sometimes he was surprised *any* of them managed to venture there. "No, not silly at all. But you'll be with me, and I won't let anything happen to you, okay?"

"It's not that. It's just..." She laid her hand on his cheek. "I'm realizing lately how very small my world has been."

Her fingers were soft. Her skin smelled like her lotion, something vague and floral he couldn't place and would never forget. He turned into her touch and brushed a kiss to her palm. "Let's go make it bigger."

Her eyes got even wider when they stepped out into the sunlight again, with no glass and steel between them and the rest of the city. Maricela clung to his arm, then slowly slid her hand down to twine her fingers with his.

No one stared. No one gave them a second glance except for one prim-looking matron dressed in silk and dripping jewels, who looked at their joined hands and loudly sniffed her disdain. She did the same thing when she passed a couple sitting on a nearby bench, fingers linked and knees touching.

Physical affection was still scorned by the upper classes of Eden, but a gentler sort of morality had trickled down to the middle class. Ivan could hold Maricela's hand and attract nothing worse than passing disapproval—disapproval no one would have dared to show if they knew who Maricela was.

He tugged on her hand to guide her down the sidewalk. "How does it feel to have rich ladies snubbing you?"

She laughed, delighted. "Better than I dreamed."

"Good."

Eden had changed in the nine months since the revolution. Not that Ivan had been inside the walls more than a handful of times before they'd fallen, but all the surviving Riders had been there in the aftermath. People had scurried about their business, their faces wary and suspicious. Those who weren't wary had been dazed by the sudden freedom.

A lifetime of repression wasn't fixed overnight. But he and Maricela passed a park where children chased each other and laughed, and when they reached the edge of the market, he was struck by the *sound* of it, a low rumble of people shouting greetings and luring customers and bartering.

It was starting to feel alive.

There weren't many booths set up in the small square that formed the main marketplace. Folding tables were more common, the kind that could be broken down and moved at a moment's notice. They spilled out down the streets leading to and from the square, lining the sidewalks so thickly that you could only walk on the street itself.

Maricela hesitated by a table laden with tech, mostly tablets with flaws like dinged edges or cracked screens, then moved on to a booth stocked with little pies baked in disposable tins. She covered one whole side of the square that way, studying each table with a frown of concentration, as if understanding the goods for sale was the key to understanding Eden itself.

She wasn't entirely wrong. The markets in Sector One overflowed with handmade goods and crafts.

Gideon might not frown on tech the way his grandfather had, but only a few dealers had sprung up over the past decade, and almost no one sold used or refurbished junk. There might as well have not been a world before the Flares.

Eden's markets were the opposite. Every table sagged with reminders of the world that had been. Bright digital signs flashed words like *antique* and *vintage* and *authentic* over displays cluttered with the trash of a forgotten world, buffed and polished until the memories shone.

When Maricela finally stopped, it was at a cluttered table on the north side of the square. But instead of choosing something on display, she bent to retrieve a large book from a box beside the table. It was bound with leather, worn but not scratched or torn.

When she opened it, four metal rings inside held pages and pages of old photographs, warped with age. She flipped through them slowly, lingering over snapshots of smiling faces and sleeping animals, thick forests and tall, glittering buildings. There was a small inscription beneath each picture, faded and often hopelessly cryptic.

Aria & Skylar
NYC summer trip
Big Bear - 30th birthday

"Oh, you don't want that." The older woman behind the table waved a hand at her. "That's junk, brought in by one of the scavengers. Haven't had time to pull out the old pictures yet." She picked up a thin rectangle the size of her palm and activated the digital screen with a flick of her fingers. "This'll hold ten thousand pictures, and I have 'em loaded with foreign places you have to see to believe. Huge mountains, vast oceans, trees so big three people couldn't put their arms around them…"

Maricela barely glanced up. "How much?"

"A hundred credits. A real steal, if you ask me. How else can you see the world?"

"I'll take it." Maricela closed the book and ran her hand over the cover. "If you throw in the album."

"Done," the woman said so quickly that Ivan assumed she'd been prepared to be haggled far down from the asking price. She brought out a little bar-code reader with a slot for a cred stick and typed in the total. "Here you go."

Maricela pulled one of the credit sticks he'd given her out of her pocket. She fumbled a little with fitting it into the reader, but after a moment, the machine beeped, and the vendor smiled widely as she tucked it back under her table. She came back up with a crinkled brown bag and held it open so Maricela could deposit the album inside. Then she slipped the digital photo in on top. "Come back if you want another set!"

Maricela took the bag, and Ivan guided her away from the table. They found a free spot in the middle of the square to stand, and for a moment she just *stared*, her wide eyes taking in the bustle of people, the colorful displays, the sunlight glinting off the glass windows of the nearby buildings.

It was probably the first time she'd been anonymous in a crowd. His lingering pangs of longing transformed into a fierce joy that he'd been able to give her this. "What do you want to do next?"

"I think…" She clutched the bag to her chest, the brown paper crinkling in her grip. "I want to see the City Center."

Even the words seemed to leach warmth from the sun. The City Center was where the final battle between the sectors and Eden had culminated. The place where dozens of Riders had given their lives to cut a path through the corrupt councilman's defenders.

Judging by the sudden seriousness in her eyes, Maricela knew that. She wanted, maybe needed, to see the place where the men she had known had sacrificed themselves to build a better world. Their memorials would always live on in the pictures painted in the quiet sanctum in the heart of the Rios family temple, but the City Center was still hallowed ground.

He found her free hand with his and twined their fingers together again, needing the warmth and contact more than he wanted to admit. "Okay."

If you didn't already know, it would be hard to tell from the City Center that war had ravaged Eden.

There were subtle signs, telltale things like patched spots in walls where the fresh brick still gleamed and the mortar hadn't had time to darken with exposure. Maricela even caught sight of a few tiny craters in the buildings that could only have been left by bullets. But the vast majority of the damage had been repaired. Erased.

Then there was the memorial. It looked almost like a gazebo, an octagon with a large roof hanging over stone walls that didn't quite meet each other. The spaces between them served as the only entrances to the heart of the memorial.

Inside was dark, cool, the heavy stone blocking out the midday summer sun. Each wall was dedicated to a sector, fitted with a flat screen that scrolled the names of their people who had died in the war. In the center of the room stood a fountain with a ninth screen affixed to its base. The walls and the fountain were covered and surrounded by pictures, bundles of flowers, and messages. Desperate attempts to personalize the losses, or perhaps even to do the impossible—to reach out to the dead one last time.

The only exception was the wall dedicated to Sector One. Its screen didn't scroll with names, and no one had left bouquets of wilting lilies or goodbye letters. Instead, the screen bore one static sentence—*In honor of Gideon's fallen Riders*—and the wall had been painted.

Maricela recognized Del's work instantly. Skillful brushstrokes covered the entire wall with the skull and tree that comprised the Riders' tattoo, only instead of having ravens circling, there were dozens of brightly colored leaves drifting down from the stark, bare branches.

"One for each." Ivan reached out to touch a leaf. "So many of us died that day."

And Ivan could so easily have been one of them—unnamed, memorialized here only with a single leaf smaller than her hand. Her stomach twisted, and she had to take a moment to focus on her breathing to quell a sob. "What was it like?"

It took Ivan forever to answer. "Bad. It was just... bad. Our job was to break through the Special Tasks forces who were protecting the building where Peterson had holed up. It was a lot of chaos. A lot of *noise*."

Maricela had begged to come along that day. Not to the front lines, of course—she'd only have gotten in the way—but the allied sector forces had set up an aid station just outside the city, a place to treat mild injuries and stabilize more critical patients. She could have helped there, but Gideon had been implacable in his denials.

So she'd stayed behind, secreted away in the bunker beneath the palace with Isabela's family, while

Gideon and Mad and the rest of the Riders rode out to fight. She tried to imagine doing that now—sitting in tense silence, waiting for her loved ones to return.

For *Ivan* to return.

The memorial was suddenly claustrophobically close. With the eight stone slabs blocking out most of the sun and air, it felt like a mausoleum. A tomb. She turned and half-stumbled outside, where she could breathe again.

She still had to lean against the outer wall for support. "Were you scared?"

Ivan leaned against the wall beside her. "Not for most of it," he said finally. "But there was one moment..." His fingers started to curl into a fist, and he slowly flexed them. "A Special Tasks soldier had his gun trained on your cousin's back. I didn't think I'd get to Mad in time."

Maricela blinked. "But he was fine. What happened?"

"I tackled him." Ivan exhaled roughly. "Half a second slower, and we both probably would have been dead. But somehow I got there."

No one had told her about it, no doubt to save her from worrying. But Ivan's grudging admission had a deeper import, one he didn't even seem to realize. "You saved his life."

"No. I mean, yes, but not... It wasn't like my father or anything. I didn't take a bullet for him."

He had such a narrow view of what it meant to protect the Rios family, and it did more than frighten her. It broke her heart. "You don't have to die to save someone, Ivan."

He looked away. His gaze drifted across the open square in front of the towering City Center building, and she couldn't tell if he was seeing the people hurrying about their business, or the battle he'd fought. "I know. In my head, I know. But my mother…"

She reached for his hand and waited.

"It wasn't her fault." The words held the forceful edge of repetition, of something he'd said too many times. "Everything she went through was bad enough. She lost my dad when I was a baby. And then her brothers turned traitor. The sector shunned her."

He gripped her hand harder and closed his eyes— but only for a moment. Even now, he couldn't stop scanning their surroundings, watching for danger. "Kora was the one who saw it. She called it major depressive disorder. Some sort of chemical imbalance in the brain. She ran a bunch of tests and had the guys in Five fabricate a custom implant."

"Is it working?"

"Like magic. Like she's a totally different person." His sudden laugh was edged with pain. "All those years, I thought I was taking care of her. Covering for her when it got bad, making sure no one ever found out. In my teens, I *resented* her for it. And she just needed help. Real help. I'm the reason she never got it."

The lump in her throat made it hard to speak. "Ivan, that's not true. You were a child. What could you have done?"

"Maybe nothing. I don't know." He finally looked at her. "But it makes it harder, do you understand? All the stuff she told me when she was in the dark places. She ground it into my head over and over that the only way to be *good* was to be like my father. To die for the family her brothers had betrayed. And it wasn't her fault, but it still…"

It still hurt. She could hear it in his voice, see it on his face—along with a simmering frustration, maybe even a hint of anger. But he couldn't be angry with his mother, a woman who'd only wanted the best for him, whose only crime was being *sick*.

Maricela stepped closer. "You did the best you could. So did she. She thought she was telling you the truth. She just...happened to be wrong, because she wasn't well."

A breeze caught her hair and tugged it across her face. When he reached up to smooth it back, his warm fingertips lingered on her cheek. "I saved Mad's life," he said, as if testing out how the words felt.

"Yes. Your father saved Adriana, and you saved her son." It was the kind of irresistibly poetic parallel that people wrote songs and plays about. "They're going to make you a saint."

He stared at her, unblinking. "What?"

"Sainthood, Ivan. There must be plans in place already."

The realization swept over him slowly. His furrowed brow gave way to widening eyes. Clear. Bright. *Joyous*. But she only had seconds to savor it before something dark intruded, sinking over him until the light of the moment vanished.

Glimpsing that light made the darkness even worse. "What is it?"

He shook his head and pushed away from the wall, tugging her after him. "Nothing. It's a lot to take in. I need to think about it."

She dug in her heels. He was already overwhelmed, and there had to be a better time and place for grand declarations, but she couldn't hold it in any longer. "None of it changes anything, not for me. Whether you're a saint or a Rider or just *Ivan*, I like you anyway." She swallowed hard. "I love you."

He turned to her slowly, his expression unreadable. "Maricela..."

Don't. She bit back the word. She'd begged him to talk to her, and she couldn't stop him now.

They were standing in the shadow of the memorial. He cupped her cheek, tilting her head back so she stared up into his eyes. "I still can't give you forever. I'm a Rider. I took oaths. I have a duty."

It should have sounded like he was letting her down easy. Instead, all she could hear was what he hadn't said yet. "But?"

"All my life, I've only had one mission. One goal. I've been numb for years." His thumb ghosted across her lower lip. "You're the first thing I've ever...felt."

Heartbreak and elation, all rolled into one quiet confession. "If that means you want to keep feeling me, I'll take it."

He smiled. "I wouldn't know how to stop."

"You don't have to." She wound her arms around his neck. "I'm right here."

Ivan kissed her there beside the memorial. It was a bittersweet thing, to be so happy in a place that had seen so much death, but wasn't that what the Riders fought and died for all the time? They gave their lives so that other people could carry on, keep *living*. Find their joy whenever and wherever they could.

Maybe one moment of pure, blissful peace wasn't just the best way to commemorate the friends they'd lost.

Maybe it was the *only* way.

20

Ivan's emotions were still roiling when Ana arrived to let him know Kora was waiting for him in Gideon's office.

He wasn't in any condition to face his leader. He could still taste Maricela on his lips, and it didn't even feel like blasphemy anymore. It felt *necessary*, like she'd taken her place alongside all the other things he needed. Air. Water. Food.

Maricela.

But a Rider didn't disobey a summons. He walked into Gideon's office and found both Gideon and Kora seated at the round table in front of one of the huge windows overlooking the orchard. Bright sunlight filtered through the panes, gilding Kora's golden hair and catching the colored glass of the huge chandelier above them.

"Sit," Gideon said by way of greeting, nudging a third chair back from the table. When Ivan obeyed, Gideon tilted his head. "Kora?"

She opened the thin white folder sitting in front of her. "You didn't kill Javier Montero."

Ivan wasn't prepared for the relief that washed over him. Though he'd never enjoyed death, he'd never regretted a life he'd been forced to take, either. But the people he killed were usually scum—killers and bullies, those who preyed on the weak.

Javier Montero had been an asshole, but *asshole* was a far cry from *evil*. "Do you know what did?"

She nodded, her expression grave. "He had an astronomical amount of alcohol in his bloodstream. The highest level I've ever seen, well into lethal range. My first thought was that someone forced him to drink it—poisoned him, essentially. But then I remembered what Gabe said..." She glanced at Gideon uncertainly.

Gideon inclined his head. "The Riders should know."

"Right. I remembered that he said Javier could drink anyone under the table. So I checked his liver enzymes." She took a deep breath. "Javier was an alcoholic. The night of the ball, he drank himself to death."

Ivan had been prepared for poison, for an *enemy*. No, not just any enemy. In those dark places he couldn't even acknowledge, he'd been waiting for it to be Lucas, the Prophet's lost heir. His ultimate proof that bad blood always won out, that betrayal was hereditary.

Maybe it really wasn't.

"There's something else," Gideon said quietly. "I know you've heard the rumors by now."

"Yes, sir."

Gideon's expression turned sympathetic. "If I could wave my hand and make them go away, I would.

But this...is not the sort of thing you announce. It's a private matter of grief for the Monteros, and even if I *did* make it public..."

He didn't have to finish. None of the devout would dare defy Gideon to his face, but unthinking devotion left ample room for quiet hypocrisy. People had always found ways to justify their mistreatment of Ivan's mother. If they wanted to believe in Ivan's guilt, they'd rationalize it somehow.

Ivan didn't care, as long as Gideon still believed in him.

And Maricela.

Her words came back to him. Those tempting, beautiful, terrifying words. *They're going to make you a saint.* She'd sparked a reckless hope in him, one he'd done his best to quell before it grew so strong that the disappointment of having it dashed would crush him.

Because there weren't any plans in place to make him a saint. There couldn't be. The final battle had been a chaotic nightmare. In its aftermath, Mad had been busy with his O'Kane family in Sector Four. He might not even remember that moment, one near miss among dozens. He certainly hadn't announced it to Gideon.

And Ivan hadn't told anyone, not until Maricela.

What was he supposed to do now, nine months after the fact? Blurt it out? Brag? It would sound like he was grasping for something flattering to counter the rumors. Like he was seeking glory.

"Ivan?" Gideon's brow furrowed with concern. "Is there something you need to say?"

Of course he knew. The hair on the back of Ivan's neck stirred as Gideon's gaze focused on him, intense and knowing and maybe just a touch otherworldly.

The thought of Gideon seeing deep enough into his soul to find Maricela there was so terrifying that

Ivan blurted out the truth. "I saved Mad. During the battle inside Eden. I saved his life."

Something very close to surprise flashed across Gideon's face before he schooled his expression. "Really? Ivan, why didn't you—?"

"It was nothing," Ivan interrupted, already self-conscious. "It was just my job. I knocked him out of the way of a bullet and didn't even get a scratch. I didn't want to make a big deal about it, but Maricela found out. And now she thinks... She thinks I'm going to be..." He couldn't say the word, but it hung there between them, so loud it filled the room.

Sainted.

"I understand." Gideon reached out to squeeze Ivan's shoulder. "She's fond of you, and she wants to see you honored. And you will be. Del and Isabela are already planning the memorial to mark the one-year anniversary of the final battle. Let them recognize you. For Maricela, if nothing else."

It wasn't a promise of sainthood. Ivan hadn't really expected one, but disappointment still pricked. How convenient it would have been to tie everything neatly up in a bow. Pre-sainted, already saved from damnation.

Good enough for her.

Gideon was rising from the table. "If that's all...?"

For Maricela. On a whim, Ivan turned to Kora. "I need to talk to you, too. About a medical issue."

"Of course." Kora flipped the folder shut and addressed Gideon. "Medical matters are private. You'll have to leave."

He arched one brow at her. "You're kicking me out of my office?"

"Yes, I am."

He heaved a sigh. "Sisters are an eternal delight

and an eternal irritation. Come find me in the court-yard when you're done, Kora."

When he closed the door firmly behind him, Kora turned to Ivan. "Now, what's going on?"

The moment the words were out of her mouth, Ivan regretted speaking up. His tongue felt heavy. Frozen. He'd gotten so used to talking to Maricela that he'd forgotten there was some magic in her that made it easy.

But he had to find a way to get this out. He had to *know.* The darkness inside him that whispered of bad blood and told him he deserved every scrap of pain and discomfort that came his way had been a part of him for so long, he'd assumed it was all there was to living. The numbness. The hopelessness.

The fantasies of dying as a martyr so he could live on as a saint.

It had never seemed to matter before. As long as the broken pieces fit together well enough for him to do his job, Ivan hadn't cared why he was broken. Why poke at all those painful memories when pain was only a distraction? It wasn't worth fighting through it when he could take a bullet tomorrow. Damned men didn't need fixing.

But men who wanted to live, who wanted to *love...*

"What my mother has," he said abruptly. "Could I have it, too?"

"Depression?" Kora asked gently. "It's possible. But if this is about the war, you should know that post-traumatic stress isn't uncommon."

"I don't know what it is," he ground out. "It's always been there. It just never mattered, because I could still do my job. Not caring if I lived or died made me even better at it."

"I don't think that's true," she murmured. "At

least, I hope it's not."

The sympathy in her eyes scraped his raw nerves. He felt exposed. This wasn't something he knew how to fight. He needed the cool, familiar steel of a blade in his hand and a tangible enemy. Not *feelings*.

He clenched his fists on the table as panic nearly choked him. "This is stupid. I should go."

"Wait." Kora laid her hand on one of his clenched fists. "If you're worried that your mother's depression is hereditary, we can run the tests. There's no harm in it, and no shame. If you were concerned enough to ask, then we should." She tilted her head, met his eyes, and echoed Gideon's words. "For Maricela, if nothing else."

Ivan went utterly still.

It was easy to forget that the same genetic experimentation that had produced Ashwin's terrifyingly adept military mind had also produced Kora, except that she'd been designed for empathy and healing. Ivan studied her sweet, heart-shaped face. Her blue, blue eyes. There was an understanding there that went deeper than her words. An understanding that dared him to deny the truth.

"You know," he said flatly.

"About Maricela's feelings, yes," she admitted. "She doesn't hide them, does she? But I didn't realize they were mutual until the night of the ball, when we were all getting ready in Nita's suite."

Before they'd given in. Before he'd taken Maricela to bed and learned all the sounds she could make when he stroked her just right. Before he'd become so enamored, he'd started to wonder impossible things, like whether he could make himself into a man worthy of a princess.

How much more obvious must it be now? "Does Gideon know?"

Kora smiled. "Trust me, there are some things Gideon couldn't imagine, even if he tried. His baby sister, all grown up and in love, tops the list."

Gideon, fallible. Another sacrilegious idea to add to the list. He was getting rather good at ignoring blasphemy. Ivan swallowed hard and closed his eyes. "She sees something in me that I never saw. Something good. And she makes me think..." That he wanted to live. That he could be the sort of person who had something to live for. "Maybe I'm worth fixing."

"Ivan, you—" Kora bit off the words. "I understand. We can run the tests, and then you'll know. But, Ivan..."

"Yeah?"

She waited until he opened his eyes to continue. "What if you don't get the answer you want? What then?"

He wanted to protest that he wasn't looking for any *one* answer, but Kora would see through the lie.

The fantasy had already formed inside him. Kora would run her tests and tell him that everything dark and hard and wrong in his life had been a chemical mistake, and then she'd give him one of those implants and he'd be *different*. Good enough.

Fixed.

He was grasping for miracles again. For sainthood, for a medical cure. For anything that might wipe away his past and offer him a brighter future on a silver platter.

Ivan had to be braver than that. He clenched his hands and forced out the words. "Then we talk about post-traumatic stress, or whatever else you think I should talk about."

"All right." She smiled again, the expression as gently encouraging as everything else about her. "I can take the blood samples I need to get started now. If you want."

For Maricela. He'd used the words as a talisman and a token, but if he wanted to be the man she saw, the *good* man, this couldn't just be about her. He could lean on her courage, her faith and hope, but if he was going to face down his past and his legacy and his traitorous blood, he had to do it for himself.

He didn't have to be a saint to be worthy of happiness.

gabe

People kept trying to comfort him.

Gabe sat in the Riders' gym and took the time to wrap his hands. If he didn't wrap them, someone would notice. He'd scrape his knuckles raw or he'd injure his wrist, and Kora would start fretting at him again about PTSD. Ashwin would get agitated about the fretting, and Gabe would be forced to talk to someone.

He didn't want to talk to anyone. Not about his brother, not about his family, and not about what had happened to him at the Suicide Kings' compound.

Especially not about the nightmares.

Hands wrapped, Gabe strapped on some gloves and moved to the heavy bag. Before the war, he would have shaken off his mood by dropping into the meditative beauty of his sword forms. Now, every time he tried, all he could remember was Joaquin, the grizzled old Rider who'd trained him with a blade.

Joaquin had been the first Rider to go down as they charged the City Center. Gabe had grieved for brothers before, but Joaquin had been more, like a father who actually *understood* him, who agreed that you should deeply feel every life you took. That violence was a necessary but ugly weapon you should never be comfortable wielding.

Joaquin would be disappointed that Gabe couldn't let him go. He'd be even more disappointed at the *rage* that roiled inside Gabe, dark and unrelenting. The only outlet he had was hitting the heavy bag until his body was too tired to sustain the anger.

If he seemed calm, maybe people would stop worrying. If they stopped worrying, maybe they wouldn't notice him falling apart.

"You alone for a reason?"

Laurel's voice prickled over his skin in a way a voice shouldn't have been able to do. He could *feel* it when she talked, like wires had gotten crossed in his brain somehow.

He swung at the bag and let the impact shiver up his arm to erase the sensation of her words. "Don't need a partner for this."

"Obviously." A zipper rasped. He tried not to imagine what it belonged to. "I just wanted to make sure the gym wasn't empty because you need some space."

It figured she would ask. Laurel respected personal boundaries, and she wasn't the kind of person who'd show up and try to smother you with hugs and make you talk about your pain. Based on what he knew of her upbringing in Three, she'd probably *laugh* at his pain. *Poor, sad rich boy.*

He swung again, hitting the bag a little harder. "It's fine. I'm fine."

"Yeah, you look it." A beat passed. "I don't suppose I could persuade you to hit me instead of that bag."

Gabe froze. The bag swung back and slapped him in the arm. He steadied it and turned to find Laurel slipping her arms out of a hoodie. She was dressed for a workout.

Or some hand-to-hand.

"Ashwin says I'm too dependent on weapons. I need to use my fists and feet instead, because you can't drop those." She laid her sweatshirt across a bench. "I beg to differ about that fact, but I do acknowledge his point."

"You want to spar?"

She rocked up on the balls of her feet, her eyes gleaming. "I want to *fight*."

It was a terrible idea. Gabe could think for a long time and not come up with a worse one. Laurel's voice did wild things to him. He wasn't sure what her touch would do.

The dark places inside him wanted to find out.

He took a slow step away from the bag, watching her body for any signs that she was about to pounce. "What kind of fighting is Ashwin training you in?"

"Close quarters." She grinned. "Street fighting—the dirty kind."

It made sense. Laurel was taller than Ana, but she was leaner too. Less muscle, probably less speed. If someone got past Laurel's guns, she'd have to be mean. No fancy maneuvers or showing off, just quick and nasty.

Quick and nasty suited his mood just fine.

He moved to the center of the mat, still watching her. "So come at me."

She rushed him, straight on, then feinted left at the last moment for a leg sweep. It would have worked on a lot of people.

It wouldn't work on a Rider.

In seconds, he had her on the mat, on her back, pinned with an arm across her shoulders. He only had a moment to process the feel of her beneath him before she surged up, reversing their positions.

She was better on the floor. Vicious. Getting her down had been easy, but getting her pinned was a nightmare. Every time Gabe thought he had her, she wriggled away. She flipped their positions with surprising strength. She dug fingers and elbows and once even her chin into impossibly sensitive spots, like she'd mapped out every vulnerability on the human body and could nail someone right on the rawest nerve with her eyes closed.

After a particularly painful jab in the ribs, he tried to roll away. Laurel followed him, grabbing a fistful of his hair to haul him back. When her knee collided with his side, he grunted and twisted desperately, using his superior strength to flip her onto her back again.

This time, he didn't take chances. He restrained her with his body and slammed her hands down to the mat.

He also kept his face out of the range of her teeth. Just in case.

She stared up at him, her chest heaving but her hands lax beneath his. "Does not thinking help?"

He couldn't understand her question. He couldn't understand *thinking*. Her thin shirt clung to her breasts, and her quick breaths did fascinating things, and maybe she'd crossed *all* his wires, because he could taste how good her skin looked.

He was losing his damn mind.

He shoved away from her and rolled to his back, staring up at the ceiling as his body roiled with conflicting instincts. "If he just started training you, you don't need much help. You're gonna be really good at this."

"That's Sector Three for you." She sat up and wrapped her arms around her legs. "But thanks. That means a lot."

That chilled the lust in his body. Gabe might be in here hiding from the raw truths about his family, but he couldn't imagine growing up in the sort of place that taught you to fight like your life depended on it. Worse was knowing Laurel's life undoubtedly *had* depended on it. Daily.

Poor, sad rich boy.

"It's just the truth," he said, covering his discomfort. "We can go again if you want."

"No, that's all right." She turned her head to meet his gaze. "I heard about Javier. That's real rough, Gabe. I'm sorry."

She wasn't laughing at him. There was sympathy in her gorgeous brown eyes, but somehow it didn't make him feel trapped. "Yeah. It's... It's rough."

"What are you gonna do?"

What he had to do. What it was his *duty* to do. He'd sworn oaths to Gideon and the Rios family, and nothing would make him forsake them. But being born to one of the noble estates came with a different set of obligations. Hundreds of families depended on the stability of the Montero businesses for their livelihoods.

If something had gone so wrong that Javier had resorted to drinking himself to death, the ripples wouldn't stop with his brother. Thousands of lives could be ruined, and the chaos that would follow had the potential to consume the sector.

What were a few nightmares compared to that?

"I'm going to do my job," he said quietly. "I'm going to find out what's going on in my family, and I'm going to fix it."

21

The bar in Sector Three was a place out of time, like someone had picked it up from another century and dropped it here.

It was clean but not polished. Posters lined the walls, most with references that Maricela didn't recognize, and some she only knew because of Zeke and his seemingly endless collection of pre-Flare T-shirts. There was a large stage at one end of the room, an even larger dance floor, and booths around the perimeter.

The stage was empty, the music spilling instead from tiny speakers affixed to the ceiling, but the dance floor was full. Even the fans blowing on high speed couldn't do much to dispel the heat of so many bodies moving, and a trickle of sweat slid down the small of Maricela's back.

It throbbed through her—the music, Ivan's hands

on her hips, the grinding rhythm of their dance. His face was in shadow as he rocked and swayed with her, but she could feel the intensity of his gaze fixed to her face.

"Relax." She wrapped her arms around his neck, her skin slicking over his. "We're the only people here."

One of his hands skimmed up her spine to where the plunging back of her dress revealed her skin. His rough fingertips glided in a slow circle as he pulled her even closer. "I can take a night off from acting like your bodyguard," he murmured, one thigh slipping between hers. "But I'll always be protective. I'll always be thinking about punching anyone who gets too close."

Maricela swallowed a moan, torn between the sweet note of confession in his words and the hard heat of his thigh between hers. "If you can still think about anyone else, I need to try harder." She rocked her hips, grinding against him.

His grip on her hip turned to steel, and he made a hoarse noise, muffled against her temple. His lips skated across her cheekbone on their way to her ear. "Stop trying to distract me," he murmured, "or I'll have to start trying to distract you."

Another slow, lazy rock. "Is it a competition?"

Ivan chuckled, hot and low. "Look around, Maricela. Stop trying to ignore the other people. *See* them."

She didn't want to. The only thing she cared about right now was him—his body against hers, the look in his eyes. His hands on her.

But she did it anyway. She looked, and there was no one looking back, not like at the dances and balls back home. Every single person on the floor was caught up in their own little world, oblivious to her very existence.

"They don't know who you are. They don't care

what you're doing. That's why I brought you here."

The freedom of anonymity was heady, but it couldn't compare to the sheer seductive power of Ivan's voice. "All I see is you."

He nipped at her ear. His hand skimmed down her spine to the small of her back, and with one tug he had her up his thigh, riding so high only her toes touched the floor. Her dress hiked up her thighs, and the friction as he rocked her against his leg made her shiver despite the heat. "Then don't hold back. Nobody else is. Ride the pleasure, Maricela. Ride it all the way."

"Right here?"

"All you see is me, right?" His teeth found her jaw. His tongue swept out, quick and hot. "Now feel me, too."

It was scandalous, the kind of thing the temple acolytes whispered and giggled about when they thought she couldn't hear, and Maricela wanted it more than her next breath. She drove her fingers into Ivan's hair and licked his cheek as she picked up the rhythm, moving her body against his.

The music rolled from one song to the next, something slower. Hotter. The bass line trembled up through the floor, throbbing through her as they both matched it effortlessly. They moved together like they were meant for this, like he knew what she needed and was right there before the craving could fully form.

Harder. Firmer. Deeper.

His breath blew hot against her cheek. "You're beautiful."

Giddy with pleasure and the illicit thrill of it all, Maricela moved faster. Everything was charged, electric—the music, the movement. The heat of skin through clothes. Ivan panting in her ear. Then her hip nudged his cock, and Ivan's groan shattered the tension in one blow, like a hammer on thin ice.

He sank his hand into her hair and pulled her tight against his chest, muffling her cries with a kiss and holding her as she shuddered. When her knees would have given way and she would have slid to the floor.

She kissed him back, gliding her tongue over his, as the dizzy aftershocks rippled through her. She was trembling, but so was he—a different kind of tremor, fine and taut, that she could feel every place he was touching her.

Their swaying rhythm took on new purpose. When she opened her eyes, he was coaxing them toward the edge of the floor—not toward the posh VIP booths that dominated one side of the room, but the smaller, shadowed ones in the opposite corner. "Sit," he told her softly, nudging her toward a leather bench.

"Might as well." She slid into the booth, smoothing her hair as he joined her. "Can't stand up right now anyway. Wonder why?"

Something smug sparked in his eyes as he waved down a server and ordered them two beers. They came in chilled glass bottles with condensation on the outsides that made the bright O'Kane labels peel up at the edges. Ivan took a long sip before nudging her knee with his. "Having fun?"

He wasn't the only one who could tease. "Maybe a little."

He smiled, rare and real and so damn beautiful that it almost hurt to look at. Almost. He smoothed back a few damp strands of her hair that had stuck to the side of her face, and his fingertips traced the outer shell of her ear. "You deserve to have fun. All your life shouldn't be service to the sector."

"It doesn't feel like I've been doing much of that lately." She sipped her beer and waited, but the anticipated flash of guilt didn't come. "But maybe you're right. I needed a break. A break full of wild, naked sex with my bodyguard."

His lips quirked, and the dark warmth in his gaze promised the sex would be extra wild tonight. "You needed to see this. What life can be. Maybe you'll stop being so hard on yourself when you're not happy and grateful all the time."

"A little perspective can be a good thing," she agreed.

"Yeah." He picked up his beer again, and his leg tensed against hers. "There was something I didn't tell you when we were inside Eden."

For a moment, the fear that filled her was all out of proportion to the situation. "Are you all right?"

"It's not that, it's—" He exhaled and gripped the bottle. "Nobody knew that I saved Mad. I don't think it would have occurred to him to tell anyone. There was so much going on, and your cousin has never liked the fact that we still risk our lives for his."

Her first instinctive reaction was anger. She wasn't a child—she knew that battles could be chaotic, not to mention traumatic. So much so that people sometimes couldn't remember details, or even forgot entire swaths of time as their minds fought valiantly to protect them from the horrors they'd seen.

But Mad was supposed to be *different*. He was a Rider himself. He knew the sacrifices they made for Gideon, for the sector. For the royal family. Their only reward was to have those sacrifices recognized.

And he hadn't bothered to do that for Ivan.

The second the thought formed, she was ashamed of herself. Her cousin had his faults, but he had never been thoughtless. And Ivan had also remained silent. "Why didn't you tell me?"

"I don't know." Ivan kept running his thumb over the label on his bottle like the pattern was of the utmost importance. "I think...it still feels like it shouldn't count. All my life, I've been told to be like my father, and that's the only thing he did that anyone ever talks about. He took a bullet for Santa Adriana. Anything else feels like cheating."

"Ivan—"

"I told you that the shit you thought you had to put up with wasn't okay, and you listened to me." He finally looked at her. "Maybe the shit I've always thought I had to put up with wasn't okay, either. So I listened to you. I told Gideon."

She'd been prepared to argue her case, but his sudden confession cut off the words in a knot of tears at the back of her throat. "That couldn't have been easy. I'm proud of you."

"I don't know if it changes anything. I don't know what we're doing, Maricela. Your brother's going to murder me if he finds out, and not just for the sex." He drained his beer and waved the empty bottle to take in the room. "I'm sneaking you into the city and out to grungy sector bars. I'm bending my oaths so hard I feel guilty every time your brother looks at me. I keep rationalizing it, but this is out of control. *I'm* out of control."

There was only one thing worse than losing him—hurting him. "Do you want to stop?"

"No." He reached for her, sliding his fingers through her hair to cup the back of her head. "I've said more to you in the last few weeks than I've said the rest of my whole damn life. You look at me and see..." His voice roughened. "You see a good man."

"The love of my life." She had to say something glib and light-hearted, because if she didn't, she'd say something— "Marry me, Ivan."

The *wanting* in his eyes nearly broke her heart. "If I was anyone else, I would."

"You're not anyone else. You're you, and I need you." She pulled his hands free of her hair and held them between hers. "You *have* shown me what life can be, but it doesn't have anything to do with this bar or sneaking off into the city. It's us, together."

He groaned and closed his eyes, letting his forehead drop to hers. "I'm out of control," he whispered roughly. "I know it's impossible. But when you touch me, nothing else matters."

Because they were inevitable. She understood now that it never could have been any other way. Even if Gideon had never assigned him to guard her, even if they'd never been in the same room alone, not even once, part of her would have belonged to Ivan. The same part that had drawn her to him at the training day ceremony, when she'd clumsily asked him to be her date for the summer festival.

It already seemed like a lifetime ago.

She brushed her lips over his. "Think about it?"

His kiss was deeper, more desperate, and she couldn't tell if it was a promise or the start of a goodbye. But they were both breathless when the kiss ended. "Anything for my princess."

She had to touch him, a literal physical need that raked at her, so she laid her hand on his chest, right over his thudding heart. "Anything?"

"*Anything*," he growled.

"Then it's your turn to feel me." Her options stretched out before her like a carnal tapestry—a slow handjob under the table, a faster blowjob in the car or a nearby alley. Finally, she settled on rising from the booth and heading for the darkened back hallway.

She made it to the bathroom door before he reached

for her, his hands sliding over her hips and his breath stirring her hair. "Is this what you want?"

Maricela turned in his arms, reached back to open the door, and stepped back into the dark room.

He followed her. He *prowled* after her. Intent, focused. He was made of scarcely contained energy and heat. Her heart was beating so loudly, the blood pounding in her ears, that she barely heard the door shut and lock.

The only light spilled in through a tiny window near the ceiling, a distant streetlight shining through the reinforced glass. It was enough to find him in the shadows, but that was it.

He locked his hands around her waist and hoisted her up on the edge of the counter, where his hips forced her thighs wide. "You want me to feel you?"

She dragged her nails over the back of his neck. "It's only fair."

He hooked one finger under the neckline of her dress and tugged it down, revealing the swell of her breast. "I like this. Not as much fabric in the way as your usual dresses."

"No. I borrowed it from—" her breath cut off as his open mouth brushed the skin he'd just revealed, "—Grace."

His tongue followed the edge of her dress, teasing her skin. Soft, gentle—until he jerked the fabric down. The thin strap slipped from her shoulder, leaving her exposed to the cool air, but only for a moment. Then his mouth was there, hot and intense.

He sucked her nipple between his lips, and she gripped his head, pulling him closer. As the rest of her body started clenching in time with the rhythmic suction, he lifted his head and switched to her other breast. Maricela arched against him, nearly slipping off the counter in her eagerness to get closer. More.

Just when she felt like she had a handle on the pulsing pleasure, he gave her a hint of teeth. The soft nip dragged a hoarse cry from her throat, and he pulled back and braced his hands on the wall on either side of her head. His strong arms formed a cage, and he leaned in until her whole world seemed to be made up of him.

"Open my pants," he ordered softly, then kissed her.

He didn't relinquish her mouth, so she did it by touch. They moved in harmony—his tongue tracing her lower lip as she unbuckled his belt, then driving deep as she unbuttoned and unzipped his jeans. When she freed his cock and wrapped her fingers around its stiff length, he moaned into her mouth and thrust into her hand.

She rubbed her thumb over the slick head of his cock and tore her mouth from his. "Help me, Ivan."

"Always." He slid his hands under the short skirt of her dress, hot and impatient, grasping at her underwear as she lifted her hips for him. In moments, he was skimming them down her legs. They slipped past her feet and disappeared into the darkness, and Ivan dragged her ass to the edge of the counter as her skirt hiked up.

Her hands skidded on the tile when he thrust into her, but she caught herself with a moan.

The doorknob rattled, followed by a hollow pounding on its dented metal surface.

"Fuck off," Ivan growled, his voice menacing enough to stop the pounding immediately.

And low enough to curl Maricela's toes in her heeled sandals. She reached back, bracing one hand on the edge of the sink, and arched against him. One of his hands hit the wall beside her, and the other gripped her hip.

And then he fucked her. There was no other word for it. He drove into her with a groan and pulled back with a hiss, moving slowly until she met his thrusts. Then *fast*, each thrust so forceful it would have driven her back against the wall if she hadn't been ready for him.

Ready and eager. She wrapped her free arm around his neck, her legs around his hips. Her spike heels dug in to the backs of his thighs, but he barely seemed to notice. He was so *intent*, as lost in her as she was in him.

"Yes." Another snap of his hips, and he dropped his forehead to hers, their panting breaths mingling. "Fuck, you feel so good."

Impossible but inevitable. She felt the words in her bones, as deeply as she felt him, and nothing—not a desire to hang on to her control or make this last forever or even another angry patron breaking down the door—could have stopped her from coming.

Pleasure shook through her, exploding and imploding at the same time. Ivan didn't falter as he rode her orgasm straight into a second one. She didn't have the breath to scream, just to beg him in harsh, quick whispers—*harder, more.*

Yes.

"Tell me," he groaned, sinking his hand into her hair to drag her head back. He forced her to stare up into his eyes, and the longing there was endless, so vast it threatened to swallow everything else. "Tell me."

Only one thing mattered right now. Only one truth existed. "I love you."

He made a tortured noise and kissed her. Deep, desperate, his tongue driving between her lips in the basest of claims even as the pace of his thrusts quickened. She *felt* the moment before he came in the tensing of his muscles, the trembling of his body.

And she held him as he spilled into her with a helpless moan that sounded like surrender.

She listened to his heart, pounding in the darkness, and stroked his back until the galloping rhythm began to slow. Promises hovered on the tip of her tongue, but she kept them to herself. He needed time, space. No one with a lick of sense ever backed a Rider into a corner and expected it to go well.

As his breathing steadied, his hands began to move. He guided her dress back into place and smoothed the neckline above her breasts. Tenderly, he brushed her hair back from her face and dropped a kiss to the side of her neck. Her jaw. Her temple.

"You make me lose control," he murmured against her skin. "I never knew how much I needed that."

Everyone did. Ivan had taught her that. His rigid control was mostly internal and self-directed, while her pressure came from a hundred different places and directions—her siblings, her followers, even her friends. Her *life*. The life of a Rios princess.

"I'm glad you can escape with me," she whispered. "At least for a little while."

"I'm glad we can escape together."

Someday, somehow, they'd build a life full of things they'd chosen for themselves. They'd face every day together, secure in the strength afforded by their mutual support and comfort, and they wouldn't have to escape at all.

Maricela had to believe that.

22

The first thing Ivan smelled when he walked into the barracks was donuts.

"Hey, stranger." Zeke was straddling a chair backwards, a tablet on the table in front of him. A 3D holographic image hovered over it, something that looked like words too small for Ivan to read. Zeke swiped his fingers in the air and made them scroll, and Ivan suppressed a shiver.

That shit was *not* getting any less creepy.

Hunter nodded from the other end of the table. "Day off?"

"Afternoon. Maricela's having lunch with Isabela." Ivan usually avoided Zeke's donuts, but he dropped to a bench and reached for one. They were still the tiniest bit warm, with a sugar dusting that spilled all over the table when he broke off a piece.

It was worth it when he popped it into his mouth, though. Sweetness filled his senses as the pastry melted on his tongue, and there weren't enough saints in all of Sector One to pray to for deliverance from the trouble he'd gotten himself into.

Food tasted better. Sunlight felt warmer. The birds singing made him *happy.* Just knowing that Kora was running her tests and would be there to help him navigate the results felt like kicking free of a hundred pounds of misery.

And Maricela loved him. She'd snuggled up against him in that dirty Sector Three bar, ground her way to a shuddering orgasm on his thigh, and then she'd stared up at him with her dreamy, sweet brown eyes and asked him to marry her.

The princess and her loyal bodyguard. Impossible. Forbidden. A trite fairy tale whose brutal tragedy had already played out once in Sector One. And Carter Maddox hadn't even broken any vows when he married Adriana Rios. Ivan would probably be breaking all of his.

He'd almost told her *yes* anyway.

Across the room, Reyes snorted and rolled his eyes. "What are you so jolly about? Half the sector thinks you murdered someone in cold blood. It's not your best week ever, Ivan."

"*Reyes.*" Ana chucked the book she was reading at him, hitting him solidly in the chest. "Could you *not* be an asshole for five minutes?"

"Mmm, no. Wait—" He tilted his head back and pursed his lips, as if in thought. "Yeah, no."

She stood and retrieved her book before thwacking him on the arm with it again for good measure. Then she slid onto the bench next to Ivan. "Ignore him. *We* know you didn't murder anyone."

"Not yet." Ivan shot Reyes his best brooding scowl. He didn't usually have to *try* for the expression, but the whole world felt surreal right now. Bright. Loud. *Real*, like he'd never quite been a part of it before.

Reyes laughed out loud.

For the first time, Lucio looked up from the topographic map spread out in front of him. "That was a joke," he said to no one in particular before turning to Zeke. "Ivan made a feeble attempt at humor."

From anyone else, it would have sounded like an insult. From Lucio, it was a simple observation of the truth. It *had* been a feeble attempt at humor. Ivan had never spent a lot of time trying to be funny, because being funny wouldn't earn his sainthood and redeem his family name.

But being funny could make Maricela laugh, and that made it worth practicing. "Everyone has to start somewhere."

"Uh-huh." Zeke reached through the hovering display to snag a donut and waved it in the air. "So how long are we gonna keep doing this? Just give me a ballpark."

Hunter grunted. "Do what, watch you stuff your face?"

"No," Zeke drawled out the word. "Sit here and pretend we don't know that Ivan has been full-contact naked bodyguarding Maricela all over the sectors."

Ivan froze with the donut halfway to his mouth, his cheerful mood evaporating.

Ana dropped her head to the table with a groan.

Reyes stood and walked across the room to rack his barbells. "I would like to point out, just for the record, that at least I wasn't a big enough asshole to say *that*." He paused. "Even though I knew about it before any of you other motherfuckers."

Ivan snapped his mouth shut. Opened it again.

He had no fucking *idea* what to say.

"Zeke." Ana lifted her head. "I'm going to murder you."

"What?" he protested. "I'm sorry, but we're all a bunch of badass warriors trained in observation. Surely he didn't think no one would notice. I mean, you didn't, right?"

Ivan gritted his teeth against the damning truth—he hadn't really been thinking about it much at all.

"It's not like everyone knows," Hunter volunteered. "Just us. And Laurel. And Ashwin and Kora." He turned to Ana. "Did Bishop figure it out?"

"Bishop said Ivan was too smart to go there." As soon as the words were out, she winced and glanced at Ivan. "Obviously, he was wrong. Not that you're stupid, just—oh fuck, you know what I mean."

Ivan did. If Ana was the closest thing Ivan had to a sister, Bishop had always been the closest thing he had to a mirror. Bishop didn't have the fucked-up childhood or the traitorous family, but he'd been born with an inner darkness, and he'd long since grown comfortable with the idea that his darkness destined him for solitude.

It certainly didn't make you the kind of person who should be wooing sweet, sunny princesses.

Then Ivan realized what name was missing from the list Hunter had rattled off, and his stomach sank. "Does Deacon know?"

"Uh, no. Deacon keeps thinking Maricela's still a kid." Ana held up both hands. "And we compartmentalize. I decided not to kick that hornet's nest until I knew if Maricela was just..."

"Scratching an itch?" Reyes suggested.

Ana picked up her book and threw it at him again.

"What do you mean, *if?*" Zeke made a face. "C'mon, you and Deacon may be bunking it up, and no one's gonna set off an extinction-level event by trying to pry Ashwin off Kora. But Maricela's a princess, sweetheart of the whole damn sector, and Ivan's—"

"A potential traitor who probably murdered someone," he snapped, his stomach twisting at the truth in the words. His hands were drenched in blood, and Maricela was so fucking pure she glowed, just like her white gowns.

"No." Zeke exhaled impatiently, as if Ivan was being particularly obtuse. "You're a *Rider.* And I'm pretty sure we're not supposed to be setting up house and having cute little squalling heiress babies."

Hunter stopped peeling his apple and pointed his knife at Zeke instead. "Don't be a dick."

"I'm not! I mean, those are the rules, right? That's what I agreed to when I signed up."

"No, you didn't." Ana held up a finger. "You swore to forsake family ties and pledge your loyalty to us as your family." Another finger. "To protect the people of Sector One and help them when they need it, even if it means killing so they won't have to." She held up the third finger. "And to protect the Rios family and obey Gideon Rios. That's it. *Those* are the rules. Everything else is just…tradition that got made up along the way."

Reyes toyed with the book Ana had thrown at him, turning it over and over in his hands. "Traditions can be as unbending as rules."

"They can also change." Ana turned to Ivan, her brown eyes brimming with the earnest intensity that made her so dangerous. "You're not saying anything. Are you giving her a safe outlet, or is it more?"

Everyone was staring at him. His face felt flushed, and he didn't know if it was from embarrassment, anger, or fear. The words that had come so easily lately tangled on his tongue.

A few wiggled their way free. The absolute worst ones. The truest ones. "I love her."

Silence.

Then Reyes sucked in a sharp breath. "Holy shit."

"Damn," Zeke said. And when it was *all* he said, Ivan knew he'd really fucked up. Stunning Zeke speechless was a sign of impending catastrophe. Lucio and Hunter were both staring at him, too, and Ivan wasn't sure if he'd shocked them all by having feelings, or by presuming to focus them on someone he couldn't possibly deserve.

The silence was starting to hurt when Ana leaned in and hugged him.

Her arms were strong around him, and her long braids brushed his cheek. She smelled like almond soap and the faintest hint of Deacon's aftershave, and she was hugging him like he'd said the most brilliant thing in the world. "That's good, Ivan. It's *good*. Love is always good."

"Well?" Reyes grabbed a chair, turned it around backwards, and sat, staring expectantly at Ivan. "Come on, what are you gonna do about it?"

"Is there anything I *can* do?" Ivan waved a hand at Zeke. "He's right. I'm a Rider. There are traditions."

"Traditions that Gideon wants to change," Ana interjected. "He told me so himself. He never meant for us to be totally shut away from *any* kind of love."

Zeke snorted. "Yeah, even if that's true, he probably didn't mean he wants us to find it in his baby sister's pants. Little sisters are off-limits, man."

Reyes waved him away. "Don't listen to him. He's full of shit."

The defense surprised Ivan. "What happened to

traditions being as unbending as rules?"

Reyes nodded. "Sure, since when have I given a goddamn about *either*?"

Oh, damn. Now the hope was coming back. Just a warm little prickle of it, but it fluttered in his chest like it was struggling to grow. Ivan struggled to remember why he shouldn't nurture it. "Zeke's still right. Gideon's going to kill me when he finds out."

"Maybe," Zeke agreed. Then he grinned at Ivan. "But hey, maybe I'm wrong. I mean, Gideon was going to let her marry *Reyes*, and you're nowhere near as bad as him."

"See, you're talking, and you think it's clever, but it's really just the sound of you being an asshole." Reyes turned back to Ivan. "You're happy, right?"

Happy was never a word he'd considered before. He could remember being satisfied by a newly honed skill, or coming home to find his mother smiling and *there* and being relieved. He knew determination and focus and even the contented peace of being around his brothers and listening to their banter and knowing he belonged.

None of it had ever felt strong enough to qualify as *happy*. Not until Maricela.

"Yes," he said finally. "Yes, I'm happy."

"And she's happy?"

"I think so."

"Then fuck the rest of it. Fuck the rules, fuck tradition. Even, God help me—" He crossed himself. "Fuck Gideon."

Hunter barked out a laugh. "Say that to his face."

"Let's hold off on the revolution." Zeke twisted his fingers in the air above his tablet, and the floating text vanished. He rested his elbows on the table and leaned in. "Listen, man. Reyes is right. I'm being a dick. I just don't want to see you get hurt. This is a really mean wall you've chosen to fling yourself against."

A mean, angry wall, built not only of rules and traditions, but of all the lofty expectations for Maricela's eventual marriage. All the rumors about him. His family's bloody history. The nobles who would be furious that a commoner—a man dripping with ravens, a *killer*—had snatched their useful prize out from under their noses.

So many reasons to walk away. So many ways he could break all the bones in his body against this wall, to say nothing of his fragile hope and the mind and heart he was trying to heal.

Their useful prize.

One reason not to.

The darkness was still inside him. He felt it in the rage sparked by the thought of Maricela sacrificing her happiness in a marriage to someone who could never see *her*. Someone who only wanted the glory of her name, the prestige of her position.

Someone who would shove her back into her cage to slowly smother.

"Hey." Zeke's voice called him back. "You're getting the scary eyes, man. Yeah, it's a nasty wall. But when's the last time we met a wall we couldn't get over?"

"Never," Hunter said fervently. "If this is your thing, man—your fate, your destiny—then you've got to see it through. You don't just skip out on fate."

Reyes nodded once. So did Lucio. Zeke gave him a double thumbs-up.

Ana squeezed his arm. "We're family," she reminded him softly. "That's the first oath we take, the one to each other. You know we have your back."

The emotion surging inside him *hurt*, like a bone being set. Sharp, blinding pain and then...

Relief.

The first oath they took might have been to each other, but the vow every Rider held dearest was the promise to protect the Rios family. No one knew the most dangerous parts of Ivan better than the people around this table. They'd seen him fight, seen him kill. They knew how easily he did both.

They knew about his family, his darkness, and none of them thought he was a threat to Maricela.

"Well, one thing's for certain," Lucio said gravely.

Ivan turned to him. "What's that?"

He broke out into a grin. "When you decide to rebel, you don't do things small."

When Isabela meant business, she brought out the big guns.

In this case, it was a lovingly polished silver tea tray that had belonged to their mother, engraved with simple, sweeping scrollwork—as well as the Rios family emblem. It had been commissioned by their father as an anniversary gift, and Isabela meant it, no doubt, as a tangible reminder of the royal legacy entrusted to them.

Maricela munched on a tiny cucumber sandwich and tried not to sigh.

"Estela came to visit last night." Isabela poured tea into Maricela's cup. "We had a long talk about what we want for the future of the sector."

And neither of them, for even a moment, would have stopped to consider that everyone else in the sector already had their own wishes for the future. Maricela would have bet her shoes on that. "Oh?"

"Mmm." Isabela filled her own cup and reached for the little container of precious honey. "She made us a very intriguing offer. Do you remember her younger son, Rafael?"

"Of course. He's very sweet." And shy, and awkward, and Maricela felt terrible for him every time Estela practically shoved him her way.

"Apparently, he was quite taken with you." Her sister stirred her tea slowly. "With his two elder brothers ineligible to inherit, his father has begun grooming him as the heir to the entire Reyes estate."

It was another of Isabela's treasured tactics—when she knew her topic of conversation wouldn't be welcome, she danced around it. Normally, Maricela found it amusing, but she knew where this was heading, and irritation prickled over her.

She set her tea cup in its saucer with a clatter. "Luckily, Rafael still has time to petition the Riders. He could have his ink by autumn."

The only sign of her sister's annoyance was a slight narrowing of her eyes. "That's no joking matter, Maricela. I've spoken to Gideon about this. He can't accept any more noble heirs. There's been enough tension between our families over Reyes joining, and I had to work hard to smooth things over with the Monteros. That's *why* this is so important."

The idea of her brother turning away potential Riders because of their noble circumstances made as much sense as him turning away lowborn commoners: none. "Gideon would *never* make that promise."

"I didn't say he promised, just that he's aware it's a concern." She waved a hand. "Besides, Rafael is only twenty-two. He can't join for another three years, and he's hardly suited to it in any case. I know what you're doing, and I wish you wouldn't. Would it hurt you to *listen* to the offer Estela made?"

"Not at all. But it won't help, either." Maricela

shrugged. "The only thing Rafael is less suited to than joining the Riders or running the Reyes estate is marrying me."

"Estela made a *good* offer, sweetheart. It includes some binding agreements that would offer the sector stability—"

"Besides," Maricela interrupted, folding her hands in her lap to still their trembling. "I'm going to marry Ivan."

Isabela froze with her spoon above her cup. A drop of tea rolled off the end and splashed audibly in the sudden silence.

It took forever for her sister to break it, and when she did her voice was rigidly controlled. "You're going to do what?"

"Marry. *Ivan.*"

The spoon clinked against the saucer as she set it down, and sympathy flooded Isabela's face. "Oh. Oh no, this is all my fault, isn't it? You listened to me and took him as a lover."

"No. I mean, yes, but no." Maricela retrieved her cup and sipped her tea, which had grown cool. "There's no need to blame yourself. Not everything in this sector happens at your command, Bela."

"Maricela..." Her sister reached out to touch her arm, infinitely tender. "Sweetheart, having your first real lover can be an intense experience. When I suggested it, he wasn't your bodyguard. I never would have otherwise. I know this must seem terribly romantic, but you can't read too much into it."

For a moment, annoyance flared again, then died just as quickly. Sure, Isabela was treating her like a child, but how could she not? She'd helped raise Maricela, had become like a second mother to her.

Maricela sighed again. "I know what you're

thinking, but this isn't an infatuation. I'm not blinded by sex. I love him."

"I know it feels that way." Isabela patted her arm. "Maybe it's even true. But he's a Rider. He has duties and sworn vows. Vows I know he takes very seriously."

"Incredibly," she admitted. "But it's not exactly without precedent. Ashwin is a Rider, and he and Kora have managed to work things out."

"You know their situation is different. I've come to love Kora a great deal, and I welcomed her into our family. But she didn't grow up here. The people barely know her. Her choice of partners was never going to upend the stability of the entire sector."

"Neither should mine." The protest almost lodged in her throat, but Maricela pressed on. "Do you talk so much about stability because you can't call it what it is, Bela? *Business*."

"Survival," she countered. "You're too young to remember what it was like before your brother's sacrifices and my marriages established peace. Our family members were dying so often they couldn't paint the saint portraits fast enough."

"You're the leader of our religion, for Christ's sake." Maricela's throat ached now, tight with tears she refused to shed. "We're supposed to value love above everything else, but you want me to marry someone you know I don't love, and for what? To keep the nobles in line. To buy their cooperation."

"*No*." Isabela cupped her cheek. "You are my baby sister. I would *never* want you to marry someone you didn't think you could love. I have only ever wanted you to consider them, to give them a chance."

For a horrible, endless moment, Maricela stared back at her older sister, and she couldn't tell if she truly believed the claim or not. If she honestly saw all the endless pressure as *suggestion*. Gentle, easily resisted nudges.

She had to believe, at the very least, that Isabela believed it.

"Then I know," she said firmly, pulling Isabela's hand away from her cheek. "I couldn't love Rafael, not like that."

"All right." Isabela rested her hand on the table, her gaze roaming Maricela's face. A hint of worry filled her eyes. "Have you... Have you made *promises* to Ivan already?"

"I asked him to marry me, yes."

"And he said...?"

If I was anyone else, I would. "I didn't expect an answer right away. He has a lot to consider."

"Maricela." Her sister closed her eyes and drew in a breath. "Do *you* know how much he has to consider? Have you truly thought about it?"

This time, she couldn't control the sharper side of her tongue. "Not really. It's just my life I've asked him to share. That thing I've been living for decades now."

"No," Isabela said, opening her eyes. They were deep brown, filled with tears. "It's not just your life. It's his, too. Find me a painting of Carter Maddox. Find me a token, a charm. Find me anyone who remembers that you had an uncle at all."

A chill seized Maricela. "That is not the same thing. The Prophet wanted everyone to forget him, because if they remembered Carter, they'd remember that there was only one person willing to try and save their precious Adriana, and it wasn't Fernando Rios."

"Oh, I wish it were that simple. Carter was erased from our history because he disobeyed the Prophet. The people *wanted* him erased."

"They what?"

"You have to understand," Isabela pleaded. "They were the first generation after the Flares. People who had watched the world burn. Belief can be gentle now, but back then, it was the only thing keeping them alive. Grandfather's word wasn't just law, it was *divine*. They didn't see Carter's disobedience as a man trying to rescue Adriana. They didn't believe she *could* be rescued. He was spitting on their beliefs."

A handful of those followers were still around, adults who had entered worship as children or young adults. And they had taught *their* kids to believe, not only in the word of the Prophet, but in his divine mission.

In his family's divine mission.

The first frisson of doubt swept over Maricela. If people then had viewed something as human—something as *vital*—as Carter's desperate bid to save his wife and son from captivity as blasphemy against the Prophet, what would they think of Ivan? Would they see him as a man celebrating the love upon which their religion had supposedly been built? Or as a Rider turning his back on his sacred vow to Gideon?

No. "This is different, Isabela. Ivan isn't breaking faith, and he's already proven himself. He—he saved Mad's life during the war. They wouldn't turn their back on someone who's going to be a saint."

"Carter saved Mad's life, too," Isabela replied quietly. "And I can honor Ivan for what he did during the war, but you've listened to me and Gideon often enough to understand what we're trying to do. My word isn't divine. It shouldn't be. The priestesses decide now who our saints will be, and they listen to the people."

People who were already whispering about Ivan, falsely condemning him for a murder he hadn't committed.

"You have to consider this, Maricela. For his sake. Before you do something you can't undo, you have to ask yourself if it's fair to risk his chance at eternity, at the legacy he's sacrificed *so much* for."

An image flashed before Maricela—standing in that sunlit square in the heart of the city, watching joy slowly overtake the darkness in Ivan's eyes as he realized that he could secure his legacy, redeem his family. Wash away the lingering stain of his uncles' heresy and betrayal.

How would he ever be able to look at her if she took that away from him?

There was no good answer. Even if Ivan felt their relationship was worth the risk, it had the potential to endanger Gideon's position. The fact that she and Ivan had been carrying on a secret affair under her brother's nose wasn't public knowledge—yet. As soon as the heads of the noble families learned that she'd passed over their lucrative offers of marriage for *Ivan*, they'd realize the truth. And they would talk, every hint and careful insinuation meticulously crafted to make Gideon look ignorant, fallible.

Human.

"I already asked him to marry me," she whispered. "I can't take that back."

"He didn't accept." Isabela's voice was gentle. Sad. "He still might, if you make it clear that's what you want. Ivan's loyal. If you asked it of him, I don't doubt for a moment that he'd sacrifice everything. You have to decide if you're going to let him."

Anything for my princess.

Somehow, she had to do this. Tear out her heart and stumble through the agony, no matter how much it hurt. She could survive the pain. But she'd never survive ruining Ivan's life—or his death.

23

Ivan knew it was over before the door swung shut behind him.

Maricela was waiting for him at the table in her sitting room. She'd been waiting for him just like this after they'd had their *moment* in the temple, her spine perfectly straight, her hands folded in her lap, her expression careful, polite, precisely gentle and completely distant.

Back then, he hadn't understood what the expression meant. He hadn't understood until he'd spent interminable days at the Reyes estate, watching her deploy it on an endless stream of suitors, her rejections so soft and adept most of them never felt the sting.

Her smile didn't reach her eyes. "Did you have a good time?"

Too good of a time. He'd relaxed and let his guard

down, had let insidious, devastating *hope* bubble up inside him.

Hope was always a fucking lie.

She was still staring at him, waiting for an answer. He didn't know how to disappoint her, even now. "It was fine. Was everything okay with your sister?"

"Not really." The smile vanished, and she clenched her hands until her knuckles turned white. "We were right before. We can't do this."

It broke something in him, something worse than the feeling of hope being snuffed out. She was *hurting*, her sheltered heart bruised, her sweet brightness dimmed.

He didn't have to wonder what had happened. She'd told Isabela, or Isabela had found out from someone else—if the Riders were whispering, maybe the guards were, too. Nothing they'd tell an outsider, but few people in the sector could defy Isabela.

Not even Maricela.

Zeke had been right all along. Gideon and Isabela might want the Riders to pursue happiness, but that didn't mean they got to start with their beloved baby sister.

And Ivan had done this to her. He'd done it the first time he crossed the line, and he'd known how wrong it was with every inch he pushed past it. He was the one who understood the harsh realities of who they were and how vast a chasm separated a Rios princess from a Rider with traitors' blood.

He was the one who'd set her up for a broken heart.

"It's all right," he lied, crossing to the door that led to his quarters and her bedroom beyond. "We just won't talk about it again."

She went very, very still. "We won't?"

He couldn't bring himself to walk out of the room

with her staring at him like her world was crumbling, but he couldn't comfort her either. He couldn't touch her. Couldn't fold her into his arms and bury his face in her masses of brown hair and promise it would be okay.

He could do nothing but watch her heart bleed and hate himself for getting both of them into this mess.

"Won't it be better that way?" he asked gently.

"I don't know. But we—" She sank her teeth into her lower lip. Slowly, her confusion faded into something even worse—horror. "You never said it."

"I never said what?"

"Of all the things you told me..." She rose and faced him fully, every movement precise and careful. Like it hurt. "Do you love me, Ivan?"

Stillness filled the space between them. The silence burned.

She was right. He'd never said it.

And now he couldn't.

Tears brightened her huge brown eyes, and he curled his fingers toward his palms. Telling her now would be selfish cruelty. It would be sheer manipulation.

Worst of all, he was *tempted.*

Six steps. That was all it would take to cross the vast, echoing emptiness between them. He knew her body. Whatever Isabela had said to Maricela, he could erase it if he wanted. Drive it from her mind with his hands, his mouth, his tongue. He could make her *feel*, the way no one else had ever even tried. Alive, wild, wanted.

He could convince her to stay with him.

And then what? Turning Maricela away from her sister would shatter his vows. He'd be just like his uncles, a traitor to the Rios family. There'd be no place for them in Sector One.

And that was assuming Gideon didn't kill him,

straight out. Not a safe assumption to make.

If her family wouldn't support them, then all Ivan could offer Maricela was a hard, brutal life on the run. The allure of browsing in a marketplace or dancing in a dingy bar would fade rapidly when faced with the stark reality of life without the luxuries she knew.

Ivan didn't even like seeing mud on the hems of her pristine dresses. How could he subject her to that?

The tears in her eyes gathered on her lashes as the silence stretched and stretched, straining under the pressure. He knew what he had to do. A swift blow, a clean cut, a wound that would heal.

Maybe hating him would give her some comfort. "We're supposed to meet Nita soon—"

"No." Maricela's spine straightened. "Not until you answer the question."

He reached for the blank numbness that had been there his whole life but got painful, prickling misery instead. Apparently, these newly intense feelings weren't something he could turn back off when they were inconvenient. That seemed unfair.

This lie was going to hurt. "I care about you. I respect you. You're my princess. But I warned you there were some things I could never give you."

She bent over a little, like she'd just taken a sucker punch to the solar plexus, and the pain of it ripped through Ivan, like he'd plunged a knife into her heart.

Like he'd plunged one into his own.

By the time she straightened, she'd blinked away her tears. Without them, her eyes were flat. Dull. "Yes, you did warn me. I'm sorry that I misunderstood. I didn't mean to make things difficult for you. I'll speak to Gideon after dinner—"

"It's not necessary," Ivan interrupted. If Maricela went to Gideon looking like this, her brother really *would* murder him, and he'd deserve it. But the scandal would taint her for years. The best thing Ivan could do for her was vanish from her life as neatly as possible. "I'll take you and Nita to meet the architect, and when we get back, I'll talk to Deacon. He'll assign you a new guard."

Maricela nodded vaguely. "Whatever you think is best. But I—" She indicated the door through his room to her own. "I need a minute, please, before we leave."

He stepped aside and let her flee.

He tracked her movements as the pain sank into him. Soft footsteps across carpet. The loud slam of her bathroom door closing. The sudden gush of the water in the sink.

She was probably crying.

Ivan dug his nails into his palms until they cut the skin. His knuckles ached. He wanted to ram his fist into the wall, *through* the wall, any sort of tangible expression of the emotional wreckage inside him.

He didn't. He'd done enough damage to her perfect world.

Maricela was keenly aware of image. You couldn't grow up in the Rios family—in *any* of the noble families—and be ignorant of the fact that people were always watching you. One ill-timed frown could set off a flurry of gossip.

The same was true in the company of your friends, but for a different reason. If you seemed upset, they couldn't help but want to make it better. So she was careful to prepare herself for meeting Nita. After crying until her chest hurt, she'd washed her face, pressed a cool cloth to her eyes, and steeled herself against the pain that made it hard to stand up.

It didn't work.

Desperate to avoid Nita's questions, Maricela stared out the car window and kept up a steady stream of inane chatter. It was exhausting, but she didn't know what else to do.

After a particularly chipper comment about something she already couldn't remember, Nita's hand crept across the space between them and squeezed hers.

Anything but that. If Nita comforted her, she'd break down again, and she couldn't. Not with a stone-faced Ivan in the driver's seat.

She pulled her hand free and turned to Nita. "Your brother made me an offer."

Nita blinked. "My broth—you mean Rafael?"

"Yes. Your mother is...determined."

Nita's gaze flickered briefly to Ivan, who had a white-knuckled grip on the steering wheel. "I'm sure she is. Rafael is growing into a good man. Papa used to be hard on him. He never liked being outside with the rest of us, and he hates to ride, but he's smart. He researches things in the old archives. More efficient irrigation, stuff like that."

"I'll have to ask him about it." Not that it mattered. Gideon and Isabela could choose her spouse, and she'd make the best of it.

Not the most romantic notion, but Maricela was too tired to care. Her own judgment was too suspect to be trusted—Ivan had made that much clear the moment he'd looked her square in the eye and admitted that everything he'd given her, he'd given out of obligation. Because she was his princess.

Because he couldn't say no.

She bit her tongue until it bled.

Nita glanced at her again, quiet sympathy in her eyes. But her voice was relentlessly cheerful as she launched into a rambling monologue about the pottery sets she was making for the refugee homes, and Maricela made a mental note to thank her.

Later, when it was safe to finally unclench her jaw.

Pulling up to the refugee housing provided a welcome distraction. There were dozens of shipping containers now, some already under renovation, placed in gently curving rows that seemed to surround a central courtyard. She couldn't see it very well from the car because of the placement of the containers, but she caught flashes of green as Ivan parked a few feet from the contractor's vehicle.

"They've planted the garden already," she murmured.

"They're rushing to have it ready for harvest," Nita said, reaching for the door. "We can—"

"Wait," Ivan snapped, his voice lashing through the vehicle. Nita froze as Ivan slid from the car and dropped to check under the contractor's truck, as if someone might be waiting to lunge out the moment Maricela set foot outside the vehicle.

That single-minded focus on her safety reminded her of too many other things now—including the way he'd applied that same focus to touching her. She swallowed a curse, pushed open the door, and climbed out of the Jeep.

He glanced up, his lips flattening into a disapproving line. But he didn't snap at her the way he had at Nita, just finished his inspection and rose, a silent, painful shadow.

Nita watched them both nervously for a few seconds before inching out of the Jeep after Maricela. "Come on, Murph's waiting for us."

The man was even more nervous than he had been

at their last meeting, but he was eager to show them the progress his crew had made. Maricela listened carefully, asking questions as he began to lead them around the complex.

Forcing her attention on the matter at hand helped her ignore Ivan's quiet presence at her back.

Almost helped her, anyway.

24

Ivan's skin felt turned inside out.

Everything scraped at his nerves. The drone of the contractor's voice. The hesitant obsequiousness in his nervous movements. The wind, bringing air that was too warm to be pleasant and thick with the annoyingly domestic scent of freshly turned earth.

Nita's voice. God, Nita's voice *scraped*, because that husky, warm-honey tone that she deployed like a weapon was gone, replaced with a high-pitched, forced cheer that made every word sound like a backhanded accusation.

He'd broken Maricela's heart, and Nita was never, ever going to forgive him.

Ivan was never, ever going to forgive himself.

The back of his neck prickled, and Ivan tensed to keep from spinning around to check for somebody watching him. It wouldn't do any good. The layout of the shipping containers made excellent use of space, but it was an absolute nightmare for visibility. Ivan's muscles had tightened from the first moment he'd stepped into that circular courtyard, and the nagging feeling that something was *off* wasn't helping.

Everything was off. His whole fucking life was off.

The conversation stopped abruptly, and Ivan watched as Murphy began to roll up his plans. Nita turned to give Ivan a cutting look he was surprised didn't actually flay his skin from his body. "You can go do your...whatever with the car. We'll be along in a moment."

It was a dismissive command worthy of her mother, but it wouldn't have slashed so deeply if Maricela hadn't ignored it, her gaze still fixed on the empty table as if she couldn't bear to turn around until the sight of him wouldn't pain her anymore.

Her shoulders were slumped with misery. Ivan's throat hurt. He turned, swallowing the discomfort as he started back toward the Jeep. He was halfway there before he realized the lump in his throat was tears.

He couldn't remember the last time he'd cried. He couldn't remember if he'd *ever* cried.

The grass was scrubby in the dirt where they'd parked. Ivan dropped and slid beneath the car, his body moving on muscle memory until he spotted a shorn length of wire.

Someone had cut the line from the battery to the starter, disabling the vehicle.

Ice flooded him as he rolled free of the undercarriage, lunged to his feet, and broke into a run. The panic button Zeke had programmed for him was clipped to his belt next to his favorite knife, and it only took a moment to jam the trigger on it.

Zeke would get the alert, and the Riders would come, armed to the teeth. Ivan just had to keep everyone alive until they got here.

His heart didn't beat again until he crested the tiny rise and caught sight of Nita and Maricela, still standing in a triangle with the contractor, who'd turned to wave an arm in the direction of the community garden.

"Maricela," he shouted, covering the space between them as fast as he could. "Get—"

It was all he got out before the contractor's head exploded.

Maricela clapped both hands over her mouth and lunged after him as he slumped to the ground. She pulled him into her lap, dirt and blood grinding into her white skirt as her chest heaved.

The back of Ivan's neck prickled again, and he dove into an evasive roll as another shot cracked through the air, drowning out Nita's scream. The bullet whistled past Ivan—close, too close—and he came to his feet again in a dead run.

He reached them just as Nita went to her knees. He caught her arm and pulled her back to her feet. One glance at Murphy told him there was no hope. Ruthlessly, he dragged the man out of Maricela's lap by his shirt and hauled her to her feet, shielding her with his body as he herded both women into the shadow of the closest shipping container.

It was the model home. Nita was still staring at him in horror, her brown eyes huge with shock. He kept his voice even but firm as he guided them toward the door and opened it. "Get inside."

"*No.*" Maricela's hands were slick with blood and slid over his arms when she tried to grip them. "Ivan."

"*Inside,*" he roared. When she didn't move fast enough, he wrapped an arm around her waist and lifted her from the ground, knowing that if he released her she'd try to scramble back to check on a dead man.

Nothing was harder than keeping a Rios alive when people started dying around them.

Nita stumbled inside, and Ivan dragged Maricela across the threshold. "Get down, Nita. Maricela, *down*."

She didn't release him. "Stay here," she begged. "Please."

Her eyes were huge and terrified, and her fingers dug into his arms hard enough to bruise. Blood splattered her pretty white dress, so much of it. It stuck to her throat, too, and her cheek. He wiped a bit from beneath her eye and only left a smear.

He couldn't fix this. All he could do was take care of the problem—or at least hold out long enough for the Riders to get here.

He went to his knees, dragging her down with him. Nita was already there, her back pressed to the unfinished wood of one of the kitchen's little cupboards. Ivan freed a hand from Maricela's grip and took the beacon from his belt. "Keep this," he told her, folding her bloodied fingers around it. "Zeke will be tracking the signal, and he'll come to wherever it is. I'm going to lead this guy as far away as I can."

"You can't," she whispered hoarsely. "You can't leave me."

It would have hurt less if she'd driven her hand into his chest and ripped out his heart. He cupped her cheeks, wishing for more time. Wishing he could take back the last few hours.

"I love you." He didn't mean to say the words, but they came out anyway. He pressed his lips to her forehead. "I'll always love you, Maricela. I'm sorry."

She stared up at him in shock, and he left part of himself behind when he tore free of her arms. He was

empty and cold again, cold enough to ignore her stran-
gled, "Wait—"

He slammed the solid wooden door behind him
and wished it was steel.

But it wasn't. The thick walls of the shipping container might stop a bullet, but the doors and windows
wouldn't.

Ivan had to find the shooter.

He shoved away from the container, his mind
replaying the last few minutes. The shot had come
from high ground. The closest thing was the containers
themselves.

A heartbeat later, he heard the soft thud of boots
hitting the ground somewhere to his left. He spun and
cursed the layout of the containers again as he darted
across the open space to find cover.

Visibility was shit. He was trapped in a maze as
aggravating as the one in the Reyes family gardens,
nothing but narrow pathways and blind corners. Gravel
skittered off to his right, and he whipped around the
edge of the container, pistol in hand, only to find himself facing down an empty alley.

The sounds had been too far apart. The second he
thought it, metal creaked a few rows over.

Fuck, how many *were* there?

More than one could be too many. It felt like hours
had passed in agony, but it had only been minutes since
he'd jabbed the panic button. The Riders were fast, but
not *that* fast.

Gravel pinged softly off the other side of the container, and he whirled around it to find nothing, again.
Someone was playing mind games, taunting him like a
cat with a trapped mouse.

He sprinted across another stretch of empty space,
heading for the courtyard. If he could get to the other

side and find a vantage point—

Instinct screamed. His skin crawled. He could *hear* Ashwin in his head, scolding him for letting someone herd him into an ambush.

Ivan whirled and saw the gun barrel three feet from his head.

Training took over.

He ducked and threw himself at the man holding it. The shot went off over Ivan's head with a deafening crack as he hit the man square in the chest and bore him to the ground. The gun went flying, skittering across the gravel.

Ivan reared back, swinging his own weapon around. He was already squeezing the trigger when brutal fingers dug into his wrist and shoved his arm aside. The bullet went high, shattering a window on a nearby house.

Dead, frozen eyes stared up at Ivan, eyes with the same chilly detachment he'd seen in Ashwin's scarier moments. White-hot agony shot up his arm as his attacker squeezed with impossible strength, grinding the bones in his wrist together.

Impossible—or genetically enhanced.

Ivan ripped his knife from his belt with his free hand and went for the man's throat. The blade almost grazed him, but the man—the *Makhai*—heaved them both up and flung Ivan aside. He hit the ground with stunning force, dropping his gun.

He scrambled after it, but the Makhai was faster.

Ivan saw the blow coming and rolled to one side. The man checked his punch before driving his fist into the dirt and shifted his momentum with superhuman speed, changing his attack into an elbow aimed at Ivan's throat. He rolled again, this time with a desperate kick to the man's knee. It barely landed.

Ivan had trained hours upon hours with Ashwin. He knew what a Makhai soldier could do. There was no way a single Rider could take one down without a miracle. His only hope was to hold on, to keep the man too busy to go after Maricela.

To die as slowly as fucking possible.

He kicked out again, drilling his attacker's ankle. It bought him a few seconds to scramble to his knees and raise his blade. Before he could use it, the Makhai kicked his hand so hard Ivan *heard* bone shatter. The knife fell from Ivan's suddenly useless grip.

He ignored the agony. He ignored the probability that at least three of his fingers were broken. He came up with a smaller throwing knife in his left hand and flung it from the hip.

It sank into the Makhai's shoulder, but Ivan's momentary relief died when he reached up and jerked it free without even flinching. Ivan wrenched his body out of the path of its return flight and made a split-second decision—no more throwing weapons that could be used against him. He had to get close enough to sink that knife into the Makhai soldier's throat.

This was going to hurt.

Ivan loved her.

It didn't feel *real*. There was too much going on. Maricela's hands tightened and relaxed around the tracker Ivan had given her as her brain struggled to process everything that was happening. Her head pounded, her mouth was dry, and she couldn't stop shaking.

A man was dead.

Ivan loved her.

And he was out there now, searching for the killer.

Her fingers closed around the beacon again. Its blinking green light should have reassured her—the Riders knew they were in trouble. The Riders would come.

But would they make it in time?

She huddled closer to Nita. "I don't know what to do."

"What Ivan told us to do." Nita pulled away far enough to roll to her knees. The vase of flowers sat on the table where the contractor had placed it, the blooms bright and fresh, obviously picked that morning just to please them.

And now he was dead.

Nita grabbed the vase and ducked back beneath the table next to Maricela. She tossed the flowers aside and used the water to wet one of the hand towels that had fallen from the counter in the chaos. "Here, let me—"

The blossoms were scattered on the floor, like the poor man lying outside in the dirt. And Maricela couldn't even remember his name.

She brushed Nita aside as her friend tried to clean the blood from her face. "I can't just sit here."

"You *have* to." Nita caught her hand and squeezed it hard. "Whoever is out there is here to hurt you. You have to make it as hard as you can."

Nothing could be harder than this—waiting, helpless, as Ivan confronted danger all by himself. That was the part that made her skin crawl. Not that he was headed into a potentially fatal fight—he was a Rider, after all—but that there was no one at his back. If he died out there, he would do it alone.

No.

Before she had a chance to say it aloud, a shot rang out, stopping her heart for agonizing seconds. When a second shot exploded, Maricela sprang from her hiding spot beneath the table. "Are you armed?"

"Maricela—"

"*Show me.*"

Reluctantly, Nita eased up her skirt and pulled a knife from her boot. "I just use it for practical stuff. I don't even think it's big enough to be useful in a fight."

"It won't come to that." She shoved the tracker into Nita's hands. "The rest of the Riders are on their way. Stay here. That's an order."

Nita scrambled to her knees again, her eyes full of panic. "No, Maricela. If you're going, let me—"

"I said stay, Anita."

Another heartbeat, and Nita sank back, her gaze dropping to the floor. "All right."

"I'll be back," she promised. Maybe it was a lie and maybe it wasn't, but it was all she had.

Maricela eased through the door, closing it as silently as she could. Then she ran, determined to get as far away from Nita's hiding spot as possible. Her sandals slapped against the dirt and gravel, but she barely heard it over the sound of her pounding heart.

Where *was* he?

The way the converted shipping containers had been laid out made it impossible to see anything off in the distance. She moved between them, staying as close to the sanded metal surfaces as she could. If she lived, this would be her new nightmare. Not stumbling to Gideon's study, but helplessly trying to find her way through a labyrinth of chipped green and murky blue and rust red.

Somewhere to her left, she heard grunts of pain and rage, the kinds of primal noises that raised the hair on her arms. She followed the sounds—

—and walked into the rest of her nightmare.

Ivan was grappling with a man dressed head-to-toe in mottled brown, the kind of color that blended into the desert landscape. Except now those clothes were stained dark with blood, and she couldn't tell at first whether it was his or Ivan's.

Then she saw they were both bleeding, and more crimson spattered the ground with every kick and punch. Maricela stood, frozen to the spot, too horrified to hide as the man—the *soldier*—bashed his elbow against the side of Ivan's head.

Ivan wheeled back, groaning—

And saw her.

Their eyes clashed for an instant that felt like an eternity. She read the horror there, the fear. She saw his jaw work, knew he was biting back the urge to shout at her to run.

The moment snapped as he lunged forward with a roar, swinging straight for the man's face with a renewed fury.

This was her nightmare—and this time, she didn't know how to stop it.

25

Ivan had three broken fingers, a rapidly swelling eye, knife wounds in his shoulder and in his side, and a burning pain in his chest that might have been fractured ribs or internal bruising—it was hard to be sure when everything *hurt*.

All of that vanished when he saw Maricela.

Panic roared through him, giving him a second wind. He drove his good fist into the man's face, taking out his rage at himself on his opponent. It should have bought him time to get to the backup gun in his boot, but the bastard was on him again in a heartbeat.

He'd known better. He'd *known better*. He should have found a way to lure the Makhai soldier away, because you couldn't trust a Rios to stand back when the people they loved were in danger.

Now all he could do was keep the man from

realizing his target was right behind him. No more dragging it out. No more playing it safe.

Ivan had to kill an unkillable supersoldier.

The next blow hit him in the gut. Ivan stumbled back more than he had to, drawing the man with him. With his good hand, he groped for his last throwing knife, staying bent over his bruised stomach to hide the movement.

Too slow. The Makhai was *so fast*, on him before he managed to straighten. The weight of the other man's body slammed into him, and his ears rung under the force of another blow upside his head.

His vision wavering, Ivan spun and lashed out, driving the tip of the knife toward the Makhai's unprotected face. His blade grazed the man's cheek. Skin split. Blood ran.

Ivan's feet left the ground as the Makhai hauled him up and *threw* him at the table in the courtyard.

The wood shattered. Fresh pain erupted from a dozen parts of his body in the moment before his head crashed against a rock. Dirt stuck to the blood on his face, and he groaned as he rolled, frantic to find Maricela.

To make her *run*.

To see her one last time.

She was there, hovering in the shadow of a shipping container. Blood splattered her dress. Her arms. Her face. Her eyes were huge. Hurting. Time slowed, and he lived a lifetime of regret in the space it took to draw in one pained breath.

He wanted to take back his impulsive *I love you*. His death would have hurt her less that way. Now, even if she survived this, she'd never be able to escape him. He'd haunt her forever—on the walls of the temples, on cards they sold in the market, in the artwork inked onto people she passed in the street. A saint and a ghost, her first heartbreak. A soul-crushing world of *could-have-been.*

Don't turn me into a saint. Let me vanish into darkness. Let her heart heal.

The crunch of gravel snapped the world back into focus. The Makhai soldier was walking to pick up Ivan's discarded pistol. Every stabbing breath hurt, but Ivan tried to make his broken hand move, to grasp the gun in his boot.

He couldn't even feel his fingers.

He switched hands, twisting as far as he could as fire from his broken ribs grayed out the edges of the world.

But he could still see well enough to glimpse Maricela stepping out of the shadows.

Maricela didn't realize she was going to move until she did. But the moment she took that first step into the courtyard, she knew what she had to do.

With Gideon, she'd stumbled across the botched attempt on his life almost by accident. She'd intervened—unthinking, out of pure reactionary instinct. She'd rushed Donny, heedless of the gun in his hand or any other weapons he might be carrying.

Heedless of the very real, very mortal danger.

She wasn't that naive anymore. She knew now what it felt like to stare down your own demise, to see it racing toward you like a summer thunderstorm, violent and unpredictable. It was all around her here, that sensation of inevitability and tragedy, raising the fine hairs on the back of her neck.

But she wasn't scared. Ivan kept a backup pistol in his ankle holster. If she could buy him enough time to reach it, her death would be worth it. It fit with the narrative of her life, of what it meant to be a Rios—courage, sacrifice. They'd plaster her image all over the temples and their skin and write songs about her, and they'd never know the truth.

She was too selfish to watch him die.

Somehow, the soldier didn't notice her. It had to be tunnel vision, an adrenaline-fueled artifact of the fight, but a tiny part of her whispered that it was a sign. She was meant to do this. Maybe they'd sing about that, too—a small, perfect miracle at the hour of her death, grace where there should have been none.

Looking at Ivan *hurt*. He groped at his boot with his good hand, his face lined with pain, his eyes begging her not to do this. His shirt was soaked with blood, and even more dripped from the wound on his head. He was in bad shape, but not too far gone to make it.

"It's all right," she whispered, and she believed every word.

She even believed it when the soldier swung around, the pistol in his hand pointed toward where Ivan lay on the ground. She stepped between them, her heart pounding a hard but steady beat.

"No." The word came out clear, no hint of unsteadiness, because she'd never been more certain of anything in her life.

The man's blank expression didn't waver. He stared back at her, his eyes flat except for a spark of something vaguely like surprise tinged with annoyance.

But he didn't squeeze the trigger.

Maybe this was that trick of the brain the Riders talked about sometimes, time stretching out until it felt like all of eternity was swirling around you, seconds ticking by in excruciatingly slow motion. Or maybe she was already dead, and this was her existence now.

If so, it was closer to heaven than hell. Ivan was alive, and nothing hurt. She'd take it.

The soldier's eyes narrowed, and he pulled the gun back just a little. For the span of a heartbeat, Maricela almost let herself hope that he was relenting, that somehow the brashness of her command had driven him to surrender.

He stepped to one side. Around her.

Before she could react, a gunshot blasted through the stillness. For the second time that day, hot blood spattered her skin, and she squeezed her eyes shut, her ears ringing painfully.

Irrational fear seized her as she turned, but it was Ivan who held the smoking gun, and the nameless soldier who slumped to the ground, dead.

Ivan's arm wavered. Agony twisted his features. But his gaze locked on her, raking over the blood on her skin. "Are you—?"

He sounded even worse than he looked. "Don't." She dropped beside him, half-crawling to him across the dirt and gravel. "The other Riders will be here soon."

"No." The gun fell from his hand. He gripped her arm instead, his fingers digging in with a fraction of his usual strength. "Don't *ever*...do that...again. *Promise me.*"

"Oh, Ivan." She tried to wipe away the half-dried, sticky blood on his face. "I can't."

"Mari—" Her name dissolved into a broken cough that filled his eyes with agony. His hand found her cheek, clumsy but intent. "Promise me," he rasped. "Promise me you'll live."

The rumble of engines in the distance saved her from having to lie. She pulled his hand to her lips instead. "We'll talk about it all you want. *After* Kora fixes you up."

His thumb shifted, brushing the corner of her mouth. "My princess."

My love. Before she could whisper the words, his eyes rolled back in his head, and he went limp. She prayed it was just the pain driving him out of consciousness, but the specter of possible internal injuries haunted her as she threw back her head and screamed for help.

26

The numb detachment that had gotten Maricela back to the palace had settled firmly around her, making it hard to focus. Gideon and Ashwin were deep in conversation, but she couldn't hear what they were saying. Some of the other Riders were arguing. Zeke was bouncing out of his skin, Deacon glowered from the corner, and Nita was clinging to Hunter, sobbing as if her heart would break.

At least everyone had stopped staring at Maricela.

It was all happening very far away. When Ana tried to press a glass of water into her hand, she was far away, too, her words echoing and dreamy, like they'd drifted to her ears from the other end of a long tunnel. There was an odd sort of safety in that distance, and Maricela clung to it even as she shoved the glass away, just like she'd shoved away Ana's attempts to get her cleaned up.

There would be time for that. Later.

In another room specifically outfitted for life-threatening emergencies, Kora was taking care of Ivan. She literally held his life in her hands, and Maricela wasn't ready to deal with the tension and fear lashing through the room. It had all been so clear in her head—if she managed to give Ivan enough time to take down his attacker, then he would be okay. But the thought of winning the fight only to have Ivan succumb to his injuries...

It didn't make any sense. It had terrible narrative flow. Even defeat could carry a measure of glory, tragedy that still managed to sing triumphant. Those tragedies became songs and murals and tattoos and epic poems whose recitations were reserved for the holiest of days. Things worthy of Ivan.

A win that slipped, whimpering, into loss was just sad.

She knew she was being stupid. She knew. She was fixating on this because she needed it to make sense.

She needed it to make sense.

A sharp, vicious curse from the other side of the room drew her sluggish attention. Even braced for the worst, she wasn't prepared for the next word to penetrate her haze of confusion.

Makhai.

"What are you saying?" Deacon demanded.

"I'm saying the dead man in the back of your truck is Wyatt," Ashwin answered in a firm, sure voice. "A Makhai soldier two classes ahead of me."

Reyes drove both hands through his hair. "Does this mean there's going to be a squad coming in behind him?"

"I don't know. It seems unlikely that the Base would send another Makhai soldier into Sector One to execute a mission objective when I'm already here, but I can't rule out the possibility, either."

Deacon stepped forward. "Then get in touch with your buddy on the inside and find out, because that's necessary information, goddammit."

Gideon spoke for the first time, his voice rigidly controlled and somehow still dripping ice. "And ask them why they sent an assassin after my sister."

No wonder it was taking Kora so long. A Makhai soldier, someone seemingly trained in every kind of deadly combat that existed, had tried to kill Ivan. He could have done more damage with his bare hands than a group of heavily armed bandits.

And he'd tried to kill *Ivan*.

"No," she said, her voice still rough from screaming. "Not me."

"I can send a message. It won't take him long to get here."

"Do it. Deacon, until we know what's going on, put the royal guard on alert and send a message to Bishop. I want all of my sisters under Rider protection."

They didn't even hear her. She was eight years old again, eavesdropping on the balcony while Gideon discussed important things with important people. She was traumatized and shaken, blood on her hands, babbling madly as she tried to explain that she'd killed Donny. *She'd* held the knife, *she'd* taken his life—

No one ever listened. They soothed and petted and reassured and sedated her, and then they kept talking right over her.

Not this time.

"I said *no*." She rose, swaying on her feet. Ana reached for her, and Maricela shook her off. "That's not

329

what happened."

Ashwin stopped talking mid-sentence. Gideon turned to look at her, his face already softening into his concerned-big-brother expression, the one that meant he was about to assure her everything would be all right. "The details aren't important right now, sweetheart. Why don't you let Ana take you to get cleaned up?"

She stared back at him. He'd be horrified to know what sort of prison he and Isabela had created for her. It was warm and luxurious and safe and loving—

And she was dying in it.

"The devil's in the details, Gideon." She turned to Ashwin. "That man—Wyatt. He was trying to kill Ivan."

"It would have been one of his objectives," Ashwin confirmed, his tone making it clear he still didn't understand. "Ivan was the dominant threat. He had to eliminate him in order to reach his target."

"If he had been trying to kill me, I'd be dead." If they kept going around in circles, she'd start screaming again, and then they'd never hear her. "They were fighting, and Ivan was down. I stepped between them."

"You did *what?*" Gideon's voice rose until the final word was a roar that had all the Riders on their feet.

Maricela didn't flinch. "You heard me." She pinned Ashwin with a questioning look. "Would you have hesitated to take that shot? Would you have moved around me at that point to get to the *dominant threat?*"

Ashwin studied her for a moment. "No. I would have shot you, then him."

"Precisely." She turned back to Gideon, who was still flushed and damn near trembling. "I wasn't the target."

"It may have *seemed* that way—"

"Gideon," Ashwin interrupted in a quiet, firm voice. "If she stepped in front of Wyatt's gun and he didn't shoot her, there's no way she was his intended target. If anything, he had to be under explicit orders *not* to hurt her. Makhai soldiers rarely attempt to avoid collateral damage."

Gideon held up both hands. The room fell silent, and her brother drew in a slow, measured breath before exhaling. Then he turned to face Maricela, and it wasn't her overprotective big brother staring at her now. He was looking at her the way he looked at Isabela—like she was one of the grownups who had to make the hard decisions. "He was targeting Ivan."

She nodded. "Ashwin, when you're asking your Makhai contact questions, make that one of them. Why Ivan? Is someone still trying to kill Riders...or just him?"

Ashwin inclined his head and took a step toward the door. But he hesitated until Gideon waved him away. "Go. We need to know."

When Ashwin was gone, Gideon turned to study her again. His gaze roamed her face forever, as if he were seeing her for the first time. She was a mess, covered with dirt and blood and God only knew what else, but she felt *strong*.

Without taking his eyes from hers, he raised his voice. "We need the room."

When Gideon spoke, the Riders obeyed. Within moments, they scattered, with Nita sparing her one worried, red-eyed look before her brother herded her through the door. Then they were alone, staring at each other across two feet of empty air.

"Why did you do it?" Gideon whispered. "Maricela, *why*?"

Part of her had been so afraid of telling him the

truth for fear that he would be hurt or, worse, disappointed. But that part of her was gone. She knew now that she would face death itself for Ivan. Next to that, a little familial disapproval was nothing.

"I had to," she admitted. "I love him, Gideon."

Most of the sector viewed Gideon as all-knowing and infallible, a wise man who could stare into their souls and read every sin they wanted to hide. A man who could tilt his head and listen to truths no one else heard, as if God himself passed his time by whispering in Gideon's ear.

She doubted anyone had ever seen him gape in wide-eyed, open-mouthed disbelief.

"You—" He sputtered. Stopped. Stared at her for another endless moment as his eyes narrowed. "You're serious."

"Yes. Ivan and I are—" No, that wasn't right. "I mean, we were—" That was even worse, because her throat tightened, and tears blurred her vision. "Not anymore."

"Oh, Maricela." He gathered her into his arms, as solid and comforting as when she was a child.

But this wasn't a skinned knee, something he could soothe with ice cream and a trinket. She stepped back, shaking her head. "I don't know what to do. I asked him to marry me, but Isabela says he'd wind up like Carter—hated and forgotten. I can't do that to him. I won't."

"Shh, shh." He reached for her hair, smoothing it back where a blood-soaked lock had dried to her cheek. It wasn't anger or disappointment that clouded his eyes. It was hurt. "Why did you tell Isabela and not me?"

"I didn't want either of you to know, not until I figured some things out. But Isabela brought me another marriage proposal, and I had to tell her."

"And she said that Ivan would end up like Carter."

Something about the way he phrased it was so strange that she had to ask. "You think she's wrong?"

"I don't know." He laid his hands on her shoulders. "But neither does she. The people can be fickle, Maricela. If you marry Ivan, they might turn their backs on you both. Or they might embrace him. Your sister and I have lived our lives for the whims of the people, but I don't want that for you."

She didn't care—but Ivan did. "I would leave the sector if that was what Ivan wanted," she confessed. "But all he wants is to create a decent legacy for his family. That's one thing I can't risk."

"I know, sweetheart." Gideon pulled her close again, mindless of the blood drying on her clothes, and his voice dropped to a whisper. "I've tried to make the world easy for you, to protect you from what it really means to be a Rios. But you're a grownup now, and this is the hard truth. Sometimes the kindest thing we can do for someone we care about is not bring them into this world."

"Yeah." She leaned her head on his shoulder. "It doesn't feel very good, does it?"

The door opened, and Deacon leaned against the jamb. "Ashwin heard from his contact."

Gideon looked up without releasing her. "Already?"

Deacon snorted. "The guy was having some dinner in the market district. Ashwin says he'll be here as soon as he finishes his steak."

"He's already in Sector One?"

"Guess so." Deacon bumped his fist against the wall and shook his head. "I don't think it's a coincidence. Whatever he knows, it must be big."

"All right. We're going to get cleaned up. When he

arrives, put him in the old audience room to wait for us. I want every Rider there. And the royal guard."

"How many?"

"A Makhai soldier just tried to kill one of us, so I'd say all of them."

"I'm on it."

As Deacon shut the door behind him, Gideon gripped Maricela's shoulders again and met her eyes. "There are a lot of downsides to being a Rios. But we have one very, very important power."

"What's that?"

"We can find the people who hurt the ones we love." His eyes went cold and hard, and Maricela shivered. "And we can make sure they never hurt anyone else again."

Gideon preferred to call it the audience room, but the thrones on the dais told a different story.

There were three now, a gradual change from the Prophet's singular seat. Even his wife, Ana, had been forced to stand beside him while he held court. *No one* had been allowed to claim equal status with Fernando Rios.

The rest of the room was unchanged. Marble pillars rose from the stone floors to brace the arched ceilings, which were painted in rich hues of blue and red and gold. Those same colors were replicated in the single strip of carpet that ran down the center of the room, from the oversized double doors to the dais.

Isabela sat, unmoving and regal, on Gideon's right side. On his left, Maricela fidgeted in her huge chair. She'd showered and changed, and her fresh white dress cut a stunning contrast against the gilded wood and deep red upholstery. But she felt like she was going to jump out of her skin, and she didn't know whether to blame the events of the day, the events still to come, or the fact that dozens of people were watching her sit on this dais for the first time.

Del had come up from the palace temple with a complement of guards. She ignored the ornate chair reserved for her near the foot of the dais and stopped next to the cluster of Riders. She folded her fingers together in front of her and offered Maricela a gentle smile of sympathy.

She almost returned it but had to press her lips together at the last moment when Ashwin came through the wide doorway. A sandy-haired man walked beside him, and the knot of Riders on the left-hand side of the room tensed.

It was odd, not seeing Ivan's steady countenance among them, but not as odd as the other missing Rider.

She touched Gideon's arm. "Where's Reyes?"

Gideon scanned the room again and frowned. "I don't know."

Maybe he was still with Nita. Maricela didn't have time to wonder, because the man who had come in with Ashwin stopped in front of the dais and bowed his head.

Gideon straightened in his chair, his frown vanishing. He studied the Makhai soldier for just long enough for the silence to turn heavy. "Samson, is it? Ashwin told me I can trust you."

"No, he didn't." Samson shrugged. "But you can, for what it's worth."

"I suppose I'll have to." Gideon's pose stayed casual, but Maricela was close enough to see his muscles tense. "Why did the Base attack one of my Riders?"

"They didn't. It wasn't an official op." He gestured to Del's ignored chair with an upraised brow, then dragged it around to face the dais and dropped into it. "Here's the thing. I'm not sure you've noticed, but Makhai make excellent mercenaries. We don't ask too many questions, and we're not overly encumbered by conscience." He paused. "Someone hired Wyatt to take out your boy. Could have been off the books, could have been approved by his CO. That, I don't know."

Gideon glanced at Ashwin, who inclined his head. "Makhai soldiers are generally deployed on long-term, solitary missions and given a great degree of autonomy. Even if his CO didn't issue the command directly, they wouldn't necessarily disapprove if Wyatt could make a case that his freelance activities furthered his active mission."

Samson scrubbed a hand over his face. "Jesus Christ, you still sound like a robot when you talk."

Ashwin's brow furrowed. "And you're still irritating."

Maricela clenched her hands on the gilded arms of her throne. "Who hired him?"

One of the doors slammed open, causing the guards to close ranks as Diego Reyes stumbled through, followed by his son. Maricela had never seen Reyes in the heat of battle before, but she'd seen him angry. This was something beyond that, a rage so cold and boundless it could freeze the world.

He snapped at the guards nearest him, then pushed his father toward the dais. "Go on. Tell them what you did."

Diego jerked away from his son, his spine stiffening as his gaze landed on the dais. "This is inexcusable behavior."

"Confess, and I'll let you live," Reyes growled. "Or you can test me. I'm already damned, remember? What's a little patricide on top of that?"

Blood pounded in Maricela's ears, almost blotting out the older man's haughty protests. "Diego?"

His chin came up as fury filled his eyes. "I killed no one."

"Rafael was their last chance with Maricela." Reyes dragged a hand through his hair. "Ivan was in the way, so Dad decided to get rid of him."

It was unthinkable. Even in her worst moments, Isabela had never made the issue of marriage seem this vital, something serious enough to kill over. And yet, Diego Reyes had tried to murder Ivan because he was *in the way*. Because of her.

Or maybe Isabela *had* tried to tell her, and Maricela simply couldn't fathom it.

On Gideon's other side, Isabela had transformed from a warm, exasperated sister to the intimidating high priestess of the Prophet's true religion. Ice dripped from her words as she delivered each one like a blow. "If this is true, then you've presumed too much, Diego. Maricela's hand in marriage is her own to offer or deny. If you thought you could entrap her by murdering—"

"I didn't murder anyone!" he exploded.

"Murder," Isabela repeated harshly. "There are no loopholes when you take a life. Your weapon may have been money instead of a blade, but you wielded it with the cruelest of intentions. The fact that you failed to achieve your objective earns you no amnesty."

Flushed with rage, Diego spat at their feet. "You disgrace your grandfather's legacy. You are unworthy to sit where he did."

"Probably," Gideon said in a deceptively mild tone. "Of course, my grandfather's legacy has some very specific things to say about murder. It doesn't look kindly on it."

"And what of my legacy?" Diego demanded. "You

take our sons and turn them into killers, too." He flung an arm out, pointing at Reyes. "I lost my heir to your precious Riders, but you'll let that *traitor's son* put his hands on your sister. Will you let him join your family, too? Are there any rules you won't break if it suits you?"

Maricela started to rise, but Gideon grabbed her arm. "Diego Reyes, you are accused of paying someone to take a life. The life of one of my honored Riders, the son of a revered saint. Now would be a very good time to unburden your soul in confession."

Diego wasn't even trying to pretend anymore. "So what if I did? I will not stand here and be judged by the false heir of the Prophet."

"I'm afraid you don't have a choice." Gideon glanced at Maricela, then Isabela. At her tight nod, Gideon sighed. "It is our judgment—"

"Eleven lives," Samson cut in. "For accuracy's sake."

Gideon blinked at him. "What?"

"The best time to hire a Makhai assassin is when no one else will take the job," Samson elaborated. "After what happened to the Suicide Kings, your friend's options for contract killing must have been...somewhat limited."

For an interminable moment, no one moved. No one *breathed*.

Then Reyes pulled a gun and leveled it at his father's temple. "You greedy, grasping piece of shit."

"Reyes!" Gabe lunged and took an elbow in the eye for his trouble. He swore and dragged at Reyes's shirt, hauling him back a step. Ana appeared on his other side, grappling for the gun. He shoved her away as well, his fingers tightening on the pistol grip.

"Fernando."

Del's authoritative voice cut through the scuffle.

She stepped up to Reyes's side, her fingers brushing his shoulder. His arm trembled as she slid her hand down to his wrist with painstaking gentleness. When she reached his hand, her fingers curled over his. "Let go."

After a few tense heartbeats, he relented, dropping the magazine and clearing the chamber before handing her the gun. "You'll do worse than burn in hell," he promised his father. "I'm going to make sure of that."

Maricela shuddered. The guilt over Ivan's brush with death—all because of *her*—still burned like acid in her gut, but now it was joined by anger and a rising swell of something that felt dangerously like relief. She wasn't the prize here, just a stepping stone. Another pawn.

They couldn't win if she refused to play the game.

"It's a coup," she murmured. "Eliminate the Riders, marry me off to Nita or Rafael or whoever will get you into the Rios family, and get rid of Gideon. Then you step in—favored godson and confidant of the Prophet."

"His family abandoned him in his old age." Diego's voice dripped disdain. "His daughter defied his will, his son stripped away his power, and his *grandchildren...*" He turned the word into a curse. "You mock the faith. You undermine it at every turn. We should be a power to rival Eden by now, but you waste the tithes you steal from us to feed outsiders. I'm trying to save this sector."

"No," Gideon said coldly. "You're trying to save yourself. You want to restore us to a time when the nobles ruled over this sector as petty tyrants who took as much as they could get and gave nothing in return but promises of eternal reward. I'm afraid I won't allow that."

He gestured to the royal guard. Two members hurried forward and caught Diego by either arm. "Take him to the dungeon," Gideon ordered before smiling poisonously at Diego. "You'll have to excuse the dust. We haven't used it in a while. But since you're so *fond* of the relics of my grandfather's rule, you should be very comfortable there."

"You can't do this," Diego hissed. "The other families—"

Hunter stepped up. "The other families also have children you tried to murder. I wouldn't expect a hell of a lot of support from the Wests."

"Or the Monteros," Gabe added in a low growl. "The Kings almost killed me. They broke my bones, beat me half to death. How did you look my father in the eye at that party and smile like you were still best friends?"

"Your father should understand." Diego lunged toward Gabe but was stopped short by the guards, who jerked him half off the floor. "Gideon stole your future, your *afterlife*. That traitor killed your brother."

"No, he didn't." Gabe shook off Laurel's restraining hand and stood face-to-face with Diego. "My brother died of natural causes. But I'm not surprised anymore that the rumors about Ivan spread so fast and far. I'm sure you helped with that."

"I only did what was—"

Gabe grabbed him by the throat, choking off his words.

Gideon rose. "Gabe..."

"I could kill you before anyone managed to stop me," Gabe snarled. "But I'm not going to. You're not worth a raven."

Gabe released him abruptly and walked away while Diego sucked in a coughing breath. Gideon waved to the guards. "Get him out of here."

The guards dragged him, spitting and cursing,

toward the exit while Reyes watched, his face devoid of all expression. Maricela was mad as hell and more than a little shocked, but he had to be devastated to learn that his own father had tried to have him killed. And *Nita*—oh God, poor Nita.

As the heavy doors slammed shut, Maricela silently vowed to do everything in her power to protect the rest of the family. The thought made her pause, then stand a little straighter.

She *had* power. All she had to do was use it.

27

Ivan spent a thousand years drifting in and out of consciousness, grateful in one moment that he had survived and wishing fervently for oblivion in the next. Kora was always there, her cool hands soothing as she reassured him and added something to his IV that wrapped soft, sweet numbness around him.

When he finally woke up completely, the worst of the pain had receded to a dull, wearying ache. He squinted against the light and shifted on the bed until a sharper stab of pain from his ribs convinced him not to move.

"Hey, now." Gideon appeared next to him, one hand dropping to his shoulder. "It's nice to have you back among the living."

"Is—" His voice cracked, and Gideon vanished again before returning with a cup and a straw. Even taking a few sips took more effort than he wanted to expend, but the cool water soothed his throat. He tried again. "Is it?"

"Oh, I'm still mad at you." Gideon set the cup on the table next to Ivan's bed and dragged his chair closer. "You showed a stunning lack of judgment. And you made me look like a fool."

The casual way he said it made it cut deeper. Ivan might have been able to rally in the face of shouting rage, but not this quiet, wry, terrible *disappointment*. He had to swallow twice to get out two simple words. "I'm sorry."

"You should be." Gideon sat back in the chair and stared at him. "All the Riders knew. Diego Reyes knew. It will be quite a blow to my reputation if I admit that the infallible Gideon Rios couldn't see what was happening right under his nose."

Ivan opened his mouth to apologize again, and Gideon held up a hand. "No. I didn't see it because Maricela's still so young. And I want to shake you and say that you're too old for her, you should have known better, and you should have *told me*."

Bleak, helpless despair rose inside him, the kind of pain that made his broken fingers and ribs feel like pinpricks. He wished fervently for Kora and more of her oblivion drugs, but there was no relief. Just the disappointment of the one man he'd always wanted to honor, the man to whom he owed *so much*. "Gideon—"

"Let me finish, Ivan." Gideon folded his fingers together and let them rest across his chest. "I'm angry with you because you kept a secret. Distraction could have gotten one or both of you killed. My baby sister went out into the sector with a bodyguard she loved so deeply, she was willing to step in front of a bullet for him, and if I had *known that*, I would have assigned her to someone else."

"You're right." Gideon didn't interrupt him this time, so Ivan continued, each word shredding him. "She could have died, and it's my fault. But I didn't know. I swear, Gideon, *I didn't know* she'd do that. I told her to stay—" He faltered, because it was almost a lie.

He hadn't known that Maricela would step in front of a bullet for him. But he wasn't surprised, either. It was what the Rios family did. They protected the people they loved with their own blood.

He just hadn't realized how deeply she loved him until that moment.

"I know," Gideon said softly. "I'm mad at you, Ivan, but I'm more mad at myself. I tried to pretend Maricela hadn't grown up, and I let that make me blind. Not just to your affair, but to all those suitors and the pressure she was under. You gave her something no one else could—a chance to be happy."

Ivan struggled to follow what his leader was saying. He didn't sound disappointed anymore. He sounded almost...

No. No hope, not this time. "I want Maricela to be happy," he said carefully. "I'll do whatever you want me to do. Whatever it takes."

"Be careful with promises like that," Gideon replied wryly. "Because what I want you to do is stay away from Maricela until you've thought this through the way you should have thought it through from the beginning."

"Thought what through?"

"What it means to be a Rios—or to be married to one." Gideon braced his elbows on his knees. "The life of a Rider is bleak and hard, but it still can be your own sometimes. A Rios doesn't have that luxury. You belong to the people, from the moment your feet hit

345

the floor in the morning to the moment you close your eyes at night. You even belong to them after you die. There's no privacy. No respect for the fact that you're just a human being, one who has good days and bad. Who gets tired and sad sometimes. You aren't a person anymore. You're a symbol. An object. A holy relic."

"Gideon—"

"You like interrupting me, don't you?" He shook his head. "My sister loves you, and you make her happy. There's a part of me that wants to throw you right into her waiting arms, because I can be selfish when it comes to making that girl happy."

His voice dropped as he leaned forward. "But you need to know all of it. If you marry Maricela, the nobles will hate you. The people might, too. They could make you disappear after you die. No sainthood, no legacy. And while you're alive, it will be difficult. You'll be visible all the time. You'll have to learn to make small talk and shake hands and smile at people you hate. And if you start to resent her for that, you'll make her miserable. But how could you not resent it?" A wry smile curled his lips. "I wouldn't wish it on anyone I cared about. And I care about you."

It was so much, too much to take in. Ivan's head throbbed just trying—or maybe Kora's drugs were wearing off. Everything felt too bright and too sharp, and he couldn't tell if Gideon was trying to scare him away or offer his blessing.

Gideon stood. "Kora will be here soon to look you over. We've discussed what's best for your recuperation. It'll take a few weeks before you can even think about going back to work, so I took the liberty of sending a message to your mother. She's getting a room ready for you at the temple where she lives. You can rest. And you can think."

Ivan stared up at the man who had rescued him from homelessness, who had encouraged and defended him all his life.

The man who was offering him a chance. "And if I decide I want to marry your sister?"

Gideon held up both hands. "All I can do is say the family would welcome you. The rest, you'll have to work out with her. But, Ivan?"

"Yes?"

"She's worth all the shit that comes with being a Rios. Don't even think about marrying her if you don't know that."

Kora arrived then, flashing Gideon a disapproving look. Gideon laughed and kissed her cheek. "I was nice."

Ivan didn't hear her response. He barely heard anything she said as she examined the cuts and bruises and broken bones that riddled his body. Even the pain seemed distant.

The family would welcome you.

It was more than he'd ever dared hope.

But Gideon was right. He wasn't ready to be a Rios, standing at Maricela's side under the harsh light of public scrutiny. Not until he'd faced his own inner darkness.

Not until he could face his past.

It was a lot easier to set up private meetings now that Gideon didn't think there was someone trying to kill her.

Well, *actively* trying to kill her. Knowing what she did now, Maricela wasn't sure she could ever be blasé about security again. But the royal guard could stand post outside the courtyard just as they did her quarters, and no one had to sleep in her antechamber anymore.

It wouldn't have felt right. As desperately as she missed Ivan, it was just that—she missed *Ivan*, and having any of the other Riders take his place as her guard would have been torture. She couldn't let them see how miserable she was, because they were all a bunch of meddling bastards.

The breeze lifted her napkin from the table, and she set her glass of lemonade on its corner to keep it from flying away. "Thank you for meeting me, Nita."

"Of course." Nita was unusually subdued, clad in a plain brown dress with her hair pulled back in a messy braid, her eyes red-rimmed with dark shadows underneath. She worried at the edge of her napkin but didn't look up. "How's Ivan?"

"Better." Not that she'd seen him, but Kora had been kind enough not to make her ask about his condition. "He has some injuries that are trickier to treat with regeneration therapy, so he's taking some time off to recover."

"Good. That he's better, I mean." Nita finally looked up, revealing a haunted expression. "Maricela, I'm so sorry—"

She held up a hand. "Nita, you know me better than that."

"Maybe I don't know anyone at all," she replied, swiping angrily at a tear that rolled down her cheek. "I still can't believe my father would *do* that. To Ivan, to the Riders... To his own son. How much does he hate us for not being what he wanted?"

Maricela wasn't sure that Diego hated them at all—but was that better or worse? She reached for Nita's hand. "What he did is no reflection on you. None."

"To you." Nita choked on a laugh. "You should have seen my mother. She *fainted* when they told her.

She's scrambling to convince everyone she had no idea. It would be funny, watching Estela swear she's just a powerless pawn...if anything about this could be funny."

"I believe her." Estela would probably have been delighted to have Ivan out of the way, but her methods ran more toward manipulation than murder. And she never, *ever* would have would have killed her own son to facilitate a coup. "Nita, I have something to say, and I need for you to let me say it."

"All right."

Maricela took a deep breath. "I think we should consider getting married, after all."

Nita blinked teary eyes at her. "You—what?"

"I'm not going to fall in love again," she confessed. "That's...not an option. But I can get married for other reasons. Not the mercenary ones everyone seems to toss around, but good ones. I can protect you, Nita. You and the rest of your family."

"Oh, Maricela." Tears spilled over Nita's cheeks again, and she hid her face in her hands for a moment, her shoulders shaking. Then she wiped her face and shook her head. "No. I can't. I love you, you know I love you. And that's why I can't let you do that. You can't marry a Reyes. You can't give my mother so much as a toehold. She may not have known about the mercenaries, but she still wants power. And when she's done playing subdued and contrite, she's going to grab for it."

"All right," she soothed. "So tell me what I *can* do for you."

Nita twisted her napkin around her fingers before letting out a rough sigh. "There's one thing, but it's kind of big."

"Name it."

"Can I live here for a while? Not over with the initiates, but *here*." Nita gripped the napkin until her knuckles turned white. "I don't think anyone else will consider marrying me until my mother finds a way back into the sector's good graces, and if I'm at home, she'll try to use me to do it. And I just... I can't."

"You can have the suite next to Avery's." In the palace, at least, she'd be shielded from the rumors about her father's betrayal as well as from her mother's aspirations.

"Thank you." Some of the tension seemed to leave Nita. She reached for her lemonade and drained half of it, but her eyes were still haunted as she carefully set her glass down. "Can you sleep? I can't sleep."

"No." When Maricela slept, she tended to dream—not the nightmares she'd anticipated, but soft, sweet dreams of Ivan, snatches of moments that felt more like memories.

Somehow, that was worse.

"I keep hearing the shots..." Nita stared past her. "I know why you ran out there. I was so angry with you then, but I understand now. There's nothing worse than being helpless."

"Not even close." Maricela had spent most of her life just letting things happen to her. Sometimes it seemed like the only option when you were surrounded by powerful people, and you just felt like you were in the way all the time. "So what do we do about it?"

Nita managed a ghost of her usual smile. "We're a couple of smart, super-hot heiresses. I think we should stop letting anyone make us helpless."

28

Every time Ivan so much as twitched, his mother was there. "I'm fine."

"Are you sure?" Her brows drew together, and she pursed her lips as she studied him. "Are you hungry? I can make you something."

Now that she'd found her footing in the world, Irena Wolff wasn't a woman who took *no* for an answer—at least, not from her son. He'd been there for just under a week, but a week was long enough for the reversal of their roles to shift from mystifying to annoying to poignant.

Ivan had always had a mother. Now he was being mothered. "I'm fine," he insisted, then relented before she could take it on herself to cook him another meal. "I could use a drink. Those painkillers make my mouth dry."

She broke into a smile. "I made lemonade this morning."

Lemonade had been his favorite expensive treat when he was young. Sometimes, after a particularly rough time, his mother would splurge and bring him a glass bottle still cool from the vendor, though knowing she'd probably skipped lunch to afford it had usually spoiled the pleasure in it.

That wasn't a problem now. His mother's suite at the temple wasn't much compared to Maricela's quarters, perhaps, but it was lavish for a cook. She had her own small kitchen and dining table, a sitting area with two comfortable chairs, her own bathroom, and even the spare bedroom she'd prepared for Ivan.

Everything was clean and bright and tidy and *happy*, and he still felt a little lost dealing with her. Their weekly visits had always been perfunctory, over before they had a chance to get awkward. Now that he was here all the time...

They didn't know how to be a mother and son, not really. But Irena was trying, so Ivan tried too. "Thank you," he said when she brought the glass back to him.

But the first sip didn't remind him of his childhood. It reminded him of Maricela, who loved lemonade and always closed her eyes just a little with the first sip, as if she had never gotten jaded about having freshly squeezed lemons and real honey at her fingertips.

"Is it too sour?" Irena asked anxiously. "You don't like it."

"No, it's perfect." He took another sip and didn't fight the feelings that came with it. That was what the priestess had told him during their first meeting, anyway. To stop fighting the things he felt.

So far, Ivan wasn't loving it.

His mother sat across from him and rested her

chin on her hands. "You look so much like your father. When something was bothering him, he used to get the same—" she rubbed the spot between her eyebrows, "—scrunched-up look, right there."

Ivan barely kept himself from running a finger between his eyebrows. *It's nothing.* The words hovered on the tip of his tongue, born of a lifetime of habit. He'd never wanted to burden his mother with his problems, always worried that any extra stress would be the final straw that sent her to her bed to stare at the wall.

But his mother was doing a hell of a lot better than he was. And maybe, in this, she really could help him. "I saw how much the medicine Kora got for you helped. When she told me that my tests didn't show the same imbalance... I guess I just wanted an easy answer."

"Ah." She chuckled. "I have it easy, do I?"

"No," he protested quickly. "No, it's just—it's a thing you can measure. It's an enemy Kora knew how to fight. I don't know how to fight something I can't even wrap my head around."

"Isn't that why you've been talking with Minako?" she asked gently. "So you can work through all the terrible things you're still carrying?"

"I guess so."

She went on. "I know it's not just what happened recently, or even the war. Growing up was so hard for you, and a lot of it is on me." She took a deep breath. "It's taken a long time for me to be able to say that I did the best I could. But I still wish things had been different. For your sake."

It was the one thing Ivan had never doubted, that Irena had always done the best she could. Harder was trying to reconcile the very first thing Minako had told him—that he'd done the best he could, too. Life had dealt them a shitty hand, but they'd scrapped and fought the best they could to protect each other.

And that was the crux of it, wasn't it? Everything Gideon had warned him about, all the consequences of drawing the ire of the sector...

They wouldn't just fall on him.

Ivan cleared his throat. "All my life, all I've wanted to do is make you proud. And to make our family's name into something good, so you never have to worry again."

She shook her head, her dark blonde hair swinging. "That's never been your responsibility."

"I know, but—" There was no way around it. He was going to have to say the words. "Irena. Mom. I'm in love with Maricela Rios."

Her sheer confusion would have been comical—if it hadn't given way almost immediately to joy. "But that's wonderful! She's a lovely girl."

She hadn't even asked if Maricela felt the same way—and it was maybe the most *motherly* thing she'd ever done. As if she simply couldn't imagine a world where anyone wouldn't adore her son. Not even a princess.

Ivan loved her for it.

He still had to pierce her joy. "She is, but her life is complicated. If I married her, we wouldn't be invisible anymore. *You* wouldn't be invisible. For all we know, everyone in the sector could get really, really mad that someone like me had seduced their beloved princess. I can't put you through that again, not when you've finally got a life."

"*Ivan.* Listen to me." She reached across the table and gripped his hand. "I lived through it once, for the worst reasons imaginable. I can make it through that again, especially for the best reason possible. Your happiness."

His eyes stung as he clutched her hand. "It might not happen anyway," he told her hoarsely. "I kind of fucked it up. I don't know if she still wants to marry me."

"So you'll fix it. Make it right," she told him resolutely. "You can invite her for dinner. Ed's coming over."

"Ed? The blacksmith?"

Irena blushed and cleared her throat. "Ed, my fiancé."

It was Ivan's turn to stare in confusion. "You—you're marrying Ed?"

"We planned to tell you tonight," she admitted. "We didn't announce it—it's nothing that formal. But he's been sweet on me for years. And once I gave it a chance..."

She was glowing. When he reached for her other hand, a smile curved her lips—the kind of smile he used to wonder if he'd imagined, because his hazy memories of the time before his father's death always came in tiny snapshots with blurry edges.

But here it was. Older, a little world-weary...but still beautiful. And so, so happy. His mother had lost the love of her life and had gone through seven different kinds of hell on earth...but here she was, brave enough to love again.

Her courage humbled him.

"I'm glad," he told her, and he'd never meant the words more. "I'm really glad. You deserve to be happy again."

"So do you." Irena's smile faded a little. "It doesn't have to be tonight. When you're ready. Just...don't let her slip away without a fight."

His body was still sore, but it was healing. And his heart... Well, that might be a work in progress for a while. But if he could figure out the right words, maybe Maricela wouldn't mind.

"Don't worry," he told his mother, squeezing her hands again. "Fighting is the thing I do best."

29

In her haste to make a good impression, she'd gone overboard with the gifts.

Maricela shifted the wrapped box in her arms as she climbed the last landing outside Irena Wolff's apartment. Though the dinner invitation had come from Ivan, she had no doubt that his mother was the one behind it. The poor woman probably had no idea what had happened between them and was simply trying to extend a courtesy to a member of the royal family.

That made the evening even more nerve-wracking. Maricela would have to sit at a table with Ivan and make pleasant conversation, with no indication that, until very recently, they'd been lovers.

She took a deep, bracing breath and pressed the door chime with her elbow.

The door opened before the sound had entirely faded, and she found herself face-to-face with Ivan.

It was the first time she'd seen him since Kora took him away, and looking at him was harder than she'd imagined it would be. Bruises lingered on his face, and tape wrapped three of the fingers on his right hand. He was barefoot, clad in loose black sweatpants and a T-shirt that hugged his chest tightly enough to reveal the bandages wrapped around his torso. Dirty-blond hair fell over his forehead—he still hadn't gotten it cut—and new lines bracketed his eyes.

"Maricela." He said her name with a soft rasp that shivered over her as he stepped aside and pulled the door wide. "Thank you for coming."

"Thank you for inviting me." She dropped the gift box on the dining table with an accidental *thud*. "Sorry. The guards offered to carry it, but I wanted to deliver it myself."

He poked at one edge of the box. "You didn't have to bring anything. I just wanted to see you."

Her heart thumped painfully. "They're for your mother. Cookbooks. I told you that I'd help you find some for her."

"She'll love them." He turned and gestured toward an open door that led out to a tiny little balcony with a table and two chairs. "She put out some lemonade and cookies before she left. I don't think she trusted my manners. Do you want to…?"

There was no sign of Ivan's mother, or of a dinner in progress in the immaculate kitchen. "Am I early?"

"No, she's just using the big kitchen." Ivan's lips quirked. "She wants to show off for you."

Maricela had expected to have a buffer between them, someone else to focus on for the duration of the evening. How was she supposed to sit with Ivan until then, pretending that everything was fine?

"I can't do this, Ivan." She indicated the balcony. "I can't sit and eat cookies with you and make small talk like I'm okay. Because I'm not."

"I know." His hand came up, like he was about to reach for her, but he stopped with his bandaged fingers hovering a few inches from her shoulder. "I don't want to make small talk. I just—I need to get this out in the right order. Please."

If he had things to say, she'd listen. She owed him that much. "What is it?"

He drew in a deep breath. Exhaled. She could see him gathering his courage. "There's—there's a priestess here. Minako. She helps people who are struggling."

"I know who she is. She trained as a therapist before she took her vows."

"I've been talking to her." Ivan rubbed at his shoulder with his uninjured hand, staring somewhere past Maricela. "About the shit that happened when I was a kid. About the war. About a lot of stuff. I don't really like doing it. I don't know if I ever will, but...I need to try. I need to see if I can find the person you always saw when you looked at me."

"Not saw." Her throat ached. "The person I *see.*"

His gaze snapped to hers. "Even after what I did? I hurt you, Maricela. And I told myself it was some noble shit, that you were better off hating me. But I was just so fucking scared. I'd never imagined a future before you. I'd never *hoped.*"

And she'd gone back on her word, retracting a marriage proposal that she'd offered out of love, with all her heart. The worst kind of betrayal. "We all do terrible things sometimes. All we can do is make amends and move on."

"Yeah." He reached out again, and this time his

fingertips grazed her cheek. "I'm sorry I hurt you."

She ducked away, ashamed that she couldn't let him touch her at all, not even in comfort or apology. "It's in the past, Ivan."

"Do you still love me?"

Grateful that she wasn't facing him anymore, she leaned on the back of a dining chair and tried to blink away her tears. It didn't work. "Yes."

"Then marry me, Maricela. If you can forgive me, marry me."

The words pierced her like a blade. But she'd earned this pain with her carelessness and naivety, with all her blind promises, and she had to face it.

She turned to him. "Nothing has changed. All the reasons you couldn't accept when I asked—they're still there. I can't give you what you need. I can't guarantee your father's legacy."

"My father already has a legacy." He took a step closer. "I spent so much time trying to be him that I never thought about what losing him meant. I grew up without a father. My mother had to live alone, without his love or support. His legacy isn't just his sainthood. It's also all the ways his death broke the people he left behind."

"What if they hate you?" She could survive that, but there was one thing she'd never get over. "What if that makes *you* hate *me*?"

"Why would that make me hate you?" Another step, and he was almost touching her again, so close she could *feel* him along every inch of her body through the empty space between them. "I survived it before, and I had nothing. So what if they hate me again? This time, I would have everything. I'd have *you*."

The temptation to throw herself into his arms nearly overwhelmed her as she drank in his words.

In the end, she touched his arm, brushing one of the ravens inked into his skin. "Are you sure?"

"For the first time in my life." He cupped her cheek again, and this time she didn't pull away. "I don't care if I die and disappear from history. I don't care if I never become a saint. Making you happy for the rest of my life is the best legacy I can imagine."

It seemed like years since he'd last touched her, and she leaned in to his caress as the tightness in her chest slowly began to ease. "You love me."

"I love you." He stroked her cheek with his thumb. "I want to show you the world. All the parts you never got to see."

"And you want to marry me."

"If you're still offering."

"Always." She stretched up and brushed her lips over his. "I'll never want anything else. Just you."

Ivan caught her up in his arms and hauled her close—then hissed out a breath and winced. "Okay, sweeping you off your feet might have to wait for my ribs to finish healing."

"Oh, my God." She hustled him toward the nearest padded surface, a plush, dark blue loveseat in the living area. "Sit."

He dropped obediently to the loveseat but pulled her down to sit on his lap. "I'm okay. Just...you know. Remind me not to wrestle with a Makhai soldier who actively wants me dead. Now I know how much Ashwin's always holding back."

"You're still here. Not only that, you won." She combed his hair back from his forehead. "Ashwin's *flabbergasted*."

"I was highly motivated." He inched her a little closer, his fingers curling around her waist with a possessive pressure that made her stomach clench. "But I didn't win, not really. *We* won."

"You know what that means, then."

"What?"

She whispered the words against his lips. "That we really are perfect as long as we're together."

He kissed her. Slow, sweet, like it was the first time, his lips warm and soft. His fingers flexed on her hips, and when she opened her mouth, he lifted one hand to the back of her head, his fingers tangling in her hair as he licked her lower lip.

Maricela fell into the kiss. For the first time, there was no *danger*, no risk of discovery. If anyone caught them, they'd see a woman and her beloved, not a princess and her bodyguard. It was freeing in a way that even confessing the truth to Gideon and Isabela hadn't been.

Ivan was hers. And everyone was going to know it.

His fingers clenched tight in her hair for a heartbeat, and the urgency in his kiss thrilled her. But then he broke away with a groan. "We shouldn't do this. You have a habit of making me lose control, and my mother will be back any minute."

"She *what?*" Maricela scrambled off his lap and tried to smooth her hair. "I thought that was an excuse. Ivan, I can't meet your mother looking like we just— like we—"

He rose with a wince and used his fingers to comb her hair down. "Like we were about to defile her loveseat?"

"*Shh.*"

Ivan's warm laughter spilled over her as he tugged on her dress to straighten it. "Okay, I'll behave. But you don't have to be nervous. She's going to love you."

He sounded so certain. "What about my family?"

"Your brother's still pissed at me." The words

sounded damning, but he was smiling as he ran his hands up her arms. "But he also told me he'd welcome me into the family—if I was smart enough to love you."

Maricela bit her lip to hide an answering smile. "And Isabela?"

He leaned closer and lowered his voice. "I was thinking about hiding behind you until she forgives me."

"Good answer." Some of her humor faded. "If it were up to me, we'd go to the temple tomorrow and get married. But there will be parts of this we don't get to avoid. You know that, right?"

"I know. Your brother told me that, too." His hands slid from her shoulders up to her face. "I'm ready for it. The big wedding. All the people staring at me. Being a Rios and everything that comes with it. Because you're worth it, Maricela. You're worth anything."

Maybe defiling the loveseat wasn't such a bad idea. Or the floor. Or even the balcony. She leaned closer, twisting her hands in the warm cotton of his shirt, and—

The front door chimed.

Ivan chuckled against her lips. "Are you ready?"

"No." She laughed. "Yes. Maybe?"

Ivan kissed her one more time before answering the door. He plucked a huge basket out of his mother's arms and waved her inside. Irena Wolff was tall and curvy, with long blonde hair silvering at the temples and Ivan's blue eyes and ready smile.

She glanced at Ivan, who nodded once. Then held open her arms to Maricela. "Can I hug you? Is it okay if I hug you?"

"I..." No more words would come, but that was okay. Maricela reached out to Irena, who folded her in a hug so tight she could barely breathe.

"Thank you," the woman whispered against her ear, her voice wavering with tears. "Thank you for making him happy. Thank you for loving him the way he deserves."

All Maricela could do was nod.

Irena hugged her again, then pulled back and swiped at her cheeks. "I'm so happy to have you here. Come, come..." She drew Maricela over to the table where Ivan was unpacking the food. "I want to hear everything."

"Everything?" Ivan flashed her a warning look, which Maricela promptly ignored in favor of pulling out a chair. "Well, I suppose it all started on the last ceremonial training day for the Riders. I tried to ask Ivan out on a date, something he *completely* missed..."

As Irena's laughter pealed through the room, Maricela caught Ivan's eye again, and she knew he was remembering that day as clearly as she was.

My hero.

My princess.

They were still those things, but they were also more. Friends, lovers. Confidants. Everything that had happened—all the trauma, the danger, the forbidden yearning—had brought them here, a winding path that had led them exactly where they needed to be.

And she couldn't imagine anything more perfect.

gideon

Gideon wasn't sure he'd ever seen the Riders' barracks so full of love.

Parties were common. The Riders would throw open the doors, and Del's girls would flood in. They'd dance and laugh and flirt and celebrate life. There was joy, to be sure. Brotherhood and kinship.

Tonight, the celebration was smaller. Just the Riders and the family—and the Rider who was about to become family.

Ivan still moved stiffly and tired easily, but no one was letting that detract from the celebrations. When he wanted a drink or a snack, a Rider leapt to fetch it, and Maricela was glued to his side, radiating enough pure happiness to fill up the room all on her own.

Gideon resolved to lock away his own lingering reservations. Anyone who made Maricela smile like that deserved his unswerving loyalty.

Isabela handed him a glass of wine and leaned against the wall beside him. "Diego Reyes is dead."

She said it so casually that it took a moment for the words to penetrate. It took another to control his expression, so they wouldn't disrupt the party. "When did that happen? *How* did that happen?"

"Poison, if I had to guess." She cut a look at him. "Estela went to visit him earlier. Should we connect the dots?"

No one had to. The only real question was if Diego had known he was receiving the mercy of a swift death over lingering humiliation and eventual banishment. "She probably did us a favor. If we'd exiled him, who knows what sort of trouble he would have caused down the line?"

"That's a pretty bleak statement, coming from the benevolent god-king of Sector One."

Gideon rolled his eyes and took a sip of his wine. It was one of the more common vintages from Isabela's vineyards, fruity and pleasantly dry. He wished it was beer. "We still have to deal with Estela. I don't know if she's entirely innocent, but I can't imagine she would have signed off on the Suicide Kings hit. She wouldn't have risked a single hair on her precious baby boy's head."

"Never." Isabela looked around. "It's a nice party."

"It is." Gideon swirled his glass. "I'm glad you came. I know this isn't what you wanted for her."

"It's never been about what I *wanted*, Gideon." She blew out a breath. "This is a difficult path, and not just for Maricela. You're setting a precedent with your Riders, whether you realize it or not."

Diego's accusation echoed in his head still, the one thing he'd said that had struck a nerve.

Are there any rules you won't break if it suits you?

Gideon had spent a decade dancing along a knife's

edge, struggling to reconcile the sector's most beloved traditions with the future he wanted to see. And he was fucking *tired* of being patient. "Maybe it's time to set some new precedents."

"Even if they don't benefit you?" Isabela asked sharply. "If you turn the Riders into something other than a cloistered order of warriors—if you make it clear they can have *lives* just like anyone else—then you can bet your ass Estela Reyes will find a way to drag her son back into the family business. Will you let him go, Gideon?"

Estela might want to sink her hooks into Reyes, but Gideon knew him better than his mother ever had. Nothing would send him back to the family estate to pick up the reins of leadership. But Hunter was still close to his parents and siblings. And Gabe...

The Monteros were clearly struggling. They'd lost their heir. If Gabe asked to be released to take his place as their new patriarch, could Gideon deny him that? *Should* he, when so many people's lives and livelihoods depended on the Montero businesses?

"Yes, I'd let him go," he said quietly. "The world has changed, Isabela. Eden isn't a threat anymore. The boundaries between the sectors are blurring. I ask too much of my Riders to hold them against their wishes to vows they made in a different time. If I forced them to sacrifice their lives at my whim, how would I be any less of a murderer than Diego?"

"You wouldn't." Isabela paused. "Maricela filed with the priestesses this morning—a petition for canonization."

"Not for Ivan, surely?"

"No, not Ivan." She rubbed the heel of her hand quickly over her cheek, catching a tear that had just begun to fall. "Uncle Carter."

That hit him in the chest. Carter Maddox had been a good man. He was the one who had given Gideon his first lessons in combat, who'd taught him how to throw a punch and hold a gun. He'd loved Gideon's aunt with every atom of his being, so completely and unwaveringly that the disapproval of her family and the Prophet and a whole damn sector hadn't been able to sway him.

Just like Ivan.

The way he'd treated Carter was one of the many things Gideon had made his grandfather answer for at the end. "Good. That's good. Do what you can to make sure the priestesses agree."

"I plan to, though I'm not sure it'll be necessary." Isabela flashed him a rare smile. "Things are changing, big brother. Are you ready for it?"

"You know I am." Gideon raised his glass, and she clinked hers against it. "Tell you what. I'll handle the angry nobles and the conspiracies and the rogue Makhai agents and all of it—if you promise me one thing."

"Don't even try it. I will *not* plan a Rios wedding on my own."

Gideon heaved a tortured sigh, but inside, his heart felt as light as Isabela's laughter. As bright as Maricela's smile as she leaned in to kiss Ivan's cheek. As brilliant as Avery's grin as she leaned over the back of the couch to whisper something to Kora.

It would be months of planning. Hundreds of guests. Endless days of celebrations. A year's worth of tithes. But maybe if he made the wedding big and splashy enough, he could buy himself another decade of reprieve.

Because Gideon had sworn himself long ago that he'd never damn anyone he loved to the hell of being married to him.

about the author

Kit Rocha is the pseudonym for co-writing team Donna Herren and Bree Bridges. After penning dozens of par-anormal novels, novellas and stories as Moira Rogers, they branched out into gritty, sexy dystopian romance.

The Beyond series has appeared on the New York Times and USA Today bestseller lists, and was honored with a 2013 RT Reviewer's Choice award.

acknowledgments

As with every book, we have an entire team to thank for helping us to the finish line. Our editor, Sasha Knight, our Keeper of Bibles and Timelines, Lillie Applegarth, our sharp-eyed proofreader, Sharon Muha, our assistant, Angie Ramey, our new agent, Sarah Younger, and our community moderators, Jay and Tracy. Without this fabulous group of women, we would be lost and our books would be abandoned manuscripts. Thank you, a million times thank you.

We want to thank all of our patrons over on Patreon, whose support gives us a little breathing room to concentrate on writing. Special shout out to the members of the VIP Booth: Adrienne Lovelace, Andrea Porfirio, Brenda Oster, Courtney Foster, Ilene Gerber, Jacki, Julia Broek, Pattee Gatica, Rebecca Lewis, Ritarsha Furqan, Suzii Stevens, Terri Berryhill, Treece Phelps. You are the best!

Finally, as always, thank you to our readers. Your enthusiasm for the Sectors and your willingness to embrace the Riders as you embraced the O'Kanes is a blessing and our daily motivation. We love you and are grateful to you every day.

special thanks

We owe special thanks to our O'Kane Lieutenant's from Patreon. Your support has given us a chance to focus on writing, and without you, this book would have taken a lot longer to finish.

Pattee Gatica
Rebecca Lewis
Suzii Stevens
Terri Berryhill

gideon's riders

Ashwin
Deacon
Ivan
Hunter *
Gabe *

forthcoming

the beyond series

Beyond Shame
Beyond Control
Beyond Pain
Beyond Temptation
Beyond Jealousy
Beyond Solitude
Beyond Addiction
Beyond Possession
Beyond Innocence
Beyond Ruin
Beyond Ecstasy
Beyond Surrender

www.kitrocha.com

CPSIA information can be obtained
at www.ICGtesting.com
Printed in the USA
FSHW010222230119
55189FS

9 781986 818278